**Although she couldn't see his face, she knew
that silhouette well.**

In fact, her fingers had traced every line of his body through the medium of ink and pen, replaying the brief moment when he'd wrapped his arm around her waist and pressed her to him. Had she known how their encounter would linger in her mind, she'd have taken notes. As it was, her recollection of their time outside the bookshop was etched into her memory so deeply it played behind her eyes when she heard his voice.

Even if she hadn't been able to identify him by key landmarks like the straight line of his shoulders under his caped greatcoat, she would know it was him by the way every hair on her body seemed to stand at attention in his perfectly polished presence.

Each time she laid eyes on him, the urge to muss his pressed and starched edges grew. To run her fingers through his tamed waves and kiss him until his cravat was hopelessly rumpled. If ever there was a hero who needed a good unraveling, it was him.

Praise for Bethany Bennett and the Misfits of Mayfair Series

"This is a gem." —*Publishers Weekly* on *Dukes Do It Better*

"Emma's and Mal's journey more than lived up to my expectations." —The Romance Dish on *Dukes Do It Better*

"Packed with disguises, debts, and debutantes, this delightful Regency does not disappoint."
—*Publishers Weekly*, starred review on *West End Earl*

"Delicious, sexy fun."
—*BookPage*, starred review on *West End Earl*

"Filled with gripping drama, strong characters, and steamy seduction, this tantalizing story is sure to win the hearts of Regency fans." —*Publishers Weekly*, starred review on *Any Rogue Will Do*

"Everything I adore in a Regency—wit, steam, and heart!"
—Grace Burrowes, *New York Times* bestselling author,
on *Any Rogue Will Do*

"A beautiful tale that weaves second chances, genuine characters, and heartfelt emotion into a satisfying happily-ever-after." —Kelly Bowen, award winning author,
on *Any Rogue Will Do*

"This is a fast-paced and spicy debut, with likable characters and a feel-good finale that boasts a just-right blend of tenderness and groveling."

—*BookPage*, starred review on *Any Rogue Will Do*

"This debut novel has everything Regency fans love—wit, drama, lovable characters, steam, and romance all in an entertaining story."

—All About Romance on *Any Rogue Will Do*

Good Duke
Gone Wild

Also by Bethany Bennett

Good Duke Gone Wild

BETHANY BENNETT

FOREVER
New York   Boston

Copyright © 2024 by Bethany Bennett

Cover art by Judy York
Cover design by Daniela Medina
Cover copyright © 2024 by Hachette Book Group, Inc.

Forever
Hachette Book Group
1290 Avenue of the Americas, New York, NY 10104
read-forever.com

@readforeverpub

First Mass Market Edition: August 2024

Forever is an imprint of Grand Central Publishing. The Forever name and logo are registered trademarks of Hachette Book Group, Inc.

The publisher is not responsible for websites (or their content) that are not owned by the publisher.

The Hachette Speakers Bureau provides a wide range of authors for speaking events. To find out more, go to hachettespeakersbureau.com or email HachetteSpeakers@hbgusa.com.

Forever books may be purchased in bulk for business, educational, or promotional use. For information, please contact your local bookseller or the Hachette Book Group Special Markets Department at special.markets@hbgusa.com.

ISBNs: 978-1-5387-4048-4 (mass market); 978-1-5387-4049-1 (ebook)

Printed in the United States of America

BVG-M

10 9 8 7 6 5 4 3 2 1

For Court. Because you're where I go when I need to run away from home. Thank you for being my person, for having the good sense to marry a prince who's generous with his air miles, and for living in a house with the best shower in two hemispheres.

Acknowledgments

I seem to always have the same people listed here, and it's because I have an enviably awesome inner circle.

My love, devotion, and eternal gratitude go to the Let's Get Critical group. You ladies show up for everything from therapizing Marco Polo sessions, to pet sitting not-quite-potty-trained puppies. Y'all are the actual best. Thank you.

Alexa and Ambriel read early copies of this book, and somehow still believe I can write. Thank you both for your time, insight, and enthusiasm. Ambriel, I promise your girl Constance's story will be a blast.

Massive thanks to my amazing agent, Rebecca Strauss. Thank you for being my advocate, cheerleader, guide, and professional 'Oh honey, no' friend. You're phenomenal, and I'm damn lucky.

The Forever team and my kick-ass editor Madeleine Colavita worked miracles and turned 'the book that just might kill me' into a beautiful thing. This cover is ten kinds of perfect. Because of your hard work and passion for the romance genre, my books are in the hands of readers all over the world. (Hi, reader! I am so grateful you're here!) Thank you isn't enough.

And finally, to Hotness, Ladybug, and the Mini. You are my world.

Good Duke
Gone Wild

Prologue

✒

London, summer 1812

The next villain she wrote would be a vicar. Perhaps a vampiric vicar, who survived by sucking the blood of sheep while the villagers slept, unaware of the danger they fostered in their midst. Although, now that she considered it, vampires might be more loyal to their offspring than her vicar father.

Caroline Danvers hugged the oilskin folio containing all her worldly goods tighter to her chest and pivoted to avoid the circle of men blocking the pavement. Or more accurately, dodged their hands and cries of "Pretty bird, where you off to so fast?"

There'd been worse on the road from Staffordshire to London. A few men drinking away their wages outside a pub in the middle of the day were no more annoying than a gnat. On her third day of travel, she'd traded her pewter ink-pot for a small blade, which she tucked in her walking boot. If one of those men tried to do more than call to her, they'd be missing a finger, and she wouldn't feel bad about it.

So much could change in such a short time. Today she was ready to pull a knife. Not long ago, she'd been the spinster daughter of a vicar, making her biweekly visit to pick up the post for the perpetually ailing (and entirely imaginary) widow Mrs. Delia Wallace.

Traveling merchants and myriad other people used bookstores and lending libraries to hold their mail until the next time they passed through the area. When she'd begun writing erotic novels a few years ago under the nom de plume of Blanche Clementine, she'd gone to a nearby town and established an account under Mrs. Wallace's name to handle correspondence with her publisher.

The day had been sunny and warm, like this one. Except, instead of the scents of roasting meat pies, sweat, and waste, she'd breathed in fresh country air and the honeysuckle growing over the cottage. She'd gathered her latest manuscript in its oilskin folio, along with the usual writing tools in anticipation of stealing time to work while she enjoyed an afternoon of freedom with the pony cart. When the bookshop had a small display of Blanche Clementine novels in the window *and* the mail had included royalties, she'd thought the day couldn't get any better.

Until she returned to the vicarage to find her father standing over the open metal lockbox that held her savings, contracts, and letters from her publisher.

The money in her pocket was enough to pay for meals and cots in stables along the road to London. She'd hailed passing farmers' carts to give her poor feet a rest as the miles, then days passed. Parting with her coins one by one, she'd clung tighter to the half-finished manuscript—all she'd been able to take with her.

If she were more delicate in nature, and of a less vengeful bent, she'd be able to cry. That's what one of her heroines would do. Except, she was an ugly crier, and any excess water in her body was otherwise occupied by seeping from her pores, not her eyes.

London in the summer was like wandering through hell's furnace with thousands of other people who appeared to be having a better day than she was.

Having a better day than a woman who'd been thrown from her home wouldn't be hard, all things considered.

Rounding a corner, Caro nearly sagged with relief when a sign came into view. Carved wood swung from an iron post mounted to the front of a stone building with multipaned windows of wavy glass.

Martin House Books.

Finally. Just a few yards away.

Without conscious thought, her weary feet slowed. Mercy, it had been a journey to get here, and part of her didn't fully believe she'd arrived safe and whole. The travel had seemed to take forever. Yet in that next instant, with her goal so close she could almost touch it, time stretched until a second could have been a year or a lifetime, rather than a blink.

A hard body connected with her back. Instinctively, Caro stuck out her arms to stop her fall, which sent her precious manuscript tumbling to the ground. The oilskin landed with the center flap open, and the top pages fluttered in the breeze of passing feet. Fully expecting to fall, she arched to cover the papers with her body.

Except, hard cobblestones didn't hit her palms. Her knees didn't connect with stone. Nothing hurt. It took a second to realize she hung suspended, pulled against the firm body of whoever had bumped into her. He'd wrapped an arm around her waist, and a rough voice said in posh tones, "Terribly sorry, miss. No harm done, I hope."

He set her on her feet, and Caro bent to gather the pages of her book. Large hands dusted with gold hair appeared in her peripheral vision, plucking a piece of paper from the ground and tucking it into the oilskin folio.

"Is that all of it?" he asked, and she had to swallow around a lump in her throat.

So close to her destination, and she'd almost lost all she had left in the world. "Yes. Thank you for tidying the mess you made." The words were thick with accusation and emotion. Frustration, anger, sadness, exhaustion, but not quite tears—more proof she wasn't the kind of heroine she wrote about.

He wrapped the leather thong around the bundle and held it out to her with one hand, while steadying her with his other arm as they rose. "Please accept my deepest apologies."

Accepting the folio, she clutched her precious manuscript to her chest where it belonged. Caro finally looked up.

He had the bluest eyes she'd ever seen. Clear blue, like the sky in Staffordshire, rimmed in straight dark lashes, lit with obvious interest as he took her in. A firm chin under a serious, concerned mouth. At least he appeared genuinely apologetic, which soothed her ire.

After all, he'd apologized prettily and been kind enough to make sure she was unharmed after literally knocking her off her feet. The budding smile didn't have a chance to bloom before she took in the rest of him.

Pristine white cravat, starched collar, dark coat cut to perfection over his shoulders. The clothing he wore was of the finest quality. Combined with the elegant pattern of speech, he was the walking, talking human equivalent of a heavy purse. Money. She'd bet her last farthing there was a title in front of his name, and he wooed the kind of women who drank orgeat on purpose.

Women who wouldn't dream of traveling alone out of desperation. Women who would faint dead away at the thought of appearing on the street in all their travel dirt as she currently was.

"Thanks to your quick reflexes, I'm unharmed. Thank you." Caro stepped away from his clean bergamot scent, and the bustling city street snapped back into focus around her.

"May I make it up to you? Perhaps help you get to wherever you're going?"

"That's kind but unnecessary. I've arrived." The smile she'd held back slipped free as she gestured toward the bookshop sign.

"I was heading there myself. Here, if I may." He held open the shop's door.

A bell overhead tinkled in welcome as they entered. Honey-hued wood, rich with lemon oil, gleamed everywhere. Plank floors squeaked under their feet as they approached a long wood counter. Rows of bookcases held more books than Caro had ever seen in one place, and tables scattered about the sales floor displayed artful piles of specific titles and writing supplies.

It was beautiful. Heaven and, hopefully, a haven.

"Caro? Caro, oh my God—what are you doing here?" Blonde curls and a wide dimpled grin registered an instant before her cousin, Constance, wrapped her in a warm hug.

Days of travel and worry, the fatigue, the pain of her father's accusations and actions, the handsome stranger on the street—it all disappeared in a flood of relief. "I can't believe I made it."

Her cousin pulled back, her smile disappearing as quickly as it had come. "Did you ride the mail? Hire a coach?" Connie's eyes widened when Caro shook her head.

Their other cousin, Hattie, hurried from a doorway behind the counter. "Caroline! What a wonderful surprise. How did you get here?"

"I walked. Sometimes rode in a cart." Caro cleared her throat, painfully aware of the man standing behind her.

Surely his polished perfection only served to make her scruffy appearance and desperate straits stand out in stark relief.

Constance gripped Caro's arms and inspected her as if looking for damage. "You walked? From Staffordshire. *Are you mad?*" Caro knew the exact moment her cousin noticed the man she'd entered with because Connie sent him a distracted smile. "Pardon the family drama, Your Grace. Our cousin has taken us by surprise."

Your Grace. Sweet mercy, he's a duke. Well, she'd been correct in her evaluation, hadn't she? Caro turned to give him a tight-lipped smile. "Thank you for your help, Your Grace."

"It was the least I could do," he said simply.

Now she could push his presence from her mind entirely. Even if his curious gaze lingered like a caress on the side of her face, Caro would likely never see him again. And that was as it should be.

Perhaps it was knowing she'd achieved some modicum of safety that allowed each ache and pain to make itself known. She licked her lips, desperately wishing for something to drink. As if reading her mind, Hattie ducked back into the room she'd just come from, and returned within moments with a teacup. "Here, luv. You must be parched."

"I'd think so, after walking halfway across the country on a whim." Constance shook her head.

"I had no choice." Caro sipped and found the tea to be tepid. Hattie must have sacrificed the cup she'd already prepared for herself. In a few gulps, she emptied the cup as she clutched the package closer with one hand. "I didn't have anywhere else to go."

Like mirror images, each woman pressed her lips into a line and drew in a deep breath as they heard everything she didn't say. They knew her father, after all, and could fill in the missing information.

Hattie spoke first. "Let's get you upstairs to Uncle Owen and Aunt Mary."

Caro raised a brow and wiggled the folio, asking a silent question. *Would they throw her out as well when they learned of her writing?*

Somehow, Hattie understood. "They'll be thrilled you're here. Uncle Owen was just saying he needed to hire someone to handle the account books. Besides, you're family. We take care of family."

Right. They took care of family. Her father often said the same thing but in a way that sounded like the task was a burden, rather than a privilege. Caroline let another layer of tension leach from her shoulders.

Constance turned toward the man—the duke—who'd stood silently watching. "Are you here for the books you ordered? I'll have them wrapped for you in one moment. Our apologies for the wait, Your Grace."

"No apologies needed. I'm happy your cousin is safe and sound." Like the duke he was, he sent Caro a shallow bow before taking a seat by the window to wait.

As Hattie led her upstairs to the family's living quarters, Caro didn't look back.

The next book's villain might be a vicar, but the next heroine she wrote would have two supporting characters who would carry her to her happiness.

"Is she in there?"

"Well, I can't exactly see in the dark, now, can I? I'm not a bloody fruit bat. Caro, are you in here?"

"I could have yelled, Constance. I'm trying to be respectful. She's had an awful time of it; she doesn't need us hollering like fishwives, does she? Especially if she's crying in the dark."

The sound of her cousins bickering in the doorway washed over Caro, bringing a smile. "I'm here. And I'm still not crying." Caro sat up in bed, flinging the lightweight linen covers down to her waist. "A proper sort of woman would be weeping after all this, wouldn't she?" As she knit her fingers together in her lap, she worried at her lip. "Father called me unnatural. Do you think he might have been right—about part of it, anyway?"

Someone lit a candle, and Caro blinked against the tiny flare of light. While Constance tended the flame, Hattie crossed to the bed and nudged her arm. "There's nothing unnatural about you. Scoot over, darling. There's a girl. You're talented and brave, and I won't hear another word to the contrary." Hattie spoke with the same tone one would use with a distressed child.

"I still can't believe your father threw you out. What kind of monster would do such a thing?" Constance hung her apron on a hook behind the door, then stripped out of her gown and petticoat. They were wearing the barest layer of clothes in deference to the summer heat. The room was nearly stifling after a long day of sun and soot in the great city of London. Despite the late hour, the calls of merchants and neighbors on the street below entered the room along with a welcome evening breeze.

Caro eased back onto her pillow. Growing accustomed to the noise and bustle of so many people living in such a small area would be impossible, yet Caro would have to do it.

"He thinks having a successful author for a daughter is *so* disgusting." Connie let loose a dark laugh. "What I'd give to meet him in an alleyway and show him the error of his ways."

A lifetime of defending her father had Caro speaking before she thought it through. "Not just an author. An erotic-novel author. His sense of right and wrong is rigid. The people in the village expect their vicar to be perfect, and by extension, me too."

Constance settled the candle into its holder on the bedside table and made a shooing motion with her hands.

"Your father should be horsewhipped," Hattie said, crawling over Caro to claim the space by the wall. "I refuse to refer to that man as my uncle from this day forward. He's no family of mine."

The bed dipped as Constance climbed in. "Bloody vicar. I hope he falls in love with a cow and dies of the pox. But not before his willy falls off."

"Good God, what have you been reading to give you such ideas? Does Uncle Owen know what his daughter is pulling off the shelves and filling her mind with?" Hattie asked, jerking her head off the pillow beside Caro's.

"My father encourages us to read, and I'll read whatever I like, thank you. Don't think I haven't noticed the books you hide under the counter at the shop, Hattie MacCrae. Check your chemise—your hypocrisy is showing."

"Fair enough," Hattie grumbled.

Constance wrapped her arms across Caro and rested her hands on Hattie, linking the three of them together.

Yes, she was safe here. Caro drew in a deep breath, then paused. "Connie, why do you smell like men's cologne? Is that...sandalwood?"

"I swiped it from James. He thinks it's romantic that I want to wear his scent."

"James is the beau of the week," Hattie explained without

prompting. "Poor fool doesn't realize she's trying to see if she can stand smelling him for longer than an evening."

Caro glanced between them. "Beau of the week? I thought James was last month."

"This is the third James. Or maybe fourth. I don't know. I've lost count," Hattie said around a yawn.

"Ah, that makes sense, then. I thought I'd somehow missed something since our last letter." She relaxed deeper into the mattress. "Have you decided, Connie? About the cologne?"

Constance answered with a dramatic full-body shudder. "Too much musk. I think he's overcompensating. Doesn't bode well for the relationship when their cologne screams *I'm a man* so aggressively. I'll return the bottle and break things off with him tomorrow."

"Add another name to the rejection list. At this rate, you'll either be an old maid or have to wander Mayfair to catch some swell's eye. You've run through all the men in the rest of the city." Another yawn distorted Hattie's teasing.

"Surely not *all* the men." If Constance was worried or insulted, she didn't sound like it. As she burrowed under the thin blanket, it rose and tickled Caro's nose.

Sharing a bed would take some getting used to as well.

Constance's burrowing seemed to be her way of releasing the rest of her energy, because she now sounded as tired as Hattie. "It has been quite the day, hasn't it? Tomorrow, we all start fresh. I'll end things with James, Hattie will make a plan to publicly ruin your father and get your savings back, and you can tell us about the new book you're writing."

"I look forward to ruining him," Hattie whispered. "It will be so satisfying."

"I don't know how we can get my savings back, short of marching into the house and stealing it ourselves." A pang of sadness cut through the feeling of safety Caro had been enjoying. "There was almost enough. I was going to buy a cottage closer to London, so I could see you two more often, but far enough out of the city to have peace and quiet. I'd garden and write more Blanche Clementine novels, and no one would ever expect me to be perfect again. It was going to be wonderful."

"You can still do all that, luv," Constance said. "Even if we don't get your money, you'll eventually save enough again. We've sold quite a few copies of your books, and that's without our customers knowing of our connection to the author."

Caro tensed. "We can't tell anyone. I'll be a scandal and drive away your more conservative patrons. It would kill me to cause problems for you all, especially after your kindness today. Uncle Owen and Aunt Mary didn't even hesitate when I showed up on your doorstep. Promise you won't say a word outside the family, Connie."

"Relax. We've managed to hold our tongues this long, haven't we? No one needs to know your secret identity unless you choose to tell them."

Gradually, one breath at a time, Caro relaxed once more. "All right. Maybe it will all turn out in the end... eventually."

"Of course. Thankfully, my bed is big enough for all of us. Now that Betsy's married, there's room. I'll clear out her old shelves and drawers for you."

"As long as you don't kick like Betsy did, this will work out perfectly," Hattie said, exhaustion weighing heavy in her voice.

Connie kissed Caro's cheek. "Good night, luv. You're not alone anymore. You have us, and now you have Martin House Books too."

Chapter One

Eighteen months later, February 1814
On the River Thames, London

I've seen the elephant. Let's call a hack." Dorian Whitaker, fifth Duke of Holland, blew on his gloved fingers, hoping to bring some level of sensation back to the tips.

"How can you be such an old curmudgeon during a day like this?" Oliver flung his arms out to gesture to the mass of London's population teeming atop the frozen Thames. "There hasn't been a frost fair since we were children."

"Every part of my body is frozen."

"Not every part, surely," Oliver said with the complete lack of concern only a longtime friend could show and still be considered an ally.

"If my ballocks fall off from frostbite, I'm sending them to you in a box," Dorian grumbled.

"And I'll sell them to the highest bidder. The best bits of the Duke of Holland should fetch a fair price, don't you think?" Oliver held out a paper cone, sending spirals of steam into the frigid winter air. "Roasted chestnut?"

Dorian popped one in his mouth, welcoming the temporary warmth.

As promised, the elephant had paraded up and down the river as a testament for any doubters that the ice was thick enough to walk on. Although who could doubt it at this point he didn't know.

Booths lined the river, offering an astonishing array of wares to thousands of Londoners from every walk of life. Games of chance and more than one card table provided ample opportunity to lose yet more coin. There was even a makeshift pub serving drinks behind a plank bar they'd constructed sometime overnight.

"Is that wise?" Oliver gestured toward the pub, where patrons warmed their hands and feet around a roaring bonfire. "Building a fire atop ice seems like a risky choice to me."

Dorian wanted to say something snide about asking the elephant to test that patch of the river but held his tongue. "Then let's not linger. Just in case."

Happy cries of squealing children carried on the air along with the scents of roasting meat and a general din of conversation, haggling, and the metallic scrape of sharp skates on ice. All of it together was a little overwhelming, while also being rather delightful. If he could have the happy children, the delicious food, and the genial crowd without losing random body parts to frostbite, Dorian would be far more enthusiastic about the whole thing.

For his part, Oliver had approached the entire affair with a wide-eyed wonder he'd rarely shown toward anything. Those in their circle would describe the Earl of Southwyn as logical, a bit cold, but fair and loyal. Few were allowed to see this side of him. But then, there wasn't anyone else in Oliver's life who'd stood beside him when word of his dissolute father's death reached the school. He and Dorian had been school chums until that day. After the news, they'd empathized as boys who'd both lost their fathers, and became the next best thing to brothers.

"I'm out of nuts." Oliver shook the paper cone upside down, frowning.

Dorian wandered toward a stall filled with books, pens, and a small table of cards bearing an ink print of the frozen river. The illustration showed the giant blocks of ice that had broken free over the last week from the pier by London Bridge, then floated along the Thames, only to be caught as the river froze again. Along the riverbank, sheets of ice stood like massive walls of a quarry. It was quite the sight, and the artist captured the scene perfectly with a few deft pen strokes.

The ingenuity and speed merchants had shown in creating items to sell for the fair was impressive. Dorian paid for a card, then slipped it inside his coat before moving on. For a moment, he'd wondered if the stall was that of Martin House Books, but the man who took his money wasn't familiar.

Holding a wood stick speared with roasted meat of some kind, Oliver rejoined him. "They have interesting mementos to commemorate the event. Looking for something specific?"

"I bought a print showing the ice blocks. I'd have lingered, but the stall wasn't run by the bookshop I like."

They passed a cobbler, a game of skittles, and a woman roasting whole rabbits on a long spit. Another fire built on ice. Dorian shook his head at the sight. If people wanted to be warm, they should return to their homes, rather than risk drowning in their attempts to avoid freezing to death.

"Is this by chance the bookshop that employs a certain brunette you keep going on about?" Oliver asked.

"I do not go on about her. That is blatantly false." An urge to bat that stick of roasted meat to the ground out of petty defensiveness reared its head, but he ignored it.

Ticking off the instances as he sucked meat juices from his bare fingers, Oliver recounted, "Approximately eighteen months ago, you mentioned bumping into a woman outside the bookstore. A brunette. You estimated her to be near thirty. She'd been disheveled and travel weary but remarkable after such a journey. Your words, not mine. A year ago, you commented over port in your study that although the woman at the bookstore had smiled and been perfectly polite, you didn't think the smile was real, because it didn't reach her eyes. Nine months ago, you said that even if you hadn't known the connection between her and the Martin family, it would have been obvious to anyone who spent more than two minutes looking at her. Apparently, there is some resemblance with one of her cousins."

"She and the blonde have similar mouths. Their lips are practically identical," Dorian muttered in a half-hearted attempt at a rebuttal. "A handful of mentions is not 'going on about someone.'" He stalked down the row of vendor stalls to get away from the conversation.

"For you, it's comparable to lurking and spying from behind bookcases." Oliver followed, looking quite pleased with himself.

"Noted." Oliver's worst trait was his tendency to be correct about nearly everything. Although Dorian had opened himself to speculation and analysis by admitting to looking for the bookshop stall. "You're a bloody nuisance. Why are we friends again?"

"Lack of options. No one else would put up with us. You're a private and deeply personal man who doesn't like to show his soft underbelly to anyone. And I, as you so eloquently put it, question everything and everyone until I become a bloody nuisance. We annoy each other to exactly the right extent."

The verbal sparring might have gone on all afternoon if he hadn't spied the blonde curly-haired cousin leaning against a vendor booth up ahead, flirting with a red-haired young man. Upon further inspection, the object of her flirtation seemed to be having a conversation with the curve of her bosom rather than her face, but she didn't seem to mind. In fact, she rather cheekily reached a finger out and tilted his chin slightly so he was looking her in the eye.

"That stall there." Dorian pointed.

"The blonde? Is that the cousin with the mouth?"

As they approached the stall, he could make out tidy displays of books on several tables and what appeared to be wood crates draped with eye-catching cloths. On the far side of the booth stood a familiar curvy form, busy pinning frost fair prints to a line of twine strung from one end of their makeshift store to the other. It didn't matter that he'd just bought a card almost exactly like them; Dorian knew he'd be purchasing another.

Several seconds, counted in heartbeats, passed as they approached and he waited for her to turn. As always, the anticipation of that first fizzle of awareness sang under his skin, catching his breath and holding it hostage until he saw her round cheeks and pointed chin. It was a heady thing, the buzz of attraction. Just like that first day when he'd briefly held her body against his outside the bookshop, desire swept through him with the potency of whisky. Unable to help himself, he'd returned to the store time and again to experience the feeling and subtly check in on Caroline. Even after she was clearly settled in and thriving in her new life, he'd searched for a sign that she wasn't as fine as she pretended to be. If she wasn't genuinely well, he didn't know what he'd do to help her circumstances. Yet, the compulsion to see her remained. And with each visit, instead of finding a woman in need of rescuing, he saw someone who wore confidence like armor. It was intriguing as hell after glimpsing her vulnerable reunion with her family.

"Damnation. Brace yourself," Oliver muttered, a split second before a man blocked Dorian's view of the bookseller.

"Well met, Holland. After weeks of trying to catch you at home, I run into you here of all places." Timothy Parker paired the comment with a wide-eyed expression innocent enough to set off alarm bells in Dorian's mind.

"Here I am, along with half of London." He kept his tone bland, clean of any emotion Timothy might twist to his advantage.

A tense silence stretched, and the false geniality on Timothy's face slipped into a familiar sneer. "You're going to make me beg for what I'm owed, aren't you?"

It wasn't a script per se, because the words were slightly different each time. But after countless reiterations over the years, Dorian knew how this conversation would progress. Timothy would play the part of victim, at the mercy of the tight-fisted ogre duke. If that didn't work, there would be insinuations and snide comments about Dorian's marriage and character. Finally Timothy would make overt threats he lacked the clout to carry out.

Over Timothy's shoulder, the brunette bookseller spun in a playful pirouette on the ice. In moments like this one, when she didn't know he was there, he caught sight of the woman she'd been on the cobblestones that first day—annoyed that he'd bumped into her, peevish over him helping pick up her papers from the ground. She'd snipped at him, then met his gaze, and he'd forgotten how to breathe. Even covered in travel dirt and so clearly exhausted it made him ache to tuck her in bed and stand guard while she slept, she'd been undeniably vibrant.

Winter sunlight hit her hair, turning it auburn and illuminating her face, just like it had that summer day. While her lips moved, saying something to her cousin he was too far away to hear, Timothy began to wheedle and whine.

"If anyone knew how you treated the family of your duchess—"

Dorian muttered a curse. Tearing his eyes from the bookstall, he stared down the last remaining family member of his late wife. Like the proverbial straw that broke the camel's back, enough was enough. Having to deal with Timothy when Dorian had been savoring a rare moment of feeling like a whole, unbroken man used any remaining patience he had with the situation. "Let's skip to the end of this farce, shall we? You've been a financial nuisance for fifteen years. My wife has been dead for five of them, and yet I'm still supporting you. Why?"

A red rush of color surged over Timothy's neck and face. "When a man marries a woman, he marries her family as well. Especially when he has funds to spare."

Dorian stepped closer, faintly aware of Oliver placing a hand on his arm in silent warning. "Juliet is gone, and it's time we all moved on. You already have everything she left behind. The jewelry, the gowns, the coach. Everything, as well as a generous allowance. The only thing left to sell is her library. Take it and leave my life for good."

"Oh, I've heard all about your plans to move on." Timothy puffed his chest in an aggressive movement anyone who had read about apes would recognize, but Dorian didn't retreat. "All of London is talking about the great Duke of Holland deigning to take another wife. The ladies wouldn't be so eager if I told them how things really ended with my cousin, would they?"

There were the threats. Once upon a time, they would have made Dorian furious, or fearful of people learning of

Juliet's infidelity. Now they just made him tired in a way sleep couldn't solve.

Oliver's voice, cool and logical, cut into the conversation. "Holland might not want the scandal of shooting you on the heath and leaving your body for the scavengers, but I have no such compunctions. Watch your threats, lad."

A white line rimmed Timothy's lips as he hissed, "What the hell would I do with a library? Burn it to keep warm? I don't need fucking books; I need money. Do you have any idea the kind of men I owe? They don't accept poetry as payment."

"Books are worth quite a bit to the right person, you troglodyte," Dorian began, but Oliver cut him off.

"Holland is being more than generous by offering valuable property that by rights is his. Think it through," Oliver said.

A glance beyond Juliet's cousin showed the stall of Martin House Books. Thankfully, their conversation hadn't caught the attention of anyone in the booth, although a few passersby had slowed their pace to eavesdrop.

In the shop ahead, the blonde cousin sent the flirt on his way and returned to work. The quieter cousin was kneeling next to a crate of books as Caroline took money from a gentleman with the polite smile she reserved for patrons. The smile she gave her family was wide and unfettered.

Another difference he'd noted between the woman she'd been on the street—and occasionally glimpsed with her cousins—and who she was with customers. Not only was her smile subdued, but he suspected she chose her words carefully during the times they'd spoken in the store. A telling pause marked her conversation, as if she sorted through a list of replies in her head before choosing the most banal.

It was the contradiction that made him return again and again, not only her physical appeal. For whatever reason, she'd decided to make herself smaller and quieter, as if trying to escape notice. Yet the way she carried herself, even when silent, held an arresting confidence that countered her efforts.

Dorian forced his attention back to Timothy, who droned on.

With the shop so close, there was an obvious way to end this conversation.

"Timothy, your debtors are your problem. However, as an act of good will"—Dorian ignored the derisive snort that earned him—"I'll sell the library for you. In fact, my favorite bookshop has a stall right over there. I'll speak with them now. All proceeds will be yours to keep. In return, you and I sever all ties." Dorian held out his hand. "The alternative is, I cut you off with nothing. This is my final act of charity toward you. Do we have an agreement?"

Tense seconds passed as Dorian waited, palm extended. Finally, Timothy took it but made his real feelings known by spitting on the ice beside their shiny leather boots, before stalking toward the nearest pub.

Oliver shook his head. "I don't know how you've not let him rot in debtors' prison before now."

Because Juliet had adored her cousin. But as was the case concerning most areas in his life, Juliet's opinion mattered less and less as time passed.

"There's still time for him to land in gaol before the Season begins," Dorian said. "Would you like to wander on your own for a while? I believe I have a library to dispose of." He gestured toward the booth.

"Are you sure about this?"

"I've been considering it anyway." Dorian lowered his

voice. "Think about it. No matter which dewy-eyed debutante I agree to wed, she's going to be marrying a man known for his previous love match. The poor woman will have to battle Juliet's ghost with all of society watching. The least I can do is ensure she doesn't have to live in a house surrounded by Juliet's things." He may not expect to love his next wife, but she would be the Duchess of Holland, deserving of respect and kindness.

"Perhaps we can convince your bookseller to save you from the horrors of the Season and marry you as a mission of mercy."

"Tempting as that thought may be, Mother would faint dead." Dorian laughed.

"Then you'd best not flirt with her in front of your mother. This is the first woman you've been attracted to in years."

Dorian averted his eyes from the shop and the women inside it. "I never said I was attracted to her."

Oliver made a moue of disappointment, then ruined the effect by taking a giant bite of roasted meat from the stick he still carried. "You're a terrible liar. It's a miracle you didn't single-handedly lose us the war."

"The king valued my diplomatic skills greatly, and you know it."

"Yes, well. We all know he's mad. Not the ringing endorsement you think it is, Holland."

Chapter Two

🖋

"Three pages," Hattie hissed from where she crouched beside a crate of books, reading a copy of her own. "Blanche Clementine has gone on for three pages about this man's hands. His *hands*. How special can a pair of hands be when they aren't even touching the heroine yet?" She widened her eyes comically, and Caro clearly heard everything she wasn't saying. *What were you thinking, Caroline? Hands? Really? Is this what readers expect from one of your books?*

If her cousin had any idea how compelling the inspiration had been for this last book, Hattie would be congratulating her on her restraint. As if summoned by her thoughts, a shadow fell over them, barely preceding a waft of bergamot that somehow wove its way through the scents of the fair.

A customer entered the small square of ice they'd claimed for store space. But not just any customer. *The* customer. The man who'd unwittingly inspired an entire erotic novel— one they'd already sold several copies of that day. Inking each sale with their hastily made PURCHASED ON THE RIVER THAMES stamp was the closest she'd ever come to signing her books, and it gave her a thrill each time.

In the middle of the booth, the Duke of Holland paused, backlit by the bright winter sunlight that did little to dispel the bitter cold. Caro forced a serene smile of greeting.

Although she couldn't see his face, she knew that silhouette well. In fact, her fingers had traced every line of his body through the medium of ink and pen, replaying the brief moment when he'd wrapped his arm around her waist and pressed her to him. Had she known how their encounter would linger in her mind, she'd have taken notes. As it was, her recollection of their time outside the bookshop was etched into her memory so deeply it played behind her eyes when she heard his voice.

Even if she hadn't been able to identify him by key landmarks like the straight line of his shoulders under his caped greatcoat, she would know it was him by the way every hair on her body seemed to stand at attention in his perfectly polished presence.

Each time she laid eyes on him, the urge to muss his pressed and starched edges grew. To run her fingers through his tamed waves and kiss him until his cravat was hopelessly rumpled. If ever there was a hero who needed a good unraveling, it was him.

Caro wasn't the only one to think so, as the gossip rags speculated with a wild sort of glee over whether London's most eligible widower would marry this next Season. No doubt women all over the country were preparing to dampen their petticoats and pinch their cheeks in hope of being lucky enough to do the honors.

According to the papers, close friends of the dowager duchess claimed he'd turned over the entire bride hunt to his mother. *God help the debutantes this year. I wouldn't wish the dowager's critical eye on my worst enemy.* She'd served his mother tea several times in the store, and the older woman would intimidate anyone. "Good afternoon, Your Grace. I hope you're enjoying the frost fair." Caro dipped a shallow curtsy as another man joined the duke.

Before he could answer, the man with him stumbled forward. As if watching the moment suspended in time, Caro reached out a hand to no avail and was left staring at her cousin. Behind the men, Constance stood with her mouth agape, gripping a small wood crate to her chest—presumably, the object responsible for shoving a grown man off his feet.

Like dominos, one man fell against the other, then tilted at an alarming angle until gravity won the battle and both tumbled to the ice in a heap of limbs and fine clothes that cost more than a year's income.

"Bloody hell, Connie, what have you done?" The exclamation escaped before Caro could call it back.

"I won the game of ice bowling for nobs, didn't I?" Constance joked weakly before the gravity of the situation hit her and she sobered. "I'm terribly sorry, gentlemen. Is anyone hurt?"

Caro desperately wished she could close her eyes and unsee the events of the last few seconds, or perhaps have the ice give way under her feet and sweep her away into the Thames. Not only had Connie just physically assaulted a duke and—judging by the clothes—another lord, but Caro had sworn in front of them.

He'd never return. They'd lose the patronage of their highest-ranking customer, and the considerable income he brought to the store. And it was all because Connie couldn't watch where she was going, and Caro's mouth had momentarily allowed her inner thoughts an outside voice. *Damn it*.

The duke met her eyes from where he lay sprawled half under his friend, and Caro clapped a hand over her mouth to muffle another curse. They were probably furious. Any second now, he'd erupt and they'd have an entirely deserved aristocratic tantrum on their hands.

Every time she'd seen him, her heartbeat thundered in her ears as she met those blue eyes, and today was no different.

Blue, serious, sometimes sad. Never laughing, and rarely relaxed.

Until now. Creases fanned from the corners of his eyes, and a huff of laughter broke the horrified silence in the booth. "We seem to struggle with gravity in each other's presence. Have you noticed?" he said, meeting her gaze and sending a riot of awareness frolicking through her blood. She couldn't help a smile at his jest. The moment didn't linger, because he elbowed his friend and said, "Oliver, you're heavy as an ox. Move."

For a man who was always so terribly perfectly turned out, the incongruity of his deliciously rough voice was enough to make it linger in her mind each time she saw him. A voice like that was made for whispering in the dark, not making polite conversation in ballrooms. Hearing it laced with humor made the expected flutter in her belly turn warm.

Later, she'd allow herself a moment to remember the feeling, that voice, and the lines framing his eyes when he smiled. There'd be extensive pondering of the rare sighting of a smiling Duke of Holland. But first, she needed to get him upright.

"Please let me help." Caro offered a hand to the duke's companion, since he was on top, but was waved away as he lumbered to his feet.

The duke's first attempt to stand resulted in one boot sliding in the wrong direction and his—*rather spectacular, not that she'd spent considerable time staring at it*—bum thumping back to the ice.

Despite the air being cold enough to freeze her eyelashes

together, when His Grace accepted her outstretched hand, his leather-clad fingertips felt as if they'd leave a permanent imprint on her skin. Inside her gloves, Caro tingled at the contact with the same broad palms and strong, tapered fingers she'd written about.

If he'd spent time at his desk today, his gloves might be covering the one less-than-perfect part of him—the right pointer finger with its dark smudge of ink that sometimes lingered after hours of work doing ducal things.

Whatever those were. Writing bills for Parliament? Sending chatty notes around to Prinny? She had no more idea what a duke did with his time than she had a say in the fashion choices of Queen Charlotte.

Frankly, Hattie should be grateful Caro had limited the descriptions of his hands to only three pages. But then, her cousin hadn't reached the erotic scenes yet.

As he released his grip, their surroundings returned to sharp focus, just as she remembered from that summer day so many months ago. The frost fair surged around them in a cacophony of smells and sounds. Constance was apologizing again to the men, while Hattie took the wood box before anyone else could be hurt and set it on a nearby table.

The one called Oliver dusted off bits of snow and ice clinging to his breeches as he sent Connie a charming smile. "Nothing hurt besides my dignity."

"There wasn't much of that to begin with," His Grace commented wryly.

A jest. A smile and a jest? He was handling the situation with far more good humor than she'd expect. All day they'd watched people slipping and sliding about on the ice, and rarely did the falls result in a well-dressed man laughing. Much less the handsome but stoic Duke of Holland.

"After such an entrance, I hesitate to ask if there's anything we can assist you with." *Now that we've thrown you to the ground and possibly ruined your clothing.*

His Grace smoothed a hand over his greatcoat, then tugged his cuffs into place, putting himself to rights. The perfect duke once more, albeit with a smile lingering at the edges of his mouth. "There is something. I'd like to speak with someone regarding the sale of my late wife's library. I imagine there are a few titles that might be of interest to private collectors. The rest can be sold as a lot, or perhaps go to your lending library as a donation."

"We are honored to be considered for such a project, Your Grace. I can begin that process for you and review our standard fees. My uncle is expected to return within the hour; if needed, he can help with any questions I can't answer," Caro said.

Hattie and Constance began unpacking the contents of the box. With a deliberately casual air, Hattie said, "Perhaps it would be best if Miss Danvers examined your collection in person, Your Grace. Most of our collectors deal with her directly, so she is the logical person to inspect your library and make arrangements for transportation and private sales."

Constance's laugh was muffled as she began stacking and arranging books as quickly as Hattie set them on the table.

A warm flush bloomed under Caro's breastbone, and she desperately bid the blush to stay there and not travel to her cheeks. Between Hattie's too-innocent tone and Constance's giggle, they'd definitely noticed this inappropriate and entirely inconvenient fondness she harbored for the duke.

Sharply intelligent eyes on the stormy side of blue focused on Caro. "Miss Danvers, I presume?"

She couldn't help a small wince at his words but quickly smoothed her features into a neutral expression. *Indeed, the same woman who waits on you each time you walk through our door and has now served tea and biscuits to your mother on three separate occasions while you perused the store. You've held me against your body yet didn't bother to learn my name.* Instead, she said, "Miss Caroline Danvers at your service, Your Grace." She offered a small curtsy, trying not to be cheeky about it.

"Assessing the collection in person is an excellent idea. Whatever your normal fees are, I'm sure they're fair. This will be a significant undertaking, and you should be compensated for the work," he said.

How large was this library? Possibilities tickled her brain as the list of customers looking for specific titles circled. Those sales would be a welcome boost in revenue, even if it was only their usual consignment fee.

Although the store was not failing, as the one handling correspondence and bookkeeping, Caro knew exactly what a boon an influx of money would be. Perhaps they'd be able to replace the weather-beaten back door that had let in rain and snow during the last thaw and frozen shut during this week's temperatures. Or they could set aside funds for Aunt Mary and Uncle Owen to visit their other daughter, Betsy, and her family. With their first grandchild due in a few months, it would mean so much for Aunt Mary to be there.

The duke's companion interrupted her thoughts by picking up one of the books on display. "*A Dalliance for Miss Lorraine.* Holland, isn't this that author you like?" Without waiting for a response, he flipped through the pages. "Is this picture on the front page the only one? Where are the others?"

The duke turned and glanced at the burgundy cloth-bound cover. "What are you talking about? It's a novel."

"A dirty novel. What good is a dirty book if there aren't pictures?"

Caro bit her lip against an entirely inappropriate urge to laugh.

Bless him, the duke's sigh spoke volumes and, honestly, made him more appealing. "Oliver, you use your imagination. Blanche Clementine's writing offers plenty of fodder for your mind to make its own pictures. And the stories are erotic, not dirty. They've earned devoted readers because they are also emotional. Making someone care about the lives of imaginary people is the sign of a writer of merit, regardless of content." He plucked the book from his friend's hand, shaking it in his face. "I'm buying this for you. You're going to read it and you're going to like it—even without pictures." Picking up a second copy, he handed them to Caro. "We will take these today. As to the library project, if you are available this Friday at one o'clock, I'll tell my secretary to expect you."

Visiting the ducal residence? Back in the village, she'd gaped at the ostentatious furnishings in the squire's home when she visited with her father. A duke's house would be ten times grander. How was she supposed to act? Were there protocols in place? "I'll need to check with my uncle."

Hattie nudged Caro's shoulder. "If the river is still frozen, Aunt Mary can watch the store with Constance, and I'll work the booth with Uncle Owen. Unless you have other plans, you're free to tend to the duke on any Friday you like."

Pasting on a close-lipped smile, Caro addressed him. "It appears I'm available."

As she marked the copies of her book with the frost fair stamp, then wrapped them in brown paper and twine, her stomach roiled. The previous butterflies had drowned in a rising tide of nerves. It was too easy to imagine herself in his grand library, surrounded by all those bergamot-scented personal items that might offer clues about who the duke was in private. Was he the pressed and perfect society gentleman? Or the apologetic man who'd looked at her with such interest and concern when they met, even though she was bedraggled? Or was the real Duke of Holland actually the laughing man who'd joked with his friend while sprawled on the ice? Sure, he could be all of them, but that only led to more questions.

Despite the rather pathetic uselessness of her attraction to the man, she still wanted to examine the pieces of him like a puzzle to see what made him laugh, or what caused his eyes to turn stormy with emotion, or why he'd chosen to part with something as valuable and personal as his late wife's library.

Rumor had it he'd spent years serving as a diplomat on the Continent and did it so competently the king couldn't spare him long enough to return home to bury his wife. Was that why he wanted to get rid of her books? Guilt?

I have a weakness for tortured heroes. The duke was usually the picture of a somber, tortured, controlled hero—a heroine could unravel a man like that, given enough time and bravery.

The duke tucked one book under his arm and passed the other to his friend. "It's settled, then. I'll let my staff know to expect you next Friday."

A little of her worry drained away as the two men left the stall. In such a grand house, someone could probably spend an entire month under his roof and never lay eyes on the man. Caroline rested a palm over her thundering heartbeat, drew in a deep breath, then turned to her cousins. "There are two more sales toward my cottage...which I'll need when I have to run away in order to escape your painfully obvious scheming."

Hattie gave her a cheeky wink. "You're welcome. Enjoy his massive...library."

Chapter Three

❧

*T*hat night, her introduction still rang in his ears, despite the quartet playing across the ballroom.

Miss Caroline Danvers.

Dorian had known that. However, when faced with either a potential awkward silence after pretending he didn't know her name or the guaranteed awkward silence sure to follow the revelation of his uncanny ability to remember everything she'd said within earshot since they'd met…he'd faked ignorance. With Oliver looking on, and having literally just fallen on his arse, saving himself further embarrassment seemed the safest thing to do.

Especially when what he'd wanted was to ask if she'd won the ongoing war with her cousin's cat for her pillow—something he'd heard about in bits and snippets of conversation for months now. The women were far chattier on the sales floor when they didn't know they had a duke in their midst.

When he'd entered the temporary shop booth, Miss Danvers's cheeks were pink, and her eyes were bright. She'd appeared the picture of health. A relief, because when he'd stopped by two weeks ago, her voice had been strained from a sore throat. Thin lines of discomfort had pinched her lips.

Yes, he remembered everything. Now, added to the list of memories, was the brief flash of emotion she'd shown when

he'd pretended not to know her name. His feigned ignorance had stung, and frankly, he felt like a jackass when he
remembered that barely-there-then-gone wince, followed by
a pause. He'd bet his last shilling that she had considered and
discarded several replies before settling on a simple introduction. The harder she tried to be cool, calm, and collected, the
more he wished she'd firm that pointed chin at him and fire
off the first thing that came to mind.

She didn't look like a Caroline. Dorian knew several Car-
olines, and each was blonde and so cool they might as well
have been carved from marble.

Exactly like the woman his mother was pointing toward
with her glass. "Lady Caroline Stapleton. Her father's connections within the Whigs would be helpful should you pur-
sue politics someday."

Dorian tried not to choke on his champagne. God, politics. No, thank you. The diplomatic service on the Continent
had been interesting. Sitting in Parliament would bore him
to tears.

Lady Caroline Stapleton looked like a Caroline, in all the
worst ways.

Blonde hair curled around her face in the current style,
while a variety of decorative objects turned her coiffure into
a sculptured affair that risked poking a dance partner's eyes
should they move wrong. Although beautiful, she was so rig-
idly composed he worried her face might crack should her
lips veer beyond the polite curve she'd worn all evening. She
would certainly never swear at her cousin for knocking him
over. But when Miss Danvers had cursed, the professional
mask had slipped, and he'd thought, *Ah, there you are.*

A smile teased his mouth at the memory as he drank
again. "No."

Either Gloria Whitaker, Dowager Duchess of Holland,

had taken her name to be aspirational, or she'd been chris-
tened in a moment of prescient clarity. Even standing on the
edge of the room, she was glorious. A sheer veil fluttered
from the back of her turban, secured with clusters of what he
hoped was faux fruit. Pom-pom tassels bobbed and swayed
from a long wrap that seemed to serve no purpose except to
drape fetchingly from the crooks of her elbows as she raised a
glass of champagne to her lips.

The dowager examined the women present again with
the focus of a general assessing unruly troops. And like a
general, she'd be happiest if people would simply put her in
charge and stop meddling in her plans. Given permission,
she'd be a benevolent dictator in his, and everyone else's,
life. Unless he disagreed with her on something; then the
benevolence faded into terse negotiations. His mother loved
him to distraction, and Dorian knew that. However, her
confidence that she knew best was equal to—if not greater
than—the feelings of maternal adoration toward her only
child. Her plan frequently trumped affection, until Dorian
raised a fuss. It had always been thus.

This evening, his dismissal of a third potential wife made
her sniff in annoyance.

"Miss Edwina Humphry? The freckles are unfortunate,
but she's charming. Keep your children out of the sun, and
you will be fine."

"She is charming—I'll grant that."

"That wasn't an outright no, so we shall call Miss Humphry a maybe."

He rather liked Miss Humphry's freckles, but if he said
so, his mother would be sending wedding invitations to the
printers by the weekend. A chandelier overhead cast flickering light through the room, making Miss Humphry's dark
hair shine becomingly.

Rather like a certain bookseller's. In the sunshine, would Miss Humphry's hair also turn auburn?

Miss Danvers might not look like a Caroline, but Miss Humphry did look like an Edwina. Whether that was fortunate or terrible was a topic open for discussion. But not a topic he'd discuss with her, obviously. Perhaps Miss Humphry had read an interesting book recently, and they could talk about that while they danced. For expediency's sake, if he wanted to speak to her for more than two-second passes on the floor, it would have to be a waltz.

Right, then. Dorian straightened and handed his glass to a passing footman. "I'll ask Miss Humphry to dance, shall I?"

His mother's smile was a bit smug, but as he'd agreed to this bride hunt, he would have to accept the natural consequences of Gloria feeling she'd successfully coerced him into doing her bidding.

Truth be told, doing her bidding more often than not was simply easier. It wasn't as if he had conflicting plans. Not when most days, he struggled with a general feeling of disillusionment regarding the future. His mother had mentioned he would feel like himself again after the initial grief ran its course.

It might be grief, but not just for Juliet. If anything, this feeling might be grieving everything else he'd lost—the confidence born from knowing his place in the world, the belief in true love overcoming all obstacles, and a rather irrational conviction that he'd somehow done everything right to lead such a blessed life. He hadn't only lost Juliet five years ago.

Crossing the room, Dorian tried to concentrate on the familiar faces lining the walls and filling the dance floor, reminding himself he was among friends—or at least not enemies. This was a small gathering, since many families of the ton wouldn't return to Town and join the lords sitting in Parliament until the spring. Yet even in this more intimate event, the number of eyes watching to see whom he'd lead to the floor made him want to retreat to his study with a glass of brandy and a book, never to be seen again.

This past Christmas, the dowager had approached him about taking another wife. After years of marriage, he and Juliet hadn't secured an heir to the title. There had been three pregnancies, all of which ended within a few weeks of realizing she was with child. By the third, Juliet had been subdued when she'd told him they were expecting, then treated the miscarriage with a fatalistic sort of acceptance. Not long after that, he'd been called to the Continent to help in the war against Napoleon.

Gloria hadn't been unkind when she asked about his plans for an heir. In her usual way, she'd laid out her concerns, strategies, and anticipated outcome. After thinking on it for a few days, he'd suggested they assess marriage prospects before the beginning of the official Season. The sooner he could choose someone, the better. And if he could avoid ballrooms rank with the crush of bodies, even better.

Once upon a time, he'd looked forward to events like this. Loved twirling around the floor with his wife in his arms and the world at his feet. A stab of emotion in his throat warned against further progress down that mental pathway—it would only hurt. Like the old mapmakers wrote at the edges of the known, hic sunt dracones. *Here be dragons.* He had no intention of fighting those dragons in a room full of dancers and onlookers sipping champagne.

Instead of feeling relaxed amidst friends, he couldn't get past the distracting ache of his feet after being on them all day. With each passing minute, a faint throbbing grew behind his left eye, and something on his cravat was making his neck itch.

Despite those general discomforts, Dorian was having a better night than Oliver. The Earl of Southwyn and his fiancée, Miss Althea Thompson, moved gracefully through the steps of the dance, social masks firmly in place while not facing one another. During the brief intervals when they were partnered, there appeared to be a hushed argument happening.

Or rather, Althea was having an argument, while Oliver wore a blank expression as if his mind was elsewhere.

Dorian shook his head. He and Juliet hadn't argued often. Hardly ever, in fact. But they'd had one disagreement at a ball. Biting words in hissed whispers flung like arrows, two or three seconds at a time. It was miserable, as he recalled. Funny that he could remember going to bed angry, but he couldn't for the life of him remember what they'd been fighting about.

Time might be the greatest force in nature. It erased and healed so much.

Bowing to a matron his mother had entertained in the yellow drawing room yesterday, Dorian offered a few polite phrases before moving on. On the far wall, Miss Humphry appeared deep in conversation with an older woman. Her mother? A chaperone? He'd find out soon enough.

Like most of the marriage prospects, Miss Humphry was young. To be honest, younger than he'd like. They'd shared several brief exchanges over the last few weeks at events like this one, but he'd never singled her out for a dance. Although he couldn't imagine her in his bed, once Dorian knew her better, that might change. She had a sly wit, which indicated she was an excellent conversationalist. No way of knowing until he spoke with her beyond the pleasantries. If she had a sharp intellect, Miss Humphry could be tolerable, at the very least. They might even get on well and be content.

There would be no grand romance this time. He had already lived that and dealt with the bitterness that followed. At the moment, the shock and pain of reading Juliet's death-bed confessional letter rose in his memory, despite having faded over the years. Most days he didn't taste the heart-break on his tongue—especially after realizing cynicism was sweeter than pain.

And it was cynicism paired with logic that allowed him to see the wisdom of the dowager's suggestion to remarry. As she'd gently but devastatingly pointed out over wassail and stuffed goose, there was a good chance Dorian wouldn't need to deal with his new bride for long. After all, his father had died at the age of thirty-six, and his grandfather passed before the age of fifty.

In a few months' time, Dorian would be thirty-six. If his father could clutch his chest and suddenly collapse in the hallway on a random Tuesday, so might he. Should that happen, Dorian needed to do right by the duchy and leave an heir.

Thus, a bride. An aristocratic woman who would have the training and social connections to deal with not only his strong-willed mother, but the rest of society, and in his absence, to raise the next Duke of Holland.

Miss Humphry's eyes—green, not the rich brown of Caroline Danvers's—widened when he stopped and offered a bow.

"Miss Humphry, may I have your next waltz if it's not already taken?"

"Of…of course, Your Grace."

Dorian forced his cheeks into a smile. He'd told his mother he would try, and try he would.

Half an hour later, Oliver found him in the hall outside the card room. "Going to play a few hands to pass the time?" he asked.

Except, Oliver already knew the answer, because he leaned against the floral papered wall beside Dorian. As he relaxed, his shoulders settled into their normal place instead of up by his ears. They both needed a break, it would seem.

"Hiding, and I'm not afraid to admit it," Dorian answered. "It's worse than it was the year before I met Juliet. Everyone is watching. I'll have to constantly be on guard against mamas trying to catch me alone with their daughter. Women don't talk to me—they simper or go silent and expect me to carry the conversation. Makes a man feel hunted."

"Such a trial it is to be a young, rich, handsome duke. You can't see the tears, but my heart sheds them for your plight."

They were quiet a moment, attendants of the event buzzing down the hall and around the corner from their dark hiding place.

"So...Miss Humphry," Oliver ventured.

"We danced one waltz. No more, no less."

"The whispers are already circulating. I counted three women glaring at Miss Humphry during your dance and overheard others speculating on your wedding date."

Dorian pressed the heel of his palm against the persistent ache behind his left eye. "It wasn't even the supper set."

"One of the dowager's suggested brides?"

"Yes." The word was part answer, part sigh. The waltz could have gone better. Miss Humphry had been quiet, but there were myriad reasons to explain that. Surprise, worry, or even a blasted headache like the one he was dealing with. Unfortunately, holding her in his arms for the dance hadn't brought an immediate feeling of rightness, and her company hadn't offered additional clues to assure him they'd suit. "I'd rather the whole ordeal be done and over with as soon as possible."

Oliver's crooked grin held little sympathy. "Don't relish the idea of choosing an infant bride from this year's debutantes?"

"You have no idea what it's like. You've been promised to someone since the cradle." Dorian's shudder was genuine.

Oliver shrugged. "I may not be familiar with the hunt, but I can understand feeling more like a title or a role than a man. My engagement—or rather, engagements—hasn't exactly been romance and roses either."

Wincing, Dorian cursed his flippant words. If anyone understood marrying for duty, it was Oliver. "Have you heard from Dorcas?"

"Actually, yes. We're friends. I suppose growing up believing you'll marry someone has that effect. She writes regularly to tell me how much she enjoys married life. Never a word about the muddle she left me to unravel, though. Thanks to that damned betrothal agreement, when Dorcas eloped, her father was well within his rights to hand me Althea instead. I feel like a pair of old boots, passed down from one sister to another."

"At least you didn't love Dorcas. That would have been devastating. Althea seems nice, though. Pretty, and from the same good family."

"Althea is fine, except she acts like she hates me now. We used to get along famously when I was marrying her sister. Now it's practically pistols at dawn every time we meet. Bodes well for our marital bliss." Oliver straightened. "I need a drink. Something stronger than champagne."

Dorian pushed off the wall and tugged his waistcoat into place. "Game room should have brandy."

As they walked, Oliver asked, "Miss Humphry—yes or no?"

"The dance was stiff and awkward, despite my best efforts." As they'd danced, he'd tried admiring her eyes but found himself wishing they were brown. The wit and intelligence he'd encountered before had been absent, perhaps because she felt the pressure of everyone's eyes on them. "I'll call on her later in the week. Try to strike up a real conversation before moving on. But it's probably a no."

It hadn't been disappointment he'd felt as he returned her to her mother but relief. What that meant for his desire to find a bride before the height of the Season, he'd rather not contemplate. One day soon, he'd have to settle on someone. But the relief that the decision wasn't going to be made right then had been immediate. While he didn't harbor fanciful notions of finding love again, surely marrying a woman he could imagine living with wasn't too much to ask.

Chapter Four

As agreed, Caro arrived at the imposing marble facade of the ducal townhome in Bloomsbury on Friday and had been shown inside by a polite but aloof butler who introduced himself as Hastings. Within minutes, she'd been handed off to the duke's personal secretary, Howard.

After a three-second perusal of the collection, Caro reassessed her initial expected timeline. The duke had warned that this wasn't a small undertaking. She'd envisioned a shelf of books, maybe a couple of bookcases—not several shelves twice the length of her bedroom that towered over her.

The turmoil in her chest might have been excitement at the challenge or a mix of dread and anticipation at seeing the duke regularly for the weeks it would take to complete her task. Maybe even months, since she had only a few afternoons per week to devote to the donation.

Yet three days of pulling, sorting, stacking, and listing the duke's collection had come and gone in peace and solitude. Apart from Howard, of course. The secretary moved with the silent steps of a ghost, so she often forgot he was in the room. The expectation of seeing the duke waned, and her nerves diminished with it, but the feeling of being on edge in case he showed up never quite went away. This was a job like anything else, and the location turned out to be surprisingly free of blue-eyed distractions.

During those quiet days in the opulent library, she developed a rhythm of sorts as she lost herself in her own little world of books and the seemingly endless list of items the shop's wealthier collectors were looking for.

But now? Caro sighed. *Hell and blast.*

Turning the book over in her hands, she admired the way the sunlight streaming in through the tall windows flashed off its gold-edged pages. A collection of Shakespeare's plays—one of many on the shelves. While it was a nice copy, there wasn't anything particularly noteworthy about it.

Except for the folded piece of paper that moments ago had fluttered out of the book to rest on the toe of her leather walking boot. Alas, the paper wasn't anything so helpful as a pound note or instructions for something useful like hair tonic.

No.

My dearest Juliet,

Was there ever anyone so perfectly named? The Bard himself surely envisioned someone like you when he wrote of a woman with whom a man could fall in love at first sight. Like that Montague in the play, I saw you from across the room and knew my life was irrevocably changed. I treasure every word you have graced me with since, and the memory of your lips keeps me company during the lonely nights when my arms ache to hold you.

From there, the letter writer—signed Romeo, naturally—meandered long-windedly through declarations of eternal devotion, more than a few innuendos about masturbation, and one misspelled quote from the referenced play in question.

Funny, but the duke didn't strike her as the kind of man to wax poetic, then end with a paltry *You're in my heart and mind always*. But who was she to cast judgment on his marital correspondence?

Due to the mentions of self-pleasure, this particular letter probably shouldn't be returned to the duke through his secretary.

On a normal day in the shop, Caro easily braced herself for talking to Holland. But these circumstances were beyond what she encountered on a normal day. Grappling with an inconvenient attraction to an aristocrat was bad enough without the additional embarrassment of discussing a letter in which he wrote about touching himself.

Yet if someone found a letter she'd written to her spouse, she would want it returned to her. No matter what she thought of the contents, this was a piece of their history and belonged to the duke.

Last night, Constance had regaled her with gossip about Their Graces, the Hollands. A romance for the ages, entirely out of place amid the family mergers and financial couplings of the ton. She held proof in her hand of their passion for one another, as this letter was dated a year before the duchess's death.

So, time to face him. Caro neatly refolded the paper along well-worn creases that told their own tale of hands opening and closing it countless times. Perhaps she would get lucky and could leave it on his desk, then scurry from the room like a frightened mouse.

"Howard? Might I have a word with His Grace?" She waved the folded paper. "I've come across correspondence of a personal nature I believe the duke would prefer to remain as private as possible."

Howard raised a brow but sent her a nod. "I'll enquire with Hastings as to His Grace's schedule. Wait here."

And that's how she found herself ushered into the personal study of the Duke of Holland, where the man himself sat at his desk, with sunlight making the curly hairs of his exposed forearms appear dusted in gold. No coat, shirt cuffs rolled high, pen in hand, and a composed, closed expression on his perfect face.

And the project had been going so well too.

Orange-blossom water. When Caroline Danvers entered a room, she brought spring with her.

Howard, Hastings, and Oliver all had access to this study. Howard tended to use a gentle rap to announce his presence. Hastings preferred a more direct knock. Oliver just walked in.

Moments ago, Hastings had knocked, then said Howard needed a meeting. Dorian nodded and returned to his work.

But Howard didn't smell like orange blossoms. When the door opened, Hastings's voice carried from the hall saying, "His Grace will see you now."

The scent she wore hit one's senses with a freshness that made a man want to picnic on a lawn under the sun in those early bright days after the gray of winter had slipped away.

Despite her alluring smell, the clothes she wore were serviceable, sturdy, and more than a little drab. The dark-brown gown looked thick enough to block any breeze that dared tease at her skirts, and she'd covered her décolletage with an equally thick fichu. In the bookshop, he was often distracted by the subtle tint of her skin peeking through the semitransparent fabric of her typical fichu. No chance of that today.

With enough starch, the whole ensemble might stand on its own and retain the shape of her.

As much as he wished to linger on that shape, Dorian averted his eyes to the neat lines of numbers on the page in front of him. Rather than consider how often her curves appeared in his dreams, or sauntered through his more heated thoughts, he forced himself to focus on the sharp black ink strokes that created notations and amounts in tidy columns. Those numbers served one function—to tally properly and balance in his favor. This particular ledger was for the estate in Dorset.

The Dorset house had an orangery, an entirely unhelpful part of his brain supplied, where the orange blossoms were fragrant and sweet, promising luscious fruit if tended to properly. Fruit that would explode in your mouth with bright notes of happiness and drip down your chin.

What he wouldn't give for the chance to take her sweetness in his mouth. Images assailed his brain, causing a predictable response in his lap.

Damn it all to hell and back—he couldn't possibly rise to his feet now without embarrassing the both of them.

Dorian cleared his throat and inhaled a shallow breath intended to limit his senses to ink, paper, and the bergamot aftershave he'd used that morning. "May I help you, Miss Danvers?"

He risked a glance in time to see her hesitate for a brief moment before crossing the room. When she paused by the chair on the other side of his desk, he waved his hand, silently inviting her to sit.

Even at rest, she appeared poised for action. Perching on the edge of the seat, back ramrod straight, and fingers clenched in her lap around a piece of folded paper. "I'm terribly sorry to interrupt your work, Your Grace. I won't take up too much of your time."

She laid the paper on the desk in front of her. "This was tucked in the pages of a book. Due to its personal nature, I wanted to return it to you myself and not involve the staff."

He realized he was scowling when the space between his eyebrows pinched, making him wince as he unfolded the paper.

That wince traveled down his body in a sharp path as he read the words. A gaping pit of dread opened in his chest, seeming to swallow his whole body in an emotional ebony tar that threatened to drown him completely.

He'd known, hadn't he? The letter Juliet left for him as a sort of last confessional when she realized she was truly ill had mentioned a lover. She'd said the betrayal and shame had been too great a burden for her to bear, that she couldn't die with the lie on her soul. The dire tone of the letter had made his heart ache. She'd been in so much pain, and he hadn't been there. In the end, the fever ensured she wouldn't have to live with her guilt. But he did. Damn her eyes, he had to live with all of it, as well as a million questions he'd never have answered.

Without thought, Dorian shoved his chair back from the desk and rose, gasping for air like a man surfacing from a hard swim across an icy lake. Distantly, as if observing the consequences of someone else's actions, part of him noted Caroline jump at his abrupt movement, before he turned his back on her to face the window. Shaking fingers tunneled into his hair and stayed there as if he could contain the whirling thoughts through sheer pressure on his skull.

Fuck. There was the proof. A love letter to his wife, written by a man fancying himself to be her Romeo. Intimate and sexual. Romantic and graphic. Handwriting he'd never seen before, wooing with words of devotion and lust. And Juliet, damn her, had saved it. Carefully hidden it away in her books.

"I apologize for the invasion of your privacy, Your Grace. It was entirely accidental and won't be repeated."

As much as he hated that uncertain tone in her voice, he was too deep in the clawing panic and shock to turn around and reassure her. Hell, he'd been in here trying to convince himself for the third day in a row to visit her in the library. If for no other reason than to be a good host. Instead, he'd sat in the study like a coward because he didn't know what to say; in a stellar example of irony, the one woman who lingered in his mind and held his attention for longer than five seconds was entirely unsuitable. Night after night he was out with the dowager assessing potential brides, and the only woman he wanted anything to do with was in his bloody library while he hid behind his desk.

She'd found her way into his personal sanctum for reasons he'd never imagined.

He couldn't breathe. Fabric rustled as she either shifted in the chair or stood, but he couldn't turn to see when it felt like his ribs were crushing his lungs. Low and as if reaching him from a tunnel, the sound of her voice rose above his shallow, frantic gasps. A slight echoing in his ears gave everything a tinny quality as her words jumbled together with the lines of that fucking letter repeating through his brain.

"...People speak of the Duke and Duchess of Holland's romance, and after reading that, I see it's all true. I am so terribly sorry for your loss. I realize one would never choose such circumstances, but perhaps there's a small comfort in knowing the legacy your marriage left in others' minds is one of true love. The kind we read about in fairy tales."

Was he going to faint? No. Not if he managed to breathe again. This was a familiar hell. Panic had stolen his breath when his father died. He'd fought for air when he discovered his wife died loving someone else. These iron bands squeezing his lungs could be managed if he found the corner of his mind where the calmest version of himself lived. Because that part of him recognized this experience for what it was—an emotional reaction to the worst surprises life could throw at a man.

Through clenched teeth, Dorian hissed in vital air as he told himself the truths that could conquer the emotions turning his body and mind into a battleground.

Surprises happened, but life *would* go on. There was plenty of air in the room. He was safe. He could breathe. He could think. The shackles around his ribs opened ever so slowly.

A touch on his arm sent a shock through him, cutting past the anxiously racing thoughts, slicing through the emotions. It was only a hand, but he clung to it like a drowning man thrown a line and let it pull him out of the muck. Another breath, easier this time. Heavier with the scent of orange blossoms. He curled his hand around hers and let the solid realness of her presence act as an anchor.

As much as he hated his personal battle playing out in front of her, especially since she clearly found it concerning, he was grateful for the incentive to return to the moment.

"I am sorry if this reopens the grief for you. That is certainly not my intention. If I find more letters, I will deliver them to you directly. You have my word." She sounded hesitant, like she didn't know what to say but was still compelled to try.

"Thank you." The words were hoarse, pared down from everything he wanted to say but shouldn't. *Thank you for providing proof.* Even though it destroyed lingering hopes he hadn't realized he held—hopes that he'd somehow misinterpreted Juliet's last letter.

Her hand pulled out from under his, and he turned, drinking in the sight of her like the air he'd struggled to find seconds ago. "Wait. Miss Danvers...I'm sorry. I've handled this poorly. Caught me off guard, to be honest."

Caroline offered a crooked smile. "It's gratifying to know you're capable of being taken off guard, Your Grace. Please don't apologize to anyone for mourning a woman you loved. Grief is a tricky business."

If only it were that simple. He tried to return her smile, but his mouth wouldn't make the shape. "Marriage is a tricky business as well. Complicated."

The urge to sit down and tell her everything nearly overwhelmed his good sense. However, their relationship—if one could call it that—was not one where spilling his secrets was appropriate.

"I'll be on my way, Your Grace. Again, I'm sorry for any pain this caused."

Before he could reply, she was gone, leaving him alone. Just him, a love letter he didn't write, and the lingering scent of spring beside him.

Chapter Five

"Constance, what is this made of?" Caro held the makeshift hairpiece between her forefinger and thumb as if it were a rodent. It did look rather ratlike.

"Burlap, wool batting, and hair from Gingersnap's brush." Constance glanced between the women, then rolled her eyes. "What? Gingersnap and I have essentially the same hair color."

"Gingersnap is a cat, luv. What possessed you to make a hairpiece out of cat hair?" Hattie's dry comment made Caro grin.

"My hair will cover it. This makes my bun larger." Constance snatched the furry hairpiece out of Caro's hands and positioned it at the back of her head, then pinned her coppery gold in place over top. "See? Otherwise, my bun is a pathetic, puny thing. I have a lot of curls, not a lot of hair. In the styles everyone is wearing, the difference is quite obvious." The result was rather fetching. But still. Cat hair.

"You look beautiful, as always. However, the method by which you achieve that look is revolting," Caro said.

Constance shrugged, completely unconcerned with another's viewpoint, as always. It was an admirable trait to be able to roll opinions off your back like a duck with water.

"The end justifies the means," she said. "Help me into

this?" She held up the gown they'd made over with bits and bobs harvested from other gowns and bonnets.

While the frost fair had lasted less than a week, London was still dealing with a frigid February, which meant limited options for romantic outings for a woman with as many beaus as Constance. A line of beaus. A veritable herd of them. She held court over her suitors like a queen, never choosing one. She liked them all equally, and in the end, she disliked them all equally. But tonight, she'd dance, and Caro was happy for her.

Hattie secured the wool overdress with a brooch whose pin could double as a weapon in a pinch. "There. That will do nicely."

"Mr. Hudson will be enthralled," Caroline said.

With a swish of skirts and partially faux hair, her cousin kissed them each on the cheek, then left.

Hattie collapsed on the bed and stared at the ceiling. "Mr. Hudson struck me as rather staid. What does she see in him?"

"I have no idea. Perhaps opposites do attract."

"I don't think I'd like to fall in love with my opposite. Would you?"

Caro cocked her head and considered the question. Finding a husband who would cherish her the way her heroes adored her heroines seemed impossible. It was difficult to imagine a man who would not only accept her writing but support it. Although nearly two years had passed, there were days when her father's betrayal still felt fresh. He'd treated Caro's mother with similar controlling bully tactics.

When she died while trying to bring Caro's sister into the world, he'd claimed the labor would have gone differently if she'd been pregnant with a son instead of another useless daughter. They'd buried them together, since her father refused to pay for two caskets. Even though he'd denied her little sister her own burial plot, Caro found comfort in the thought of her being held forever by their mother.

Was it any wonder she'd started writing stories where everything ended happily? There'd been so little joy in her world Caro had to create her own. Wrenching away from the painful memories, Caro returned to the topic at hand. "I'd think there would need to be enough similarities to have common ground. A like-mindedness. But too much might eventually be...boring, perhaps? Yet to have him be entirely my opposite seems like a lot of hard work." Had the duke and his wife been similar in disposition? According to the gossip she'd heard and read since word got out about his desire to remarry, the late duchess had been part of every social gathering, seen and adored everywhere...which was the opposite of everything she'd observed about the duke.

Hattie shook her head. "Not that I plan to marry. But if I did, it seems there are already enough opposites at play by virtue of a husband being a man. Putting up with a man seems like enough mental labor, thank you. We needn't add contrary interests on top of that."

Caro bit back questions, as she always did when Hattie spoke of her aversion to marriage. A few years ago, she'd been hurt. Badly. While she refused to share details, Caro and Connie knew enough not to challenge Hattie's assertion that she'd never marry.

"Perhaps the cousins with the empty social calendar shouldn't be the ones passing judgment," Caro said. "Mr. Hudson might be exactly what she wants."

"My social calendar is exactly as I wish it. However, I can't help feeling you're made for romance and all that—"

"You want to say *nonsense*, don't you?"

Hattie laughed. "I was going to say *rot*. You're made for all that rot. I am not."

A pair of blue eyes rose in her mind. Now she knew they had an equal impact on her system when smiling as they did when flooded with pain. She'd touched him. It was meant to comfort, but she'd still been surprised at the way he clung to her hand rather than pushing her away. "I have my books. Besides, who could possibly compare to the heroes I write?" Caro shrugged.

"Girls? Last chance to come with us! You haven't been to a social gathering in an age." Aunt Mary's voice carried down the hall.

"I have correspondence to see to," Caro called back.

"Do you really?" Hattie hissed.

"I always do." Especially after spending so many hours at the ducal townhome instead of her desk.

"How about you, Hattie? There are several young men I'd like you to meet."

Hattie widened her eyes at Caro, silently pleading.

Caro tried to disguise her laughter when she raised her voice. "I'm afraid I'm stealing her for office duties, Aunt Mary. Please give our regards to the gossipy matrons. We can't wait to hear all the latest when you return."

"You're an angel of mercy," Hattie whispered.

Downstairs, their family chattered, doors opened and closed. When all was quiet, the women made their way to the office.

"I love it when it's like this. When everything is dark and still," Caro said, keeping her voice low. Not that there was a reason to be quiet, but it felt profane somehow to disturb the space.

"When I can't sleep, sometimes I come down here, curl up in the chair by the window, and soak it all in." Hattie sighed happily. "All those stories, all that knowledge. On the shelves for the taking."

On the other side of the wavy glass panes, Londoners went about their night in a mix of horses, carts, carriages, working clothes, and evening wear. Hattie dragged a wood chair from behind the sales counter to the office and plopped down beside Caro at the desk. "Hand me a stack."

Caro stifled a yawn. "Thank you for the help. I don't know why I'm so tired already."

Hattie took a few of the letters from the pile on the desk and began scanning one. "Perhaps you're exhausted from the mental circles you've been spinning all day, matching books to collectors. At least it seems there will be plenty of valuable titles in the duke's collection." She drew out a sheet of paper and penned a quick reply to whatever the letter said.

The first note in Caro's pile was from her friend Gerard, who lived on the top floor a few buildings down. Gerard and his partner, Leo, wanted her to join them at the theater when she was available. The men had adopted her in a sense when they realized she rarely went out in the evenings and had few friends beyond her cousins. Smiling, she dashed off an agreement to check her schedule, then moved on to the next one.

"Being in the duke's home is unsettling." As much as she wanted to share about the letter she'd found, it didn't seem right to discuss something so intimate. Especially when he'd reacted the way he had.

Hattie's gaze flew to hers as a pinch between her brows appeared. "You don't need to go alone. If you don't feel safe, Caro—"

"No, that's not it. I don't feel threatened. I'm a bit embarrassed, to be honest." A wry smile tilted her lips. "I . . . I don't want to look like an arse in front of him. If he catches me staring cow eyed, I will quite literally die of mortification.

Wither and turn to ash on his no-doubt priceless carpet."
Except, when you touched him, he welcomed it.

"He might return your regard. Or be flattered. Or look
down his ducal nose and sniff about commoners. We won't
know until we know." Hattie held out a letter from the general delivery pile. "This one is yours. From your publisher,
looks like. He's still pressing for the next book?"

Caro sighed as she took the square of folded paper with
its familiar green wax seal. "I'm sure that's what it's about."
After arriving in London, she'd established a mail account
for her publishing correspondence, under the same name.
Only this time, everyone who worked in the bookstore knew
Mrs. Delia Wallace was actually Caro, and not a reclusive
widow.

"Well? Open it. No use putting off bad news. It will still
be waiting for you tomorrow."

Wrinkling her nose, Caro muttered, "You're overflowing
with pithy pragmatism tonight, aren't you?" As she unfolded
the sheet, she continued, "The duke would never be so
undignified as to experience attraction, least of all to me. All
that emoting might rumple the perfect fit of his coat..." The
letter revealed no surprises. Mr. Mathers needed a date—
preferably a close one—for when he could expect the next
Blanche Clementine manuscript. "My publisher's patience
with my lack of progress is wearing thin, I think."

Hattie winced in sympathy. "In that case, perhaps the
duke can be inspiration. Spending time in his company
might spark a story."

Did Hattie realize the Duke of Holland had inspired the
last book? Caro bit back the question and focused on reply-
ing to her publisher. In black ink, she scrawled a few breezy
lines about the story being ready soon and promised it would

be worth the wait. A twist of anxiety in her throat spoke of her worry that she could deliver on the claim.

Thus far, the characters in this story were wooden and uninspired, making them uninteresting and difficult to push through the plot. Something had to change if this book was ever going to make it to print. In the past, if words weren't flowing, she'd tried writing letters as the heroine or hero to explore them deeper. If the letters were decent, she would incorporate the material into the story somehow. Given how long she'd been struggling with the current couple, it was probably time to try that approach.

Thinking back on how the duke had looked in his study earlier that day, and the way she'd felt witnessing his pain, she wondered what kind of woman would know what to do in that scenario. Instead of feeling helpless, as she had, what kind of heroine could turn such raw emotion into something intimate?

"Caro, look at this." Hattie's excited voice pulled her from her thoughts. A piece of paper nearly hit Caro in the face as her cousin waved it about before she managed to grab it and read.

Mrs. Adams, a matron from Kent, needed tips on preparing a wild goose and asked that a cookery book be added to her husband's account. Mrs. Adams was a chatty woman and a regular customer, so she explained she'd been given wild fowl, but after following instructions for cooking a domesticated goose, even the dogs would not eat the result. What followed was news about their upcoming move to her husband's family farm, and personal details about people Caro would never meet.

Hattie pointed to the bottom of the page. "Did you read the last bit? About them moving?"

"Yes; pity about his father's gout, but I don't see why it's cause for you to be grinning so madly."

Hattie wiggled in her chair, barely containing her excitement. "Their cottage in Kent is perfect. Absolutely perfect, Caro. It's everything you need, and all the things you've said you want. Uncle Owen and I delivered an order last fall. Don't you see? If they're selling their cottage, *you could buy it.*"

The clock on the mantel chimed, and the second hand filled the expectant silence. Slowly, Caro leaned back in the chair and drew in a careful breath.

"Caro, why aren't you saying anything?"

A million questions, scenarios, and what-ifs tumbled through her mind. Finally, she asked, "Do you think I have enough saved?" Before Hattie could answer, Caro shook her head. "Probably not. But I have to be close, don't you think?" As Blanche Clementine's popularity grew, so had her royalty checks. The last one brought her savings back to the amount she'd lost to her father. "This next book should bring my funds to where they need to be." *If I can write the damned thing.*

Hattie waved her pen in the air. "I'll ask about their price and tell Mrs. Adams you'll be delivering the cookery book in person as soon as the roads allow. You can see the place for yourself. It never hurts to have details."

A home. Her own bed. It was all she'd wanted for so long. A place where she could fully relax and be herself. No one watching. No meeting expectations from others that involved pinning down or pruning off parts of her personality. A place where being Caro was enough. The idea of it being within reach—once she finished the book—was downright scary. Exciting, but scary. Owning a house wasn't as fantastical a dream as marrying a prince or duke. However, life had taught her that dreams came true on paper, not in real life. Only heroines had their dreams come true. Everyone else was teased with hope.

Hope was terrifying. Resentment rose in the wake of the fear. "I'd have enough saved if Father weren't such a scab."

Hattie grimaced. "I wish we'd been able to retrieve your savings." She brightened. "Speaking of your worthless parent—I sent out the packages today. I'm sorry it took so long. The fair was entertaining but a lot of extra work. I didn't have the time before now."

Some of Caro's emotions faded to satisfaction. "Thank you for handling that."

"Trust me—it was my pleasure. Few things are more enjoyable than tormenting sanctimonious men of the cloth." Hattie finished her reply to Mrs. Adams with a flourish, then sealed the paper with wax. "It's my favorite part of release day. Sending notes and books to all those village lending libraries. I wish I could witness their reaction every time they open a parcel with erotic literature, seemingly donated by their local vicar. I hope they write each man and thank him personally. Your father and his friends deserve every bit of the confusion and discomfort it brings."

"And then some."

Hattie nudged the letter to Mrs. Adams toward Caro. "You'll have enough money soon."

Caro's gaze flitted over the pile of correspondence, then the mostly empty story journal pushed to the edge of the desk. "If not with the sales from this book, then the next one. Perhaps Mrs. Adams and her husband aren't in a rush to sell."

At last, excitement filled her, lending a warm glow under her sternum. If the timing worked in her favor, Caro could have a home of her own soon. There was that hope, again, rearing its head.

"I see you eying your story journal. Between the duke and this cottage, you may have enough incentive to write those characters into compromising positions." Hattie wagged her eyebrows and handed Caro the journal. "I'll leave you to it."

Within moments, the ticking clock was the only thing to keep Caro company. As tempting as it was to join Hattie upstairs, the blank pages on the desk wouldn't fill themselves.

The earlier pondering over the heroine had created a tickle in her brain, which was better than the desolate moor of blank space her creative well supplied when she'd thought about her before. Imagining the hero, Caro's mind offered nothing except blue eyes and a serious mouth. Groaning, she rested her forehead on folded arms atop the empty page. Damn Holland for being so appealing. Even when broken-hearted and so tightly wound it made her fingers twitch with the need to muss him.

One book already existed with him as the hero inspiration. Could she get away with writing another? Average men didn't sell as many books, so this hero needed to be a count or a duke, or maybe a prince. Details spun, twisted, then sorted themselves into a version of the man living in her imagination full-time these days.

Fine. The hero would have blue eyes (which may or may not deepen with his mood), but rather than explicitly stating the color of his hair (dark upon first glance but turned gold when lit by the sun), she'd focus on the wavy texture. Everyone appreciated windswept curls. Out of contrary impulse, she decided he'd be a little bumbling in the bedroom, and the heroine could be the experienced, confident one. With that, the spark of idea caught flame, and a familiar rush of excitement pushed through her.

Yes, the heroine would be the teacher this time, capable of

handling every situation that came her way. Picking up her pen, Caro began to write.

> *I fear, Your Grace, you have much to learn. While you hold the power to command parliament and advise the king himself, your reach does not extend to me, or our bed. In this domain, I reign and demand your vow of fealty. It is not a ring you must kiss, however, but parts of me I will only share for as long as you please me…*

Two hours later, Hattie slipped into the room with the tin of spiced biscuits Aunt Mary had baked earlier.

Caro blinked as the real world asserted itself. "I thought you'd gone to bed."

Hattie shook her head. "I was reading. Constance will wake us when she comes home, so it's no use trying to sleep. How's the story coming along?"

Caro flexed fingers that were cramped from holding a pen. "The characters are talking again." The characters in her head had been loosed to speak, and goodness, how they'd shown up. A flush warmed her cheeks at the things the heroine had written to her lover. Being so bold may be beyond her personal experience, but that was what imagination was for.

A murmur of voices reached them as their family arrived home.

Uncle Owen peered into the office. "You two still working?"

Hattie waved a biscuit in greeting. "Caro is."

He raised a brow at the open journal on the desk. "New book?"

"If I can ever finish it, yes. But I made progress tonight."

Aunt Mary entered the room, Constance trailing behind. "I overheard three different conversations tonight about your latest one. The hero really has everyone talking. We're so proud of you, sweetheart." She kissed the top of Caro's head as she walked by. "Don't stay up too late working."

"I was finishing for the night. How was your evening?" Caro closed the journal and capped her ink.

"Such fun. I'll let Connie fill you in on what happened," Aunt Mary said wryly, then shooed her husband up the stairs.

Constance collapsed in Hattie's abandoned chair, then let loose a high-pitched giggle, which turned into a rolling laugh.

Hattie raised a brow, then held out the biscuit tin to Caro. *Settle in for story time.*

"Lord, it was the funniest thing. Well, not for him. At the time, I was horrified, but now I can't stop laughing." A snort punctuated Constance's statement.

"Whatever happened, you're clearly not heartbroken about it," Caro said.

Connie shook her head, still giggling. "It started with Eloise Graham. Remember her?"

Hattie scrunched her nose in thought. "Too many curls and has those stays that lift her breasts so high she nearly smothers herself in church?"

"That's her. She's been walking out with Bugsy Peterson."

"I can't believe a grown man calls himself Bugsy. That alone should disqualify him for an adult relationship," Caro commented.

"Absolutely agree. However, darling Bugsy is quite the attentive beau. Either that, or Eloise is finally bringing him up to scratch. Tonight, she was showing off a nosegay of hot-house flowers."

"In February? Those cost a pretty penny. Bugsy is wooing in earnest, then." Hattie perched on the corner of the desk and bit into another biscuit.

"Indeed. So, we're sitting next to Eloise and Bugsy when Mr. Hudson starts sneezing. Not once or twice, but violently sneezing. He says he needs me to scoot over because flowers make him sneeze. I scoot, but he's still sneezing. His eyes start watering, nose turns red, and he keeps inching away from the flowers. Everyone around us is gaping, open-mouthed, as the poor man practically sits on my lap to get away from them." Constance, a natural storyteller, was completely in her element. Caro exchanged a grin with Hattie.

"There we are, shocking all the matrons around us—" Constance snorted midgiggle, then paused for dramatic effect. "He says, 'I don't know what's wrong. The only thing that makes me sneeze worse than flowers is *cats*.'"

Hattie gasped. "Gingersnap!"

"Yes." Constance was wheezing now. "My hairpiece."

"This might be the first time a beau's been felled by a hair accessory," Caro said through her laughter.

"It's a personal first. I'm quite proud of myself."

Hattie shook her head. "Will you give him another chance? Sans cat hair next time?"

"Of course not. I love Gingersnap. Where I go, he goes. If Mr. Hudson can't be near a fur hairpiece, imagine how he would react to the whole cat. No. My future husband will be perfectly content allowing Gingersnap to sleep on the pillow next to our heads."

Since Caro and the animal had been locked in a battle of wills over that exact subject for nearly two years, she kept her skepticism to herself. Instead, she raised a biscuit in the air, and the women raised theirs as well, in a cinnamon-spiced toast of sorts. "Farewell, Mr. Hudson. We hardly knew ye."

Chapter Six

Oliver stared at Dorian with the same patient and analytical look he'd worn for the past half hour. "Have you heard the phrase *nervous as a cat*?"

Dorian squirmed in his leather chair and answered with an arched eyebrow.

"You could give the proverbial cat lessons in twitchy behavior. Which isn't like you. What has you in a lather?"

Having someone in your life who was so bloody observant could be a real pain in the arse. "I don't know what you mean."

"To steal from the Bard, let me count the ways. You're shifting in your seat approximately every thirty seconds despite that being your favorite chair. After so many years, the cushion has no doubt conformed to the shape of your buttocks in a way that makes you feel like you are being hugged every time you sit. Yet today you are uncomfortable."

Dorian laughed. "That's your evidence? My chair doesn't appear to be hugging my bum in a friendly enough manner? Perhaps it lost its shape while I was abroad."

Oliver held up a finger and shook his head. "Oh, I'm not done. Your right hand has been balled into a fist for the past half hour. Your left hand has been busy. Drumming your fingers along the arm of the chair, rubbing your thigh, scratching your nose. Do you have an itch? Do you need to use a handkerchief? You're twitching like a matron fighting off a case of the vapors."

Dorian rested his head on the back of the chair and heaved a sigh. "Two things. Today I'm meeting with a solicitor to look into Juliet's financial details. A handshake on the Thames is all well and good, but I want documented legal recourse to evict Timothy from my life. The man is a menace. After our conversation with him the other week, I was curious about how often he'd approached Juliet for funds. I'm building documentation to show I've done my part in providing for him, should he try to push this to court."

Oliver nodded in understanding, so Dorian continued. "The numbers don't make sense. There are thousands of pounds unaccounted for. Then, two days after I made that agreement with Timothy, I received a bill claiming a long-standing debt in Juliet's name."

"You think he's out racking up debts in her stead."

"Unless her ghost has decided to visit London after five years to go on a spending spree, yes. I can't prove it, though, because she kept meticulous records... until the last year or two, when money disappeared into thin air."

Oliver settled deeper into his chair. "Ah. And given what happened in that last year or two, the entire situation is now suspect."

"Exactly."

A moment of silence passed, then Oliver said, "You said there were two things on your mind."

Dorian felt his neck grow hot. "Miss Danvers from the bookstore is expected today. Last time we spoke, I didn't handle it well. It seems there are letters from Juliet's lover floating about the library, and Miss Danvers found one."

All levity disappeared from Oliver's expression. "Was it signed? Did it offer any clues about who he is?"

"Clues, yes. A definitive answer, no."

"Where there's one, there could be more. With the curvy brunette sorting your library, she might discover the rest. Since you're back on the marriage mart, a juicy story about your perfect match being a sham would fetch a pretty penny with the gossip rags. She could sell the story easily enough."

A feral sound akin to a growl escaped before he could catch it. Gritting his teeth, Dorian forced a calmer response than his initial reaction. "Your analytical nature will think me mad, but I don't believe Miss Danvers would do that."

Oliver twisted his mouth in a vaguely sympathetic expression, but Dorian knew his friend would ruthlessly level all counterarguments with logic. "Your trust is based on what evidence? Your attraction to her?"

He'd said something similar on the ice, and at the time Dorian had made a feeble attempt to deny his obvious attraction. Now he didn't see the point in lying. "Every instinct I have tells me Miss Danvers will keep mum about anything salacious she finds here." Dorian pressed the heels of his palms against his eye sockets to block the sight of Oliver's pursed lips. "I know. I know what you're thinking. My gut isn't reliable." Yet if he thought about it, the feeling of her hand on his arm returned like a welcome ghost, free of any feelings of foreboding.

"There is some irony in you being willing to trust your intuition regarding a matter where your intuition failed you entirely."

Dorian heaved a sigh. Juliet's affair had taken him so entirely by surprise it ripped the landscape of his life apart in more ways than he could have predicted. He might have grieved that more deeply than her death during those first weeks. And what did that say about him?

Letting his hands fall to his lap, Dorian voiced the most

prominent thought from those swirling in his head. "If there are more letters, they need to be found before the books leave the house."

"It sounds like you're going to have some long hours in the library with Miss Danvers. Best to decide now how you're going to handle her before you find yourself in the moment and floundering madly in conversation."

"I don't flounder madly in conversations. I was a diplomat, for Christ's sake."

"Not in the traditional sense of floundering, no. You turn icy and ducal, which everyone mistakes as confidence. Works well in situations where men are making decisions based on assumed cock size, but it won't win you a lady's hand. Admit it—if you go in that library without a plan, your brain will be like a swan frantically paddling to stay afloat."

"Oh, fuck off," Dorian said without any real heat as he got up and stalked to the tea cart. "This has gone cold. Do you want a cup anyway?" Having something in his hands always calmed him, even if it was room-temperature tea. He poured himself a cup.

"No, but I see Cook sent up strawberry tarts. Pass me a few of those, if you don't mind."

Dorian placed a selection of tarts and tiny sandwiches on two plates, then popped a sweet in his mouth. The fresh burst of well-preserved summer exploded on his tongue along with buttery, flaky crust, and it made him moan in appreciation. Cook was exceptionally good at her job.

When he handed Oliver a plate, his friend immediately did the same and made a similar noise. "Lord, can I steal Cook?"

"No." Sipping his cold tea, Dorian sat again. "That woman is a treasure. You can't have her."

"But if you die, you won't haunt me from the grave if I hire her and live out my days full of strawberry tarts, right?"

"You're ridiculous." Dorian laughed.

"I'll take that as a yes."

As they ate in silence, Dorian was acutely aware of the low sounds drifting through the wall from the rest of the house. The soft drone of servants' voices, a door closing, footsteps on the marble foyer floor. Any minute, a feminine laugh he'd recognize anywhere as hers would enter into the background noise, and he welcomed it. It had been several days since he'd last seen her. While she had been in his home during the last week, he had been out each time. But she was expected today, so he was acutely aware of every person coming and going from the house.

From the door, Hastings cleared his throat. "Your Grace, the solicitor has arrived. I've taken the liberty of ordering a fresh pot of tea. Shall I show him in?"

Saved by the staff. Dorian settled behind the desk so he'd appear ducal and in control of the situation, instead of like a man being henpecked by his best friend over a woman.

Oliver returned his empty plate to the tea cart. "I will leave you to it." He pointed a stern finger at Dorian. "Don't trust someone just because you fancy what's under her skirts. Don't be a ducal swan. Those two things are all you have to do."

Dorian laughed, and some of the tension drained from his shoulders as Oliver left.

The duchy had retained the same law firm since his grandfather's time. When he'd talked to them about Timothy's probable debt-making in Juliet's name, they'd responded with advice to pay the man in order to prevent him making a fuss and creating scandal. Essentially, they'd proven their loyalty to the dukedom over Dorian himself.

And that wouldn't do.

Maintaining the dukedom, with its vast estates and countless employees, could easily take up every moment of his life. He'd done a piss-poor job of dealing with it all while abroad, leaving the bulk of everything to his managers and foremen. He'd stayed on the Continent for a while after Juliet's death, at the insistence of the king. Grief ate up another block of time after he returned home, during which he'd left the dukedom's business in the hands of those already dealing with it.

About two years ago, the heaviness in his chest that he'd carried since losing his wife began to lessen, and he'd stopped living with the sensation of drowning all the damn time. Bit by bit, he resumed his duties. Since then, the days often felt filled to the brim with account books, meetings, and visits to estates to learn what was going on. However, it had given him a chance to reconnect with those he'd left in charge and realize some changes could be made. It was a tedious, time-consuming process to address outdated farming methods, the managers resistant to the newer machinery that could increase productivity as well as the health and safety of laborers, and to weed through people like the lawyers who had access to private information yet whom Dorian wouldn't choose to trust with his secrets.

Sometimes, change was good. With his birthday looming in the months ahead, he'd felt more driven than ever to set the properties on the road to long-term success.

Hastings entered again, with a man following behind. It was the work of a split second to assess the representative this new firm had sent over. Tall, slender, fair hair neatly trimmed along the neckline. The man's jacket fit well but was not flashy.

He stood to greet the newcomer. As the solicitor bowed,

the rest of Dorian's first impression fell into place. Everything about the man screamed competence and confidence. The kind of confidence that didn't need to wear fashions from elite tailors when solidly made garments of quality material would do nicely. There was a deference to the man's gaze but no awe or intimidation. Excellent.

Sycophants had no place in business.

"Your Grace. I am Gerard Bellmore, a solicitor with Morris, Haredale, and Wilson. It's a pleasure to meet you," the visitor said.

Dorian motioned for the man to take a seat, then he resumed his own. The chair squeaked under his weight in a familiar, comforting sound. Precious few hours had been spent at this desk in those years after Juliet's death, while he hid from his duty because he felt as if he'd been run over by the emotional equivalent of a night-soil cart.

An apt comparison when everything he'd held dear had been covered in metaphorical shit. Literal shit would have been easier to clean.

Shoving the thoughts away, Dorian jerked his attention back to the matter at hand. He'd never been one to prevaricate. Honesty was simply easier, even if it meant picking and choosing what he shared. Yet every time he thought of Juliet's deception, his usual aplomb became hard-won instead of easy.

"Thank you for meeting with me today, Mr. Bellmore."

"Our firm is honored to be representing Your Grace in whatever manner we can. They sent me because you requested someone with a special knack for numbers and money trails. I would have been an accountant, but my father insisted on the law," Mr. Bellmore said with a charming smile.

"I'm happy to hear it, because I need a bloodhound to find answers regarding a financial matter, and a legal mind to ensure the outcome is fair to the ducal estates."

Mr. Bellmore nodded and removed a pocket-size pad of paper. "Sounds like I'm the man for the job. Where would you like me to begin, Your Grace?"

"My late wife's account ledgers. Specifically, payments she made during the last two years of her life. There are thousands of pounds missing but no notations regarding charities or projects where the money was sent."

"Did the duchess have any pet projects during that time?"

"There was a village school she spoke of rather often during the last year she was alive. Details are hazy, but I remember the village was in Kent. Also, look for anything that might lend legitimacy to recent debts that have come to light. I believe her cousin has been spending in her name, but I cannot prove it. You have your work cut out for you, I'm afraid."

The solicitor raised a brow. "Interesting. This will be a challenge, and I haven't had one of those in too long. Perhaps you could start by telling me about this cousin character."

Anticipation made Dorian smile. Hiring specialized counsel had been the right thing to do. Timothy would be dealt with legally and thoroughly and might even suffer lasting consequences.

Excellent.

"With pleasure. Fresh tea will arrive momentarily. Get comfortable, Mr. Bellmore. We might be here awhile."

Chapter Seven

Tidy penmanship swam on the page in front of her until Caro sighed and leaned back in her chair to rub at her eyes. Long days were what made up a life, but today the twenty-four hours she'd been allotted felt more like thirty.

She'd planned to spend a few hours in Bloomsbury but hadn't been able to get away. Just as well there wasn't a set-in-stone schedule at the townhouse, because the store had been like literary Bedlam. Instead of people throwing food and bedpans, they were throwing money on the counter and demanding copies of *A Dalliance for Miss Lorraine*.

Which, while gratifying, was baffling as hell. Blanche Clementine had loyal readers, and each book did well enough to warrant her publisher asking for more. Every new release gained readers as her popularity grew, and that growing audience sought out her previous books. But they'd never sold so many copies in such a short period. Caro glanced through the doorway to the dark sales floor and the empty table that had started the day with a display of her latest book.

London readers had gone mad, in the best way. Perhaps it was the holiday. Valentine's Day put everyone in an amorous mood, or so she assumed. Not that she knew from personal experience, since she'd never received a valentine from a beau.

Uncle Owen had winked at her as he sent an order to the

publisher this evening. Higher sales, no matter the book, would help the store, so everyone was grateful, if puzzled by the situation.

Hopefully it would be easier to get away from Martin House tomorrow so she could put in a few more hours on the Holland library. His Grace's donation would mean a windfall of potential income, as well as a near-immediate influx of money from direct sales to collectors. All she had to do was finish sorting, categorizing, and boxing well over a thousand volumes, in addition to completing the paperwork and letters needed to connect individual titles with wealthy buyers. All while maintaining the shop's sales records, lending-library records, customer mailboxes, and the store's regular mail. Plus, with the end of the quarter around the corner, there would be a flurry of notices sent out for lending-library subscriptions.

That she slept or had written anything since beginning the donation project was a miracle. Each day, she rose with the sun to tackle the shop's account books and correspondence. Then, if there was time, she crossed town to the duke's townhome to put in a few hours there, before returning to the store for more office work.

Despite everything packing her schedule, the writing threatened to take over her brain entirely. When she'd responded to her publisher last week, her assurances about the next book had been wishful thinking wrapped in an outright lie. The book hadn't been working *at all* until she allowed the duke the starring role. Again.

Being in the duke's home, even when she didn't see him, was inspiring, to say the least. The titillating thought—or maybe threat—that he could open the door at any moment and fill the space with his serious, amazingly blue eyes and grim mouth, kept goosebumps primed and ready under her skin all day. However, it wasn't until she found that letter, and showed him, that the story began to pound at her brain.

At the end of the night, regardless of how exhausted she was, that anticipation she'd felt all day transformed into something the likes of which Blanche Clementine had never produced. Words flew from her fingers to the page, faster than she'd ever written before. It was a wonder the paper didn't set itself aflame from the friction of her pen, and the intensely sexual scenes filling the pages.

The heroine, Phoebe, had a mind of her own and was taking over the tale with fantastical scenarios Caro hadn't known existed in the depths of her brain. But then, Caro's physical experiences in the real world were limited to three sadly disappointing encounters involving awkwardness, a few minutes of possibility, then a mess that ended the whole sorry thing.

Fiction was better. Phoebe and her duke, Lysander, had passion and intimacy in spades and never experienced muscles cramping from limbs placed at strange angles, or were left wondering what all the fuss was about sex.

One thing nagged at her conscience. In *A Dalliance for Miss Lorraine*, Holland had been less of a man and more of a role. He was the inspiration. A rather one-dimensional figure who served the purpose of being broody and attractive enough to massage her creativity.

Last week, as he stood in his study in his shirtsleeves, burrowing fingers into his usually perfect hair, he'd been oblivious to the picture he presented against his window. The sight seared into her brain, changing the inspiration source material irrevocably. The one-dimensional character he'd been as her muse paled in the face of reality.

God, that letter had nearly leveled him. The grief on his face, the way he'd turned his back to hide his vulnerability as mourning surfaced anew. That letter, and everything she'd heard about the duke and duchess, painted the picture of passionate, romantic partners she'd thought only existed in fiction. Yet there he was. A grown man, allowing her to witness a sliver of his heartbreak.

Even if that sliver showed itself in the rise and fall of his shoulders as he took deep breaths and unknowingly provided her with an excellent view of his trim torso under a fine lawn shirt, and a distractingly perfect bum in snug breeches.

The duke had been on the verge of weeping, and she'd been admiring his arse, unable to think of a way to help. Because Caro felt entirely at sea and rather useless in the face of his pain, she'd created Phoebe to be perfectly capable of soothing a man's emotions.

Since then, the scene in the study had rewritten itself into a version of events fitting Phoebe and Lysander and was pounding at her brain to be released onto the page. However, the idea of writing it had her in knots. It felt exploitive of the duke's very real emotions to write what she knew came next in the story.

This version of events would have Phoebe on her knees in front of him, licking his cock, but with the command that she'd only suck on him if he was talking. Opening up, speaking what was on his mind. Phoebe knew how to make a man enjoy vulnerability.

Whereas Caro had run like a frightened rabbit back to her den. Which, in this case, was a dimly lit office area comprised of the stacked folders she called a filing system, a desk piled with bills, letters, and account books, and a looming headache behind her eyes from working so many hours without a break.

Above her head, shuffling told the tale of her uncle and his family going about their nightly rituals as they found their beds. Aunt Mary, bless her, had brought Caro a plate of food several hours ago. Constance and Hattie were probably already asleep, warming the covers for when she'd eventually crawl in beside them.

Or at least that's what she thought until one set of feet veered toward the far wall above the office, then trotted merrily down the stairs.

"I knew I would find you here." Constance threw herself into the only other chair in the room with her usual dramatic verve, then placed her darning bag on her lap, pulled out a pair of stockings, and set to work.

"Is there something in particular on your mind, or did you just want company?"

Constance all but forgot the stocking and needle as she leaned forward with a wide grin. "I found the man I am going to marry."

"I thought Mr. Hudson was disqualified because of the cat."

"Not Mr. Hudson. He was last week. Right after Mr. Hudson, I met Walter." Constance rolled her eyes and huffed, "What is that look for?"

"What look? I didn't do anything."

Waving her finger in the air in a vague sort of circle, Constance said, "Then your face just had an entire conversation without your knowledge."

Caro laughed, shaking her head. Constance wasn't exactly known for her, well, constancy. Since the marriage of her twin sister, Betsy, Constance seemed determined to find a husband as well. The sisters were mirrors of one another on the outside but couldn't have been more different in temperament. Betsy was calm, orderly, and focused. Constance was... well, cheerful chaos incarnate, most of the time.

"After declaring him your future husband, I have questions. Admit it, Connie. We've had meals fill our bellies for longer than some of your relationships. What makes Walter any different?"

"Clearly I was waiting for the right one. You can't find him if you are not willing to look. I was looking." Constance sat up straighter and donned a prim expression as she returned to sewing the hole in the toe of her wool stocking.

Fair point. Granted, her cousin may have looked longer and harder than most people. However, you could not claim Constance had not done exactly what she claimed. If one thought of her relationships as interviews for the position of husband, she had been interviewing rather intensely for quite some time. It sounded like the position was finally filled.

Caro relaxed in her seat and forced aside her reservations. "Tell me about him. How do you know he's the one? How did you meet?"

The darning forgotten in her lap once more, Constance beamed. "His name is Walter Hornsby, and he is a cloth merchant. I met him at the milliner's when Hattie was looking to retrim that old straw bonnet she refuses to get rid of. She was extremely particular about the shade of blue she wants. And"—Connie spread her hands wide—"there he was. He'd visited the shop to deliver an order and was ever so polite and polished when he spoke to us. He treated me like a lady, and I swear his eyes are the exact shade of blue Hattie was looking for. I even said so, which started our conversation."

Only a week ago, she'd been out with poor sneezing Mr. Hudson. Caro bit her lip and dug for appropriate questions besides *What are you thinking?* or *How can you consider a lifelong commitment based on the shade of blue God gave a man when handing out eye colors?* "I struggle to see how that's a basis for a decision of this magnitude, darling."

Connie's expression shifted from excited to stubborn in a blink. "Just because you're as sentimental as a mud puddle doesn't mean those of us who use instinct to guide our decisions are wrong."

"You say instinct, I say emotions. And emotions are wildly unpredictable and unreliable."

Connie shook a finger at her. "See? That's exactly what I'm referring to. You are practical to a fault, Caroline Danvers."

Caro closed her eyes and silently counted to three before opening them. "Then I'll focus on practical questions. Have you spent much time with Mr. Hornsby? Does he return your high regard?"

Constance relaxed in her chair, accepting the questions as the olive branch they were. "When he visited the bookshop the following day, he called me enchanting, and we've seen each other since. In fact, he dropped by this afternoon to give me a valentine he made with a short poem. I think he wrote it himself. You've been so busy with the duke; I doubt you noticed."

Only literally biting her tongue kept Caro's response inside her head. *Of course he said you're enchanting, Connie. It's a well-established feature like your hair and dimples. A long line of broken hearts litters the ground in your wake, because you're so enchanting.* Instead, she said, "I'm glad your valentine made you happy. Has he met your parents yet?"

"He's shaken hands with Father in the store, obviously. Tomorrow night he's taking me dancing at the pub, with Mother and Father accompanying us."

Caro couldn't remember the last time Constance had been this excited about a man taking her out. Perhaps Walter Hornsby was special, and those instincts she relied on were guiding her in the right direction after all. "I hope everything works out the way you want it to." She reached over and squeezed her cousin's hand.

"I'm sure it will," Constance said, all cheerful confidence. "Now it's your turn. Tell me about your duke."

A disbelieving laugh escaped before Caro could stop it. "*My* duke?"

"Holland visits this store more often than the average patron. He can't read *that* much, Caro. It's obvious he's here to see you. And I notice the way you look at him. Given the chance, you'd lap him up like a bowl of cream."

Caro's shoulders slumped. "Oh God, am I that obvious?"

"If it helps, your covert glances are very covert."

Caro mustered a smile. "That's a relief. You know, if I could rid myself of this attraction, I would. All these fluttery feelings are about as useful as teats on a bull."

Constance's grin turned sly. "But those flutters lead to such enjoyable activities. What would Blanche Clementine do in your shoes?"

Caroline gaped through a surprised laugh. "Constance Martin, are you suggesting what I think you're suggesting? I'll have you know—" A knocking sound interrupted the faux appalled rant she was preparing. "Is someone at our door?"

Constance rose and tucked the still-holey stocking back into her darning bag. "I'll check."

After a moment, she returned with a wide grin. "You have a visitor waiting outside. I'll take my darning upstairs if you want some privacy."

"What? Who on earth is calling at this time of night?" Caro plucked her knitted wool shawl from the chair where she'd discarded it earlier. Perhaps Leo and Gerard from down the street? They sometimes stopped by in the evening. They'd settled on a date for the theater. Perhaps they needed to cancel. She made her way through the dark sales floor.

Constance stuck her head around the doorframe from

the office and said in a stage whisper, "Just ask yourself what Blanche Clementine would do."

This was madness. Dorian knew that. And yet, he stood under the gas streetlamp outside Martin House Books, the better to be easily identified after knocking on the door after hours.

While it would be easy to create a believable explanation for his presence on the street well after dark, the reality was far messier. Caroline had failed to arrive at the library this afternoon. The last time they'd seen one another, he'd inadvertently exposed her to one of his attacks, which would never not be humiliating. Even when she'd tried to comfort him, he hadn't been able to explain himself.

After a week of not being home during her visits, she might think he was hiding from her like a coward, and that wouldn't do. So he'd waited for her in the library, methodically looking for more letters in each book in the stacks she'd made, before carefully replacing them. No doubt she had a system in place, but damned if he could determine what it was. When she didn't arrive as expected, he'd worried about her. Worried his reaction to what appeared to be a simple love letter had scared her away. Showing up at the shop just to make sure she felt comfortable returning to his home was extreme when sending a messenger would have sufficed. But he needed to see her for himself.

Compared to her watching him struggle for air, it was relatively easy to open himself to the potential for embarrassment, discomfort, or her justified-but-prying questions. The way Caroline's cousin had smirked when she answered the door confirmed how unusual his behavior was, but he wasn't here for her or her opinion.

The store window showed a shadow moving toward the front of the shop, and then Caroline appeared, opening the door and sending the overhead bell tinkling.

"Your Grace, this is unexpected. Would you like to come inside? There's a fireplace in the office where we can be warmer."

Tempting—dangerously so. In his current frame of mind, it didn't seem wise to curl up by a fire in a dark and quiet bookshop. The image that brought to mind was too cozy. Too intimate. He shook his head. "No, thank you. I won't be long."

Caroline stepped into the circle of gaslight, wrapping a shawl around herself. The red garment appeared handmade and well loved. It had worn thin in several places and was fraying around the edges. Instead of the shawl making her appear shabby, Dorian thought of it as proof that someone cared enough to spend hours creating something for her with their hands. "What can I help you with?"

Lamplight was just as kind to her face as sunshine. Moonlight would no doubt be just as generous to the curves of her cheeks and the sharp dip dividing her upper lip. It was the intelligence in her gaze, the confident sense of *knowing* she wore like a second skin, that had caught his attention in this very spot so many months ago. After spending so long feeling like he'd lost a similar surety in himself, he'd been unable to look away, slightly envious of her quiet confidence.

That intelligence he respected wouldn't be satisfied with half-hearted explanations or prevarication, and he wouldn't do her the injustice of asking her to stand in the cold just to serve a paltry excuse for his presence.

"Last time we spoke, I wasn't at my best. When you didn't stop by the house today, I was afraid I'd scared you away. I had to make sure you were all right."

It must have been surprise that made her chuckle. "How kind of you to check on me, Your Grace. I'm sorry if I worried you or your staff. I've worked more hours than usual these last few weeks and was feeling run-down. Also, it was a particularly busy day in the store. I'm just now stealing a moment to look at the ledgers for the past week."

A breeze whistled down the street with the accuracy of a scalpel, making the fine hairs at her temples dance and blowing open the front of his caped greatcoat with icy fingers of recrimination. Of course she was exhausted. Between long days at the store and the additional work at his house, it was no wonder she'd needed a day to focus on just one thing.

"Is there anything I can do? If it's too many hours between your usual duties and my library, we can find a solution. Perhaps if I rented a space near here to store the books, it would be less travel time for you. Or I can hire you an assistant. Two assistants. Whatever you need."

The problem solving seemed to be gaining momentum, but he stopped abruptly when Caroline placed a hand on his arm. He could get used to her doing that. "You're very generous, but I simply needed to change my plans for the day. That's all. No storage or assistants needed."

Her hand stood out in stark relief against the oiled cloth of his greatcoat. Smudges of ink shadowed the fingers, settling into the creases to outline her short nails. Such small hands for someone so hardworking and capable. She must have realized what she'd done, because Caroline tried to snatch her hand back, but he covered it with his own.

If pressed, Dorian wouldn't be able to offer an explanation for his actions beyond wanting to keep the contact for a little longer.

Like each time they'd touched, beginning with that first day in this very spot, Dorian was painfully aware of her. The way her hand warmed his like a brand. The way he wanted to breathe her in until every sense was full of Caroline. It would be such a simple thing to pull her closer, for her to step into his embrace. To lower his head and finally know how she tasted.

For any of that to happen, one of them would have to move. Caroline's fingers curled into his arm, tightening her hold.

"Was that your only reason for calling, Your Grace?"

Checking on her may have been the primary excuse for stopping by, but he wanted so much more. Since wrapping his arm around her waist and pulling her curves against him on this street, he'd wanted more. Under his intense gaze, she lifted her chin, and Dorian took that as a silent invitation.

Dorian covered her lips with his in a firm kiss. The kind of kiss neither could misconstrue as accidental or casual. There'd be no going back after this. An act of bravery to counter the cowardice he'd shown on the Thames when he'd pretended not to remember her name.

Then, he'd feared Caroline would somehow guess that everything about her was seared into his brain. Now he desperately hoped she'd let him show her how deeply she'd slipped under his skin.

If she pushed him away, he'd take the rejection. In that case, he'd make sure they were never in the same room again for both their sakes.

Or she could . . . do that. Open her pillowy lips in welcome.

After a heated second, Caroline pulled away, gasping. She stared at him, as if searching for something. Whatever it was, he hoped she'd find it, if it would bring her back to him.

When she rose on her toes and returned her lips to his, he let her swallow his small cry of victory as he gave in to the heady desire and deepened the kiss. As he wrapped his arms around her, Dorian stepped out of the lamplight, closer to the heavy wood door of the bookshop, away from possible prying eyes.

Eager fingers clutched his shoulders, ran through his hair, cradled his jaw. At some point, his hat fell off, and he didn't care. Not when his arms were full of orange-blossom springtime, and her mouth was a marvel of heat, indescribable softness, and the honey she'd had in her tea. It all combined into the new experience of Caroline. If his mouth weren't occupied doing better things, he'd have shouted, *Finally!* to the skies.

Over eighteen months of pent-up longing poured out on a moan of relief that almost immediately recoiled into a spiral of lust. Every inch her hands explored was hers to conquer. Dorian held her close enough to feel a faint tremble rock her as he nibbled and sucked and drank her in, leaning against the shop door for support.

God help him, but if a kiss from this woman could destroy his composure to this degree, he might never recover from a night in her bed.

And not a single part of him considered that to be a problem.

The kiss could have gone on forever, but as the wind buffeted his back and he protected her from the elements with his body, logic decreed that she couldn't be out in the cold much longer with just a shawl and a lusty duke for warmth.

Even though he was the one pulling away, he still made a low sound of disappointment. "You'll catch your death out here. I should let you go."

Emotions flickered across her features in a silent reply before settling into a composed expression. "Yes, of course."

That was far less than what she wanted to say. He was certain of it. Angling his head to place a kiss at the corner of her mouth, it thrilled him to feel her arms tighten around him. "What were you thinking just now? During the pause."

"The pause?"

"Before answering, you waited." He searched for the right words. "It's something you do. Like you have a whole conversation in your head and then only say the least interesting bits."

Caroline laughed. "If I voiced every thought in my head, I would have more enemies than friends, and my days would be far more complicated."

An honest answer, and an intriguing one. "Will you tell me what you were thinking just now? Let me into the pause."

"Why?"

"Because it sounds like that's where the real Caroline Danvers lives, and I must confess I fancy her. Probably more than I should."

"Do you really want to know what I was thinking?"

"Absolutely. My God, your skin is unbelievably soft." His lips grazed her cheekbone, then trailed along the fine curls at her hairline.

"I was thinking you have some nerve to come here and kiss me like that after claiming to not know my name two weeks ago." Wicked delight curved her lips as she teased, tilting her head so he'd have better access to the delicious column of her neck.

Ah, so they were going to talk about that. As much as he wanted to wince or shy away, he couldn't help a laugh against her velvet skin. Because *this* was the woman who'd been so unguarded when they met, who griped at him about making a mess and knocking her down. This was the woman he'd watched disappear behind a polite facade. Frankly, he'd stand here all night and freeze to death if it meant Caroline spoke to him without pausing to consider her words. "I knew your name. I owe you an apology for pretending otherwise."

"Why did you, then?"

"Cowardice." Truth wasn't always pretty, but that was the truth. "I was afraid you'd realize I've been paying too much attention to you since we met."

"But that was nearly two years ago."

"And I can't forget it. Any of it. How you fit in my arms so perfectly when I caught you. How even travel weary, you were so damned pretty. Then you told your cousins what you'd gone through to get here, and I knew you weren't just beautiful. You were remarkable. I kept finding reasons to return, to see how you were getting on. From that first moment, you've demanded my attention without ever asking for it."

Her breath was coming in quick pants as he spoke, pressing her breasts into his chest and inciting torturous pictures in his imagination. Uncovering those curves, making her gasp and moan until she was rosy and satisfied. Then doing it all over again.

Caroline rewarded his honesty with another kiss. Dorian draped his coat over her shoulders as she wrapped her arms around his waist—sheltering her from the cold night as his body pinned hers to the wood door.

From somewhere beyond their cocoon of kisses, a man whistled. "Criminy! Someone's having a nice Valentine's Day, eh, luv?"

When Dorian pulled away, Caroline's laugh was infectious, unguarded. There was no pause when she said, "Happy Valentine's Day, Your Grace."

Chapter Eight

❦

"If he needs another book, I'll eat my hat," Constance hissed as she scurried past Caro the next day.

Hattie snorted from her place at the register, then called out a merry "Welcome back, Your Grace. May I help you find anything this morning?"

Panic tightened Caro's throat, and she struggled to swallow. Where she stood behind the bookcase nearest the register would hide her from anyone entering the store, and she was grateful for it. Drawing in a calming breath, she tried to settle her thoughts.

Although why they'd settle on command now, when they'd been whirling since his kisses the night before, she couldn't guess. As expected, his presence was the furthest thing from a soothing balm to her nerves. If this heart-pounding, fizzy feeling was what Constance experienced every time she had a new beau, it was a wonder the woman hadn't run away to a nunnery before now. In her books, the first meeting after their initial kiss never felt like this. Her heroines were usually swoony and a little giddy. Not this knotted tangle of anticipation and the vague need to vomit.

What had she been thinking, to lift her face to his and invite that kiss? Then to repeat the action over and over, until their tongues were tangling and his heartbeat was a drum under her palm. Caro remembered him placing his hand over hers, and asking herself what Blanche Clementine would do.

Blanche Clementine would kiss the duke and turn him to putty in her hands.

Caroline Danvers, however, was an agitated mess over what she'd done. He was a bloody duke, and she was the disowned daughter of a country vicar. This kind of pairing might work in one of her books, but expecting a relationship in real life was ridiculous.

And yet, remembering the kisses they'd shared made her knees weak. Holland had been open about his desire, perfectly willing to let the spark between them flame into something she feared would grow beyond their control. He'd seemed to welcome the passion, and in the moment, so had she.

Now that she'd tossed and turned all night, pondering their kisses incessantly, Caro acknowledged that she was scared. Because as amazing as those kisses had been, it was the gentle teasing afterward that made it the most erotic experience of her life. She wasn't a virgin, yet his gentle request that she fully speak her mind felt more personal than the time she'd spent with her last lover. Not that the experience had been all that great, truth be told. But that was beside the point. If that man had paid attention to her the way Holland had, she might think of the relationship with more fondness.

In the dark, lit only by gaslight, she'd felt seen. She'd been desired. For almost two years, she'd admired the duke in the same way a child longs to touch a pretty glass figurine. Last night, she'd been allowed to not only touch, but stroke and taste.

His footsteps sounded with quiet precision on the wood

floor and Caro realized she didn't know what to do. They were in public, so she couldn't greet him like a beau. Would he want her to if they were alone?

Or perhaps he was here for the sole purpose of telling her that last night was a fleeting moment of madness, and he regretted every second of it.

A pain around her heart made her gasp softly, then straighten her spine. If he was here to tell her he never wanted to see her again, then so be it. Better to be ready for the blow than be taken unawares like a moon-eyed ninny.

"Miss Danvers? May I speak with you a moment?"

Sweet heaven, his voice alone was enough to make her thighs damp. Caro dug for some inner reserve of aloof professionalism and turned to face him. She dipped a curtsy—a stern reminder to herself of this man's place in society versus her own.

When she finally met his gaze, it wasn't the ardent man who'd teased and kissed her the night before but the composed, stoic duke she'd grown accustomed to seeing who stared back. Ah, so he did regret what they'd done. Ignoring the stab of hurt at the idea of this man harboring her as one of his regrets, she forced her mouth into a cool smile.

A flicker of something crossed his face, so quick she almost missed it. Given his overall demeanor, she doubted he'd answer if she asked what that emotion had been.

"How may I assist you, Your Grace?"

The knot of his Adam's apple bobbed as he swallowed. Caro let her eyes rest there, on that column of skin above his cravat.

"I came by to see how you were faring after...well. I see I was correct in my instinct to call." He spoke softly, and she was grateful for it. The last thing they needed was a customer to overhear their conversation. Although she didn't think there were any others in the shop right now, except her cousins.

"I am perfectly fine, Your Grace," she said, addressing her words toward the jade stickpin securing the folds of starched linen around his neck.

"Are you, though?"

"Of course. Thank you for your consideration." Even as she said the words, Constance's singsong voice echoed in her mind. What would Blanche Clementine do? Blanche would already have her hands under that perfectly cut dark-blue coat and be rubbing against him like a cat in heat.

As she'd already realized, Caroline Danvers was nowhere near as brave as Blanche. Better to give him an easy reason to walk away than hear him list all the reasons why their kiss, and the most erotic interlude of her life, was a mistake. *This might be the lack of sentimentality Connie had mentioned. Since Connie is the one usually doing the leaving, she wouldn't understand the need to protect oneself.* She waved the dust rag covered in lemon oil toward the shelves she'd been cleaning. "If that is all, I need to resume my duties, Your Grace."

His lips worked, but ultimately, he remained silent. A moment later, he dipped his head and turned on his heel.

Carol blew out a breath. *You did the right thing.* Closing her eyes, she willed the moisture welling there to retreat as quickly as his footsteps were.

The footsteps abruptly stopped, then resumed and grew louder. The brush of fine kidskin against her bare hand made her eyes fly open in surprise.

"I apologize, but I can't walk away yet." His voice was a whisper, yet no less urgent. "I asked how you were, but I didn't share my own state."

Caro met his blue gaze and saw a fierce earnestness there that made her catch her breath.

"Unlike you, I am not fine. I didn't sleep well last night. I don't know if I am supposed to feel excited about finally giving in to the urge to kiss you, or if I am supposed to be begging forgiveness right now."

She wet her lips with her tongue and couldn't help the small thrill she felt when his eyes tracked the movement. The tiny flare of heat in his expression gave her the courage to be honest. "To be honest, I don't know either."

When he squeezed her hand, she realized he still held it. "If you don't return my regard or if you feel pressured to act as if you welcome my attention, please say so. I promise you'll suffer no repercussions and endure no further unwanted advances."

Shaking her head, Caro fought a smile. He was so very proper. The poor man probably couldn't help it. He was a duke, after all.

All urges to smile vanished.

You're a duke. What do you want from me? Am I a plaything to be discarded? A convenient distraction? Or a mistress to serve at your leisure? If you wanted me as your mistress, would I be strong enough to resist temptation and say no? Would I regret rejecting you? Would I really regret it if I said yes and had you all to myself for a brief time?

"Our positions in this world are wildly different, Your Grace."

Dark brows pinched together over blue eyes gone stormy. "Don't do that."

"Do what? Remind you of reality?"

"You paused," he said simply. He looked at her exactly the same way he had the night before. Like a man focused on something he found utterly fascinating.

She was just as defenseless against it now as she had been then. When this man, who'd caught her attention so long ago, stared at her as if he found it impossible to look away, it made her believe there could be something between them.

Caro gripped his hand tighter and spoke her fears aloud. "But it's the truth, isn't it? I don't know what you want from me. For all I know, you kiss women in doorways every night, and it was simply my turn. So, I don't know how to feel. Do I return your regard?" *Be bold. Be Blanche.* "Yes. Am I glad you slept poorly? Also yes. Because so did I."

His low laugh rippled over her like a caress, and that was her reward for speaking honestly.

Holland raised her hand to his lips, sending tingles up her arm from the brief contact. "Do you know how many women I've kissed since my wife died five years ago?" Before she could hazard a guess, he answered. "One. You. I don't make a habit of kissing women in doorways." Discomfort twisted his mouth in a wince. "Why I kissed you, I am not sure. I've wanted to do so since the moment I met you, and I seized the opportunity, I suppose."

It had mattered to him as well, then. No matter how this ended, that made her feel better.

"What happens now?" she asked.

His chest expanded on an inhale, as if he was finally allowing himself to take a deep breath. "I'm not sure. But if I may make one request?"

She nodded.

"Let me see you. The real you. Be honest with me to the best of your ability, and I will do the same."

Warmth suffused her chest, and she had to bite her lip to contain a smile she knew would make her look like the moon-eyed ninny she feared being. "You mean you won't always be serious like you were when you arrived today?"

His face slid back into the stoic mask she was all too

familiar with, and he said, "I shall do my best." If not for a playful glint to his eyes, she'd have thought him in earnest.

Caro laughed, then covered her mouth to stifle the sound, lest anyone peer around the corner at them. "Teasing? I'm impressed."

Holland's thumb slid over the top of her hand in a repetitive caress, and she wondered if he realized he was doing it. "My friend, Lord Southwyn, claims I turn cold and serious when I'm anxious. I'm often unsure of what to do or say when I'm around you."

The sweet man, to admit such a thing. Who'd have imagined a powerful duke had been nervous around a lowly bookseller? "Well, I've enjoyed speaking with you like this. Like we did last night. Beyond the kissing," she hastened to add.

"I'm finding a fondness for plain speaking as well, Miss Danvers." He kissed her hand once more. "Until next we meet."

"I have time to work in the library tomorrow," she said, a little of Blanche's bravery coming to the fore.

His wide smile, directed entirely at her, made her pulse quicken. "Then I'll look forward to seeing you tomorrow, Miss Danvers."

The top of her hand tingled as he walked away. Perhaps Caroline Danvers wasn't as bold as her nom de plume. But there might be room within her for more than practicality and jadedness. There could be space for a little bit of Blanche.

This wasn't the first time Dorian dreamt of Caroline Danvers, nor the first time he awoke from a dream hard, aching, and hungry for her. However, after he'd taken himself in hand and rose to dress for the day, there was a lightness in his chest, rather than the usual burden of hopeless longing.

When he visited the bookshop yesterday, there'd been that moment when he'd been certain one evening of frantic kisses against a door would be all he'd have with her. Turning around to reengage had been an impulsive risk but one that served him well in the end.

Speaking his mind had been a relief, but the real moment of satisfaction had come when she softened, and he witnessed the sparkle return to her eyes. Those plump lips had curved, lifting her round cheeks, making her face distinctly heart shaped, and it had taken everything he had to not kiss her again, public location be damned.

At breakfast, his mother raised one arched brow over the rim of her teacup as she studied him. "You're in an awfully good mood."

Dorian spread butter over his toast and shrugged. "I suppose I am rather cheerful this morning."

When he didn't offer more, Gloria prodded. "Has something happened? Perhaps you've come to a decision regarding your bride? There's still time to plan an engagement ball to welcome the rest of the ton back to Town."

The toasted bread stuck in his throat, forcing him to cough into a napkin and guzzle too-hot tea to wash it down. His good cheer was dissolving significantly faster than the breadcrumbs clinging stubbornly inside his mouth.

"Please don't let your mind stray too far down that path. I am not making a decision yet. In fact, I think I might pull back from that project slightly." At his mother's militant expression, he added, "Not abandoning it altogether. I have a duty, after all."

Even as Dorian prevaricated, he recognized a sick feeling in his gut. Discussing the bride hunt with his mother while nearly giddy over seeing a woman who fit none of the requirements for a duchess stole the last of this morning's optimism.

Gloria couldn't force him down the aisle, no matter how scary her glares and raised eyebrows were. Yes, he needed to marry and sire an heir. And yes, the men in his family were frightfully short-lived. Not to mention the rather emotionally fraught birthday arriving in a few months.

"It is an important decision," she said with a tone that explained she was feeling magnanimous. "I trust you're aware of your duty and the need for some haste."

It struck him, not for the first time, that his father must have been quite strong-minded to have not only won the respect of a woman like Gloria, but kept it, even after his death.

Life would certainly be simpler if his father were still alive. Father had been a wise, gentle man. A good parent and kind husband. He'd know what to do about Juliet's letters and this damned bride hunt. Dorian would give anything to have him here, teaching him what it meant to be a duke when it sometimes felt as if he was rebuilding his life one piece at a time.

Wiping his mouth on a cloth napkin, he stood. "Enjoy your breakfast, Mother. I find I'm not as hungry as I thought I was."

As he left the room, she called, "Don't forget! We've invited the Humphrys to the theater this evening. Miss Humphry's parents are feeling ill, so it will be the three of us. Please be charming, Dorian."

He paused, one hand on the doorjamb, and hung his head. Drawing in a deep breath, he continued walking. One night at the theater wouldn't kill him. It wasn't as if it were a public declaration of intent.

Even though it would guarantee more tongues wagging, building on the existing speculation. God, the gossips would talk, and he was knowingly handing them more choice conversational morsels.

A thought flitted through his mind, there and then gone. Like a timid creature skittering into the light, then darting away lest it be seen.

A man brave enough to have a relationship with someone unconventional—perhaps someone like a bookseller—would have to be immune to things like gossiping matrons. That would take the strength of knowing oneself thoroughly. Like his father had.

Dorian straightened to his full height and headed toward his study. As usual, a pile of work awaited him there—more than enough ducal decisions to occupy him until Caroline arrived.

After all, there was more than one way to do his duty.

Chapter Nine

❧

"Do you have family besides those at the shop?" the duke asked.

It had been like this for the last hour. Holland asking questions while stacking books in the piles to which she pointed and guessing but failing to discern her organizational system.

With the fire burning merrily in the grate, the library felt cozy and private, like their own little world. It hadn't taken long for Caro's initial nerves to settle and the conversation to flow more naturally.

"My father is still alive, but as he's disowned me, I no longer claim him as family either."

He froze, with his hand clutching a book over a stack. "Disowned you? What kind of father disowns his own daughter, and how mad must he be to not look at you and burst with pride? You're intelligent, beautiful, well-spoken. What's wrong with him?"

Hearing him describe and defend her in such a way made Caro smile, and she felt a tiny part of her tumble toward something sweeter than lust. "Not that stack. One pile over."

He obeyed without complaint.

"To answer your question, my father has always had very strong ideas of right and wrong, good and bad. There is no middle ground with him. Ever. No compromises, no negotiations. As a vicar, that particular trait has ensured he always sounds confident while speaking."

"I don't think pigheadedness is an admirable trait in anyone, especially a clergyman," he grumbled. "Dare I ask what happened to make him cast you out?"

Despite the warmth of the fire, a chill rolled over Caro, and she turned from him to grab the next book from the shelf. "I'd rather not say. Not right now, anyway. The bare details are that I went to town one day and returned to find him nearly frothing at the mouth with rage and refusing to allow me entry to my home. I lost everything but what I had on my person at that moment."

His face looked thunderous, and wherever her father was, she hoped he felt an inexplicable wave of foreboding threaten him. Holland appeared ready to wreak havoc on her behalf.

"What about your mother?"

Caro offered a tight smile. "Died in labor when I was young. The baby didn't make it either."

He stepped close, studying her face with so much empathy her heart ached at the knowledge that he'd suffered loss too.

"It was a long time ago," she began but stopped when he cupped her cheek in his warm palm.

"Just this morning I was pondering how different life would be if my father were still alive. I wish he were here to guide me. I miss him," he said, his thumb brushing across her cheekbone.

The admission made way for her to share as well. "I miss her. Unfortunately, Father wasn't kinder to his wife than he was to his daughter. Part of me is also glad she's away from him."

Holland nodded in understanding, then dropped a soft kiss on her cheek where his thumb had caressed her. Not

the first kiss of the day. Through some kind of mutual but silent agreement, they'd avoided the sort of embrace they'd enjoyed in front of the shop. Instead, today had been a study in kisses. Short kisses, light kisses. Teasing nips and an occasional brief, passionate embrace that brought every ounce of longing to the fore. Every time, Holland pulled back before the situation escalated.

It all seemed deliberately designed to build familiarity and comfort between them. Caro had to admit it was working. She'd caught him flexing and clenching his hands several times, as if consciously reining himself in from pinning her to the nearest bookcase and ravishing her.

She was confident it would be a bookcase. Though he'd been eying the tall, sturdy wood structures as well as the velvet lounge since she'd arrived, the bookcases were closer.

That restraint, combined with steady but undemanding affection, meant her skin was alive with awareness, aching in a way it never had before. Eventually, the duke's iron control would snap, and she could hardly wait. Anticipating that moment acted as an antidote to the melancholy their conversation might have otherwise inspired. Until then, they'd talk.

Holland pulled away and busied himself with tidying the closest pile of books—one of five intended for their lending library, not private sale. "Was that when you came to London? After he threw his fit?"

Caro smirked. "I appreciate that you make him sound like a child throwing a tantrum. Thankfully, I had a small sum of money in my pocket. It was enough to pay for various rides that got me closer to London. I knew if I could just get to Martin House, then I might have a safe place."

Dorian cleared his throat. "What you did was incredibly brave. Hell, surviving childhood with a sanctimonious bully for a father is remarkable too. But a woman traveling alone for such a distance? I think there's a lot you're not telling me about your journey. Perhaps you'll share more about that someday."

She liked the idea that they might have a "someday." A future, although what that looked like, she had no idea.

The book in her hands would be of interest to three collectors in her records, so Caro made a note of it on her growing list. The one to offer the highest price would take it home. Perhaps highly sought-after titles like this one could be included in some sort of mail-in auction. The logistics of how to make that work made her brain hurt, but she'd ask her uncle what he thought of the idea.

As she turned over the volume, two folded papers drifted from the pages. Slowly, she bent and plucked them from where they'd landed against her dirty hem. "These are yours, I believe." Caro held out the letters, watching as he unfolded and read them.

The last time she'd found one of these letters to the late duchess, seeing it had nearly brought him to his knees with grief. Despite her growing closeness with Holland, she felt no more equipped to deal with a similar situation now than she had that day.

Yet, other than a tightening around his mouth and a deepening furrow between those dark eyebrows, Holland didn't seem as affected. She wanted to ask why, to understand the difference between that first letter and these, but her tongue wouldn't loosen to form the question. Asking about his wife and the pain of losing her seemed like a far more personal question than was appropriate for their level of intimacy.

"I apologize if these letters cause you pain, Your Grace."

Holland refolded the papers into tidy rectangles and shoved them in his pocket. He appeared to search for the right words before he answered. "The last one took me by surprise. I know I've already said so, but I'm sorry you had to witness that."

Caro shook her head. "Never apologize to me for having emotions, no matter how strong. Although I understand it can be uncomfortable when others are around to see those moments. Being a vicar's daughter meant everyone was watching me, expecting me to be perfect. The villagers and Father believed he had his position because he'd been chosen by God. By extension, I was held to an impossible standard as well. I imagine a man in your position would know a thing or two about that." She gave him the book where the letters had been hidden, gesturing toward a smaller pile on his left.

Holland offered a crooked smile that was more a quirk of the lips than a real expression of humor. "Everyone feels entitled to an opinion about my actions."

Caro shrugged. "I don't. And these days, I do my best to escape notice of anyone who would think to judge me. In fact, if I have my way, I'll eventually live far from prying eyes and never suffer anyone's scrutiny, no matter what I do. I could lounge about in my garden utterly naked if I wished, and no one would say a thing."

His smile transformed to a grin. "Are you prone to prancing naked in your garden? Feel free to summon me next time you have the urge. I'd like to see that."

She laughed and nudged his arm with her shoulder. "Number one, I have no garden. And number two, I said lounge, not prance. It's the principle of the idea, and you know it."

Holland slipped an arm around her waist, pulling her close. "Don't dash my hopes like that, Miss Danvers. I'd much rather cling to my version." His lips were soft when they met hers, but he didn't linger long. "I have a garden," he said against her mouth, then nibbled her bottom lip as she laughed.

"You're incorrigible."

"Am I? Or am I a man walking the fine line between desperately wanting to taste you properly and trying to respect your need to work? Perhaps I'm trying to help instead of becoming a distraction, in hopes of being invited to assist you again." With every word, he placed a soft kiss along her jaw, then down her neck, lingering as he drew closer to the edge of her gown. Ripples of sensation shot straight to the desire that had been simmering below her navel.

Holland paused and shot an annoyed look at the stacks of books. "Even though I can't understand your sorting system."

It felt like the most natural thing in the world to laugh and thread her fingers through his brown waves. Satisfaction roared through her when the hair didn't fall obediently back in place. She'd finally mussed him, and it made her want to ruffle him more.

"Did you know," he said conversationally against the column of her neck, "when you wear fichus like these that don't let me peek at your skin through them, it annoys me?"

Her thighs trembled as his teeth grazed where her neck and shoulder met. "Does it? I didn't know you held such strong opinions regarding my wardrobe."

In answer, he muttered an oath and plucked the offensive—but warm, thank you—fabric from the gown's neckline, and she laughed. The sound turned to a moan when his tongue dipped into the crevice of her cleavage.

"I've instructed the servants to leave you to your work, but I know my mother is home." Regret and frustration colored his tone. "We'll have to content ourselves with kisses. But for your information, I've spent a disgraceful amount of time imagining these breasts. I hope to see them someday."

Another mention of someday. Caro tugged his hair until he met her gaze. "I rather like the idea of you thinking disgraceful thoughts about me, Your Grace." She couldn't contain a giggle. "Pardon the awful pun, but I just couldn't help myself."

His grin turned wolfish when he backed her against the bookcase, as she'd predicted. Kissing her in a way that made her feel as if she were the most desired woman who'd ever lived, Holland explored her curves through the heavy wool of her gown.

And for a moment, Caro let herself believe they were in a world of their own, where no one was watching.

Chapter Ten

❧

The Theatre Royal Drury Lane bustled every night the curtains weren't dark, but the crowd tended to be particularly unruly or distracted when the prince regent was in the house. After all, when else were the masses in the same building, let alone the same room, as the profligate royal? Caro craned her neck to stare up at the luxuriously appointed private boxes and their inhabitants.

With Prinny on hand, everyone else was watching the royal box to the right, leaving all of them open to her curious gaze. Silks shimmered in the flickering light of countless candles, and a veritable mine's worth of gems winked from necks, wrists, fingers, and earlobes.

"Makes such a fuss wherever he goes," Gerard muttered from beside Leo.

"Everyone is probably trying to witness a scandal in person, rather than read about it in the papers tomorrow," Caro murmured, distracted by the happenings around Lady Caroline Lamb. As usual, the woman who'd made herself infamous through her affair with Lord Byron was surrounded by a motley crew of hangers-on. While clearly Quality, those filling the seats in her theater box were likely split between genuinely caring about her and wanting to be on hand should she do something they'd pick over later like vultures.

Almost against her will, Caro's eyes strayed toward one

specific seating alcove high above her hard wood bench. A shame such a luxurious box sat empty, but then the Duke of Holland hadn't made an appearance at the theater since his wife passed away. Or so Constance had said before Caro set out for the evening.

Caro had never followed the ton's gossip beyond the usual newspaper fare, but since working in the Holland townhouse, she'd bent her ear toward tales about a certain duke. Thanks to Constance, and the few things Holland had shared, she felt she had a decent grasp on the situation. At least, as much as an outsider in every conceivable way could.

The view of certain empty theater seats disappeared as the man in front of her jumped to his feet. "Watch where yer goin', harebrained lummock!"

Leo wrapped an arm around her shoulders and pulled them both back, shifting precariously on the bench to avoid the two men. Despite his maneuver, the spilled pint of ale now decorating the front of the offended man's trousers reached her gown as well. A dark splash marred the skirt of her best dress, and she grimaced. All around them, men and women either leaned away to avoid the conflict or stood to lend their aid should the beer-soaked man's clenched fist be put to use.

"Apologies, Caro. We can move to another seat if you wish. Leo, are you all right?" Gerard asked.

"I'm unscathed," came Leo's wry reply. His hand on her shoulder tightened as if preparing to guide her from the fray.

A spike of irritation at the men around her came and went when the beer spiller apologized loud enough to be heard above the raised voices, appealing to the injured party's compassion. The offer to buy the man a pint of his own probably didn't hurt either. What was nearly a situation involving blows dissipated to nothing as the pair set off to buy beer and likely form a lifelong friendship. Neither of them noticed the sodden state of her gown as she plucked the wet fabric from her thigh in a feeble attempt to dry it.

"We will pay to have your dress cleaned," Leo offered.

Gerard nodded. "The washerwoman Leo found for us is a miracle worker. I don't know how he manages to comb the streets and find nothing but those who excel at what they do, but I'm grateful for it."

Leo grinned. "It's a gift. I found you, didn't I?" He shifted his attention to her. "Just say the word and we will move."

Caro shrugged. "No need. The danger has passed, see? Now, if people start throwing things at the prince and there's real danger in the pit, I'll happily vacate our seats."

Her friends exchanged a rueful smile, and Gerard said, "The minute someone throws a rotten cabbage, we're whisking you away."

"Let us hope these fine folks wouldn't disrespect Beethoven to such a degree." Caro smiled and clasped the playbill for the evening. "I'm looking forward to hearing Mrs. Dickens sing. The papers say lovely things about her."

It was familiar, this back-and-forth with Gerard and Leo. Perhaps as a solicitor, Gerard dealt with too many of the rougher elements of society, so he was constantly on guard to every possible threat. His protective nature was a comfort, if sometimes a bit much. It was always a treat to see him with Leo, and to witness that care and concern turned toward his partner.

The men who'd squabbled over spilled beer returned moments later, chatting merrily as predicted, and took their seats as Miss Smith finished yet another reading from *Paradise Lost*.

In Caro's opinion, the opening entertainment left quite a

bit to be desired. Or perhaps that was her ingrained antagonism toward her vicar father rearing its rebellious head. In any case, her mind and eyes wandered back to the empty Holland box.

That wasn't empty any longer.

In evening dress of black and white, looking far better than any man had a right to, sat the duke. All evidence of their passionate kisses had been erased. The curls she'd tugged to guide his mouth, and the cravat she'd left rumpled and creased, had been replaced with his usual standard of pristine polish. Holland stared at the stage with a vacant expression that could be mistaken for attentiveness by anyone who hadn't spent every available moment studying his face. On either side of him, a woman fluttered and fussed with the harried air of those arriving late to an event. Caro recognized the steely gray curls of the dowager, but the other woman was a mystery.

Dark hair, delicate bone structure, and a fine gown displaying her décolletage to perfection. She was beautiful.

Caro wanted to hate her on sight. And part of her did, which was surprising. Having never had the opportunity to be jealous, she didn't realize she had it in her.

But Lord, did she ever.

The sight of the woman and the duke attending the theater under the chaperonage of his mother might not have stung a week ago. But mere hours had passed since she'd been tangled with that man against his bookcases and wrapped in his arms, running her fingers through his hair. At last, she'd left her mark on the perfect duke, and it had been glorious.

He'd left his own mark, not as easily combed and pressed away—a patch on her neck where his late-afternoon scruff had rubbed against her skin and left a graze. Until now, she'd cherished that mark as proof that their heated kisses weren't a dream.

Caro covered the beard burn with her hand and forced her attention back to the front, where musicians were beginning to play Beethoven's interpretation of Jesus in the Garden of Gethsemane. Despite the depressing subject matter, it was difficult not to be moved by the talented layers of musicality Beethoven brought to the stage.

"We should have looked at the playbill before bringing you here tonight," Leo murmured.

"We thought this would be an enjoyable night away from your responsibilities. Instead, we've brought you to a sermon put to music," Gerard whispered.

Caro grinned. "You forget my father was clergy. As sermons go, this is far more entertaining and remarkably short-winded."

Leo, always the optimist, said, "At least the comedy sketch from Mr. Bartholomew should liven things up. I've heard he's brilliant but hard to work with. When we were in line outside, I overheard someone say he didn't get the final script to the actors until this afternoon."

"Really? Ugh, I feel for those poor actors. If he's as amusing as they say, Mr. Bartholomew should end things on a high note."

Gerard offered a crooked smile. "Don't try to make me feel better. It won't work. I'd hoped for a lighter evening, or at least a romantic drama. Maybe even *Romeo and Juliet*."

She was rolling her eyes before he'd even finished saying the name of Shakespeare's play. "*Romeo and Juliet* does not qualify as a romantic drama. Two lust-addled children making poor decisions in the name of sex is not romantic."

Beside her, Leo sputtered, "It's a classic, Caroline."

"So are any number of other questionable works written by men who liked the sound of their own voice." She shifted to face her friends, leaning close to avoid annoying those around them too terribly much. "When looked at objectively, you have to agree that Romeo was inconstant, flitting from Rosaline to Juliet within seconds, due solely to the appearance of an absolute stranger. And Juliet returns his favor based on what, exactly? Because he paid attention to her? After which, they destroy themselves and their families because they had the communication skills of beach pebbles, proving that they were indeed children in need of naps rather than kisses."

Gerard's rolling rumble of laughter—entirely inappropriate as the actors on stage sung of Christ's impending crucifixion—made her smile in return. "You see, Caro? This is why I respect you so much. You think with your head, not your heart. There's not a sentimental bone in your entire body."

Hearing Constance's words from a few nights before repeated, albeit with a slight variation, made Caro blink as she struggled for a reply. "Is…is that how you see me?" It was on the tip of her tongue to blast a cannonball-size hole through their idea of her and tell them their unsentimental friend wrote erotic novels. That she'd chosen to write erotic fiction specifically due to the genre's consistently higher sales numbers was a fact she'd keep to herself.

Before the urge could overwhelm her sense, Gerard continued. "Your logical brain is your greatest asset, my dear. You would be a fine companion for any man but especially for one like me, who values your open mind as well. To that end, Leo and I would like to have a conversation with you."

Leo placed his hand over hers. "Please hear us out before answering."

What was happening right now? Caro glanced around, but no one seemed to be paying attention to their conversation. Up in his box, the duke was lending an ear to something his young companion said. He nodded but didn't smile. Not that his lack of smile meant anything. Holland claimed to have wanted Caro for nearly two years, and he'd been unsmiling the whole time.

Gerard said, "We are realizing something needs to change. It has been made clear at work, although not in so many words, that I won't advance in the firm while unattached. They see single men as unreliable, while a married man is viewed as stable."

"They've never let an unmarried man join the higher ranks. Not once," Leo added.

"Over the last few months, there have been comments asking when I will marry," Gerard said.

Violins joined the wind section as notes intertwined and swelled around them, providing a counter rhythm to the heartbeat pounding in her ears. "Gentlemen, what are you saying?"

They exchanged a look. Leo said, "We would like to propose an arrangement that meets all our needs. Except for occasional events with the firm's partners, you could have your own life, your own schedule. There would be no other demands made of you. Between the two of us, we could provide adequate financial support. Perhaps a little cottage like you've mentioned. You could do whatever you wanted with your time."

The music softened as Mrs. Dickens finished her solo.

One part of Caro's mind was aware of the theater and her fellow patrons.

A woman in Prinny's box teetered dangerously over the railing, and the crowd below began betting on which would fall loose first—the woman herself, or her breasts from her bodice.

In his box, the duke rose and moved toward the curtain behind their seats.

But it was the practical part of her that surfaced from the shock and spoke. "Are you...are you proposing marriage, Gerard?"

"Yes, of course. What else would we be talking about?"

All around them, the audience burst into applause.

Chapter Eleven

God would smite him any moment now.

For the last hour, Dorian had been sitting in his theater box silently comparing what Christ endured while marching to his crucifixion to that of a night at the theater with his mother and a young lady vying for the role of wife. Beethoven's musical rendition wasn't nearly dark enough, in his opinion.

Miss Edwina Humphry hadn't said more than ten words to him all night. He'd tried. Lord, how he'd tried. In the carriage, he'd asked after her family ("Fine, thank you"), pets (none), hobbies (sewing, charitable acts), interests (dancing), and opinion about the domestic law Parliament was considering—which he'd made up on the spot and didn't actually exist. Each answer essentially settled into a general "Yes, Your Grace. I'm sure you know best."

Infuriating. Despite the lack of conversation, she'd pasted on a demure smile and had the audacity to flutter her eyelashes at him. Flutter. Her. Eyelashes. All evidence of intelligence and wit seemed to have vanished under the weight of his lukewarm interest. If one could call a single waltz and his mother inviting her to the theater without his knowledge "interest."

The depth of his frustration told him the earlier decision to take his time choosing the next Duchess of Holland had been the right one. A certain luscious bookseller complicated things. Even without thoughts of Caroline Danvers muddying the waters, Miss Humphry wouldn't be the right candidate.

There wasn't anything wrong with her personally. But there wasn't anything right either. Nothing to suggest they could carry on together for the foreseeable future. He'd decided to dance with her because she'd been witty during the few moments they'd spoken before that event.

Now the poor woman seemed petrified to do more than smile and nod in response to whatever nonsense he spouted. When he'd whispered as much to his mother as they'd climbed the stairs to their box, the dowager had replied coolly, "Well, I should hope so. It shows she's aware of what an honor it is to carry the Holland name."

Which was no help at all and made Dorian want to retreat to Martin House Books, where he could listen to the cousins' conversation and perhaps sneak a few more kisses from Caroline. The blonde flirt, Constance, was a whirlwind but extremely entertaining, and the mousy-haired Hattie had a sense of humor that usually had him hiding his grin behind the nearest book.

The thought he'd briefly entertained that morning of how his father would have dealt with an attraction to someone like Caroline crossed his mind once more. Their time in the library had felt easy, free of complications. She'd conversed with him the same way she did her cousins, and he'd enjoyed a blessed reprieve from the pressure that came with social interactions within the ton.

The performance droned on, until his left butt cheek tingled from sitting too long. Dorian shifted. It was impressive that Miss Humphry managed to impersonate a statue so convincingly. Did the woman not need to move occasionally? It made him want to study her face to see if she even blinked, but he didn't want her to misconstrue the attention.

As he considered the situation, he couldn't avoid drawing parallels between the woman beside him and his late wife. Both were well-bred and educated to be the wife of a man in his position. At ease in society. If he had to hazard a guess, he'd say Miss Humphry was about the same age Juliet had been when they married.

Which, given fifteen years had passed since, was too bloody young.

No wonder they didn't have anything to talk about. Of course, the letters they'd found today were proof that he and Juliet hadn't discussed everything either. Romeo—whoever that was—thanked her for helping "the children" in the second letter. For a brief moment, his brain had spiraled down twisted paths where he calculated dates to determine if Juliet might have somehow had children without anyone knowing, while he'd been on the Continent. That level of deception was impossible when factoring in the few visits he'd made home. The more likely scenario was that Romeo convinced her to financially support a cause involving children. Might this Romeo person be where Juliet's missing money had gone?

The dowager rapped his arm with her fan. "Sit still. You're squirming like a child," she hissed through clenched teeth, never taking her eyes off the stage.

Dorian turned to Miss Humphry. "I need to stretch my legs. I'll be back shortly."

"Would you mind bringing me a glass of lemonade when you return, Your Grace?" With that one request, she'd doubled her word count for the evening.

"Of course."

Dorian closed the heavy velvet drapes behind him and

stepped into the hall like a man gulping fresh air after a year in a prison cell. "Fuck, I'm in hell," he whispered.

A hell of his own making, though, and that fact was unavoidable. Not for the first time, he wondered what would happen if he didn't die young, like the other men in his family. The dowager was gray-haired but otherwise immune to the passage of time. She would likely outlive them all. What if Dorian found a wife, sired an heir, then had to live forever with his decision?

It was enough to make a man consider running away from home.

Instead, he set off down the hall, going nowhere in particular but intent on staying there as long as possible before he had to return to depressing Beethoven and a silent companion. Checking his pocket watch, he estimated he could be gone for fifteen minutes before pushing the boundary of polite behavior.

Down one hall, around a corner, and then down another hall he didn't recognize. Dorian wandered with no destination but did so with purposeful strides so he looked like he was going somewhere important. People tended to leave one alone when one looked like they were in the middle of doing something.

After a while, he became aware of footsteps following him down a passageway and around a corner. Dorian turned to see who it was and stopped in surprise. Like he'd conjured her from thin air, Caroline walked toward him. He greeted her with a smile.

"All I can think about is you, and now you've appeared." As she approached, her expression didn't change. "Has something happened? You look so serious." While his heart pounded happily at the sight of her, she appeared less enthusiastic about seeing him. In fact, Caroline had yet to meet his eyes. Part of him wondered if she'd keep walking by if he hadn't stepped in her path.

A theater hall was far from private, so he couldn't do more than brush her hand quickly and ask, "Are you all right?"

There was that damned pause again before she gave him the same benign close-lipped smile she'd offered a dozen times before. Before he'd kissed those lips. Before he'd begged to hear her thoughts. "Good evening, Your Grace." Fully weaponizing etiquette, the minx dipped into a curtsy.

Then it hit him. She wasn't being polite. Caroline Danvers was furious. At him, if he had to guess.

"What have I done?" Keeping his voice low, he gently guided her toward another turn in the hall. Perhaps they could talk there.

"I hope you're enjoying your evening, Your Grace." Never had such monotone platitudes boded so poorly for him.

"I'm not, actually. Seeing you is the best part of it." The next hall was equally well lit but had a snug, shadowed alcove off to one end, large enough to fit two. Perfect. Dorian tugged her into the space and lowered his mouth to her ear. "For the love of heaven, woman, would you please tell me why you're trying to kill me with politeness?"

"I wouldn't want to keep you from your night, Your Grace. I'm sure you have people to see other than a lowly bookseller." There was nothing self-deprecating in her tone. Instead, the words rang as a challenge, daring him to step one more foot out of line so she could flay him alive.

Wait...He met her stony gaze. "You're jealous." He reached to trace her cheek and reassure her but stopped with his hand midair when she glared.

"Touch me with that finger and I'll bite it. You don't get to caress my face and tell me I'm remarkable and make my head spin with that mouth of yours, when there's a woman sitting with your mother in your box down the hall."

"Ah, there's the real Caroline. I missed you." Instinct told him smiling would not go well, so he refrained. Barely. "The woman in my box is Miss Edwina Humphry. I danced with her once and was relieved to return her to her chaperone at the end of it. Mother invited her to join us this evening without my knowledge. Yes, she's one of the women Mother asked me to consider as a wife."

Caroline bit her lower lip and stared over his shoulder. He dipped his face to be in front of hers. "However, Miss Humphry will not be my duchess. I won't lie to you, Caroline. Remarrying was a higher priority recently, although I wasn't particularly keen on the idea. It's even less appealing after kissing you. However, if something happened to me without an heir, the title and everyone depending on it for their livelihoods would suffer. At some point, I'll have to assess my options."

Slowly, to give her time to shy away, he brought his fingers to her cheek again. This time, she didn't move—or threaten him—but her eyes were still stormy. "The only woman I am thinking about is you. The only woman I am kissing is you. I don't know what happens next, but I can assure you I'm not slipping into shadowed doorways or alcoves with anyone else."

Caroline turned her face and kissed his palm, then said, "I didn't like looking up and seeing you with her. I don't have any experience with jealousy. It's not a comfortable emotion."

Of course she'd be sitting in the pit and not in a box. It was on the tip of his tongue to invite her to join him when she said, "Overall, this hasn't been a terribly enjoyable evening. As soon as my friends are ready to leave, I'll be returning home."

Dorian shifted to lean against the wall beside her, so her shoulder snugged against his arm. He dropped a kiss on her hair. "The performers are talented, but the subject matter is a bit shit, isn't it?"

She laughed. "God, it's all so *depressing*. Next week Edmund Kean will be here playing Shylock again, which everyone claims is brilliant. Why are we subjecting ourselves to this, instead of returning in a few days?"

"I have the excuse of being dragged here by my matchmaking mother. Who are you here with?"

"Friends who live down the street."

He was quiet a moment. "I imagine it's different down on the floor. In the box, you feel like you're on display. Every reaction to a play, everything you do, is right there for everyone to see."

"I'll take the anonymity of the floor, thank you. Even if it is a bit rowdy. With the right companions, it can be fine. Some people only come to shows to cause trouble, so if you can avoid those, it's all right."

"You said it hasn't been enjoyable this evening. I hope my presence didn't ruin your night."

Caroline settled heavier against his side, and he smiled. Hiding in an alcove with her was more entertaining than anything else he'd done since entering the building. "Well, I nearly bathed in beer, warranting a thorough washing of my skirts before I can wear this gown again. Then I narrowly avoided being caught in the middle of a brawl over said spilled beer, and two men proposed to me. Frankly, I'm ready to go home."

A fiery pinch near his heart made him pause, then shake his head. "Does it make you feel better to know that hearing about two men proposing to you makes me jealous?"

She smiled up at him and rested her cheek on his shoulder. "It does, actually."

He gazed down at her, and having her so close and comfortable made a ball of tension he hadn't realized he'd been carrying loosen under his ribs.

"I like your smile. You should do it more often," she said.

"You give me reasons to smile."

When she closed her eyes and took a deep breath, he sensed their time together was ending. "I should return to my friends."

Reluctantly, Dorian checked his watch and winced. "I need to go back to the box as well." He laced his fingers with hers and pushed off the wall. "Please tell me I'll see you soon."

Her grin was saucy. "You'll see me soon."

"And will I kiss you soon?" Dorian pulled her hand, reeling her closer to his chest.

The curve of her mouth was sweet under his, opening for him immediately. Losing himself in the feel and taste of her would be too easy, and he'd be left wanting more. As they drew apart, Dorian kissed her hand before dropping his hold on her. "Do me the kindness of not accepting any offers of marriage before I see you again."

She arched one brow. "Do me the kindness of not making any offers of marriage before I see you again." Caroline held out her hand, offering a handshake agreement.

His laugh made him feel lighter than he had all evening, but he took the offer and shook on it. "Agreed."

Far more than the fifteen minutes of freedom he'd allotted himself had passed, but thankfully Dorian was able to find a glass of lemonade for Miss Humphry on his way back to his seat. And a quarter hour later, when the short comedy piece—likely on the program for the sole purpose of preventing everyone from dying of boredom—made the audience's laughter fill the room, Dorian searched the long wooden benches below for one woman in particular.

With over three thousand people in the theater, he shouldn't feel disappointed when he failed to spot Caroline in the sea of faces. But he was.

Chapter Twelve

❧

"You're older than I thought you'd be."

Caro nearly dropped the book she'd been examining. How had the Dowager Duchess of Holland entered the library without her hearing? The woman must move like a cat.

At a loss for the best way to respond to that opening salvo, Caro curtsied. "Good afternoon, Your Grace."

The dowager took her time crossing the room, examining Caro all the while, then draped herself onto the settee. For an older woman, she moved gracefully. Fluid, unhurried, but not unfocused. She wore her hair in a simple, flattering style designed for a relaxed day at home that likely took her maid considerable time to achieve. From silvery head to satin-shod foot, she looked expensive and stylish, even while achieving a calculated effect of casual comfort.

When Caro enjoyed a rare day off, she stayed in her ratty wrapper and let her wool stockings slouch down her calves until they pooled at her feet like sad little gray elephant ankles.

"My son is an important man."

Really? I'd never have known. I thought duke *was a friendly nickname given to him in childhood.* "Yes, Your Grace."

"You're a cool one—I'll give you that." The dowager assessed Caro with a raised eyebrow, then abruptly changed tactics. "The Holland men are a lovable lot. It's one of life's great ironies that the best things are often short-lived. His grandfather died in his sleep at forty-eight. My husband, God rest him, dropped dead at thirty-six. No accidents, no illnesses. Neither were fragile, sickly men."

Why is she telling me this? "I'm sorry for your loss, Your Grace. That must have been terrible."

"My husband had no siblings. We only had Dorian. There is no one to inherit the title, girl. Do you understand?"

Dorian had said as much. Although he'd phrased it as more of a worst-case kind of thinking, not an actual possibility.

"There are those who needn't think of such things. They live their lives unencumbered by obligations. As a result, they follow their impulses without consequences." A distinct chill coated her words. "The Duke of Holland is not one of those people. My son has a duty to fulfill, and since your presence in our home, he's been showing a concerning lack of enthusiasm toward that duty."

When Caro said nothing, the dowager pressed, "You are aware my son seeks a wife, are you not?"

"Yes, Your Grace."

"Then you must also be aware that said wife needs to be well-connected, young enough to bear children, and comfortable in society, in order to raise the next Duke of Holland alone, should my son share his father's fate."

An expectant pause told Caro a verbal answer was required. "That would stand to reason, yes." Having a mother speak casually of her only child dying young was unnerving. The dowager's lack of emotion told Caro this entire conversation was more about manipulation than anything.

"Then you agree. Holland must do his duty while you disappear back into your dusty bookcases."

Well, that was simply uncalled for. Martin House book-cases were cleaned constantly. "Your Grace, please pardon my confusion. But if you have concerns regarding your son, why are you speaking to me instead of him?"

A brittle smile curved the dowager's lips. "These things are best handled between women, don't you agree?"

This entire bizarre conversation was like walking a tight-rope made of spiderwebs over a pool of alligators. "Ordinarily I would concur that women are capable of navigating any situation with the aid of an ally. In this, though, I fail to see how I can be of help."

Quick as a curtain falling, the dowager's control slipped. "Don't dissemble, Miss Danvers. I'm fully aware of your affair with my son. Playing coy is a young woman's trick, and you are certainly beyond such things."

If I were having an affair, I'd expect to feel far more relaxed and satisfied, thank you. Caro drew in a deep breath, held it, then released it slowly. "Did the duke tell you he and I are involved?"

"A son doesn't speak of such things with his mother. However, I am capable of listening, and he speaks freely with Southwyn."

With her patience running low, Caro leveled the dowager with a look. "In other words, you eavesdropped. Your Grace, I understand your concerns. However, I suggest you take them to the duke." *Because I'll be damned if I promise to keep my hands off a grown man just because his mother threw a fit over me being a weathered old crone.*

"If you intend to remain in his life, I cannot stop you. However, if you distract him from his duty, I can and will make your life very uncomfortable."

Caro blinked. Had his mother just told her she could be Holland's mistress as long as he carried on with his plans to wed? Aristocrats were an odd lot. It was an inner struggle that lasted all of three seconds to realize she wouldn't be his mistress if he married. She couldn't hurt another woman like that and be able to look at herself in the mirror. Neither could she conceive of a situation where anyone fortunate enough to marry Holland could do so and remain emotionally distant. The man's sly humor and wicked grin, although hard-won, would conquer the hardest heart. Once he peered into a woman's eyes and begged to know the real her, tender feelings were inevitable.

"Your Grace, I have quite a bit of work to do today. If that will be all, I'd like to return to it." If the dowager raised hell with the duke, Caro would relay every word of this conversation as her defense. Perhaps moving the library to a storage room closer to the shop would be a better idea, after all.

The dowager rose with war in her eyes. "You dare dismiss me in my own home, Miss Danvers?"

Caro dipped a shallow curtsy. "That is not my intent, Your Grace. Since I am a paid employee, I would hate for you to feel I am not fulfilling my assigned tasks." The words ate at her pride but soothed the silver society dragon somewhat, allowing her to leave with the illusion that Caro hadn't sent her packing.

When the library door closed on well-oiled hinges, Caro exhaled on a low groan. Now that she was alone, the emotional armor she'd donned disappeared. The dowager's verbal arrows might not have landed the way she wanted them to, but Caro felt the sting nonetheless.

After seeing the duke in the theater, she'd walked away with an unsettled feeling. The man who'd pulled her into an alcove and kissed her would need to find a wife, and the universe seemed to agree that wife couldn't be Caro. Not that she wanted the position. Not after bearing witness to the pain of her parents' marriage. In Holland's defense, he and her father were entirely different animals. But still. Wife? No, thank you. Lover? More and more, yes.

Which led to a moral dilemma she had no easy answer for and opened her to attacks like the one she'd just experienced.

Caro glanced down and snorted. She was still holding the same book she'd nearly dropped when the dowager took her by surprise. A gorgeous gilded volume of Shakespeare in excellent condition. Part of a set released by a specialty publisher, if she remembered correctly.

Behind the settee the dowager had abandoned, a clock chimed the hour. She'd stay in the library for at least another thirty minutes just to prove to his mother that her actions hadn't made Caro scurry away. She refused to run like a frightened rabbit after the dowager showed her teeth.

In the meantime, she searched for the other volumes in the set. Had it released with four volumes or five? She might have to look that up when she returned to the shop if she couldn't find them all here.

"Ah-ha. There you are, my beauties," she murmured, spying three more volumes scattered among the shelves. Since running across the first letter, she'd made a habit of flipping through each book.

At the end of last week, when she'd found the other two letters, hadn't they been in a volume of Shakespeare as well? Instinct made her fingertips prickle as she opened each book in this set.

One volume was simply a book. A pretty one that, as part of a complete decorative set, would be valuable to a collector. But just a book. The other volumes offered two more letters to reward her stubbornness. "So, Shakespeare is the key."

She didn't read them, but her eye caught on a few lines as she looked for the signature. One letter was signed Romeo, the other Sherman, both in the same handwriting.

Wait. "Who the hell is Sherman?" Oh God. It was her turn to sink onto the settee with considerably less grace than the dowager. "The duke didn't write these."

The Romeo and Juliet references made sense if the late duchess stored the letters in her volumes of Shakespeare.

Letters from her lover. A glance at the dates proved these weren't from a childhood beau she'd had before her marriage.

I'll wait for you always, my Juliet.

I love you unconditionally.

Trite. And a bit pathetic when one considered the words themselves. Unconditional love? She couldn't imagine telling a man she loved him no matter how he acted, or how he treated her. If she ever declared her love for a man, it wouldn't be unconditional. Her place in a relationship was entirely reliant on the condition that he treat her well and was equally devoted.

To promise more reeked of desperation. Caro winced and glanced at the letters. She could be honest with herself now that she knew Holland hadn't written them. Pity welled for anyone who lost a spouse to such uninspired attempts at romance.

Especially when the alternative to this Sherman person was a man who kissed like the Duke of Holland.

Except the duke had to have realized he hadn't written the first letter she found. Caro covered her face with her hands. Had she unwittingly revealed his wife's infidelity? The grilled bread and cheese she'd eaten midday threatened to make a reappearance.

What was the right thing to do here? Burn them? Bring

them to the duke as promised—even if their existence hurt him? Thinking back on his reaction to the first letter rewrote that memory. What she'd witnessed probably wasn't grief over Juliet's death, but pain, shock, and possibly heartbreak. However, the last two had been read with considerably less emotion. That poor man, having to deal with these.

"Damn, damn, and double damn." Caro scanned the top letter again, then paused at a familiar phrase.

I am bereft, adrift, and needing your port to weather this storm.

Recognition made the hairs at her nape stand on end.

The double entendre wasn't lost on her, just as it hadn't been lost on the audience the week before at the Theatre Royal. Checking the date again, Caro counted backward. The play had been Mr. Bartholomew's latest—Leo said the actors barely had time to read and memorize their lines before opening night. Yet this letter was seven years old. There was no chance the author was quoting a bawdy line from the play, because that play hadn't existed yet. But Mr. Bartholomew had.

Did that mean the dead duchess had been having an affair with...a playwright? When and how had that relationship developed? Not questions she could ask without kicking a hornet's nest, but she wanted to be nosy and poke for answers anyway.

Between the duke's mother foretelling his imminent demise and Caro's suspicions about the letter writer's identity, there wasn't any way to talk herself out of giving these letters to Holland.

He hadn't been home when she arrived this afternoon. Was it cowardly to hope he was still not at home, so she could simply leave these on his desk? The man could connect the clues as easily as she had, since he'd been at the theater too.

Caro sighed, then stood from the settee. In the hall, Hastings informed her the duke had arrived home a few moments before and was in his study.

Steeling her spine, she knocked on the door.

Once Dorian finished reading this morning's report from the solicitor, he would let himself casually wander into the library, kick out Howard if needed, lock the door, and then pin Caroline against the nearest bookcase and kiss her silly. He hadn't seen her in four days, and the urge to touch her again made his palms itch.

But damn, Gerard Bellmore wrote a dry legal report. "Incentive, Holland. It's called incentive." He flipped to the next page as he sipped the cup of tea the ever-efficient Hastings had waiting when he arrived home.

A knock on the door made him glance up in irritation. Interruptions would only delay visiting the library and kissing the woman who'd been on his mind all day. "Enter."

That irritation vanished as soon as the door opened. Caroline carefully closed the door behind her, and his hopes rose in direct proportion to his cock. "Two more letters, Your Grace," she said, holding them out to him.

Hope and . . . everything else deflated. However, these letters might hold more clues that could help Mr. Bellmore in his quest to explain Juliet's finances. Dorian pushed the legal brief aside and rose. As he rounded his desk to greet her, something in her expression made him wave her to a chair instead of kissing her properly. "Would you like to sit?"

Rather than take the letters from her, he leaned against the desk and crossed his feet at the ankles. Caroline took the offered chair but had yet to smile, and the set of her shoulders was so straight she could have balanced a book on her head.

He nudged the toe of her walking boot with the toe of his polished Hessian. "Let me into the pause."

Her gaze flew to his, and she swallowed hard. "You didn't write these letters."

Dorian drew in a deep breath. "No, I didn't write them. But I'd dearly like to know who did."

In her lap, her thumbnail flicked the edge of one of the letters as she watched. "Did you already know about the affair? Is that why you reacted like you did when I brought the first letter to you?"

"I knew." His voice sounded rough, even to his ears. But his pulse wasn't pounding loud enough to echo in the room, and his palms weren't sweating. This wouldn't be like last time. He wouldn't read the letters and feel each word like a knife to the gut. This time, he'd breathe. He'd stay in the moment and not let the feelings steal his composure. "However, that letter, and these"—he nodded toward the two she clutched in her fingers—"seeing it literally in black and white made it all incredibly real. I won't bore you with details, but suffice to say, I loved my wife. Very much. Adored her, really. And I thought it was mutual. But during those last few years, I was on the Continent, and something always prevented her from joining me. Getting letters through or around enemy lines was difficult, which meant we weren't able to hear from one another frequently." The cravat his valet had tied that morning seemed to tighten incrementally with each word, but Dorian cleared his throat and pressed on. "I didn't know of the affair until she passed."

Caroline heaved a huge sigh of relief. "Then, I hadn't accidentally destroyed the memory of your wife by bringing you that letter?"

"God, no. Is that why you came in here looking like this?" She nodded. "Also, your mother said you are going to die young, so I needed to not interfere with your marriage plans."

He reared back. "My mother said what?"

Caroline canted her head and studied him. "At the theater, you mentioned needing an heir, but I thought it was just pragmatism. I didn't realize you have reason to contemplate your own mortality."

A curse slipped out on a sigh. Damn his meddlesome mother.

"You see, then, why this afternoon has left me with several questions." Rather than the wry humor he was beginning to associate with her, Caro appeared genuinely disturbed as she bit the side of her lip.

Which made him want to bite her lip. Dorian closed his eyes and rubbed at a spot on his temple where an ache bloomed. Just once, he'd like her to be in his study and not feel ill at ease. This room was a sanctuary for him, but she was going to start associating it with horrible events if this pattern continued. "It sounds like we might be due for a conversation."

It wasn't until he opened his eyes and looked at her again that she answered. "As much as I'd like to interrogate you, it's not my place. However, can you answer one question?"

She held out the letters, and he took them. Somehow, they'd become less important than he'd thought possible, considering what they likely contained.

"Yes, of course." Why did he want to follow that with the word *anything*? A problem to contemplate another day.

"Are you ill, Your Grace? Is that why you need an heir posthaste?"

He turned the letters over in his hands, noting the fraying of the paper along the folds and edges before returning his attention to her. "No. No, I'm not ill. I simply come from a line of men who don't live very long, don't sire many children, and happen to have a tremendous amount of responsibility placed on their shoulders from birth." Worry eased from her face, and she drew in a breath that made her rather glorious chest expand under her gown. Although, the word *glorious* made him think of Gloria, his mother. "What did my mother say, exactly?"

A quirk of her lips made the tension leach from his shoulders somewhat. "I understand she wanted to manipulate my emotions, so I'm not going to give too much weight to her comments. It's important to her that you marry."

"Did she insult you, Caroline?" The letters crinkled in his fist, so he busied himself by smoothing the paper onto his desktop.

She shrugged. "Nothing that wasn't true." Nodding to the letters, she said, "I'll confess I skimmed those. A line of text caught my eye. It's from the short comedy we saw the other night. The new one from Joseph Bartholomew."

"I, ah, wasn't paying attention. I was looking for you on the floor. I recall everyone laughing, though."

She tilted her head, which beckoned his gaze to the creamy skin of her neck. "Did you find me?"

"No, and not for lack of trying." He opened the first letter to see if he could spot the line in question. Maybe he'd been paying more attention than he realized. At the bottom of the page, a name leapt from the paper.

Sherman. Juliet's mystery lover who'd made him a cuckold. The swirling *S* of ink on the page blurred in his vision. A glance at the date made his heart ache. Dorian had been on the Continent, desperately pleading for his wife to join him. Yet Juliet always had a reason to delay.

Fucking Sherman. Literally, no doubt. Dark humor didn't dull his anger at the confident, cocky scrawled *S*. "This letter predates last night's play by several years."

Caroline offered a small smile. "Exactly. Perhaps it's a coincidence, but I doubt it. Sherman could be a nickname, or he might have given her a false name to hide his lower status in society."

"You think this Joseph Bartholomew person was my wife's lover." Hard to imagine but no more difficult to grasp than the idea of Juliet having a lover to begin with.

Another shrug. "Either way, it seems a pertinent clue to his identity. It could be nothing. It could be something." She stood. "I need to be going, Your Grace."

Dorian stared at the letter, then deliberately set it aside and reached out a hand to thread his fingers through hers. "You know, I'd planned to finish reading a horribly boring report, then find you in the library. All day, I've looked forward to kissing you. I planned to press you against the bookcases again, or perhaps coax you onto the settee and kiss you until you made that delicious little noise in the back of your throat."

She framed his face with her hands and brought his lips to meet hers. It wasn't the frantic lovemaking of mouths he'd anticipated, but it somehow felt more intimate. Sweeter. Surer because they'd shared secrets.

"Perhaps we can make that happen another day, when I haven't been awake since four in the morning and made to feel like a grizzled old crone by your mother."

Dorian laughed against her mouth. "I'm so sorry about my mother. I'll speak with her."

"That's not needed right now." She traced a finger over one of his eyebrows, and he nearly purred. How could an eyebrow feel so sensual? "However, I must make a demand."

He smiled at the idea of Caroline demanding things from him. Preferably in the bedroom. Or on this desk, if she was willing. "What is your demand?"

Her eyes turned serious, and he knew her mind had not been entertaining the same sort of thoughts. "When you choose your wife, please do me the courtesy of telling me. Whatever this is between us must end once you settle on someone."

Declaring an end before they'd truly begun. It was realistic but gutting to consider. Dorian placed a solemn kiss on her lips. "I promise."

Once again, he was left alone in his study with letters he didn't write. But this time he had a name to investigate and a woman to thoroughly woo before he wed another.

Chapter Thirteen

❧

Saturdays at Martin House were usually busy, but the retail gods must have heard Caro's silent plea for a quiet day and taken pity on her. Although she'd done her best to go to bed early, her brain had spun like a dog chasing its tail all night.

Her father used to claim from the pulpit that poor sleep was the sign of a guilty conscience. In her opinion, last night's tossing and turning had more to do with unmet sexual desire and confused feelings about the man responsible for inspiring those thoughts.

Damn Holland's confounding appeal.

Eventually, Hattie had sat up, thumped Caro over the head with a pillow, and demanded she talk. The sudden noise jolted Constance awake as well. By then, Caro had been ready to eject the thoughts whirling through her mind.

Everything spilled out. Kissing Dorian and wanting more. How he'd pinned her with that blue gaze and asked to know her...and then pinned her to the shop's door and a bookcase with an entirely different goal in mind. She told them of the unexpected proposal from Gerard and Leo. The dowager's visit to the library.

It had been like purging a wound, and just as messy. Bless her cousins for reacting exactly as they ought, because getting all of that out of her head meant Caro finally slept, knowing her two closest friends were on her side in all things.

They'd entertained themselves today by teasing her relentlessly about the fading marks on her skin Holland had left.

By the time the bell over the shop door notified them of the arrival of a customer, Hattie had ceased asking pointed questions about the duke designed to make Caro squirm and had occupied herself with shelving the new copies of *A Dalliance for Miss Lorraine*. Constance whisked around the room with a feather duster in hand but was doing more reading than dusting as she plucked one book from a shelf, read a few pages, then put it back and chose another book from a different shelf.

For her part, the only things keeping Caro on her feet were the counter she leaned against and the cup of strong tea cradled in her hands. She mustered a tired greeting when two women entered the store and headed straight toward Hattie and the crate of books. It was a relief to know she wouldn't have to actively sell them anything as Hattie struck up a rapport with them.

Bits of their conversation filtered through her foggy brain.

"I wish I were talented enough to write the things she does."

"Theodora, your stories are just as good as hers. I keep telling you, you need to send one to a publisher. Take the chance."

Some of Caro's mental haze cleared, and her pulse began to race. Even though she couldn't speak to them as Blanche, she could encourage this woman as a reader. "The world needs every story, miss. Especially when they end happily. Listen to your friend."

The young women glanced in her direction and smiled. "Thank you. It's terribly intimidating, though, isn't it? If only I could speak with someone who's published before. I have so many questions. More than anything, I'm scared they'll reject me."

Hattie raised a brow at Caro as if to say, *See, Blanche? They need you.* Part of her longed to answer the invitation. That part didn't have logic on its side, only emotional impulse. However, leaving another aspiring writer in the dark wasn't acceptable either.

Caro clutched her teacup tighter and offered the woman an encouraging smile. "A publisher might reject your work. But what if they don't? What if in a year, you had a book on that shelf, and I had the joy of selling it to readers? Contact a publisher and ask questions."

The woman's friend sent her a beaming grin and Caro sent her a conspiratorial wink. A few minutes later, she rang up a sale for each of them while they promised to let her know how the writing went.

It wasn't the same thing as admitting she was Blanche Clementine and having the chance to talk with a fellow writer, but it was close enough to lend a bubble of happiness to her step.

When the bell rang again, and Caro spied a servant wearing the Holland livery, she craned her neck to see who accompanied him even as she backed toward the door to the office. His Grace never brought a servant into the store with him, which left one possible visitor.

The Dowager Duchess of Holland swanned into the store with the confidence of a woman who'd rarely, if ever, been told no. Rather than peruse the displays on the tables, or choose a random aisle and begin to wander, she approached the sales counter with a serious expression that made Caro wince preemptively. Below the counter, Constance waved Caro toward the office, and like a coward, she inched backward until her bum hit her desk and she could breathe a sigh of relief.

The dowager's voice carried all the way into the office. Since the older woman freely admitted to eavesdropping, Caro refused to feel bad about doing the same.

"Everywhere I go, I'm hearing about a book written by an orange woman. I need a copy, and I'll be on my way."

Orange woman? Confusion gave way to…slightly clearer befuddlement. Did she mean—

"Are you referring to Blanche Clementine's latest release?" Constance asked.

"We've been selling so many of her books it's a challenge to keep them on hand. Can you believe we've sold more copies of this title than Byron's *Corsair* in the last week?" Hattie's voice was syrupy sweet, which immediately sent off an alarm in Caro's brain. "I've just finished setting out the new stock we received this morning. Perhaps this is the one you're looking for, Your Grace?"

"Is that the one all those featherbrains are tittering about behind their fans? They're talking about the hero, but not one of them will elaborate. They had the audacity to laugh and tell me I should get my own copy." Caro had to smile at the dowager's description of the women in her circle.

"Blanche Clementine's novel has been making quite a stir," Constance said.

"It's in such high demand three elegant ladies nearly came to fisticuffs over the last copy when we sold out earlier in the week," Hattie lied with a conspiratorial tone.

What on earth was she up to? If the dowager wanted to buy a copy, her cousins didn't have to work this hard to sell it. *Take the silver dragon's money and send her on her way.*

Of course, thinking of the dowager reading an erotic novel (*inspired by her son—which was disturbing*) was something Caro didn't want to contemplate.

"Who were the ladies?" the dowager asked, and Caro bit her knuckles to contain a laugh. Somehow, she'd known the woman was a gossip. The worst kind, who refused to see their gossipy ways and condemned others for the same sin.

"We could never betray a customer's confidence in that manner. I'm sure you understand, Your Grace," Connie demurred.

Hattie giggled. Hattie was not a giggler. Now there was no doubt her cousin was concocting a plan on the spot, and Constance was simply going along with it. "I probably shouldn't tell you, because if anyone discovered we had such a unique item in the store, customers would beat down the doors. You see, the author is notoriously elusive. Not even her publisher has met her in person."

Caro had to give credit where credit was due. Hattie had a knack for spinning a tale.

"After losing her chance at purchasing that last copy, one of the women who happens to be extremely high placed in society—who shall remain nameless, of course—asked us to negotiate a special request on their behalf with the publisher. I'm sure everyone with ears will be hearing her crow about the purchase soon enough, then all will be known. Thanks to her relentless pleas, Martin House now has the *only* signed copy *in existence* of *any* Blanche Clementine novel." Hattie dropped that blatant falsehood like a hook into the water and waited for the society matron to take the bait.

Caro plunked into her desk chair, trying to breathe quietly. Were they doing what it sounded like they were doing? Blanche Clementine didn't sign books. Ever. The idea of it sent part of her twisting in silent yearning. To claim her work in such a way was something she'd never planned to do. The rest of her wanted to place her head between her knees until the idea of inviting such pointed attention didn't make black spots dance in her vision. Discussing publishing with a reader and aspiring writer was one thing. Outing her secret identity to the Dowager Duchess of Holland was another matter altogether.

"It was Lady Jersey, wasn't it? That woman will be shouting from the rooftops after such a purchase—just you wait. Mercy, she will be absolutely unsufferable," the dowager grumbled.

A weighty pause made Caro desperately wish she could see their faces. Hattie, when she spoke, struck the perfect balance of calculating and helpful. "Our customer was adamant we try, and we sent a letter to the publisher pleading for their help getting the author to sign for her—I mean, sign for them. At no small cost either. After all, this customer wanted the social coup of owning the only signed copy of the book everyone in the ton is dying to get their hands on."

"We have an extensive clientele of collectors, and half of them would be salivating at the idea of owning this. I still can't believe this customer convinced Blanche Clementine to sign a book." Bless Constance—she knew how to play this game just as well as Hattie.

"It just arrived from the publisher by special courier this morning. In fact, I was sending a messenger this afternoon to notify our nameless customer of the successful acquisition." Hattie's tone turned downright sly. "Such a shame she hasn't paid for the book yet. Anyone willing to usurp her claim to fame could do so, and I'd be powerless to stop them."

Constance gasped, but somehow coming from her, it

didn't sound theatrical. "Hattie, are you suggesting we sell Her Grace, Lady Jers— I mean, our unnamed customer's signed copy?"

"Darling, I was merely speculating on a hypothetical scenario. After all, if someone knew of such a rare book and purchased it before anyone else, that would be a simple matter of timing and luck. One person's perfect timing and another's rotten luck."

Did the dowager just laugh at Hattie's jest? Would wonders never cease?

"Either way, we would be doing right by the customer fortunate enough to purchase such an exclusive item. After all, that patron would forever own something another customer was willing to fight so hard to have. Martin House is well respected due to our excellent relationships with customers, and for good reason. We like to make sure our very best patrons remain happy."

"Silence Jersey was one of the three ladies fighting over the last copy?" The dowager's glee was so obvious it was a wonder she wasn't foaming at the mouth. Of course, she might have been and Caro was missing it by hiding at her desk.

"I can neither confirm nor deny the identity of our customers, Your Grace," Hattie stated primly.

"How much was Lady Jersey going to pay for her copy?"

Constance named a price that made Caro's mouth drop open. Even dealing with deep-pocketed collectors on a regular basis didn't prepare her to hear that kind of price for a single book. Especially not *her* book.

The dowager trilled a laugh. "That woman has more money than sense. How very like her to attempt to purchase social leverage. Some of us are born with prestige, but her grandfather was in trade."

Caro shook her head. Lady Jersey's grandfather left her one of the oldest banks in England in his will. Lady Jersey was one of the richest people in the country, yet the dowager had to nitpick the woman's bloodline.

Just when Caro was convinced they'd overshot the price in their conversation, the dowager sighed heavily, with a studied casual air. "I will take the signed copy, if you please. Silence would be better served to spend that money on more flattering hats."

"Of course, Your Grace," Hattie chirped. "We placed the book in the safe, due to its value. Please excuse me a moment, and I'll fetch it for you."

They didn't have a safe. Caro nearly laughed out loud when she looked at the broken drawer that didn't even lock where they kept their banking receipts. When her cousin entered the office, she found Caroline shaking her head.

She hissed, "What have you done, Hattie MacCrae?"

Hattie's smile was pure devilment, but she kept her voice at a whisper. "Made the Dowager Duchess of Holland pay through the nose for mistreating my cousin." She pulled a copy of Caro's book from her apron pocket. "Now, Blanche. I need you to autograph this, please."

"I can't believe you got her to pay such a price. You're dicked in the nob. Both of you." Caro dipped her pen in the inkwell and opened the copy of *A Dalliance for Miss Lorraine*. Some of the pages hadn't even been cut yet, and it smelled of fresh ink. She ran her hand over the paper and experienced the same thrill she did every time she held one of her stories.

That the dowager was going to read. Caro winced. *Not going to think about that.*

With swoops and dips, the black liquid created the familiar lines of her nom de plume.

And despite the customer this copy would go to, signing

her work made something in Caro's chest settle into a feeling of undeniable rightness. Like a key fitting into a lock.

The carriage rocked as Oliver stepped into it, then flung himself on the bench opposite Dorian. Immediately, the carriage joined the others on the road and rumbled toward their destination.

"I'm here, as requested. Why the sudden interest in the London stage?"

Dorian cleared his throat and spun the rim of his hat in his hands between his knees. "Remember the letter Miss Danvers found in the library? There are others, and they reference something that might explain Juliet's missing fortune. Also, someone named Sherman wrote them."

Oliver's eyes widened for a second before his logical brain regained control. "Anything else, or just Sherman?"

"There's a line reminiscent of something the playwright Mr. Bartholomew wrote and premiered this past week, despite the letter predating that production by several years."

"Why am I here? Moral support? An alibi?"

"Neither, or both. Perhaps you're here because you're my oldest friend, and errands like these are what friends do for one another."

"Friends accompany one another to visit their dead wife's possible lover? I wasn't aware. Now that I'm informed, I'll do my part." Oliver's droll comment gave Dorian a reason to smile, and that alone was reassurance that he'd done the right thing by inviting him.

"I set up the appointment in Howard's name, so please refer to me that way. He won't mind me impersonating him for a few minutes," Dorian said.

Outside, the coachman called to the horses as the carriage rocked to a stop.

Mr. Bartholomew lived on the third floor of a building that stank of onions and dirty wash water. Stairs creaked and shifted beneath their feet as they climbed toward the flat a man on the street had directed them to.

When they knocked, a deep voice called for them to enter. Were he of an artistic bent, Dorian would have painted the man inside as "writer in repose." The playwright had truly set the stage, as it were, lounging on a fainting couch in a well-worn banyan, smoking a pipe, with a stack of paper and an inkwell within reach.

Just in case inspiration struck, and his muse demanded immediate attention, Dorian supposed.

The scene didn't distract from the piles of…things strewn about the room. The space wasn't full of the comfortable clutter of life debris. Instead, it spoke of a man who didn't see the need to pick up after himself. To the left of the door, one corner overflowed with what might have been costumes or clothing, or simply cloth destined for the rag bin. Every surface was littered with papers that might or might not have been important, dirty plates, and more empty ale mugs than Dorian had seen outside a butler's pantry. If the man didn't have vermin infesting the room and his person, it would be a miracle.

In the middle of the mess sat the battered settee like a velvet island in a sea of jumble.

Mr. Bartholomew jerked upright when Oliver stepped through the door behind Dorian. "Pardon me, I didn't realize you were bringing a friend as well. But"—a cheerful grin lit his face—"I'm always happy to make new acquaintances. Especially when they dress so well."

Dorian opened his mouth, but Oliver spoke first. "Mr. Howard is a terribly busy man, so if we could focus on our reason for being here, that would be much appreciated."

Undeterred, the playwright leaned toward Oliver. "I didn't catch your name, sir."

"I didn't offer it," Oliver replied.

Inserting himself into the awkward silence that fell as Mr. Bartholomew realized they weren't here to offer patronage, Dorian pulled the letter with the quote from the play out of his pocket. "Did you write this?"

The playwright narrowed his eyes and cautiously reached for the paper as if it were liable to bite him. A frown appeared on his face as he read, shook his head, then read once more. Finally, he spoke. "Ah, I see now. Is this the only letter?"

"No, there are more. So you _did_ write that?" Dorian asked. Looking at him and knowing Juliet, Dorian had a hard time believing this man was Sherman. Juliet was a duchess. And this man…didn't appear to understand the concept of bathing and lived in squalor. Where was the appeal? The connection through commonalities needed to steal someone's heart?

"I wrote it, but I didn't write this," Bartholomew said unhelpfully, then waved his hands about as if physically clearing the air of confusion. "Please sit. There's a story here."

Bartholomew bounced up to sweep the contents of a chair to the floor. Everyone ignored the faint sound of glass shattering as the pile hit the wood boards. "Here. Sit, both of you."

Oliver took the chair, and Bartholomew gestured for Dorian to clear the chair flanking the fainting couch. Dorian carefully lifted the chair's burden as a whole and set it aside instead of flinging it.

Perching on the edge of the torn tufted cushion, Dorian prompted, "You said there's a story. Explain."

"Yes. Right." Bartholomew drained a nearby mug without glancing down to verify the contents. A foolhardy risk considering the general state of the room.

"I haven't always been a successful darling of the London stage," the man began with such seriousness and lack of self-awareness that Dorian bit the inside of his lips to stop himself from laughing. "Years ago, I provided a service to a man who approached me in a coffeehouse. Since I've only done it once, I'm fairly certain that man is your letter writer."

Which explained absolutely nothing and sparked several questions.

"Please clarify," Oliver said.

"I wrote letters for him. Poor bloke wasn't blessed with good looks or charm, but he paid well. The plan was he'd copy them in his hand, then woo the lady in question after I smoothed the way with my words." Bartholomew held out his hand. "May I examine the others?"

Without a word, Dorian handed over the rest. After a moment of perusing the pages, Bartholomew grunted. "As I thought. He's pieced these together. Cobbling phrases here and there. Made them his own." Returning the letters, he said, "I hope he won the girl, though I doubt it. He was far from a catch. How did you know I wrote the originals?"

"The jest about ports in a storm. I was in the theater when your play debuted."

Bartholomew beamed. "That was a great line, wasn't it? I confess I write down the better bits and reuse them when appropriate." His attention switched to Oliver. "Are you familiar with my work?"

Oliver nodded. "I am, actually. What do you remember about the fellow?"

The playwright settled back on the chaise. "Honestly, there isn't much to tell. Have you ever eaten thick porridge without any seasoning in it? No honey, no salt, no bacon drippings?"

Oliver curled his top lip in obvious disgust. "Bit like eating paste."

Bartholomew snapped his fingers. "Exactly. Sticks to your mouth until you're desperate for a drink just to rid yourself of the experience. Now, imagine that described a person. This Sherman fellow was like that."

A dark laugh escaped as Dorian shook his head. "I should wander London asking after someone who looks like the human equivalent of eating paste?"

Oliver grinned, then asked, "Do you remember his full name?"

Bartholomew scrunched his face, searching a mental ledger. "Snood? Stupper? Slu— No, that wouldn't be right. Drat, it's right there on the tip of my tongue. Snyder. That was it." He nodded in satisfaction, then shifted back into the role of storyteller. "Sherman Snyder. Horsefaced as can be, poor bloke. Massive nose, no chin at all, just nose and neck. Sounded like a donkey when he laughed."

Oliver appeared reluctantly charmed. "Should I be horrified or amused by that character sketch?"

"Both, I'd think," Bartholomew said. "Horrified, 'cause his personality was worse than his looks. No wit, intelligence, or original thoughts in his head. Rather nasty fellow, truth be told. But his money spent well. If you're amused by my description, it's on account that I'm a brilliant writer."

And so humble too. Dorian smiled wryly. "You have a talent with words, Mr. Bartholomew. So, to sum up, his name is Sherman Snyder and he's entirely unappealing?"

"Boring. Nondescript. We can't all be blessed with my

vibrant coloring, more's the pity." With a shrug, Bartholomew concluded, "His own mother would lose him in a crowd, no doubt. Hair, skin, eyes—all the same color."

"Human porridge, indeed," Oliver mused.

"Exactly." Their host slapped his knees and stood. "If that will be all? I'm due at the theater in an hour. Unless you'd like to accompany me and consider offering your patronage…"

Dorian rose, brushing his backside to sweep away errant tufts of chair stuffing. "No, thank you. Do you happen to have this Mr. Snyder's direction?"

Bartholomew laughed. "Good God, that was years ago. Who knows if he's even in the city anymore? If it helps, I remember him waxing poetic about his village in Kent. Tip something."

Dorian froze in the process of placing his hat on his head. The school Juliet was funding and had spoken of so often was in a village called—"Tippering?"

"That's it. Been there? I'd never heard of it," Bartholomew said.

Dorian met Oliver's gaze. "I believe a visit is in my near future." He pulled a sovereign from his pocket and handed it to the playwright. "Thank you for your time, Mr. Bartholomew. If I have further questions, I'll be back."

In the carriage, Dorian heaved a sigh that released some of the tension from his shoulders but did nothing to unknot his gut. "Bloody hell."

"Tippering? Isn't that where Juliet's school was being built?"

"What are the odds she was financing a school in the same village that this Mr. Snyder person called home?"

"You're asking a rhetorical question, but I could do the maths if you'd like. Are we off to Kent right now? Or do I have time to get something to eat? I'm famished and will need to send a note round to Althea canceling our plans. Ironically enough, we'd planned to see that man's play tonight. Oh, and I'll grab a book for the road. Started that saucy one you bought me, and it's just getting to the eyebrow-raising parts. Have you read it yet?"

Dorian contemplated his hands. A smudge of ink remained on his finger from the work he'd done earlier in his study. "No, I've been busy. Or rather, I've been distracted." He glanced up at his friend. "Do you think this is madness? It's been five years since their affair ended. Perhaps Juliet built a school. Or maybe he took her money and ran. Does it even matter at this point?" One possibility taunted him, and it had nothing to do with money. Sherman Snyder was the only person who could tell him why Juliet strayed. Had Dorian done something wrong, or had the affair begun from questionable luck and bad decisions?

Dorian leaned back as the carriage moved into traffic. If he'd wronged Juliet somehow, he wanted to know. It might be too late to fix things with his wife, but he could ensure he didn't make the same mistakes twice. The thought made his chest tighten as if each inhale filled his lungs with gravel. Squeezing his eyes closed, he willed the looming episode away. Now was not the time or place to fall to pieces. Conscious of the mounting effort it took, Dorian sucked air in through his nose, felt it fill the heavy, dark spaces in his body, then released the breath.

He couldn't submit to this if he was busy concocting a plan, so he forged ahead with potential outcomes. He'd travel to Kent and see how many of his questions had answers. And if he traveled to Tippering, there damned well better be a school there. Dorian clenched his teeth, whistling air in, and noticed there was more space within him for the breath to go. That was good.

He could see where this trail to Sherman led. And if it led to evidence that the man defrauded Juliet, he'd bring Snyder before the court and let him rot in prison.

Opening his eyes, Dorian exhaled fully. There. Not so bad now that he had a plan.

Oliver's face settled into a compassionate expression. The kind of look you'd offer someone at a funeral, and one Dorian had seen too many times since his return from the war. "I suspect your desire to find him is about more than money. Whatever your reasons, if you need to find him, I will help." He paused, considering. "Unless he's dead. In which case, we'll find his grave and piss on it together. Plan?"

"Plan."

Chapter Fourteen

Sales of *A Dalliance for Miss Lorraine* continued apace with Byron's new book, *The Corsair*. In theory, that would thrill any author, publisher, or bookstore that stood to make a profit.

All around Caro, her family celebrated each time they had to order more copies of her book. The fervor surrounding that book rolled into sales of her previous stories as well. Perhaps it was that pragmatic, practical nature Gerard and Leo so valued in her, but Caro's excitement over the situation was fading into concern.

Why now? Why this book? Why was *Lorraine* such a bestseller with members of the ton? That she'd based a hero on one of their own and that that same hero was sparking conversations put her ill at ease. The chatter she'd overheard about the heroine revolved around speculation of who Lorraine might be, as if she were a real person.

Caro nibbled her bottom lip as she settled into her desk chair. She'd been careful to remove specific clues tying Holland to *Lorraine*'s hero.

Hadn't she? The unease grew, and she pressed a hand to her stomach. No, of course she had.

And even if someone made the leap and found some kind of so-called evidence within the novel, it wasn't a crime to write a romantic hero inspired by someone real.

At least, she didn't think it was. Did the fact that Holland was a duke mean different laws applied to him? Maybe. More concerning was not his place in society but his place in her life. Holland was a private man. They'd talked about how difficult it could be to be the focus of everyone's attention. No hypothetical scenario existed in which he would be unbothered to discover the woman he was kissing had written a novel describing him in explicit sexual situations and profited from the sale.

The tea she'd finished not too long ago sloshed queasily in her gut. Caro consciously relaxed her shoulders and blew out a breath. Worries were moot, because she'd never need to have that conversation with Holland, and there was no way people could prove she'd written the book about him.

Speculation was no more than pondering things without proof. Rumors, really, and God knew there was no way to stop those.

So, business as usual. No need to concern herself further, especially when there was work to be done. She plucked the mail from its basket. Gerard had written to gently nudge her toward an answer to his proposal. Over cigars and brandy, one of the older members at the firm had inquired after Gerard's plans for marriage and a family, making comments about stability and a future at the firm. At the end of the meeting, he'd shaken Gerard's hand, then offered to introduce him to a niece. Subtle the senior partner was not.

She needed to respond to the note but was dreading it. While she felt for the situation in which he and Leo found themselves, she couldn't imagine agreeing. Legally, everything she owned—and consequently, all she earned as Blanche Clementine—would be her husband's, even if the marriage was a sham. A marriage for altruistic reasons was still a marriage.

Which made her mind circle back, as it often did, to the duke and his nameless prospective bride. He'd be tied to a loveless match in the name of duty, and that would be the end of whatever was brewing between them. It felt selfish to wish that day far off into the future, given what was at stake for the dukedom, just as it felt selfish to not help her friends, given what was at stake for them.

Another letter had been a note from her publisher congratulating her on the best sales numbers to date and celebrating the need of a second printing. Uncle Owen and Aunt Mary greeted the news with cheers when she stood and went to the sales floor to tell them.

Caro did her best to muster similar enthusiasm, but her mind was elsewhere today. She didn't feel the close kinship she usually did when with her family, and that wasn't their fault.

"All your hard work is finally being recognized on the scale it should be." Aunt Mary squeezed her in a hug. "You look like you could use some air, though, darling girl. Would you mind running to the shops and buying pasties? We are all feeling a bit peckish."

And so, while her family was busy creating a window display of the Blanche Clementine books they had on hand, Caro slipped out the back door. The weather was typically dreary for late February, and her walking boots slipped and slid through the shallow puddles that had settled on top of ice.

Walking in the brisk air cleared her head. As the cold pricked at her cheeks, Caro marveled that Aunt Mary always knew what "her girls" needed.

When she returned, the store was quiet. Two customers browsed in the lending library, and the only family member in sight was Hattie, who loitered in the doorway to the office.

"Where is everyone?" Caro set the bundle of delicious-smelling pasties on her desk. Immediately, the scents of pastry, roasted meat, and carrots filled the tiny office.

Hattie's eyes were huge. "Walter is upstairs. I think he's coming up to scratch."

"Already? Do you think Connie will go through with it?" Caro draped her scarf over a chair, then poured two cups of tea from the pot on her desk. It would be lukewarm by now, but she refused to waste tea. Each cradling their cups, they stared toward the door leading up to the living quarters.

"She seems to genuinely like this one," Hattie mused.

"They haven't known each other very long. Can you imagine what a disaster it would be if Constance lost interest as she normally does, after she's said vows? I feel like this is awfully rushed."

Hattie shrugged and sipped her tea, but the expression on her face was worried. "Constance is a romantic. She wants the butterflies and sweeping passion of a grand romance. Perhaps she believes in finding the one and just knowing it's real."

Caro drained her tea, then set the cup aside. "She said something similar to me after they met. And you're right—she is a romantic. Where we see potential hazards, she sees adventure."

"Would you like another cup of tea?" Hattie knew her well enough not to wait for an answer. Instead, she shook the empty pot, then fetched the kettle and settled by the hearth to wait for the water to heat—which placed her next to the door to their flat.

"Are you going to listen at the door?" Caro hissed.

"Of course not." Hattie tossed her head in mock indignation. "It's not my fault I happen to have excellent hearing, and boiling water requires me to stand directly below the sitting room where a man is most likely proposing to our cousin."

Caro grinned, shaking her head. On the desk sat the rest of the day's post. Keeping one eye on the front counter, she flipped through the papers, sorting as she went. Several letters were for patrons who paid for mail service, which went into the appropriate basket. A bill for Uncle Owen got tossed into the accounts payable pile. Three letters were from private book collectors. With any luck, they'd mean sales of the duke's books.

Hattie scurried back from the door and dumped the boiling water into the teapot with such a lack of grace water sloshed over the rim and pooled on the wood. "She said yes; act surprised."

Constance opened the door, towing a man Caro assumed to be Walter behind her. "We announce the banns tomorrow!"

Uncle Owen followed, ruddy cheeks split with a happy grin. "I thought this day would never come."

Walter beamed down at Constance, looking like a man who was staring at everything he'd ever wanted. The expression made Caro's heart clench in her chest. Unconsciously, she rested a palm over the spot to soothe the ache. "Congratulations. May you have many happy years together."

"We have a wedding to plan!" Constance laughed, her joy overflowing like bubbles in champagne.

Aunt Mary joined their group, dabbing happy tears with a handkerchief.

For the second time that day, Caro found herself in the position of smiling wider than she'd like. She had her reservations about Constance being ready for marriage, but this wasn't the time to bring that up.

As soon as she was able, Caro retreated to her desk and her family moved their celebration to the larger space of the sales floor. The sounds of her family discussing wedding breakfast details became a soothing hum as she settled in to read the letters from collectors.

The first was payment for a recent order they'd sent. Money was always nice, and it felt rewarding to enter the additional income into the ledger. Letter number two was from a longtime customer. It was one part book request and three parts local gossip. Both made her smile.

The final letter held a familiar name, and she sighed. Mr. Lipscomb was a perfectly nice gentleman, if a bit demanding. However, he paid in cash versus on account and was a frequent customer as well as a discerning collector. When she read his letter, it was as she expected. Good news but with stipulations.

Yes, he would be thrilled to purchase three of the highly sought-after editions of mythology from the late duchess's collection, on the condition that they deliver the copies personally. Given the rarity of the books and their reflective value, Mr. Lipscomb wasn't comfortable entrusting them to the post.

The real story was simple. He wanted a visit with someone who could discuss his favorite topic—books—and he was willing to pay for it. The man was a bibliophile of the highest order. Thankfully, Uncle Owen would be thrilled to visit the old curmudgeon who'd become something of a friend over the years.

Once things quieted somewhat, Caro would bring the letter and enclosed partial payment to her uncle and inform him he was due for a visit to Kent.

Hattie slipped into the office and blew out a breath. "I don't know if I can smile that hard for much longer. Are we going to say something?"

Caro shrugged a shoulder. "Let her celebrate. There will be time to bring our concerns to her privately."

"What do you have there?"

Caro held up the last letter. "Mr. Lipscomb wants three of the duke's mythology books, but he wants us—

Hattie said the last words with her. "To deliver them. He's in Kent, right? Why don't you deliver them? You can take Mrs. Adams her cookery book and look at the cottage. The roads are passable now. The main ones, anyway."

The cottage. Caro pursed her lips, that terrifying sensation of hope rising within her at the thought. If she saw the place and loved it, it was possible the royalties from a second print run would mean she could afford to purchase the property faster than anticipated. "That's a good idea. I'll mention it to Uncle Owen." She picked up one of the forgotten pasties, broke it in half, and handed a section to Hattie. "Here, eat. We need to keep our strength up if we're going to survive Constance as a bride."

"Hickory dickory dock, the mouse ran up the clock. The clock struck—" Dorian pointed toward the mantel, and the clock obligingly rang once. "Very good. Well done. And down it ran, hickory dickory dock." A gulp of whisky drowned his laugh.

Flames danced in the hearth, jumping and flickering as they cast shadows about the room. He hadn't bothered to light a candle, since it had been broad daylight when he had entered the study with Blanche Clementine's newest book, a glass of whisky, and an intention to relax for a few hours.

It was dark now. Which meant the single chime was one in the morning, not afternoon. Time didn't matter after enough whisky. He might've dozed earlier, but there was no way to be sure. The book lay on the table, discarded when the insecurities that had threatened to steal his breath in the carriage after meeting the playwright returned. Sherman wasn't a handsome charmer, which meant their affair didn't make sense. Questions about how he'd failed as a husband cut deep, but whisky soothed the wounds.

The bottle had done its job, smoothing everything into a blur about him. There were no sharp corners left in his world except perhaps the desk, which he'd stumbled into and reeled away from before landing safely in this chair. Just as well. The wingback was far more comfortable than the desk chair had been.

Besides, this new seat allowed him to warm his feet near the fireplace. At some point, he'd lost a boot. Chilly toes clad only in a stocking were grateful for the nearby heat source. Dorian squinted as he attempted to wiggle his toes in time with the fire's irregular dance. Alas, the flames moved to a music he couldn't hear, so he gave up after a few seconds.

Perhaps the stocking was how he'd slipped and stumbled into the desk. It was a mystery.

Questions were hard. Thinking was damn near impossible. Words in general were mighty difficult. Which was how he knew he'd had exactly the right amount of whisky.

The paisley print of the fabric covering the opposite chair made his eyes hurt, so he closed them. Juliet had chosen the paisley. He hadn't been terribly fond of it, but he'd wanted to make her happy. Wanted to make her happy in all things. What a fool he had been to think he'd succeeded.

"Oh, Holland. What are you doing?" Her voice seemed to come from the chair. The last remnants of logic warned that if he looked too hard in that direction, her absence would be obvious, so he kept his eyes closed lest she leave.

"You don't normally drink like this, my love. What is on your mind?"

"You're not real." Even his voice sounded blurry.

Her laugh. God, how he'd missed her laugh. "Humor me. What has you climbing into a bottle and drinking alone like a sad little man?"

"Sad little man. Funny you should call me that. The more I learn about Sherman, the more I wonder what you were thinking." A stab of pain tried to strike near his heart, but Dorian took another drink to wash it away. "Why'd you do it, Jules? If I could just make sense of it all, maybe I wouldn't feel so ... scared."

The feeling didn't have a name until that moment. But God, he was scared. Scared of being taken off guard like that again. Scared of loving again. Scared that he'd somehow make the same mistakes or choose the same kind of woman and end up feeling all those awful feelings in the future. Scared that there wouldn't be enough pieces of himself left to put back together a second time.

Fumbling, he placed the tumbler on the table beside him. It would be easier to do if he opened his eyes, but he didn't want her to go away. Not yet.

"D'you remember how we used to pity those other couples in our set? The ones everyone knew were having affairs? *We will never be like them*, we used to say. God, how horrible we were. So arrogant. Completely confident the other wouldn't stray. I hate not knowing what happened. I wish we could sit and talk. Like we used to, in the beginning. Before everything got so busy and we became more interested in taking care of everyone else instead of each other."

He cracked open one eye and fancied he could almost

make out the pale-gold shimmer of her hair. Before the spec-ter of a memory could disappear, he closed his eye. She wasn't gone quite yet. She'd stay and let him speak. Which made a distant part of him wish he weren't swimming quite so deep in the whisky, so he could determine if Juliet was really there, or if that golden mirage was courtesy of the alcohol.

"Why didn't you join me in Vienna? And then Greece, or any of the other places they sent me? Even after your mother died, you promised to travel once you sorted her things. It was too late by then, wasn't it? Sherman was already in your life, and I didn't know it. Wish you'd told me. Maybe we could have fixed it. Or said goodbye and left you to be happy. I just wanted you happy, Jules. Wherever you are now, I hope you're happy."

"Do you really think you'd have let me go? That we'd have lived separate lives?" Jules asked.

He swallowed roughly around an immediate answer that might have been a lie. Surely a ghost would know if he lied. "I want to say yes. *Now* I'd say yes. But that's 'cause I'm ready to let us both move on. Back then...no. I'd have thrown a fit. Ranted about being away from you just as long as you were away from me, without straying. Even though it was hard. Weeks between letters. In the middle of a bloody war. I petitioned the king constantly to release me from my duties. Didn't really matter, though, because in the end, I wasn't there. I'm sorry, Jules."

It had been a special kind of hell to go out in society during that time on the Continent, to see and be seen. To make connections for the king, pass along information, and do his best to negotiate the thousands of minute agreements needed to get supplies and support to their soldiers. During it all, feeling something was wrong but not being able to go home again without his king's permission.

The only reprieve he'd found was even more dangerous— going behind enemy lines to accomplish special tasks that kept him too busy, tired, and scared to worry about what was happening back in England.

"I'm sorry too."

"Was he good to you, at least? Did he love you?"

"I can't answer that," Jules said. Her ghost would know, wouldn't she?

Dorian blindly thumped his fingers along the table until they found the glass of whisky. "I guess the only one who really knows anything is Sherman."

"Then ask Sherman. What do you have to lose? After all, you're the all-powerful Duke of Holland." Her voice held a mocking note she'd never wielded against him before now. "We both know you could drag the man through the streets, then drown him in the Thames and not see a moment behind bars."

"Don't tempt me. Might regret it the next day." Damned conscience. "Answers. I need to understand. Didn't I give you anything you wanted? Full control over your fortune. Whatever your heart desired." For a moment, all was quiet except the crackling fire in the hearth. "Because when you were happy, you'd just...glow. And I was content to be the one who saw it."

"I told you I was sorry in my letter."

"I know. Still wrecked me, though. Hard to risk feeling that way again. Even though there's a woman on my mind constantly these days."

"Your bookseller. You could be happy, but you'll need to let me go."

"Scared." It was easier to say it aloud the second time. "Caroline's special, isn't she? Strong. Brave. Braver than either of us ever needed to be." Exhaustion and whisky tugged at his consciousness, luring him toward sleep. Everything was blurrier and more slurred when he spoke after what might have been five seconds or five minutes. "Just tell me what I did wrong, so I don't do it again." Silence. "Sherman would know. He knew everything. Lucky bastard. I'm going to have to find him to understand, aren't I? Besides, I need to make sure he didn't rob you blind."

With herculean effort, Dorian opened his eyes, even though he knew it would make her disappear. This time, he chose to let her leave. Whisky made his head loll heavy on his neck until he rested his forehead on the wingback padding of the chair and stared blankly into the flames dancing in the grate.

"Goodbye, Jules. I hope, wherever you are, you're at peace. Glow for them, duchess."

The next time he opened his eyes, it was to see Hastings waving a glass of noxious-smelling liquid in front of his face. Dorian recoiled but, without anywhere to go, only managed to smash the back of his aching head against the chair.

"Drink this, Your Grace. I will not tolerate any arguments on this matter. Drink. Then breakfast is waiting for you in the morning room. After which, a hot bath will be next on your agenda."

Dorian opened his mouth to argue anyway, and the wily butler tipped the contents of the glass into his mouth. It tasted only slightly better than it smelled.

"You're fired," he groaned without any heat as he considered licking the upholstery near his face to get the taste off his tongue.

"Indeed, Your Grace. The staff will expect you for breakfast in five minutes."

Closing his eyes, he prayed to whatever deity hadn't turned his back on him quite yet that his stomach would not cast up its accounts when he stood. Footsteps he wouldn't normally notice sounded like hammers dropping on the wood floor as the butler walked toward the door.

"Not really fired," he murmured, feeling like a heel.

"Indeed, Your Grace. Five minutes, or I'm summoning the dowager to deal with you" came the reply from the doorway before the indispensable servant left Dorian to his morning-after regrets.

Two things settled in his gut alongside the tonic. One, the only person who might tell him where he'd gone wrong was the man Juliet had run to. And two, the thought of finding out was just as terrifying as the idea of never knowing.

Chapter Fifteen

The amount of money some people were willing to pay for books was truly a mind-boggling thing. Of course, Caro appreciated books. After all, she wrote them. Technically, they kept a roof over her head and fed the only family she cared about, through sales in the store and the occasional infusions of cash she contributed to the coffers under the guise of paying rent to her uncle. He fought her every time, but she did it anyway because she didn't want to feel too indebted to them for their generosity.

If the everyday customers kept the doors open, collectors and their niche interests allowed the store to grow and thrive.

Mr. Lipscomb was no different than many other collectors on their client roster. However, their other clients did not expect a personal visit to their home far from London, then corner her into conversation for three hours and supply her with enough tea to make her bladder feel as if it were floating. Only her return ticket on the mail and the coach's famous inflexibility regarding schedule allowed her to gracefully end the visit, collect the balance due on the books she'd hand delivered, and scuttle back to the inn. That she failed to mention her coach didn't leave until the following day must have entirely slipped her mind.

That was her story, in the unlikely event she was pressed for details, anyway. A bowl of stew as big as her head, a tankard of cider, and the warm bed in the room she'd taken at the inn would set her to rights again. Then, in the morning, she'd hire a mount and ride the considerably longer distance to the village where the Adams cottage was located.

She was grateful for the time away from London. Even if it meant traveling at the end of February, when March was batting away the icicles with its cold, soggy fingers.

However, as she followed the lane from Mr. Lipscomb's tidy cottage to the village, and thus the inn, the coins in her purse jingled loud enough to alert every thief within a mile. Around the bend ahead, an outhouse stood off the road, and she headed in that direction. Because tea. But also because the alarming amount of money on her person would make anyone nervous if traveling alone.

In the dark outhouse, she carefully separated each coin with a small section of her handkerchief, then rolled the fabric and pound notes around the metal until she was fairly certain she would not tempt thieves with every step she took. The resulting mass was lumpy and heavy, tucked between her cleavage at the top of her short stays. The boning of her undergarments on the bottom would keep it in place, and her breasts would serve her well to prevent the money from falling out. Finally her breasts were good for something. She rolled her eyes at the dark humor as she stood and shook out her skirts. That would be enough to get her to the inn and her room safely.

A fat *tap tap tap* on the roof made her sigh. Rain. Frozen rain from the sounds of it. Snowy, wet plops of slush falling from the sky. Just what she needed after a long day. More rain to create an even slipperier mess of the icy roads. If the weather didn't clear by the morning, her ride home would be miserable.

A ticket on the mail did not guarantee one a place inside

the coach. And a woman traveling alone was not necessarily incentive enough for some men to give up their dry seat.

She stepped out into the rain and glanced at the horizon. Steely gray clouds smothered the sky. When she'd left Mr. Lipscomb's home, the sun had already been glazing the treetops with amber light, setting the rooflines of the distant village into dark shadows, deepened by fast-moving storm clouds.

At least she'd worn her heaviest cloak over a thick spencer, and a wide-brimmed bonnet to protect her face from the rain. Small blessings. The lane crossed the main road ahead, and she paused to get her bearings. Was the inn to the left or right? This village wasn't that large, so if she made a wrong turn, it wouldn't be the end of the world. But mercy, her feet were soaked and hurting from the cold; the layers of clothes were keeping her from catching her death but not preventing much else. If she walked into the inn this next second, it would be five minutes too late.

A gust of wind whipped down the street, tugging her bonnet back. The wet, knotted ribbon under her chin ensured it didn't fly into the nearest field. However, her hair was thoroughly soaked. So much for a bonnet protecting her head.

Through the rain, a traveling carriage rumbled like a mythical beast from one of Mr. Lipscomb's books, hunting its dinner. The coachman slowed and called down, "Miss, no one in their right mind should be out in this weather. Where are you headed?"

Holding her bonnet in place, Caro replied, "Bless you, sir! I'm bound for the Hawk and Fan on the far edge of the village."

"The groom's perch is available, or I'll kick the mite back there and you can share the bench up here. Whichever you

like, miss. We'll get you to the Hawk and Fan right enough."
The younger servant in question sat huddled next to the
coachman, rather than standing on the step on the back
and hanging on to the strap, so they must have been driving
for a longer distance. Gratitude nearly made her weep, but
she couldn't spare the extra seconds in the cold and wet to
indulge in emotions.

She didn't want to make the lad move, so she said, "I'll
take the perch on back. Thank you again, gentlemen." She
sent them a wave and hurried toward the rear of the carriage.
A gilded crest decorated the door, thoroughly splattered by
the awful gray sludge of mud, ice, and other things on the
road she'd rather not contemplate. However, when the door
opened, she paused. Of course the gentry cove inside would
want to be thanked as well. Hopefully they were kind and
weren't about to yell at the coachman for stopping.

"Caroline? Why are you walking through Kent in bloody
February? Never mind. Get inside where it's dry."

Warm hands grasped her upper arms and none too gently urged her inside the carriage. The Duke of Holland
collapsed on the seat beside her and knocked on the roof
to signal the driver. "Why you insist on walking across this
cursed country when any reasonable person would at least
hire a hack, I'll never know. Do you have any idea the dan-
gers on the road for a beautiful woman like you? Hell, for
anyone? But especially for a woman like you."

The navy velvet interior smelled like him. A heady com-
bination of bergamot, peat smoke, and fresh rain filled
her nose, and she wanted to bottle the scent. The carriage
seemed like a luxurious cave, where she might be warm and
eventually dry. But at the moment, every inch of her was
wet and turning blue with cold and making her cranky in

the face of a lecturing, pampered duke. "I'm terribly sorry if my low-class ways offend your delicate sensibilities, Your Grace. We can't all travel with armed servants. As to the weather—" She glanced at the window, streaming with half-frozen droplets collecting in a slushy dam at the bottom of the glass. "I have no control over that. I do, however, have a dry room at the Hawk and Fan waiting for me, so it behooves me to get there, even if it means walking."

Silence grew between them, until she broke it with a reluctant, "All that said, I'm grateful your coachman stopped. Thank you for the ride to the inn."

"Miss Danvers," he began, then stopped. "Caroline." Holland's voice grew husky on her name. "I believe I owe you an apology. Several, probably." Thunder rumbled overhead, and he scowled out the window as if the sky had personally offended him. "I am a pampered aristocrat, but I prefer to grovel where it's warm and dry. Will you join me for a meal at the Hawk and Fan?"

Caro crossed her arms. In part because she was feeling a bit belligerent, but also because shivers were beginning to rack her body in a way that would make Holland feel he was right to fuss. He scooted closer and wrapped an arm around her shoulders. Despite herself, she leaned into the warm solid side of him and tried not to look happy about it.

Dipping his head to see beneath the rim of her bonnet, he nudged the hat higher on her forehead, then dropped a kiss between her eyebrows. Another on the bridge of her nose, then her cheek. "Have dinner with me. Please?" His mouth hovered at the edge of her lips until hers started to tingle in anticipation.

However, his high-handedness still rankled. "As I said, Your Grace—"

"Please don't 'Your Grace' me when I'm rather desperately trying to kiss you." Blue eyes lit with teasing, skin crinkling at the corners near thick, straight lashes.

Damn the man and his infernal appeal. Irritation gave way to reluctant humor. Just to annoy him, she quickly pecked his lips, then pulled back. When he growled, she ignored the sound and asked, "What shall I call you, if not Your Grace?"

"My Christian name is Dorian. Or Holland if you prefer."

Caro tilted her head, considering. "What did your wife call you?"

"Holland. She said Dorian didn't fit me as well as the title."

Caro scrunched her nose. "What utter rot. You are far more than your title. I shall call you Dorian when we are alone. You may continue to refer to me as Caroline or Caro."

"I like Caro. Although to be honest, I always thought you looked more like a Guinevere."

Her laugh wrapped around them in the velvet-lined space, like a cozy hug, and she leaned into his side once more. How was he so warm? "What, pray tell, does a Guinevere look like?"

"Like a woman capable of both leading and taking down an entire nation based solely on her charm, wit, and good looks."

Warmth lit her core and crept toward her heart. A dangerous trajectory. She peeked up at him, admiring the dark stubble dusting his chin. "I can't tell if that is complimentary or damning. Should I thank you or slap your cheek for thinking I have a destructive bent?"

Reaching around her, Dorian pulled her onto his lap, then tucked her against his body until they fit together like puzzle pieces. "I would rather you kissed me."

"You are quite persistent, aren't you?" she teased, brushing a wavy lock of hair off his forehead.

"With you, I am," he said in a serious way that sent entirely different shivers down her spine. "Now, care to tell me what you are doing in the wilds of Kent?"

"I was making a delivery. Three of your mythology volumes found a home with a collector. When I get back to the shop, I will draw up a copy of the bill of sale with your portion of the proceeds."

A deep V appeared above the bridge of his nose. "Why did your uncle let you travel alone? In this weather?" Outside, the rain turned from a *splat splat splat* drizzle into a downpour that sluiced against the windows in icy sheets.

"I'm thirty, Dorian, not a child. And as you said earlier, I'm no stranger to travel."

A slow, devastating smile grew as she watched. "Say it again."

"What?"

One hand cradled the back of her head, pulling her close enough to feel the warmth of his breath against her mouth. "My name. Say my name again, Caro."

"Dorian." Her voice was breathy, lips parted to welcome his kiss. The tip of his tongue flicked against the slick inner edge of her bottom lip.

"Again. I want to taste it on you."

"Doria—"

Mercy, the man could kiss. The taste of him was both familiar and new. Warm, earthy, with the faintest trace of peppermint. She wondered if he kept a tin of mints in his pocket, then stopped wondering altogether. Against her hip, the hardness of him grew and firmed, confirming exactly how much she affected him and stealing the last of her rational thought.

There was something so marvelous about knowing beyond the shadow of a doubt that you were desired. The feeling inspired a reckless giddiness in her.

With the carriage swaying under them, their bodies pressed together and rocked with the movement. One of his arms anchored her to him, while the other explored, caressing her bottom, then the curve of her thigh.

"Will you invite me to your room at the inn, sweet Caro? Feel free to say no." The heat of his body was already warming away her shivers, but a quiver of an entirely different nature came alive inside her. When he spoke again, his rumbly voice sent a frisson of heat down her core. "If you have even a speck of doubt, we can eat a warm meal together in the public room, enjoy one another's company, and you can send me on my way. I don't want you to feel pressured, or like I'm taking advantage of you traveling alone. Well, not taking advantage with nefarious intent anyway." His grin was infectious.

Caro plucked at the wet ribbon knotted under her chin as she returned the smile. "You don't have nefarious intent? Pity. I'd hoped you were suggesting doing something wicked in my room." Against her hip, the long line of his cock jumped between them.

"I'm dying to be wicked with you. Aching with it." His lips crushed hers in a kiss that quickly spiraled into moaned encouragements as hands wandered and teeth nipped. "How far away is this bloody inn?" His breathing was ragged.

Reaching for her inner Blanche was easy under the circumstances, as if that boldness lingered closer to the surface the longer she spent in Holland's company. Not Holland. Dorian. "If it were farther away, I would unbutton your breeches and have you here." Caro outlined the hardness of him at her hip. "But we can't possibly have time for that. The village isn't large."

He opened his mouth, paused, then snapped it closed. Caro tilted her head and grinned wide enough that she felt her cheeks rise under her eyes. "You wanted to make a play on words about the village being large, didn't you?"

He thumped his head back against the seat and laughed, even as a red blush crept up his neck. Well, that was adorable. Caro never would have imagined she could make the Duke of Holland blush.

"Tell me. I'm right, aren't I?"

"Yes," he groaned, still laughing. "I was going to leer and say the village isn't large, but I could offer things that were."

She threw her head back and cackled. "I knew it! Naughty duke." An expression crossed his face she hadn't seen before. "What is that look for?"

He winked. "Are you asking to be let into my pauses, sweet Caro?"

"Yes, I think I am." Reaching out a finger, she drew along the line of his dark eyebrow, then down the angle of his cheek and jaw to the mouth she was coming to adore. "No one has ever looked at me like that. What does it mean?"

"I was thinking how much I enjoy seeing you laugh. Makes you glow a bit." An odd quirk of his lips followed that last part, but she couldn't ask after it, because he pulled her into a kiss that threatened to unravel her from the inside out. Warm desire bloomed, then flowed into a lust with such sharp edges it sliced the tethers of self-restraint she'd lived with for so long.

His fingers deftly finished unknotting her bonnet ribbon—a task she'd begun, then abandoned. As he sank his fingers into her hair, he pulled back enough to murmur,

"I can't wait to see your hair spread all over my pillow. I've dreamt of it."

Caro clung to him, and her damp gown grew almost unbearably constricting on her skin.

Blanche would use words to tease them both, knowing they couldn't act on them right away, and she'd revel in the anticipation. Caro gave her those words, so surely she could find them for Dorian. "What else? What else invaded your dreams or kept you up at night?" Those fingers in her hair tightened, tugging at her scalp and making her moan. "I like that," she told him.

With his mouth against her neck, he murmured, "I want to bury my face between your legs until the taste of you fills my mouth. I've imagined the way you'll look when you come." Those long fingers she'd spent so much time imagining curved over her breast. "The number of nights I've spent wondering what your breasts look like is impossible to count."

Every word made her body slick and hot. "I've fantasized about your hands and fingers. I want them on me, in me. I want to suck you, to make you moan my name. I want to know how you feel inside me, how tightly I can grip you when I hit my peak."

Dorian dropped his head against where her cleavage would be if she weren't wearing so many layers. "One more word, and I'm going to take you right here. Have mercy, I beg you."

Oh, the thrill of that. As if her latest heroine, Phoebe, had taken over, Caro purred, "I like it when you beg. I wonder what else you will beg me for before morning."

His eyes were hot and nearly feral. "Do you already have a key for your room, or will you need to speak with the innkeeper? Do you want me to enter the inn with you, or wait and join you?"

Caro smirked, then dug into the pocket of her cloak and pulled out a key on a brass ring. "Top of the stairs, turn right. I'm at the end of the hall. Knock twice and I'll let you in."

Although his cheeks were flushed with desire, Dorian framed her face with his hands and firmed his lips into a serious line. "If at any point you're uncomfortable, tell me."

"I will. I promise." Suddenly a little shy, she toyed with one of his waves, forming it into a perfect curl in the middle of his forehead. "Will you stay the night? Or continue on to London this evening?" She stopped, frowning. "Wait—why are you in Kent? You never said."

"I was in a village called Tippering, looking for information on the Sherman fellow from the letters you found."

"And you were going home?"

"Until I stumbled upon a delicious reason to delay my return to London, yes." His hand traced a line from shoulder to hip and back, making her more aware than ever of the many layers of fabric separating them.

"I'd offer to go back to London and enjoy a few hours in this carriage with you, but I have another delivery to make tomorrow." She cupped one hand at his nape, because having the ability to touch any part of his bare skin was a heady thing. "The delivery is farther afield, so I'd planned to hire a mount at the inn, then return in time to catch the mail."

"If you'll let me stay tonight, I can accompany you tomorrow, then transport you home."

"But I already have a mail ticket."

Dorian's tone softened, coaxing. "You don't really want to climb aboard that death trap with all those people, when this fine carriage is available, do you?"

She sighed. Of course she didn't prefer a crowded, wet public coach to his well-sprung carriage. It had velvet upholstery that wouldn't leave mysterious stains on her gown and probably even had warming bricks and a lap rug stored under one of the seats. However, she hated to see the money spent on a mail ticket go to waste.

As if reading her mind, he said, "I'll reimburse the shop the cost of your ticket."

Finally, she nodded. "Very well. We travel together."

The coach noticeably slowed, and they locked gazes. His smoldering look made her squeeze her thighs together in an attempt to relieve the ache between them.

"But tonight, you're mine. And I'm yours. Tomorrow can wait," her duke said.

Chapter Sixteen

A harried maid scurried past Dorian at the top of the inn's stairs. "Mother Nature is all in a tizzy, isn't she?" She didn't pause for a response before continuing down the hall with two pails of water that sent up curls of steam in the cool air.

His staff were relieved to be off the roads. Jim, the young groom, had a purple tinge to his lips, and Gibson, the coachman, was soaked through. People and carriages clogged the stable yard as more travelers left the road due to the weather. Based on the number of people claiming spots on the tavern floor and the harried expression on the innkeeper's face as Dorian slipped up the stairs, everyone was damn near stranded at this point.

If one had to be stuck in a slightly dodgy inn hours from London, there was no one better to share a bed with than the delectable Caro Danvers.

The woman was a marvel, and they hadn't even fully enjoyed one another yet.

Rage on, Mother Nature, he thought. Knocking twice as she'd directed, he tried not to fidget as he waited for her to open the door. Then, there she was—wet, bedraggled, and somehow still so striking the sight of her made his chest ache. Stepping inside, he locked the door and surveyed their bedchamber.

"I think this will do nicely." Caro's statement held a note of challenge. It only took her three paces to reach the fireplace on the far wall, but her look threatened another pointed lecture on pampered gentlemen should he complain about the spartan accommodations.

Dorian removed his hat and set it beside the chipped washing ewer. There weren't many other options, especially since they'd need to dry all their things the best they could in a small space. "It's perfect. Thank you for letting me stay."

She shot him a smile, then knelt and added a log to the fire from the tidy stack beside the hearth.

He'd slept in worse places on the Continent. Of course, these bed linens might be damp or scattered with mouse droppings. Yet Caro seemed content, and that was something else he respected about her.

Calling the room snug would be generous. A bed barely wide enough to sleep two took up one wall. The opposite wall had a table with the ewer and a basin for washing. The mirror above the table reflected directly across the room to the bed, which inspired wicked ideas. Before the fireplace were two wood chairs and a table no larger than a chessboard. The room was bare of anything beyond the essentials. At least they wouldn't have to worry about their wet clothes soaking a rug.

"Traveling with you on the Continent during the war would have been downright enjoyable, I think." He'd so often felt guilty for being grateful Juliet hadn't been present to criticize the accommodations in the various camps. Such a strange thing to want someone there while being simultaneously relieved to not bear the burden of her complaints over the rustic conditions.

Juliet never, for a moment, forgot she was a duchess. In

contrast, Caro never imagined she was. The differences between the women were sometimes jarring. Like when Caro took him to task over being concerned for her safety while traveling alone.

She rose and offered a bemused smile. "That's kind of you to say." Caro reached into her curls and began to shake out the tangled mass. Pins scattered over the floor with the distinct *tink* of metal meeting wood. "With the rain pounding on the roof, it's quite cozy, don't you think?"

The curve of her bottom lip looked delicious—that's what he thought.

Dorian draped his overcoat next to her cloak on the warm tile of the hearth and enjoyed the way her breasts shifted beneath her pelisse while her fingers plucked pins and unplaited her hair.

"You're awfully quiet, but that look makes me feel like you're going to pounce at any moment. What are you thinking?"

"I need you to tell me you won't regret this later. Because Caro, I want you so much I'm nearly shaking with it." He prowled closer, until the rain-washed scent of her was stronger than the smoke from the wood in the hearth. "I want you naked and moaning, and I'm dying to watch those amazing breasts move while I pound into you... That's what I'm thinking."

At his words, Caro lifted one brow and sent him a siren's smile. "No regrets. Remove your gloves, Dorian."

The commanding tone made his cock leap to attention with such force it actually hurt, and he'd thought it impossible to get harder.

Tugging the wet leather off, one finger at a time, Dorian smiled, remembering her confession in the carriage, that she'd fantasized about his hands. "Whatever you want my fingers to do, they'll do. I'm yours to command."

A rough swallow was her only response, but that was enough for him. "Now your coat and waistcoat, if you please."

"Will you remove your pelisse?" The green satin waistcoat joined the growing pile of his clothing.

Taking her time, Caro unhooked the buttons between her breasts, and Dorian thought the anticipation might drive him mad. Her movements were deliberate and controlled as she draped the garment over the back of a chair.

Her chilly fingers unknotted his cravat then unwound the length of linen. A sound akin to a purr rose from her chest as she stroked his naked throat, then caressed the dip where his collarbones met. "I've thought so many times of unwrapping you. Unraveling all this perfection."

"Have you?" Dorian plucked the fichu from her gown and tossed it toward where she'd draped her pelisse. "We know how I feel about this thing. It's designed to torment me."

The vibration of her laugh traveled up his fingertips, and an actual sigh of relief shook him when he finally touched the valley of her cleavage. Dorian traced the swell of each breast and caressed the velvety skin on the slope of her shoulder, until he couldn't take another second without her taste, and he palmed her nape for a hungry kiss.

Any lingering control disappeared as clothing was shoved aside. "Bed," he gasped.

Caro ignored his demand and stepped out of the embrace to let her wool gown and petticoat slide to the floor in a pool at her feet. Standing in a worn shift, gone slightly gray from washing and wear, she still carried herself like a queen and had no compunction about commanding a duke. Pointing to the remaining chair she said, "Sit. I'll help you remove your boots."

"Never mind my boots." Dorian pulled her down to straddle his lap, and eager hands explored the bare flesh of her soft thighs, then slid higher to cup her bottom. Her shift was scratchy against his hand, and he frowned. His shirts were made of thinner material than her undergarments. "Your skin should be cradled in lace and satin, not this rough fabric."

"If my shift offends you, remove it," she teased. A smile played at her mouth as he untied the damp laces of her stays with shaky fingers.

He couldn't help the noise he made when her glorious breasts slipped free of the supporting garment, and the wet material of the shift let him see dark, tight nipples. "Fuck, I feel like a green lad seeing my first woman."

But when he gripped the hem of her shift to finally bare her to his hungry gaze, something heavy fell between them. A quick glance offered little clarity, because there, in the space between his chest and the breasts with which he desperately wanted to become better acquainted, was a pile of pound notes, coins, and a scrap of fabric with an embroidered edge. Were those daisies? "I'm not sure what to do right now. I wanted nipples but found money instead."

Something deep in his chest warmed at her laugh. "Mr. Lipscomb pays cash."

Dorian shook his head. "All of my blood is in my lap, not my brain. I still don't understand."

Another laugh, and he wondered what he could do to make her this happy all the time.

"Those mythology volumes brought a fine price. You'll eventually have your share, but it has to go through my bookkeeping process first."

"The delivery for the shop—right. Excellent... Why was it in your cleavage?"

Plucking the coins and notes into a tidy pile, she wrapped the embroidered handkerchief around it into a bundle and tied it closed. "Only a fool travels with this much money on their person and puts it in a purse. Jingling coins paint a target on my back for thieves." Tossing the lump toward the table, it landed with a heavy clang. "There. Where were we?"

Thinking of her on the road alone and vulnerable to thieves made him scowl. Caro sighed and pushed the heavy curtain of her hair over her shoulder. "I can see the lecture forming, and I won't hear it. As I said before, we can't all travel with outriders and armed footmen. People have to carry about their business, regardless of risk—even when those people are women. I had a task and I did it while ensuring my safety to the best of my ability. I won't tolerate your entitled outrage when I'm only guilty of existing as a woman within the real world instead of the castle on a hill you inhabit."

The ache between his brows softened as Dorian rested his forehead on her breastbone. Her orange-blossom scent was heavier here, mingled with the smell of rain and lingering body heat. "I suppose that puts me in my place. Instead of a lecture, I'll say I'm grateful you're allowing me to escort you home. Thank you."

Caro stroked his hair, and tension in his neck melted away. "Is the mood broken? I can dress again, and then we can eat if you wish," she said.

He reared back and tugged her shift over her head in response. As soon as the linen floated to the floor, Caro grinned. "I like that answer."

But his pulse pounding in his ears made her voice sound like it came from under water. "Bloody fecking hell, how are you more beautiful than I imagined? I can't believe I finally get to touch you." And he did. Every curve and dip. The cluster of three freckles beside her right nipple. He gently grazed those hard nubs with his palm, and she shivered. When she squirmed impatiently on his lap, pressing her heat against his breeches, Dorian stilled her with a hand on her hip. "I want to fall on you like an animal, but I only get to see you for the first time once."

The words calmed her movements, and her eyes softened as she watched his hands. "No one has ever looked at me like you are now."

Dorian shook his head. "Then they were fools. But thank God they were, because their failings mean you're here now." And she was his. "I've lusted after you since the first moment I laid eyes on you."

"You mean when you finally learned my name a few weeks ago?"

He sent her a mock glare, then raked his teeth over one nipple until she gasped. "It's been almost two years I've wanted you, you maddening woman. Since the first time you spoke, bickering at me, your voice has haunted me."

"My voice?" Her obvious confusion nearly made him laugh.

"It's what caught my attention first. Then I saw you and couldn't look away. You were so strong and prickly. Fearless, even though you were clearly having a difficult time."

Her smile was sweet and a little sad. "I was scared and exhausted."

"I couldn't tell." As they spoke, he couldn't stop caressing the length of her back. The dip of her waist. The extravagant flare of her hips. God, she was soft. "Something inside me woke up that day. I was curious about you but also protective. Possessive in a way I've never felt before. I fantasized about holding these curves again and exploring them properly. Marking you as mine the same way you'd inadvertently claimed me."

Caro reached her fingers between them and unbuttoned the bulging placket of his breeches. "Shall we explore, then?" She grazed her teeth along his stubbled jaw, and he lost his breath. "Shall I claim you as mine?"

Dorian thrust his hips, pressing his cock firmer into her palm. "Yes. God, yes. Make me yours."

She sank her teeth into his earlobe, then sucked the skin to ease the sting. He hoped it left a mark. "Last chance to turn back." As she said the words, she shifted to run the length of him along her drenched core.

Dorian gulped for air. "Isn't that what I'm supposed to say? Who exactly is doing the seducing here?" The laughter in his voice transformed into a moan when she placed another stinging bite along his neck, then soothed the spot with her tongue. One more pink spot, one more mark. Fuck, he wanted more. More of her taking what she wanted, leaving evidence of her conquering on his body that would linger in the mirror. "More," he demanded and barely recognized his raspy voice.

Her mouth dropped to the rounded muscle of his shoulder, and a fierce satisfaction shot through him when she left a faint purplish ghost of her mouth. Tightening his grip on her hips, he thrust toward her heat. "Please, Caro. Let me in. I need you." In the coach, she'd said he would beg before morning, and he'd barely made it half an hour.

Their lips met, seeking, in a give-and-take of control and desire, as Caro finally sank onto his cock.

"It's been so long for me I don't know if I'll last," he grunted. "I promise I'll make it good for you, no matter what." And then he stopped speaking altogether, because her nipple was in his mouth, and their language became that of gasps, the sound of flesh meeting flesh, urging one another toward a finish line she crossed mere seconds before him.

Moments passed with the two of them wrapped together in silence except for the rain outside and the muffled sounds of the bustling inn on the other side of the door. He stroked a lazy line up her spine while the other hand grasped her waist, holding her to him. Neither seemed in a great hurry to separate.

Mother Nature didn't appear inclined to settle anytime soon, but the aftermath of their storm was a thing of beauty. Somehow, the quiet of their breaths settling into cadence together, was as intimate as having his body inside hers.

He should say something. Something romantic to make Caro understand this had been more than he'd expected. Various points on his body ached in the hard chair. His flesh would show marks left by her mouth and the short, curved nails she'd dug into his shoulders as she'd ridden him like a woman possessed. He couldn't remember the last time he'd felt so claimed. So content. Every mark and bruise were badges of honor. And as they faded, Dorian somehow knew with certainty he'd need her to replace them.

He'd beg if need be.

Instead of using words, he smoothed a hand over her wild, dark waves, silently encouraging her to remain as she was. An undeniable feeling of rightness settled in him as he held her like this, with her cheek propped against his shoulder and her breath fanning his neck. Unbidden, a whisky-soaked memory from a few nights ago when he had spoken to either a hallucination or Juliet's ghost poked at the bubble of contentment. He'd confessed to Jules he was scared.

Now there was even more reason to fear. If he was betrayed by someone he'd shared a moment like this with, it would be gutting. Drawing in a deep breath, he was proud of how much space his lungs allowed to fill with air, despite the thoughts racketing in his mind.

He needed to find Sherman. Because whatever else that man was guilty of, he also might know what Dorian had done wrong last time. And right now, with Caro in his arms, sated and content, Dorian suspected he'd do anything to keep her happy. Keep her with him.

Chapter Seventeen

The Duke of Holland snored. With the bed a snug fit to begin with, there was no escaping the awful sounds produced by what she'd previously thought of as a rather wonderful face.

He snored when on his back. He snored while sleeping on his side. Sometime in the wee hours of the morning, she wondered if he would still snore if she were to place a pillow over his head and sit on it.

That plan was rejected because it involved sleeping while sitting up. Besides, the courts weren't likely to take pity on her desperate exhaustion if Dorian's snoring ceased altogether because he stopped breathing. After sating themselves on one another for the third time, he'd earned the rest, but so had she. So, despite the threat of a murder charge, smothering the sound with a pillow was damned tempting.

Muted conversation floated up from downstairs, along with the scents of sausages cooking and the heavenly temptation of fresh baked bread. It was morning. Night had finally come to an end. Thank God.

At this rate, she would need an entire pot of tea for herself and would likely bite anyone who tried to make her share. Dorian's arm weighed heavy across her chest, and he didn't stir when she slipped out from under it. Except for the noise, the man slept like the dead. Careful to not shift the mattress too much, she scooted to the foot of the bed, then picked up her chemise from the floor where it had been tossed unceremoniously the night before.

While he was an exceptional bed sport companion, she didn't know if she would ever adjust—or have the opportunity to adjust—to sleeping beside him. Perhaps it was simply the strangeness of sharing a bed with a man. Or of being naked next to someone who radiated body heat equivalent to the sun. Anyone resting next to Dorian would never be cold.

She might be wide awake, exhausted, and grumpy—but she wasn't cold.

The fire had burned low overnight, so she added another log and poked at the embers until the glow became a flame. Yesterday's gown was blessedly dry, as were her stockings. By the time she tied her walking boots, the call of nature was pressing heavily on her bladder. Dorian still hadn't stirred, but it would be just her luck that he'd wake up in the middle of her using the chamber pot. So, she donned her cloak, then stepped into the hall and closed the door quietly behind her.

The sky outside was a steely gray, with bloated clouds threatening more rain. But for the moment, the morning held a feeling of being freshly washed as she picked her way down the path to the privy.

When she entered the public room of the inn a while later, she considered returning upstairs. No, tea and something to fill her belly were the priority. While downstairs, she could inquire about road conditions and order a tea tray for the room. Dorian was likely used to that kind of thing.

She couldn't remember ever having tea or eating in bed. Not once in almost thirty years. What would that be like? Today could be her only chance to snuggle under the covers next to an adorably rumpled man and share a cup of tea.

But not until she'd had several cups by herself.

Thankfully, the inn believed in serving a strong brew, regardless of beverage type. A pleasant zing zapped her brain awake after the first sip. Another cup or two like that, and she might just survive the day on the scant sleep she'd managed.

Sometime around the third cup, the feeling of being watched itched at her shoulders. Raising the cup to her lips, Caro observed the vicinity over the brim.

Dorian stood in the doorway of the public room, scowling. Dark shadowed scruff covered his jaw, and a tuft of hair stood up at the back of his head. Not groomed, but fully dressed and looking disgruntled with the world—that was her duke this morning. *Her* duke?

The man in question crossed the room in a few long strides, then sat across from her. "You didn't leave."

"Of course I didn't. Why would I?"

His scowl softened into something she'd say was relief on anyone else. "You were gone when I awoke. I thought you'd left."

Caro shook her head. Strange that his first reaction was worry that she'd abandoned him. What that said about him was something to ponder later.

"I didn't sleep well, as my bedmate snored loud enough to scare away nearby wildlife. My plan was to fortify myself with tea, then bring you a tray. If nothing else, you deserve a hearty thank-you for keeping any vermin in our room cowering in fear and away from the bed."

Confusion pinched his brows together. "I snore?"

Caro paused her reach for the pot to pour him a cup. "You didn't know? How could you not know you snore? Was your wife hard of hearing?"

He blinked. "She never mentioned it."

Caro poured him a cup of tea, then pushed it toward him. "I am surprised the duchess never said anything."

Lips that had teased nearly every inch of her body last night pursed as he blew on his drink. "So am I. Or maybe not. Thinking back, I was the only one who brought up minor annoyances. She never complained about living with me. Not once. I'm not arrogant enough to think myself perfect, but I have to wonder what else she simply endured." He took a sip, then sighed. "I'm sorry I ruined your sleep, Caro."

She tilted her head, cradling her cup of tea between her palms and feeling far more pleasant in general toward the concept of facing the day. "Perhaps I'll nap on the drive home."

"Are the roads passable, then?"

"Carriages have been arriving and leaving the courtyard, so I assume so."

One brow rose and the serious expression he'd worn fled. "Are you still willing to let me accompany you on your delivery?"

"Absolutely." A question she'd briefly thought, then forgotten because Dorian was probably doing something remarkable with his mouth, rose in her mind again. "Can I ask? What happened in Tippering?"

Instead of drinking, Dorian seemed content to cradle his cup in his hands. "Your instinct to interview the playwright was sound. Interesting fellow. He didn't have all the answers, and I certainly don't either. But he gave me a name and the man's home village. Sherman Snyder: commoner and swindler. My wife had an affair with a charlatan, and I can't get anyone in that place to talk. Tried bribing them to no avail. They wouldn't even discuss the school Juliet had been building in the village, so I doubt it exists. Which means he stole thousands of pounds from her. Yesterday was beyond frustrating."

Realization dawned alongside a healthy dose of pity. No

wonder he'd been a little short-tempered when they met on the road. "If this Sherman person made a habit of defrauding women, and his acquaintances back home knew about it, they likely saw you as a jealous husband and wanted to stay out of it." A thought occurred to her. "Which is a clue in itself, isn't it?"

Intense blue eyes focused on her. "What do you mean?"

"If they want to stay out of it, that means there's something to stay out of. Their silence is a confirmation that you're on the right trail of clues. It also means the man is still alive. Sherman hasn't met his end in the last five years." The way Dorian worked his jaw made her ask, "Have you considered that you might actually meet this Sherman person?"

"That is the plan," he drawled with a steely edge to his voice.

"What will you do? How will you handle facing the duchess's lover?"

"Truth is, I don't know. Scenarios run through my head, and I can't say for sure which will be accurate. I know there are questions only he can answer. And knowing he's committing theft and fraud means I have a responsibility to bring him to justice if I can. Who knows who else he's hurt, and who he might steal from in the future? Not that my motivations are entirely noble. I'd dearly love to break his nose for what he did." A crooked smile tilted his lips, and they shared a look of understanding.

An honest reply, although one that left too much room for potential outcomes like regret and prison.

"Perhaps you should consider those scenarios until you have a plan you can live with. And we should go back to Tippering before we return to London today. This time, using all the tools at your disposal." Excitement hummed under her skin. What would a Blanche Clementine heroine do?

"What tools? I was charming, but they wouldn't be charmed. I offered money, but they couldn't be bribed. What am I missing?"

She smirked. "I bet they'll talk to me. I'll claim to be his latest lover. If they have any heart at all, someone will try to warn me away. We'll need an unmarked carriage and for you to stay out of sight. Should that fail, we'll call on Mr. Lipscomb, the collector who bought your mythology volumes. He's a terrible gossip and will discuss books and his neighbors for as long as you're willing to sit and drink tea. The man doesn't stop talking."

A plan came together in her mind as she spoke. They could absolutely do this.

Dorian's crooked smile made a shallow divot in his cheek. Not deep enough to be a dimple, but enchanting nonetheless. "You're excited about this, aren't you?"

Caro widened her eyes and made her voice breathy. "Pardon me, but have you seen my fiancé, Mr. Sherman Snyder? I have rather urgent news of a most personal nature and must find him immediately!"

"He's your fiancé now? He's been busy over the last five seconds." The line of his shoulders relaxed as he teased her and finally drank his tea.

Caro drained her cup and set it aside. "Yes, and not a moment too soon, as the midwife suspects twins."

He barked a laugh. "Excellent. That will get the local gossips talking."

"That's what we need. If nothing else, it could create a few moments of acute discomfort for the man and his current amour. Would you like to order food, then set off?"

"Perfect plan. Thank you for this, Caro." He reached across the table and squeezed her hand.

"You're very welcome, Your Grace. Just promise me you

won't end up in custody if we actually find Sherman. You can't get answers from inside Newgate."

It was his turn to don an innocent expression. "Surely the local magistrate would handle things. I'd end up confined to a well-appointed bedroom at the nearest manor house, not drafty Newgate." He chuckled once more. "I jest. If you could see your face..."

Caro sighed, shaking her head. "Promise."

"Fine. I promise I won't do anything that will warrant legal consequences."

"I'm holding you to that," she warned, then signaled the serving girl for food.

Later that morning, they arrived in the tiny hamlet of Tippering. Although she'd never been there before, the cramped streets and people who'd called the place home for generations were familiar. Dorian's error the day before had been in the way he'd approached the town. First, arriving in a carriage with a ducal crest and shiny brass bits that brought attention to himself. Then, he'd started his inquiries in the pub.

If his ducal-ness had spent any amount of time in a small community like Tippering or her village, he'd have known that while the pub owners and staff knew and saw everything, they wouldn't share information with a stranger. They were guardians of the town's secrets and wouldn't betray those secrets to an outsider without a compelling reason. Information was a sort of social currency, and the locals knew it.

Besides, the majority of the pub's stories would be skewed to the male perspective. Caro didn't have quite enough faith in that sex to trust their version of events. In her experience, men often got away with whatever they could by gravitating to those who would cheer on their misdeeds. Sherman coming home and bragging about his exploits wasn't beyond the realm of possibility, which made the men in the pub accomplices.

Bypassing the pub altogether, she walked down the high street and veered toward a white-paned bow window displaying hats, a rainbow of ribbons, and a rather fine pair of kidskin gloves. Outside the door, she took a moment to compose herself, discreetly adjusting the lump under her gown.

Between her short stays and Dorian's cravat, they'd managed to secure his coat to her waist in a way that would be noticeable to someone looking for it but not so large and burdensome that she would be expected to alter her gait.

Deception was a tricky business when one thought about it.

Caro rubbed at her eyes until her reflection in the window showed they were sufficiently red and shiny.

Overhead, a small bell announced her arrival, and she was relieved to see an older woman shuffle from the back room. Perfect.

"Good day, miss. May I help you find something?"

Caro put a wobble in her smile. "I . . . I hope so. Do you know where I can find the home of the Snyder family?"

The shopkeeper nodded. "Their place is the stone cottage on the right, just outside town. Pass the blacksmith, then continue straight until there isn't any fencing along the road. Their lane is between two overgrown apple trees. Don't know what you're expecting to find there, though. The family hasn't been in residence in, Lord, about ten years now. Only the son is left, and I haven't heard of him being back in a while."

Caro sighed heavily, resting a hand atop the bulge at her waist. "Sherman hasn't been home recently?" Scrunching her face, she tried to muster tears. Sad thoughts were hard to come by when her body still hummed from delicious bed sport the night before, so she shifted her expression to one of exhaustion. "I don't know what to do, then."

Concern wrinkled the woman's brow. "Miss, are you all right?"

When the woman reached for Caro's arm, she let herself lean into the touch. "May I sit for a moment?" She rubbed at the coat lump once more. "I'm just so tired these days."

The shopkeeper tsked and guided her to a pair of chairs near a looking glass at the back of the shop. "How far along are you?"

Drat. How far along was she? She hadn't thought about that. Caro drew in a calming breath and sent it out as a sigh. "Far enough that I worry about how uncomfortable carrying these babies will be before I finally get to hold them."

"More than one?"

Caro sat in the chair gingerly. "The midwife suspects two. You see now why it's so imperative I find my fiancé as soon as possible."

The shopkeeper made a sound of distress, then sank into the chair beside her. "You're engaged to Mr. Sherman Snyder? Oh, lamb. Terribly upset I am to hear it."

Blinking innocently, Caro asked, "Why do you say that? I confess I don't know my fiancé well. Certainly not as well as someone who watched him grow up. Is...is he the kind of man who would play me false?"

The older woman bit her lips together as if physically holding back words, and Caro tried not to smile in triumph.

"It wouldn't do for me to pass along tales."

"It's hardly passing along tales when people's futures are at stake, Mrs....I'm sorry. I don't know your name."

"Mrs. Cooke."

"Mrs. Cooke, you may call me Alice." Adopting the name of her first book's heroine, Caro took the woman's hand and squeezed as if it were a lifeline. "Sherman stopped returning my missives two months ago. When I went by his rooms, the landlady told an awful story about him leaving in the middle of the night without paying his rent. He's mentioned growing up here and even talked about building a school for the village. It sounded like he was still involved in Tippering, so I took the mail coach as far as I could, then walked the rest of the way. Please, anything you can tell me would be helpful."

Mrs. Cooke's clamped lips softened somewhat but didn't open, so Caro risked pushing a bit more. Surely the woman would dispense advice, if not gossip. "Should I keep looking for him and insist he marry me as promised, or go home and throw myself on my family's mercy?"

Imagining her father's response if she had shown up at his door unmarried and pregnant with twins was enough to make Caro's shudder of dread convincing. Feeling oddly protective of her faux baby, she covered the curve with her hands and waited for Mrs. Cooke's response.

She didn't have to wait long.

"Alice, if my daughter were in your shoes, I'd rather she come home than be saddled with that man for the rest of her days. Sherman Snyder isn't worth anyone's tears, luv."

"He's that bad? Goodness, I had no idea."

Mrs. Cooke nodded emphatically. "Better to birth a bastard than live with that one. He's the bad apple that ruins all he touches. I don't know what tales that slippery chap spun, but there's no school in Tippering. Our children learn at home, or with the vicar. The ones with real brains foster with families near the closest school an hour away and come home on the weekends."

Caro winced, while internally rejoicing. Once the shopkeeper decided to speak, she really didn't hold back.

The other woman wasn't without compassion, though.

"Alice, do you think you're the first to come here looking for that man? This is what he does. Woos women, takes everything he can from them, then walks away and leaves everyone around him to pick up the mess." She ran her gaze over Caro's serviceable gown and worn gloves. "You don't seem as high on the instep as his usual targets. Please tell me you didn't give him money."

"Targets? That's quite the word choice." Remembering her story, Caro hurried to add, "I cleared the debt with his landlady, but that's it."

"I'm sorry you covered a single ha'penny for that man. Especially with the babes on the way."

"To call Sherman's paramours targets makes him sound like a wolf on the hunt."

Mrs. Cooke rose to pull a tin of biscuits from behind the counter, then returned to her seat and offered Caro one. "That Snyder boy has been a problem his entire life. Never wanted to try at anything. Not a single bone in his body was equipped for hard work. If there was a shortcut to be found—no matter the means—he took it. Cheated in school. Pilfered from shops. Ran up his family's debt at the pub. His poor mum made weekly rounds through the village apologizing for his behavior."

The biscuit was delicious, lemony and sweet on her tongue, with the perfect amount of crunch. "This is exceptional—thank you, Mrs. Cooke. Did you make these?"

She preened. "I did. I'll share the receipt if you wish."

"I'd like that, thank you. But you were saying—Sherman has been a scapegrace all his life? Goodness, this is a lot to take in."

"Honestly, the women came as a surprise to all of us. A pretty thing like you, I'm shocked he caught your attention."

That seemed to require a response, as the shopkeeper

waited expectantly. Caro cleared her throat of the lemony biscuit and said, "He, ah, writes poetic letters. Turned my head with romantic words."

Before she'd finished speaking, Mrs. Cooke was nodding. "That's what I've heard, but don't believe a word of it. Once, two women were in town looking for him at the same time and compared letters. He writes the same thing to everyone. I'm so sorry, Alice. You should go home and forget you ever met Sherman Snyder."

Caro nodded and rose to her feet, deliberately shaky. The shopkeeper jumped up and offered a hand. She really was a dear. "Do you have any thoughts on where he might be? God knows my family will want to try to find him when I show up looking like this."

"Last I heard, he had rooms on Rupert Street, but you said he's let those go. Perhaps your parents would have some success asking his cousin, Lord Bixby, about his whereabouts. That man probably regrets giving Sherman introductions to the fancy folk. How they didn't throw him out on his ear, I'll never know."

Success. Caro offered a small smile. "Thank you. I appreciate your hospitality, Mrs. Cooke."

"Oh! The biscuits!" The woman scurried back behind the counter to scribble something on a slip of paper, then handed it to Caro. "If you bake them for too long, just cover them in icing. Icing helps everything."

Mrs. Cooke was a woman after her own heart. "I will remember your kindness. Thank you again."

As she wove through the streets toward the mews and the hired carriage, Caro forced herself to stare at the ground. Once she'd reached the carriage and closed the door behind her, she finally let herself grin like the victor she was.

"He keeps rooms on Rupert Street and has an entree to society thanks to his cousin, Lord Bixby. Oh, and I am far from the first woman to show up in town looking for him. Unlike me, they are usually wealthy. The shopkeeper called them targets. Also, the closest school is an hour away. If I had to guess, Sherman pocketed the funds."

Dorian's grin crinkled the skin around his blue eyes. "You did it. They talked to you."

Caro shifted his coat out from under her skirts and handed the rumpled mass to him. "Mrs. Cooke runs the milliner shop and bakes fabulous biscuits. She wrote down the receipt for me. Lovely woman."

He laughed aloud. When the urge to inhale surprised her, Caro realized she'd been holding her breath at the sight of him. The way Dorian's smile lit him from within, how he threw his head back as he laughed—how had she ever thought him humorless and stoic? Those old impressions she'd had of the Duke of Holland were disappearing, replaced by this man. Dorian, who kept her awake with his snoring and laughed easily once he let you behind his walls.

"You are a marvel, Caro." He pressed a kiss to her lips. "I don't know why I tried to do this without you."

Chapter Eighteen

❦

"What's the book we're delivering?" Dorian had shaken out his coat and attempted to put himself to rights in the carriage on the way to the Adams cottage.

Caro craned her neck to see through the window glass as the coach slowed. Even in the grayish depths of winter, the landscape promised verdant grass and full tree branches. Despite the weather, the road was in decent condition, and while they bounced and jostled quite a bit in the hired carriage, it wasn't so bad they risked a broken wheel. The book, wrapped in brown paper and twine, was clutched to her chest.

"Caro? Are you all right?"

"Oh. Yes, of course. We are taking Mrs. Adams a cookery book. But more importantly, I am looking at her cottage."

"Why is the cottage special?"

"Because I might want to buy it." Caro grinned, watching the landscape roll by. Someday, would this view be familiar? Would she walk or drive this lane each time she visited the shops or called on a friend? The village was a decent size; surely there might be a few kindred spirits there, waiting for her to find them.

"What do you mean, buy it?" Something in his tone almost made her turn, but a small wood sign on a tidy, white-washed fence read ADAMS, and she gasped.

"This is it. Hattie swears it's perfect for me, but I had to see it for myself before approaching them about making an offer."

Dorian was silent for a moment before joining her at the window. "What is it that makes it perfect for you?"

The house itself came into view, and Caro's cheeks ached with the width of her smile. "You mean besides how beautiful it is? Oh, look at it, Dorian. The porch is the perfect size for a chair in the summer. I bet those front windows let in the morning sun. Are we facing east? Yes, I think they must be perfect for watching sunrises." Caro settled back against the seat, now that the house was right there. "It's quiet. Private. No one to judge me or expect me to be perfect. When you grow up as a vicar's daughter, every move you make is under scrutiny. I don't want that life. I've lived that life, and it's hell."

"I understand. Everyone watches a duke…and a duchess," he said quietly.

"More than anything, though, this would be mine. Just mine. No one could throw me out on the street. I've been saving for years to own a place like this. Private and safe." It felt right to share this with him. Last night she'd offered her body, but this was a part of her heart. She took his hand and squeezed. He tightened his grip until the pressure was nearly painful. "I'm glad you're here. Thank you."

He dropped a kiss on her forehead as the coach rocked to a stop. "Thank you for letting me be here. Shall we go meet Mrs. Adams?"

At the gate to the front garden, an older dark-skinned woman with round cheeks and a sweet smile greeted them. "You're from Martin House?"

Caro introduced herself, and Dorian sent the woman a charming grin. "Mr. Dorian Whitaker. It's a pleasure to meet you, Mrs. Adams."

"Well, aren't you a handsome fella? Come in, come in, before the wind bites you. You two missed the weather yesterday. Mercy, it was something. I've never been so content to sit in front of a fireplace. I finished knitting a scarf for my son—he's married and grown now—and wrote three letters. Stew simmered all day, and I sat there, snug as a bug by the fire. Poor Mr. Adams was wet through every time he ventured out to feed the animals." And so she went, chattering as she led them along a stone path to the house. Caro exchanged an amused wink with Dorian before becoming distracted with trying to identify the plants lining the garden beds.

Herbs grew in pots by the door, with a particularly hardy thyme plant refusing to brown, even when face-to-face with winter. Thorny sticks of dormant rosebushes stood guard along the fence. "Mrs. Adams, what color are your roses when they're in bloom?"

"Oh, all sorts. Why grow one color when there are so many?" She unlatched the door and chuckled ruefully. "You'll see. I'm not afraid of vibrant colors in my home. Mr. Adams doesn't even argue anymore when I ask him to paint something. The man is used to me by now, bless him."

The door opened, and Caro stepped inside and felt overcome. She knew her mouth hung open, but she couldn't help it as she took in the most delightful home she'd ever seen. "As of this moment, I believe in love at first sight. Mrs. Adams, your house is an absolute treasure." With a hand over her pounding heart, Caro had no trouble imagining returning to this every day and proudly calling it hers.

What a life that would be. Behind her, Dorian closed the door and wiped his boots on the mat.

"Aren't you the sweetest thing to say so? Do you have time for a cup of tea?" Mrs. Adams was already putting the kettle on, so that answered that.

"Before I forget, this is yours. I'm sorry it has taken so long to deliver." The parcel exchanged hands, and Caro immediately went back to examining every nook and cranny she could see from where she stood.

Wood trim around the windows had been painted in blues and greens. The stone floor was swept clean and contrasted perfectly with the whitewashed walls. Colorful paintings the likes of which she'd never seen before decorated the house. If she had to hazard a guess, she'd say those were Caribbean and African motifs in the art, with strong shapes and lines that caught the eye.

This was a home. She couldn't help thinking happy people lived here—and had for a long time. They'd gathered around the scarred wood kitchen table and bundled under the rainbow of knitted blankets they'd thrown casually over every sofa arm and chair seat. More knitting spilled from a large grass woven basket on the floor.

When she tore her eyes from the room, she felt her face heat. More time than she'd realized must have passed, because Mrs. Adams watched her with an amused smile, holding out an earthenware mug. "I'm sorry for gawking. Your home is just..."

"Everything you've ever wanted?" Dorian asked gently, taking his own proffered mug.

Caro chuckled. "Yes. I can't imagine how difficult it must be to consider leaving, Mrs. Adams."

Hugging the thick book to her chest, Mrs. Adams sighed, then picked up her own cup and took a sip. "Moving will be painful, I imagine. But Mr. Adams and I, we've lived our life here as long as we needed to. We raised our children here. Welcomed two grandchildren to this house." She blinked away the moisture gathering in her eyes. "It's time for someone else to love here and live here. We're needed elsewhere.

This house needs young people." She glanced pointedly between Caro and Dorian.

Biting her lip, Caro debated the wisdom of showing her hand so early but knew she'd regret it if she didn't. "If someone wanted to lease this home to give them more time to save the full purchase price, is that something you'd consider?"

Mrs. Adams cocked her head. "It would be worth discussing with my husband if that person appreciated this home as much as I did. We aren't planning to move out until late spring, though. Just doesn't make sense until then."

Dorian studied Caro intently, but she couldn't decipher his expression. "Who knows? Perhaps by spring, this person would have rounded out her savings sufficiently to purchase instead of lease," Caro said. Hope surged, and for once, it didn't feel like a threat of loss in disguise.

"Then I imagine I will be keeping in touch with someone who would be interested in such an arrangement." Mrs. Adams winked, and Caro couldn't contain her grin.

As they finished their tea, Mrs. Adams told her about the village characters. The baker's perfect hot cross buns. The seamstress who could make magic out of seemingly nothing. How the older gentlemen couple next door were nosy but meant well, and raised goats on their small farm.

Caro listened but grew increasingly aware of how quiet Dorian had been since they arrived. Nothing about his demeanor suggested he was angry or petulant. However, after years of enduring her father's stony silences over every little infraction (always her fault, according to him), it was a habit to wonder if she'd done something wrong. As her mind wandered that path, replaying the events of the morning, searching for her error, Caro stopped herself. It would be too easy to slip back into that pattern of pacifying a man out of a mood.

Instead of dwelling on it now, she sipped her tea, let herself imagine she knew who the people were that Mrs. Adams spoke of, and vowed to poke at the duke about his odd mood when they returned to the carriage. Should the conversation not go well, there was time to return their hired carriage to the posting yard near the Hawk and Fan and catch the mail coach back to London as planned. She knew that if Constance were here, she'd roll her eyes and make a remark about pessimism pretending to be pragmatism.

It wasn't long before she said goodbye to Mrs. Adams, promising to be in touch. Since putting off the inevitable never served anyone, Caro raised her eyebrows expectantly as soon as Dorian closed the coach door. "Is everything all right?"

"Yes, of course."

She waited, but he didn't explain or fill the silence. "No, it's not. Clearly, you have something on your mind. Would you like to share what it is, or am I expected to guess, like charades? I'm awful at charades, so I suggest avoiding that." She wouldn't normally be so blunt, but the man had repeatedly said he wanted to know what she was thinking.

Dorian studied her, smiling ruefully. "Hattie was right. The property is perfect for you. I can imagine you living there, and the thought of you so far away makes my chest tight." Holding out his hand, he waited for her to take it.

It was sweet that he was upset over the idea of her leaving London. The prickly willingness to fight wilted, and she took his hand, then rested her head on his shoulder. "Caro, if you want the house, I'll happily buy it for you."

Never mind—the sweetness was short-lived. "What on earth makes you think I would want you to buy me a cottage? Weren't you listening earlier when I waxed poetic about having something of my own?"

"It would be your own." He winced, and she suspected the words were louder than he had intended. "I don't mean to yell. But the house would be in your name. It would be yours."

Caro cocked her head, studying him. Did he truly not understand why she was upset? "Property is something a man buys his mistress. Let me make one thing clear, Your Grace." He flinched again. "I let you in my bed last night, and I might very well do it again. However, I am not your mistress. Agreeing to that position, even until you wed, would mean I'd be at your beck and call. I'm my own woman, with work and dreams and aspirations that have nothing to do with you." She stopped herself before emotions could get the better of her tongue and make her say something they'd both regret. For his part, he appeared hurt, rather than mad, and she hated the idea of causing him pain. Drawing in a calming breath, she gentled her tone. "Dorian, we agreed to part ways when you choose a bride. Please understand the awkward position in which I find myself. It brings me no joy to think of the day I see you for the last time. Anticipating a move to this place is something I can look forward to. Because you and I both know you have pressing reasons for marrying again, so that day will arrive soon. I won't be the reason you shirk your duty, and I refuse to let you be the reason I give up my independence. Or worse yet, allow myself to hurt another woman by staying with you after you wed. I'm no man's mistress. Not even yours."

Dorian rubbed his palm over his face. "I don't mean it like that."

She firmed her jaw. "I see no other way you could mean it. Explain to me how a duke purchasing a property for a woman he's had a sexual relationship with does not equal some sort of payment or mistress agreement."

Silence. Finally, he sighed. Pain and frustration weighed heavily in the sound, but there wasn't a trace of anger. "I hoped to have more time with you."

The admission was an olive branch of sorts. It was Caro who now offered her hand, and he took it. He interlaced their fingers, as if needing to hold her in place.

"By the time I'm ready to move, you might have chosen a bride, and we'd be saying goodbye anyway." She squeezed his hand. "Let us enjoy the time we have."

He nodded, then raised their hands to kiss her fingers.

When they'd returned the hired coach, then settled into his carriage, the mood between them had settled back into the comfortable companionship they shared in his library.

But as the carriage wheels splashed through puddles, and a gentle rain began to fall, neither of them mentioned the coming spring.

Sleep eluded Dorian. The midnight velvet curtains around his bed kept out the drafts, but they couldn't stop the ghosts from his past or emotions of the present from finding him.

As the hours passed, Bloomsbury quieted outside the window. The murmurings and creaking footsteps of the servants moving about the house faded, slowed, then went to sleep, along with most of London.

The antique clock he'd brought home from Vienna chimed the hour from the mantel.

An eternity later, the chime broke the silence again. And again, until he stopped counting the chimes.

Hard to believe the previous morning, he'd awoken in a musty inn deep in Kent. With her marks on his skin and her scent on the pillow beside him, Dorian had been loose-limbed and content. At least, until he thought Caro had crept out and abandoned him in the middle of the night.

Relief had swamped him when he'd spied her across the public room.

A few hours later, relief was a distant memory as he'd felt his heart wither a little while watching Caro fall in love with a house. Ironic that on the morning after finally holding her, he had to stand aside as she chased a dream that would take her away from London. Attempting to insert himself into that dream by offering to buy the house had been a spectacular misstep.

To think he'd been a diplomat during a war yet couldn't negotiate a conversation with one prickly, brilliantly independent woman who'd slipped under his skin as thoroughly as she'd slipped under his body.

Dorian rolled onto his side and stared, unseeing, into the cavernous dark of his bed.

A bed that hadn't felt this empty in years.

"It was one night, Holland. One night. You're a grown man capable of enjoying a woman without throwing your heart at her feet." Never mind that the woman in question was not only beautiful but intelligent, adventurous...He rolled over again and huffed.

In his defense, it would be impossible not to be entranced by the way she'd lit with triumph as she shared the information she'd learned in Tippering. Caro had been so damned happy and proud of herself, and rightly so. No part of this hunt for Sherman could have happened without her.

The women in his life tying him in knots didn't stop with Caro. When he returned home late last evening, Gloria had been in a mood. No one exhibited righteous indignation with as much flair as the dowager, and she'd been in fine form. It would seem that while he was gone, Lady Humphry had called with her daughter. Over the course of tea, they'd informed his mother that they'd chosen to discourage any further wooing from the Duke of Holland.

Since his attention toward Miss Humphry had been

half-hearted and lackluster at best, Dorian didn't take offense at this development. If Miss Humphry had an ardent suitor, then he applauded her parents for ignoring his title and encouraging her to follow her heart toward happiness elsewhere.

Gloria, however, acted as if they'd walked into their home and spit in her face. Since he wasn't distraught over the news, she'd declared she would find more sympathetic listening ears elsewhere and stormed from the house.

Poor Hastings looked like he needed a stiff drink by the time she left. God only knew how much the butler had to hear before Dorian had arrived home.

Across the room, his door creaked open, followed several seconds later by scraping in the grate. The scullery maid going about her work.

Thank fuck it was morning.

Dorian sat up, letting the bedding pool around his hips, and rubbed his face. Rough stubble abraded his palms, and the stench of his morning breath seemed apropos to his mood.

Since rest was clearly not an option, he'd have to resort to action.

Rupert Street wasn't too far away. Oliver's home was practically on the way, and as they'd already established, visiting a friend's dead wife's lover was the kind of things friends did for one another.

And Dorian would remind Oliver of that fact when he pulled him away from his kippers and toast.

An hour later, Oliver didn't appreciate the reminder.

"There is something seriously wrong with your head, friend," he grumbled around a mouth of breakfast.

Dorian shrugged. "Be that as it may, are you coming with me or not?"

"Of course I am. You'll need an alibi if all of this goes horribly wrong. But making me do it before nine in the morning is downright vile, so you're a bastard."

"False. I have my father's eyes."

"And your mother's stubborn nature, unfortunately," Oliver grumped.

"Mother would be flattered to hear you say so. More coffee?"

Oliver waved a hand to push away the offer. "Don't rush me. Either you want my company, or you don't. And we've already established that you need me, so calm yourself. Maybe have a slice of toast. Breathe. Ask yourself why this has to happen *now*."

Beneath the table, Dorian's knee bounced with impatience. Exhaustion from a sleepless night dulled his usually sharp mind and reflexes, but an anxious urgency kept him from feeling the pull to rest. Why did it have to happen now? Because he'd crawl out of his skin if he couldn't do something.

The only person he wanted to be spending time with more than Oliver was Caro. His knee paused midjiggle, then resumed the movement. Why couldn't he see Caro? Most of the information he had was because of her anyway, and she'd been thrilled to visit Tippering and play a part. She'd probably enjoy it, and if he was terribly lucky, he might convince her to stay the night. Then his bed wouldn't be so empty.

He would have to sneak her past his mother, but that wouldn't be too difficult, since Gloria was expected at two events that night. Which meant he could make Caro scream his name well into the wee hours of the morning without fear of the dowager knocking on his door.

Motioning to a footman, Dorian asked for a piece of paper and pencil. After scrawling a note warning her of his pending arrival and plans, he sent the footman on his way. That would give Caro time to clear her day if possible. If she couldn't join them, at least he would be able to see her for a moment and ask to see her later.

As Oliver raised his cup to his lips, Dorian could swear he did it with the speed of a turtle.

"Are you moving as slowly as I think you are in a bid to annoy me? If so, it's working. Bravo."

His oldest friend rubbed a hand over his face, and that was when Dorian took note of the darker-than-normal shadows under legitimately grumpy eyes. "It might surprise you to learn, Your Grace, but the world doesn't revolve around you. I didn't sleep well last night after a particularly vexing evening with Althea."

Dorian forced his knee to still. It was on the tip of his tongue to flippantly ask if there was trouble in paradise, but he held back the works when he noticed the tight lines bracketing Oliver's mouth.

"Do you want to talk about it?"

"Not particularly. Mostly because I don't know that there's anything to tell. If I didn't know better, I'd suspect she was trying to make trouble. She seemed to be deliberately obnoxious, although to what end I can't imagine."

"Have you asked her if there's something bothering her? Discussed the friction you're sensing?" Irony tasted metallic in his mouth. How many times had he dismissed Juliet's silences and moods, believing all would be well eventually? As if her problems could be solved by neglect and magic. "Don't assume all is well if you are having misgivings."

"She'll talk when she's ready," Oliver said, offering solid evidence to Dorian's way of thinking that the survival of the human species to that point was a bleeding miracle.

Dorian sighed. "Oliver, you are one of the most intelligent

men I know. But please, as a friend and a man who discovers more ways every day that I bungled my marriage, I am begging you to talk to Althea. Ask her what she wants. What she needs. *Assume nothing.* If you intend to marry her, you need to start as you mean to go on. And if you intend to live your life waiting for her to come to you with her thoughts, then I wish you good luck on what is sure to be a lifetime of misery for you both."

Silence descended. With Oliver, silence could mean his friend was angry, was confused and puzzling it out, or had slipped out of the room while he'd been talking.

Judging by the pinched lips and furrowed brow, Oliver was pondering. After what seemed like an eternity, he spoke. "Althea and I are not like you and Juliet were. I am fond of her and am content with the engagement. She has all the qualities I want in a countess. Excellent family, pleasant disposition—usually—and enough education that she won't bore me to tears."

"May I ask which is more important to you: the impact her behavior had on your evening or the cause of her behavior?"

Oliver took a drink from his coffee but remained quiet. That was one reliable thing about Oliver. If someone asked a question of him, he would consider the answer before speaking.

"Neither. If there is something upsetting her, she should approach me with it."

That Oliver effectively spoke aloud what Dorian had been thinking about his own missteps made him blink. "What I am hearing is you don't care enough to ask."

When had he stopped asking after Juliet? After a decade together, when had he let the checks and balances of their marriage impact him less than those in the ledgers of the estates? When she'd needed time, affection, or attention, had he given it freely? Or had he treated those moments like he would the estate business—minimum effort and cost for maximum yield?

In the early years, all he'd wanted was to make her happy, to keep her happy, to see her smile. As time passed, newness faded into contentment—which he thought meant nothing could shake them. When had contentment turned to complacency? Did any of this excuse her decision to stray? Of course not. But there were things in their marriage, early cracks in the relationship, that Sherman could not help identify.

Dorian had wanted Juliet to be happy, but at some point, he had been so distracted or disconnected he'd failed to notice when he stopped being a source of happiness to her.

The realization settled on him like bricks, pinning his feet to the floor and killing the need to fidget.

How different the course of their relationship could have been if someone had given him the advice he offered Oliver, and he'd listened.

"What is the address we are visiting?" Oliver asked, changing the subject. A sure sign the conversation had ventured into sore subjects his friend had no intention of discussing further.

"First, I'm hoping to go to Martin House and pick up Caro. She's been part of this from the beginning, and it would be a shame to leave her out now. It was she who discovered that Sherman has rooms on Rupert Street in Westminster. Narrowing the search to a specific building might take time."

The cup hit the table with a finality, confirmed by Oliver standing. "All right. Let's go amateur sleuthing."

Chapter Nineteen

*Y*our Grace, you look as if you haven't slept at all," Caro exclaimed when a footman held open the door of the carriage and she peered inside. Shadows beneath Dorian's eyes made him look on the brink of keeling over, and she worried that something awful had happened since the last time she'd seen him.

"I'm glad you said something, Miss Danvers. When I tell Holland he looks like shit, he doesn't take it well. How sweet that you can get away with it." The friend he'd had on the Thames weeks ago grinned from the other seat, then caught himself. "Apologies. I don't think we'd been properly introduced. Lord Southwyn."

Out of habit, she curtsied. "Miss Caroline Danvers." Returning her attention to the duke, she said, "I received your note. Constance and I planned to shop for wedding things today. I can spare a little time, as long as your adventure doesn't take all morning."

"Bring her along," Lord Southwyn suggested. He shrugged at Dorian. "Even if you don't want to bring Miss Constance into your confidence, she doesn't need to know why we are looking for Sherman, just that we are. We can escort the ladies to the shops afterward."

Caro looked at Dorian. "Connie is loyal and will keep

mum if you choose to invite her, but she is curious. I understand if you'd rather keep our party small."

After studying her face for a moment, he nodded. "If your cousin wants to come, she's welcome."

"I'll return in a moment." Caro ducked back into the store, then up the stairs to their room.

"Connie, would you like to join a few swells for a couple hours of adventure?" She stopped and clarified. "It could be boring. But it might be entertaining and involve pretending to be someone's spurned paramour. Either way, they offered to drive us to the shops afterward."

Constance's eyes went wide. "With an invitation like that, how can I refuse?" She grabbed her winter cloak, and they hurried back down the stairs. "What have you mixed yourself up in, Caroline Danvers?"

"I'll explain in the carriage," Caro murmured, then called out to her family in a sunny voice. "We're off for a few hours."

At the sight of the crest on the door, Constance snorted. "The duke is taking us on this adventure? I didn't think he had it in him."

They entered the carriage, and Caro settled next to Dorian, taking his hand. Constance sat beside Lord Southwyn.

"Lord Southwyn, you might remember my cousin, Miss Constance Martin."

Connie, being her usual direct self, ignored the niceties and jumped right to the important question. "Would someone like to tell me what we are doing?"

"We're attempting to run a man to ground. His name is Sherman Snyder, and today we are trundling across town to his last known address," Lord Southwyn said.

"What has Mr. Snyder done to warrant a duke and a whatever you are coming after him?" Connie asked Southwyn.

"I'm an earl."

"Congratulations on the good fortune of your birth, milord. Is this Snyder character nasty? Dangerous? Does he owe you money?"

Southwyn blinked a few times, then turned to Dorian. "Holland, your turn."

"From what we've learned so far—thanks to Caro— Mr. Snyder uses letters written by a playwright in a sort of script to woo women of means, then steals all he can from them while they're offering their hearts."

Constance made an O with her mouth. "What a rotter. If we find him, am I allowed to hit him? As a representative of my gender, I am happy to give him a good whack. Wouldn't be the first time I've slapped a man."

Caro covered a snort with her hand. Dorian laughed, and poor Lord Southwyn was looking at Constance like she was from another planet entirely.

"Are you always like this?" Southwyn asked.

"Like what?" Connie smiled winningly. Southwyn appeared nonplussed when she waved a hand, casually dismissing him.

"If one of you has a sister, or maybe cousin, and this Mr. Snyder maligned them, then he sort of does owe you money."

"I'm not terribly concerned about the money, but I have a problem with fraud." A short battle waged in Dorian's expression. Caro saw the moment he reached a decision. "However, I also have questions for him regarding his affair with my late wife."

"Oh sweet baby Jesus," Constance said.

Caro squeezed his hand. He was brave to trust a relative stranger with such sensitive information.

He sent her a rueful smile. "I trust you. And if you trust her, then I trust her too."

As romantic gestures went, this was better than bringing flowers or writing poetry. Dorian Whitaker was a good man. The kind of man she'd thought only existed between the pages of a book. "Thank you. I promise, Constance is trustworthy."

Southwyn cut into their moment by addressing her cousin. "Someone has to say it. I don't know Miss Danvers well, or you at all. However, Holland is my oldest friend, and I promise, if word gets out about Sherman and the late duchess, I will come for you."

"Oliver—" Dorian warned, but Constance cut him off.

"You know, I almost believe you're capable of coming after me if need be. Unfortunately, we will never find out because I don't carry tales." She glanced over at Dorian. "I suppose that means you have a right to take the first whack at this scoundrel."

"That's generous of you," Dorian said, and Caro loved the half smile he offered as he teased her cousin.

The carriage slowed, then stopped before a block of buildings standing four stories tall, with narrow walking lanes between them. On the corner, a coffeehouse let in a steady stream of patrons, then released them back into the wilds of London.

Dorian nodded his thanks to the footman holding the door as they stepped onto the street, then called up to his coachman. "Return in a half hour."

At Southwyn's quizzical look, the duke explained. "Apparently a carriage with a ducal crest inhibits some people from talking freely. A lesson learned in Kent this week." He shot Caro a wink.

"And how did you find the bucolic village of Tippering?" Lord Southwyn asked.

"Silent as the grave. Thankfully, the locals talked to Caro. She was quite convincing in the role she chose."

Lord Southwyn gave her a questioning look. Caro shrugged modestly. "I placed Dorian's coat in a lump under my gown and told a shopkeeper I was expecting twins and needed to find Mr. Snyder."

"Is that where you got the receipt for those delicious biscuits Mother made this morning?" Connie placed her hands on her hips. "And you never said a word about seeing His Grace or being pregnant with twins. There is so much you haven't told me about your activities, Caro."

"It wasn't my place. But now that you know, I can't wait to catch you up." They all paused to let their carriage roll past.

"Did you see the school Juliet built?" Southwyn offered Constance his arm as they crossed the street, and her cousin beamed at the gentlemanly gesture.

"There is no school." Dorian deftly maneuvered Caro around a pile of horse droppings. "That's why I say he's defrauding these women."

On the other side of the street, Lord Southwyn dropped Connie's arm, then shoved his hands in his pockets as they approached the coffeehouse. "Have you told your legal fellow yet? If Juliet's school doesn't exist, that's fraud on a rather grand scale."

"I plan to send a note around to Mr. Bellmore this afternoon."

"You know Gerard Bellmore?" Constance asked. "He and Caro are good friends. Such a nice man. In fact, he took Caro to the theater not too long ago."

Dorian held open the door of Parson's Coffee House.

"Would this be the theater visit when two men proposed to you?"

Constance whipped around. "Proposed? Caroline Danvers, you cheeky wench, keeping all this to yourself. Who was it? Random drunk men or someone we know?"

Damn. If she shared it was Gerard who proposed, that would land her and the solicitor in a kettle of fish. It wasn't her place to explain Gerard's life with Leo, but if she simply stated Gerard had proposed, that might impact his working relationship with Dorian.

Rather than lie outright, she sidestepped. "Gerard didn't mention you were his client, Your Grace. Not even to me. I hope that reassures you of his discretion."

Dorian closed the door behind them, and she took in a dimly lit room thick with cheroot smoke and conversation hanging in the air.

"May I take a turn at playacting? I'd like to see what I can discover." Connie bounced on her toes like an excited child.

Dorian waved toward the room. "Feel free. He used to rent a room on this street, but I don't know exactly where, or if he still lives there. If you can get anything more specific than that, I'll be indebted to you."

Connie rubbed her hands together. "I'll see what I can do."

The men tracked her cousin's blonde curls through the crowd. Connie stopped here and there to chat, once or twice gesticulating wildly.

"She's in her element," Caro said.

"It would seem that way." Lord Southwyn watched Connie, wearing a bemused smile.

Dorian led them to a table and held up four fingers at the serving woman.

"What did you order?" Lord Southwyn asked.

"I'm not sure, but we're each having one."

The duke's friend sat and turned to Caro. "You said you're shopping for wedding things. Whose wedding?"

Caro nodded to her cousin, who had somehow produced tears and was receiving hugs from three different women. "Hers. They read the banns for the first time this past Sunday."

"Well, I wish him the best of luck."

"Don't you mean you wish *them* the best of luck?" Dorian said.

"I realize we just met, but I suspect she'll be fine no matter what. He's the one who needs the luck."

Caro laughed. The man wasn't wrong. "I am going to ask around too. Perhaps you two can chat with the men and get them talking."

While the patrons inside the coffeehouse were happy to share information on which of the street's buildings rented lodgings, and a few remembered Sherman Snyder, no one had seen him recently. One woman recalled watching him stumble home drunk, which helped them determine the building he lived in.

"Do you think this is how Bow Street runners feel?" Constance asked as they walked toward Sherman's lodgings. "It's a good time, inn'it? Makes me all tingly and energized."

"Are you sure what you're feeling isn't the thrill of befriending half that coffeehouse's patrons while making the other half fall in love with you?" Lord Southwyn leveled a look at her that Caro thought might hold a smidge of reluctant admiration.

"I can't help it if I'm likable." Constance, as usual, was entirely unfazed.

"The men liked your curves, Miss Martin. Not one of

their eyes wandered north of your collarbone the entire time we were in there." Southwyn held open the door to a tall, narrow building that lent rooms by the week.

Caro exchanged an amused glance with Dorian as they entered a small hallway.

"As long as they keep their hands to themselves, what does it matter? I can't control their eyes." Constance shrugged.

"Perhaps if you were slightly less…energetic, there wouldn't be as much to catch their eye." Southwyn sounded nothing short of grumpy.

Constance's smile showed too much teeth, and Caro recognized it for the threat it was.

"I don't feel the need to avoid notice, milord. But if your experience has shown that most women lie like blocks of wood in your presence, I'd reconsider your technique."

Dorian choked on a laugh. "Listening to Oliver and your cousin might be my new favorite hobby." His breath was warm on Caro's ear, and the sensation made her shiver.

"You're choosing to be obtuse and crude, Miss Martin," Lord Southwyn said.

"Am I? No matter. Since I don't care for the burden of your opinions, milord, feel free to keep them to yourself." Constance turned to Caro and Dorian. "How do we know which door belongs to the landlord? And why does this building smell of boiled turnips and wash water?"

Her voice echoed off the tile floor.

A door to their left opened to reveal a rather disgruntled-looking woman.

They'd found the landlady.

Unfortunately, they didn't find Sherman. He'd vacated his room at least nine months prior, and she didn't know where he'd gone. In a turn of reality mirroring fiction, he'd left in the middle of the night and owed a week's rent.

"Apparently, I judged his character correctly," Caro muttered as they found themselves back on the busy street in time to see their carriage round the corner.

Dorian heaved a sigh as they all got in and resumed their seats. "That leaves me with one final thread to pull, and I'm loath to do it."

Caro adjusted her skirts to keep her muddy hem from brushing his legs. "The cousin? Lord Bixby, if I remember correctly. Are you acquainted with him?"

"Bixby is Snyder's cousin?" Lord Southwyn said. "Interesting. I can't recall ever speaking to the man before. Never had reason to, since he's a bit of a bore, from what I understand."

"Why don't you want to speak with Lord Bixby?" Caro tucked a hand in the crook of Dorian's elbow and frowned at the tension radiating up his arm.

Dorian grimaced. "Bixby has little to recommend him as an individual, so he clings to gossip and plays information like cards. To him, social interactions are a game of whist. If I meet with him to discuss this, I am at a disadvantage."

"Apparently being a toady bastard is a family trait," Lord Southwyn commented. "I keep thinking about the way that playwright described him. Said he wasn't handsome or particularly intelligent. How did someone like that manage to sweep Juliet, as well as countless other women, off her feet?"

"To such a degree their purses emptied into his hands," Dorian mused. Some of the tension eased from him. "It is a confounding puzzle, isn't it?"

"Looks aren't everything." Constance shrugged. "If his personality is rubbish as well, it explains why he's using letters written by someone else. I would lay odds that most of the romance is carried out via those letters, and not in person."

It made sense. "I wonder if he's playacting, or genuinely wanting to find love," Caro said.

"One could almost pity the man. Never having a real romance is tragic, don't you think?" Constance glanced around. Finding no sympathy there, she shook her head. "Never mind; he's a toady bastard."

Chapter Twenty

After a morning spent listening to Constance bait Lord Southwyn, Caro was in a fine mood. Which only improved when Dorian asked her to come to him that night. With Constance and Hattie's help, Caro concocted a plan to stay out all night and return in the morning without alerting her aunt and uncle.

However, there was one more thing to deal with, before she spent the night forgetting her worries in the duke's bed. She'd put off having this conversation for too long already, for fear of hurting her friends. But they deserved an answer, and she now had an alternative option to present.

"I've never turned down a marriage proposal before, so please show some grace, Gerard." Caro squeezed his hand. "While I appreciate the situation in which you find yourself at work, I am afraid I cannot help beyond supplying the listening ear of a friend who cares for you both dearly."

Leo rubbed circles on Gerard's back and sent her an understanding smile. "We were afraid you'd say that."

"Your security matters to us, Caro. This could help everyone. You wouldn't have to work such long hours at the bookshop. You could be entirely independent," Gerard said.

She chuckled. "Always the solicitor. Perhaps you should become a barrister. You've a gift for pleading your case."

Gerard grinned, albeit reluctantly. "Guilty as charged,

I'm afraid." Sighing, he leaned back on his sofa and interlaced his fingers with Leo's. "You won't change your mind?"

Caro shook her head. "No. But I have an idea I'd like you to consider, and I've decided to let you both in on a secret I've been keeping."

That caught Leo's attention. A V of concern pinched between his brows, reminding her of Dorian. "Secret? What have you been up to?"

She squirmed in her seat, then quashed the discomfort. There was nothing to be ashamed of in her work. In fact, with the growing popularity of it, there was much to be celebrated. Even though she believed better of her friends, the risk of having them react as her father had made nerves jangle under her skin. Caro squared her shoulders. If they condemned her, she refused to cower like she had with her father. "I've been writing. Rather successfully, as a matter of fact. Under a nom de plume, due to the sensual nature of the novels."

Gerard slowly grinned. "Well done, Caro. I'm proud of you. Would we have heard of your work?"

"I write as Blanche Clementine." She hated the tremor in her voice.

Leo gasped. "Blanche Clementine? Caro, are you putting us on?" When she shook her head, he whistled under his breath. "There was even a bit in the gossip pages about you this morning. The ton is all agog over this latest book—what's it called? A something, something for someone."

"*A Dalliance for Miss Lorraine.*" Relief made her spine go limp, and she sagged in her chair. They weren't judging her or throwing her out of their home. "I didn't know I'd made the gossip pages. And I don't understand why the ton is clamoring for this last story, but I'm grateful for the sales."

"Let me see if I can find it." Leo dug through a stack

of papers on the table beside them. "Here it is. Everyone is talking about you, Caro."

She scanned the page he handed her. There, toward the bottom, sandwiched between commentary on Lady Colville's saffron-yellow gown and a pithy observation on Lord Baldridge's extravagant new carriage, was a mention of Blanche Clementine.

> *The ton might have a new darling to rival the antics of Byron himself. Under every bedroom pillow in London, you might find a copy of* A Dalliance for Miss Lorraine, *the latest salacious novel by Blanche Clementine. Some claim they recognize themselves on the page, and speculation runs rampant regarding the true identity of the author.*

"Interesting." Caro bit her lip. "They think the book is about them? Well, they're wrong. But with so many copies flying off the shelf, I'm not going to argue with them." She set aside the paper. "Now on to my idea. I'm going to buy a property in Kent." A bubble of happiness filled her, remembering the cottage. "I went to see it this week. The village is a decent size, located near larger towns, and apparently the neighbors closest to the cottage are an older gentlemen couple like you two. What if instead of dealing with the partners at Gerard's current firm, you moved to Kent? Set out your shingle near me?"

The men exchanged a look.

Her heart sank when they didn't greet the plan with immediate joy.

"It's something we can discuss," Leo said. "We have so many friends in London. But we'll consider it."

The moment Gerard's logical legal brain took over was obvious. "Caro, who is looking over your publishing contracts? Is everything in writing, or is there a back-alley handshake agreement going on? Are you banking with a reputable institution, or..." She bit her lip and he groaned. "Caroline Danvers, do not tell me you have your earnings in a biscuit tin under your bed."

She covered her face with her hands, laughing with embarrassment, then peeked through her fingers. "It used to be rolled into a wool stocking, if it makes you feel better. At least the tin has a lid."

"We need to ensure your money is safe and accumulating interest. Right now, it's only collecting cat hair. And the contract with the publisher?"

"Of course I read it." She sighed and let her hands fall to her lap. "However, I was so grateful they were printing my books without making me pay up front or giving them a larger share of the sales that I didn't negotiate."

"Now you've done it. Blanche Clementine will be his new project, and you may not have a say in the matter." Leo said it so affectionately a spot in Caro's chest ached. These two were so well matched. They loved one another without reservations, but more than that was the friendship and respect between them. Their relationship didn't come with lists of things they expected their partner to change.

If my parents had enjoyed a marriage like theirs, how different my life would have been.

Gerard's sigh interrupted her musings. It was the sound of a man choosing to breathe deeply rather than swear aloud. "All right. With your permission"—he shot a beleaguered look at Leo—"I'd like to represent your legal and financial interests with your publisher. I'll also offer advice on investments and how best to handle your financial future. If you won't marry me, at least let me donate my expertise toward ensuring your security."

"You're a good friend. Thank you. I will gladly take your counsel. I can't guarantee I'll agree with everything or act on it to your satisfaction, but I will listen and discuss it with you."

"Fair enough. None of the firm's clients are required to take our advice, so it would be disingenuous of me to expect that of you. I just want to know you're making the best decisions possible with the information given." Gerard pointed toward the stack of papers where Leo found the gossip sheet. "Pass Caro the small notebook and pencil, won't you, my love?" When Leo unearthed the items from the pile, he handed them to her. "Please write down your publisher's information. I'll introduce myself and inform them that the illustrious author Blanche Clementine has the protection of legal counsel."

"Thank you, Gerard."

"We're going to take care of you, Caro. And that means taking care of Blanche Clementine as well."

"Are you hungry?" Dorian asked. Caro's stomach let out a low grumble, and her face heated with embarrassment. The duke nodded to the maid—and just like that, Caro knew food would be delivered to the sitting room adjoining his bedchamber. Caro shook her head at the power of an imperious nod. Everyone around him did his bidding without the need for minor things like words.

Caro glanced around the luxurious room, with its gilded woodwork and dark-blue furnishings. Since arriving in his private chambers a few minutes before, she'd been doing her best to not gawk. Yes, the rest of the house was gorgeous. But this room, situated between a dressing room and the bedchamber, was fit for a princess. Or a duchess, comfortable with commanding a legion of servants to do her bidding.

"What does that look mean?"

Caro placed her small bag on the floor beside the bedchamber door and shot Dorian a teasing smirk. "I was wondering what would happen if you snapped your fingers. If a nod alone can order food, what happens if you snap your fingers? Do they have orders to perform magic tricks? Rub your feet, perhaps?" She darted away, laughing when he prowled closer wearing a stern expression she didn't believe for one second.

He caught her around the waist and stole a kiss. It had only been a day since they'd been alone like this, yet it felt like months. Resting his forehead on hers, he heaved a sigh. "Am I being high-handed?"

"Perhaps we should ask the maid what she thinks the answer is to that question."

"Apologies. I was trying to take care of you and protect your reputation by not pouncing on you like a starving man in front of the servants."

Caro laughed. "After I've shown up, alone, to join you in your private rooms? It might be too late to protect my reputation." She draped herself on a couch by the fire that turned out to be as comfortable as it looked. "Lucky for you, I have no reputation to speak of. At least not in the way you are used to thinking of women and their good names. The servants will speculate on my presence here. That can't be helped."

His eyes darkened, and the groove between his eyebrows turned cavernous under the weight of his scowl. "Their duties have nothing to do with wondering at our relationship."

"If you truly believe that, you're a fool. Maids, footmen, even the boot boy—they see everything, and they talk amongst themselves." She pushed an errant curl off her face. While she didn't mean to be confrontational, there was no way to end the conversation now. "Dorian, the servants are *people* with thoughts and opinions that are entirely out of your control. If you think they aren't discussing us right this moment, you're living in a fantasy world."

"I deserve that, I suppose. For what it's worth, you say no one cares about your reputation, but *I do*." He crossed the room to a slim table and pulled a tiny box from a drawer, then joined her on the couch. Instantly, the heat of him seeped into her skin, and she leaned into his warmth to rest her head on his shoulder.

"I'm sorry if I was high-handed just now. I will try to be aware of that in the future." She felt him kiss the top of her head, and the sweetness of the gesture made her breath catch in her throat.

"You're capable of quite a pretty apology when you put your mind to it, Your Grace," she teased.

His chuckle rumbled against her cheek. The box he'd fetched from the table appeared in her hand. "Here. I bought you this."

"I don't need gifts, Dorian." She glanced at his face when his chuckle grew.

"You'll want this one. Trust me."

She raised a skeptical eyebrow but opened the box. Inside were two oddly shaped lumps of beeswax and cotton. "I'm confused."

"I hate the idea of my snoring keeping you awake. But I *really* hate the idea of you sleeping away from me. I believe I'm greedy when it comes to you, and I selfishly want you beside me. Which led me to asking Hastings if he knew someone who might help, since Hastings knows everyone."

"A special power of his, I take it?" She was no less confused about the lumps of wax but was enjoying the tale.

"Definitely, and one of the myriad things that make him an excellent butler. He knows a man who dabbles in inventions involving the home."

"Of course he does."

Dorian nodded sagely. "That man sent Hastings these." He held up one of the wax-and-cotton lumps. "In Homer's *The Odyssey*, the sailors stuff their ears with wax to save them from the calls of the sirens. These are supposed to be more comfortable than Homer's concept. I thought they were worth trying. If they aren't sufficient, then we can find something else."

"You're a sweet man." She stared at the contents of the box and knew her smile was a little silly. "This was incredibly thoughtful. Please thank Hastings for me."

A knock at the door broke the moment. Dorian rose. She heard him quietly thank the servant, then watched as he maneuvered a tea cart into the room, set with several dishes, two glasses, and a bottle of wine.

"You should eat before I distract you and it goes to waste." He opened the bottle of wine and poured two glasses.

Caro set aside the gift he'd given her and rose to inspect the food. She plucked a red jelly from the tray of desserts. Raspberry burst on her tongue. She moaned, then sighed in bliss. "I could eat that every day and die happy." Selecting a piece or slice of everything that looked appealing, she built her dinner on a plate. Dorian sipped his wine but didn't take a plate for himself. "Aren't you hungry?"

A wolfish grin lit his face. "Very. But what I'm craving is

between your legs." He punctuated the statement with a kiss, and she smiled against his lips.

"Promises, promises, naughty duke." She reveled in the way his gaze heated the longer he looked at her.

It was only their second night together, but it was easier this time to set aside the Caroline Danvers who was cool and logical and who prided herself on making rational decisions. Here, with him, she wanted to be Blanche Clementine, who could command a duke and leave inhibitions on the floor with her clothing. Blanche felt familiar now, as if Caro was allowing the two parts of herself to knit together.

Popping another jelly in her mouth, she let the sweet and tart coat her tongue.

Dorian carried his wine to the sofa and relaxed in a casual sprawl on the thick velvet cushion. He'd met her at the door in breeches, a shirt, and bare feet. This was the duke in his natural environment. Real life, not a night out of time in an inn. Just as inviting her and Constance to join him and Lord Southwyn this morning had been letting her into his day, this evening he was inviting her into his night.

She set her plate on a small table beside him that looked so delicately carved she'd only trust it to carry the weight of a dish and a glass of wine. Holding his hungry gaze, she unfastened the tapes of her gown, then shrugged the heavy wool to the floor. The last of plain, boring Caroline Danvers was discarded for the night, along with her petticoat and stays.

His chest rose and fell like a bellows with each piece of clothing she removed. A flush covered his cheeks.

Caro turned her back, then lifted the hem of her shift inch by inch. A strangled noise told her she had his complete attention. With a flick, she whipped it over her head and sent it to the floor.

Dorian's groan was satisfying, but when she bent over a

little farther than necessary to untie her garters and do away with her stockings, he muttered an appreciative curse, and she grinned.

She turned and let him look his fill, as she did the same. Between his hard, open thighs was an even harder ridge straining the buttons of his breeches to an obscene degree. Anticipation prickled under her skin, raising goosebumps the fire did nothing to counter. As she approached him, conscious of the way his eyes followed the sway of her hips, Caro felt like a pagan goddess, bringing a man to his knees to worship her.

Her dinner could wait a little longer, she decided. After all, her duke had said he was hungry. She stopped in front of him, between his spread thighs. Immediately, his hands gripped her hips, then pulled her close. Gently, utterly at odds with the fierce desire in his eyes, he placed a light kiss on her inner thigh, then rested that leg on the sofa beside him.

His fingers traced a path from her foot, up her calf and thigh, over her hip, then around front to brush the damp curls between her legs. "Watch me, Caro. Let me see how this feels for you."

The pang of nerves made her bite her lip. "No one has ever kissed me there."

"Have you imagined it?" His breath was hot on her core, but the infernal man seemed determined to take his time.

She never would have expected the Duke of Holland, whom she'd wrongfully thought quiet and stoic, to be such a talkative and affectionate lover.

"I imagine a lot of things. My brain likes to stay occupied."

"Have I mentioned how much I admire your brain?" The usually rough timbre of his voice had deepened even more. He placed an open-mouthed kiss between her legs, then pulled back. And that's when she knew he was teasing her.

"You're enjoying torturing me, aren't you?"

"A little, yes." His eyes were dark blue and full of mischief. Any other time, she'd have relished the humor there. At that moment, though, she feared she'd burst if he didn't lick and kiss her as promised.

Phoebe, her dominating heroine, would make her needs clear. At the inn, Dorian had seemed to like it when she took control. And while she didn't need to be in charge all the time, it was freeing to know she could be.

Caro threaded her fingers through his wavy hair and, watching his face for any objection, guided his head to exactly where she wanted it. He moaned. At the first touch of his hot tongue, she gasped.

Blue eyes devoured her as thoroughly as his mouth, entranced by the way her breasts shook with each breath. When she tugged lightly on his hair, those eyes fluttered closed for a moment before opening again to watch her.

Yes, her duke liked it when she made demands of him.

It didn't take long before his wicked tongue had her legs quaking, and she feared they'd give way. Dorian's arms wrapped around her thighs, keeping her where he wanted as surely as her hand on his head held him in place.

She came with a keening cry, while black dots danced behind her eyelids.

Strong hands guided her down to the sofa. "My gorgeous Caro. You have no idea what seeing you take your pleasure does to me."

With hurried movements, Dorian pulled his shirt over his head and shucked his breeches. "We didn't take precautions against pregnancy last time, but we will from now on."

As she watched, he donned a sheath. The firelight cast his cheekbones in sharp relief. "I have sat in this room countless times imagining what we'd look like together. See?" He gently turned her to face a tall mirror on the wall, so they knelt sideways on the couch. When he hugged her from behind, their reflection made her gasp. Against the soft paleness of her belly, he spread his fingers wide. She watched as one hand drifted down to the wet curls between her legs, while the other cupped a full breast, then lightly pinched her nipple.

"Do you want me, Caro? Do you want to watch me fuck you?"

It seemed it was his turn to be in charge, and she was happy to cede control. Dorian laid open-mouthed kisses along her neck, and Caro shivered at the sensations.

"Yes. God, yes."

The smile he flashed was pure sin, then it fell away as he entered her. "Do you like watching us?"

He set a deep, body-shaking pace. Caro tried to answer, but the sound was a garbled noise that might have been *yes* or *more* or something else entirely. Tension from her core had spread until her muscles, her nerves, even the air in her lungs pulled tight with the promise of bliss.

"That's it. Fuck, you're beautiful when you come." The fingers between her thighs gentled but did not stop as her body clutched his. A moment later, he followed her to his peak.

The mirror showed her breathing slowing with the rise and fall of her chest as his hands drifted over her skin. Gentle explorations this time, rather than frantic movements. These were the touches of a lover taking the time to learn. To savor. Caro rested her head against his cheek.

She felt safe. Desired. Like she was seen without judgment or a list of things he needed her to change. In that moment, with her senses full of bergamot and the smell of sex, something inside her shifted into place.

"So beautiful, sweet Caro. You absolutely undo me."

The words rumbled in her ear.

She'd been undone for years. Trying so hard to keep disparate parts of herself from touching. Whether Dorian knew it or not, he was helping her gather those pieces and knit them together. Caroline, Blanche, a cousin, a friend. A woman too full of goals and dreams to pay any mind to the shame that had been heaped on her for so many years.

And at that moment, her heart was full.

Chapter Twenty-One

❧

"Lady Waterstone, it has been too long." Dorian's mother greeted their hostess with the faux society fondness everyone in their circle seemed to accept as authentic. It was an affectation he'd known since childhood, listening to his mother preside over tea and gossip during her days at home, but today it struck a discordant note. Lord and Lady Waterstone responded in a similar fashion.

Dorian made his bow to the couple, then stepped to the side of the hall and tried to blend in with the other guests.

In the carriage on the way here, the dowager mentioned a few women she'd like him to meet who had returned to Town in the past week. He'd sent her a quelling look, but she was immune to his lack of enthusiasm.

Thanks to the servants, whom he appreciated more than ever for their discretion, he'd fallen asleep with Caro in his arms every night this week. During the afternoons, she worked in the library, which looked emptier each time he went in the room.

Every volume of Shakespeare had been pulled and searched, yielding another dozen letters. She'd sat with him last night as he read them. And yes, the pain of betrayal was there. Thankfully, the edges of the emotion were no longer sharp enough to shred his soul.

Except for one letter. That one had taken his breath away.

Juliet had written to Sherman, recalling the last time Dorian had been home. And while there were plenty of failings she could have complained about—he saw that now—she'd lied. Flagrantly, without any tether to factual events. The injustice of being maligned by someone he'd thought he could trust had been compounded by the agonizing knowledge that he'd never know why she did it.

Iron bars had clamped his lungs, and he'd struggled to find air. Caro had knelt between his knees, cradling his face, and breathed with him. Inhale. Exhale. Soothing words. Complete acceptance, even when he was showing weakness.

No one at the Waterstones' ball would do that for him.

Unless Oliver is around somewhere, Dorian corrected himself.

If he could, he'd leave here, pick up Caro from the shop, and bring her home to bed. Forget the gauntlet of her aunt and uncle and his mother they'd maneuvered through before now. They were fully grown, not children hiding an illicit affair. He hated having to lie or hide their times together and knew the subterfuge would wear thin quickly.

Wandering through the rooms full of people, he offered smiles but little conversation.

What would Caro think of these events? All the watching eyes and polite nodding to people you hoped you wouldn't have to engage with in actual conversation. It was the exact opposite of the life she said she wanted.

There were similarities to how she'd described growing up as a vicar's daughter. Everyone watching, expecting perfection. He suspected she'd feel the ton was familiar territory. Just with more satin and diamonds.

Inside the ballroom, couples mingled and laughed while a quartet provided ambiance to the evening. As he turned the corner to join the fray, the scent of orange blossom stopped him in his tracks.

He searched the assembled company for Caro's dark, shiny hair and eyes sparking with intelligence. Alas, no beauty assessed him from across the room with full lips and a stubbornly pointed chin. Instead, potted orange trees lined the sides of the room, lending their color and scents to the space. The stab of disappointment actually made him wince.

A blonde woman he vaguely recognized sidled up to him and stepped too close for comfort or decorum. Her bottom pressed against the fall of his trousers, and Dorian tried to step away. Was she Lord Stropford's wife or mistress? He couldn't remember. "Terribly sorry, Your Grace," she murmured. When she leaned into him, Dorian reared back but didn't have anywhere to go. "Blanche was right, wasn't she?" The woman shot a deliberate look at his groin, then winked. "Remember me when you're ready for a new, ahem, heroine, Your Grace."

However much she'd had to drink, it was three glasses too many. A shudder of revulsion made him twitch. Half of what she'd said made no sense, but the inuendo hadn't been subtle. "You should seek out the retiring room." Dorian stepped to the side, squeezing between a planter and the wall. While he might not remember if she was Stropford's wife or mistress, he was positive she wasn't his problem, and he'd be damned if he allowed her to be.

The dowager approached, making the blonde flounce away instead of following him. "She should be ashamed of herself, rubbing against you like that. One can't blame her for the attempt, but I don't like her methods."

"If she's on your list, the answer is no," he said.

She cringed. "I should think not. However, we should

find the newest additions I mentioned in the carriage. I'd like a grandchild or three to keep me active in my dotage."

Dorian rolled his eyes but smiled. "You're hardly an old crone needing children to give you a reason to get out of bed in the morning, Mother."

She shrugged. "And yet, neither of us grow younger." Surveying the room, she flicked the tip of her fan toward the wall near the quartet. "Miss Frances Simmons has been creating quite a stir. Good family, healthy dowry, and rather nice eyes."

He followed the tip of her fan and recoiled. "She looks like she's slipped away from her governess to play dress-up. No. Besides, I told you I'm not looking right now. Not yet."

Undeterred, the fan turned toward another corner of the room. "Mrs. Marshall, widow. Excellent connections, independently wealthy from her first marriage but quite vocal about wanting to remarry and have a family."

Dorian ignored his mother. After all, she was ignoring what he wanted; he'd do the same to her. He plucked a glass of something he prayed was alcoholic from the tray of a nearby footman. "Thank you," he murmured to the servant. Then, "I said no," to his mother.

"You can't even spare her a glance?" Gloria sighed heavily, the picture of put-upon motherhood. "If this stubbornness is due to your little bluestocking bookseller, you and I shall have words at the end of the night."

"Kindly leave my relationship with Miss Danvers between her and me." The times during his life when he'd outright defied or argued with his mother could be counted on one hand. But the way she spoke about Caro made him clench his jaw. He would fight over this. And that, perhaps more than the constant thinking about Caro and wanting her near, told him his emotions were thoroughly engaged.

Damn, he was falling in love with her. Absently, he rubbed at his shoulder, where he knew she'd left a mark the night before. This morning, she'd kissed it and whispered, "Mine," when she thought he was asleep. The spot warmed at the memory.

The dowager huffed, dragging him back to the moment. "If this is how you're going to be tonight, I will need a drink to see me through."

He turned back toward the footman. Caro's voice echoed in his brain. *The servants are people... If you think they aren't discussing us right this moment, you're living in a fantasy world.* "Another glass for my matchmaking mother, please." The man's lips quirked as he held out the tray. "Would you care to weigh in on the matter? If you had to dance with one of them to satisfy your mother, which would you choose? The blonde with the nice eyes or the widow with the eager womb?"

The footman's jaw worked for a moment before he answered. "The blonde often sneaks away to the balcony with... people. The widow seems nice. If it was me, I'd ask the miss with red hair over by the large fern. When she calls with her mother, she's kind to the staff."

"The redhead, you say? Excellent. Might I convince you to leave the tray of champagne? I fear this will be a long evening."

The footman set the tray on a nearby table, bowed with a smile, then departed.

Gloria watched Dorian with an expression he couldn't decipher. "What does that look mean?" he asked.

She took a glass from the tray. "Do you know him?"

"Know who? The footman? No. Why do you ask?"

Confusion wrinkled her brow. "You were quite familiar; I assumed you knew him. I've never seen you so friendly toward a servant who isn't in your employ."

"Am I not permitted to speak to people I'm not paying?" Dorian theatrically wiped his brow in relief. "I'm relieved to hear it. Now I needn't speak to a single person in this room."

His mother grumbled, "Frustrating man. You know what I am saying. It *isn't done*."

Perhaps it should be. Perhaps treating servants and shop-keepers as if they were people instead of furniture should come into fashion. The thought was so clear in his head he nearly said it out loud. Except in his mind, the person speaking wasn't him, but Caro.

Following an impulse, and refusing to contemplate its source, he changed the topic. "Which is more important to you—me marrying a woman from a good family, or me being happy and possibly giving you grandchildren?"

She pursed her lips. "Couldn't you be both happy and married to a woman of good standing? Must one cancel the other?"

"I'm asking about your priorities. Is my happiness, regardless of who I find it with, more important than making a socially prudent match?" Why he was pushing this line of questioning, right this minute, he didn't know. Except that he couldn't look around this room without wanting to turn to Caro and comment on something. Or slip down the hall to a dark room and make her laugh, then moan.

The woman had burrowed under his skin, nearer to his heart than he'd realized.

"I'm afraid I don't understand the question." The dow-ager gestured to the room at large. "You're surrounded by excellent marital prospects. Even the redhead the footman mentioned is an option, although her dowry isn't terribly impressive. The only choice you need make is which one to court. They're all excellent candidates for your next duchess. Again, is this about your Miss Danvers?"

Yes, actually. "Merely speaking in hypotheticals."

Gloria emptied her glass in one long swallow, like a woman in the desert at an oasis. Shooting her son an annoyed look, she exchanged her empty glass for a full one. "I'm going to enjoy the evening socializing with my friends. Perhaps you can befriend the maid while I'm gone, or offer to help washing up in the kitchen, should you grow bored of hiding in this corner." Shaking her head, she swanned away and was soon lost in the crowd of velvet, feathered turbans, and glittering jewels.

Dorian sipped his champagne as he leaned against the wall near an orange tree. After a moment, he spied Oliver amidst the sea of black coats. Finally, a friend. Dorian met him at the edge of the dance floor.

"Bixby is in the card room. Fancy a round of whist and some light interrogation?" Oliver said.

"Not particularly, but an opportunity is an opportunity."

In the card room, a cheroot haze settled above the heads of the guests—men in black jackets and one woman in shining red satin. When he and Oliver entered, a hush fell over the players, then dissolved back into chatter after a few seconds.

Lady Agatha Dalrymple sat across from her husband, Mr. Alfred Dalrymple. Together they seemed to be dominating a game of whist, communicating silently in a way Dorian suspected could only happen after decades together.

Lord Bixby and another man Dorian couldn't recall the name of were no match for the older couple, if their grumpy expressions were any indication.

"Ah, Lord Southwyn, Duke. Are you here to offer more of a challenge than these two? I am afraid their boasts overstated their ability," Lady Agatha said. Mr. Dalrymple smiled at his wife, obviously enjoying her. Dorian had always liked the man.

"Southwyn and Holland can wait. We'll rally during the next trick, won't we, Dobbins?" Lord Bixby said.

Oliver shrugged. "We'll wait until there are seats available at the table, milady. Don't mind if we watch, do you, gentlemen?"

The trick went to the Dalrymples. Bixby's jaw hardened until the man's teeth were in danger of cracking.

Lady Agatha, bless her, kept up a stream of increasingly blunt questions interspersed with pointed commentary as she and her husband claimed trick after trick. "Lord Southwyn, will we soon hear wedding bells for Miss Althea? I'd thought you would rush down the aisle, given your interesting history with her family." She tsked at the other players. "Lord Bixby, hearts are trumping this round, so do not try to claim that trick. Is that your problem? Do you not understand the rules of play?" She plucked the four cards from the middle and added it to the others at her elbow.

Oliver pulled a chair over from the nearest table and settled his lanky frame into the seat. "Long engagements are unremarkable. Miss Althea and I will walk down the aisle when the time is right."

Pulling another chair over to flank his friend, Dorian heard what Oliver didn't say. That it was Althea who refused to set a date, not Oliver.

"Hurry it along, if you please. I would like to celebrate your wedding before my bones are too old to climb the church steps."

"Rushing into marriage hasn't done anyone favors, my love," Mr. Dalrymple commented.

The older man's wife shot him an exasperated look, although fondness warmed her tone. "Says the man who danced with me only twice before asking for my hand."

"You were the tallest girl in the room and a beautiful widow. You knew what you did and did not want in a second husband, and I hoped I fit the requirements. Besides, I had to act quickly if I was to avoid spending the rest of my life with a crick in my neck from looking down at my bride," Mr. Dalrymple teased. "When it's right, it's right. Best not to rush if they aren't feeling that rightness. Not everyone will be as lucky as we are, Agatha."

Lady Agatha laid down an ace, then faced Oliver, ignoring the groan from the other team. "Is it not right, Southwyn, and that is why you tarry? Your Grace, what say you about all this? You are well-versed in the joys of a love match. And I expect we shall see rather interesting things from you yet, given the talk about Town. Should your friend sweep Miss Althea off her feet or wait?"

Shifting in his seat, Dorian didn't know what talk about Town she referenced, but he suppressed those questions as well as his doubts about the compatibility of Miss Althea and Oliver. Instead, he opted for diplomacy. "Like your husband, I believe finding the right person is more important than a predetermined timeline. But I also trust Oliver to always act in the best interest of his fiancée. Besides, she has an excellent family, who will help her navigate the path to matrimony. A useful asset, wouldn't you say, Lord Bixby?"

The other man jerked his gaze from the cards he held. "What was that?"

"Family. Aren't they a wonderful asset while out in society?" Dorian tried for a casual, friendly tone. "I only have my mother and my late wife's cousin, I'm afraid. I seem to recall you have several family members rattling around London to keep you company."

Oliver, bless him, picked up the conversational thread

and played his part to perfection. "Not so great when they're a burden to the family tree—am I right?" In a loud aside to the Dalrymples, he said, "Doesn't everyone have a few calling themselves family they'd rather not claim? I'm sure Bixby can relate. We've all heard stories."

The corner of Lady Agatha's lip—rouged red to match her gown—twitched as she exchanged a look with her husband. "Not all family is worth claiming, in my opinion. And not all family arrives by blood. I am relieved to know Miss Althea need not be a matter to concern myself with. But I do worry that you have been listening to gossipy chatter, Lord Southwyn."

Oliver reared back with a hand to his chest in a theatrical response that made Mr. Dalrymple chuckle. "Not I, my lady. I am a man of logic and science. As such, I only give credence to stories that show predictable patterns." Dropping his playful tone, he turned his head to speak directly to Lord Bixby. "Not all our family members are dearly beloved, and one must question when some still coddle those who make repeated offenses."

Dorian accepted a snifter of brandy from a footman but did not imbibe. Multiple glasses of champagne were turning his head as fizzy as the drink. So, he watched. With Oliver speaking, this chat-turned-interrogation seemed less personal, leaving Dorian to observe. If Bixby knew and approved of his cousin's actions, his response would show it. In theory, anyway.

Lord Bixby and Dobbins were having a silent conversation of their own. For his part, Dobbins looked positively gleeful. Dorian decided on the spot that he didn't like him. If Dobbins was enjoying the conversation, it was reasonable to assume Bixby knew of Sherman's activities as well.

So it came as a surprise when Bixby glared at his friend. "Unfortunately, some of us"—he paused meaningfully—"bow to familial pressures and provide introductions for extended family members. Once those connections are made, there's no going back, and we cease to be in control of the situation."

Then, Lord Bixby did something Dorian hadn't predicted. As he placed his cards on the table, he folded his hands over the pile and spoke directly to Dorian. "Our family members might do things we find appalling, and we are left with little recourse but to distance ourselves the best we can. I believe you also know this feeling, Your Grace, regarding your late wife's cousin. In this matter, you and I are aligned in our disapproval. I offer you my deepest sympathies as you muddle through potential ramifications that are entirely beyond your control yet impact you directly."

Interesting.

Lady Agatha clapped. "Well said, Lord Bixby. Lord Dobbins, now would be an ideal moment to take your sniggering elsewhere. Like minds are welcome in our game of whist, and you fail to meet that criterion." She smiled at her husband. "Darling, would you be so kind as to bring me a drink and something from the refreshment room? Winning makes me peckish."

Mr. Dalrymple winked, then set his cards face down on the table. "Absolutely. Holland, would you mind stepping in? Southwyn, you can take Dobbins's place." He walked around the table to kiss his wife's creased cheek, then removed her empty glass and leveled a stern look at Lord Dobbins until the man shuffled off.

Oliver and Dorian took their seats and picked up the cards.

Lady Agatha said, not unkindly, "I am not sure what this is all about, but I hope we are not sitting to play with our enemies."

Offering a hand to Dorian, Lord Bixby said, "I offer no ill will, and I will do nothing to harm you or yours. If you'd like to meet in private, I can equip you with valuable information."

Dorian shook his hand, accepting the offer of peace. For now. "I appreciate that. Thank you."

"Excellent. I am happy to see everyone getting along. Despite the color of my gown, a bloodstain would have been a beast to clean if this had devolved to fisticuffs."

Chapter Twenty-Two

*I*f he has a penis made of gold, you can just say so." Hattie locked the door of the shop behind Caro, then hung the key on its hook behind the counter.

"Excuse me?" Caro laughed and shook her head, wondering if she'd misheard through her weariness. After working a few hours this evening in Bloomsbury, while Dorian and his mother were out, Caro was ready for some time with her lately neglected manuscript and her bed.

However, Hattie was not in a laughing mood. One by one, they worked together snuffing the lights until a single lantern illuminated the bookshop. The mass of humanity that made up London still buzzed and surged on the other side of the windows.

With the store locked tight for the night, Hattie finally turned to Caro and resumed the conversation. "What are you doing, Caroline Danvers? I saw the letter you wrote to Mrs. Adams. You should be planning your move to Kent and writing every night. Instead, Connie and I are concocting stories to explain your absence, while you spend every moment you can playing tickle the pickle with the duke. The Caro I know would write the damn book, finish his bloody library, and protect her heart. So, what are you doing?"

Caro crossed her arms to buffer the sting of truth. "Has

this been brewing all week? You haven't said a word about being concerned before now."

Throwing her hands in the air, Hattie gestured toward the street beyond the shop. "I thought it was a one-time thing. Something to get him out of your system. But the longer this goes on, the more likely those people will find out you're enjoying bedroom activities with a damned peer of the realm."

"Those people? What people?" Caro shrugged off her pelisse and tried to untie her bonnet ribbon, but her fingers were shaking.

"Everyone on that street would judge you for tupping a duke, and you know it," Hattie hissed. "Any sort of safety you have outside these doors could disappear in a blink if the menfolk decide your affair means you're open for business. Your father shaming you for writing erotic stories is nothing compared to what they can do to you. *Nothing*. You want to know what it feels like to be hunted every time you leave the house? To constantly jump at shadows and see danger in every stranger's eyes? All it takes is the wrong man discovering you aren't above reproach, and they'll run you to ground faster than a hound on a fox." Hattie's voice broke, and Caro's heart splintered with it.

This was fear, then. Fear for her because of whatever had happened to Hattie. Those events had hurt her so deeply she eschewed the possibility of a romance. "Hattie, darling, if you ever want to talk about it, you know I'm—"

Her cousin cut her off with a wave of her hand, effectively closing the topic, just as she had each time Caro or Constance tried to bring it up. "I am trying to protect you. The longer you let this go on, the worse it will be for you. Heartbreak isn't the worst-case scenario, Caroline. No matter how much time you spend in his fancy townhome, you still have to come back here. To a bookshop in a part of London that isn't safe to venture out in after dark." Hattie clutched Caro's biceps, her gaze hard. "You aren't one of them. He's from a different world, and if anyone finds out about you two, they will chew you up and spit you out. Think, for the love of God."

A tear slipped down Caro's cheek, unnoticed until the salty drop reached the corner of her mouth. Cupping her cousin's elbows, they stood locked together. Hattie, a woman who thrived on practicality, logic, and routine, shook like a leaf under her palms.

Hattie's fear for her was honest, and Caro would be a horrible friend if she met that with anything less than vulnerability.

Even so, she was loath to admit aloud what she knew deep inside. "It's going to break my heart no matter when it ends. When he chooses his society wife, it will be over. Until then, we are living a fantasy. Yet that fantasy feels more real every time I fall asleep beside him. I'm too far gone, Hattie."

Tears flowed freely now, and her laughter tasted bitter in her mouth. These feelings had grown too fast over such a short time. "Did you know I actually am coming to *like* his snoring? He bought these wax plugs for my ears." A watery laugh escaped. Of all the things to mention when speaking of loving him. "They work, though. They change the sound, and now his snores are a sort of reassurance that he's there." Caro sat on the padded chair by the window and stared up at Hattie. "I can love him for as long as possible, then keep breathing when it's over. That's it. But I am being careful. He always sends a carriage for me. I'm never walking alone after dark."

Pink stained her cousin's cheeks, but Caro couldn't name the specific emotion. Then, as if reaching a decision, Hattie's jaw firmed, deepening the dimple in her chin. "I would feel better if the carriage was unmarked, to protect you. You cover your face with a veil and don't stop anywhere between your door and his."

Caro nodded. "I promise. I'll be smart and safe."

Hattie sighed. "It's too late for smart."

Deep in the store, a door closed, and they both turned. Faint light wavered from the office, glowing brighter until Constance stepped into view. The lantern she held illuminated her puffy face.

Immediately, thoughts of Holland, and Hattie's dire predictions were cast aside. "Connie, what's wrong?" Caro hurried over and pushed a damp tendril of blonde hair off her cheek.

"Walter has to meet a shipment on the coast and may not be back in time for the wedding." Fresh tears overflowed her large blue eyes.

Caro and Hattie exchanged a glance. Their reservations about Walter had fallen on deaf ears. But neither wished to see Constance hurting like this. Hattie approached more slowly, and Caro could tell their conversation from moments ago still strained her composure.

"You're not getting married for another two weeks. What business could possibly take him so far as to miss his own wedding?" Caro asked.

Constance sniffed and wiped her nose with the back of her hand. "We might have to postpone. But the order has already been placed with the butcher for the breakfast, and we've paid a portion of the bill up front."

"Surely the butcher will apply the funds toward a new date. There's plenty of time," Hattie said.

Shaking her head, Constance wailed, "But what if this means he doesn't want to marry me after all? *Who* is fine with postponing a wedding, just because a shipment is arriving earlier than expected? And yes, he says those people are not the sort you want to keep waiting. He sounded so reasonable, and I absolutely hate all of it!"

Caro sighed. Smuggling and merchants went hand in hand, but something about this didn't make sense. "Are you more concerned with the inconvenience to everyone because you may have to reschedule, the danger your muttonheaded fiancé is putting himself in, or the worry that this is the first delay of many, and your dream man might not be so perfect after all?"

Hattie's eyes widened. "That's a bit blunt, don't you think?"

Caro gestured toward their watering pot of a cousin. "Constance is the most obnoxiously cheerful person we know and supremely confident with every man she meets. Yet she's like *this*. Clarification is needed, wouldn't you agree?"

Hattie glanced between them and sighed. "I'll make tea. Connie, find your mother's biscuit tin. Caro, check that the back door is secure, then meet us upstairs in the bedroom."

Like dutiful soldiers, war-torn after their emotional battles, they each toddled off in different directions to follow orders.

Several minutes later, Caro entered their room to see Constance on the bed, wrapped in a blanket. Cradling the tin of sweets in one hand and Gingersnap in the other, she didn't appear to be actively crying anymore. Caro scooted to sit at the head of the bed on one side. Shortly after, Hattie arrived with the tea tray. Connie nibbled despondently on a biscuit. Down the hall, a clock chimed the hour, breaking the silence.

Caro's stomach growled, reminding her she hadn't eaten yet, so she reached for the tin. If they waited long enough, Constance would eventually share what was on her mind.

Hattie poured them each a cup, then settled in beside

Constance. Several more moments passed and two more biscuits were consumed before their cousin spoke.

"What if the wedding doesn't happen? Everyone knows I'm getting married. If Walter postpones, or calls it off altogether, I won't be able to show my face on the street for months. Maybe years."

"Is that the main worry?" Hattie asked.

Constance shrugged one shoulder as she stroked Gingersnap in her lap. "We quarreled. I've always known he deals with smugglers. Show me one cloth merchant who doesn't with this damned war. I wanted to go with him, but he wouldn't hear of it. Said it wouldn't be proper. So I said it would be perfectly acceptable to travel together once we're married, and I was excited to join him on the next trip. He got angry. Like that." She snapped her fingers, making the cat jerk his head up at the sound. "Walter says I will be too busy taking care of our home and children...but I don't know if I want children right away. I thought we'd have so much to do with his business and my work here. It was as if he was suddenly someone else. Instead of the man who wants to make me happy, he was yelling and unilaterally deciding how I'll spend my time."

"No wonder you're emotional. If it were me, I'd be irate." Caro cradled her cup to her chest, hoping the warmth would soothe her.

Constance gave them a sad smile. "I know I'm not the calmest person. It's kind of you to say I'm not being too emotional."

"Not too emotional," Hattie confirmed. "My response would be more like raging curses at his ancestors rather than tears of worry. But it would be equal in scale, I'm sure."

"What were you two arguing about when I came down?"

Caro sighed. "My feelings are too deep with Dorian. Hattie has concerns."

Hattie snorted. "An understatement."

Constance rested her head on Caro's shoulder. "Why don't you end it?"

Leaning her head against the wall, Caro sighed as memories of the last few weeks replayed in her mind. His wide smile that day on the ice. Kissing him for the first time. How he'd begged to know her. The way he held her at night, as if she was precious. "Because the desire for him can be so overwhelming I think at times I'll forget to breathe with wanting him."

"You've fallen in love." There was no question in Connie's voice.

"Yes. Or so near as to not be able to tell the difference. It's too late to save myself from the fall."

"Might as well enjoy the tumble, then, eh?"

Hattie snorted. "Excellent pun, Constance. Blanche Clementine would be proud."

"I had a suspicion I'd find you in here with her." Dorian's mother entered his study after the most cursory of taps.

Annoyance made him level a glare at the dowager. "Good afternoon, Mother. May I help you with something?" Thankfully, he and Caro were sitting in the paisley wingback chairs by the fireplace—fully clothed and each in their own seat. Continuing the conversation they'd been having before the interruption, he said, "The chairs are ugly. I've been considering having them reupholstered. Tracking down Sherman, and everything else that's happened, has been a higher priority. But I agree—they're ghastly."

Caro rose and offered her seat to his mother. Dorian stood and motioned Caro to his. "There, if everyone is settled"—he sent a pointed look at Gloria—"what can I do for you?" While Caro had never gone into detail about what Gloria had said during their little tête-à-tête a few weeks prior, he knew his mother. The realization he'd had at the Waterstones' ball earlier in the week held true. As much as he loved Gloria, he wouldn't let her hurt Caro.

Seeing them together in his study sent a pang of longing through him. At once, he could see a future so clearly where these two strong women grew to respect each other. A child played with a puzzle on the floor, and Caro's waist curved with another. He'd hear her laugh well into their dotage and watch silver overtake her hair.

"Are you quite well, Dorian? You look like you're about to swoon." Gloria's voice yanked him bank to reality. The dowager settled her accessories and drapes of fabric about her. The little ritual was so familiar it eased some of his annoyance at her intrusion and soothed the ache left by the scene he'd imagined.

"I believe men faint. Women swoon."

"What rot," both women said, then glanced at each other in surprise.

"If you're well, then kindly explain what I interrupted. You two sounded like co-conspirators." Now that her bits and bobs and fluttery fringes were in place, she faced him with an expression he was all too familiar with. Dorian sighed and brought the chair from his desk and placed it beside Caro's ugly paisley seat.

Gloria had learned long ago to weaponize silence. Not in a petty way...usually. More often in a "I have no intention of deviating from this topic until you give me the information I require" kind of way.

One thing she'd always done well as a parent was communicate her expectations. Whether it be the education standards she and his father held for him as a child, or now, when she made it clear they'd be discussing nothing else until Dorian cracked like an egg and shared his troubles.

An ache began behind his left eye. "Mother, Caro, would either of you like me to order a tea tray?" He had to try.

In answer, Caro shook her head, and the dowager raised one imperious eyebrow. "If you mean to distract me with cakes and tea, it won't work. Just as it hasn't worked since you were six. Something is weighing on my only son's shoulders—something distracting enough to interfere with my plans. And we both know how I feel about interference in my plans."

He glanced at Caro. "She won't leave until she's satisfied. Mules are less stubborn than my mother." And maybe telling Gloria how vital Caro had been to his search for answers would soften the dowager toward her. After all, as a deeply intelligent woman, she respected that trait in others.

Wanting these two women to find common ground might be a losing battle. Hell, it might be the most far-fetched aspect of that future he'd envisioned. If there was any chance of that coming to fruition, they needed to start somewhere. He heaved a sigh.

"Juliet was having an affair."

The bald truth of it should have been a conversational bomb, sending disbelief and denial like shrapnel. And yet, Gloria merely nodded.

Dorian bit back the acidic words he wanted to spew. The only one he'd told back then had been Oliver. "You knew."

"I suspected. But I didn't know with whom, and without that knowledge, my hands were tied."

Gloria had written often during that time, urging him to

either return home or demand Juliet come to him posthaste. In fact, he'd quoted her letters in several of his pleas to the king for release from diplomatic service.

"Thanks in large part to Caro, we've solved the 'who,' but I have yet to reason out the 'why.' We've been trying to find the man and are getting closer to doing so. I was about to tell Caro about my plans to meet with his cousin, Lord Bixby."

"His name is Sherman Snyder. We're hopeful Lord Bixby knows his whereabouts." Caro had been silent until now. Dorian sent her an encouraging look.

Gloria's eyebrows pinched together in such a familiar way; it was impossible to miss the resemblance between the dowager and himself. "Sherman Snyder? Are you certain?"

"Do you know him?" Caro asked.

"Well, yes. Timothy brought him to tea one day, said they'd been friends since school. They were in Bath doing the usual things and stopped in to pay their respects. Timothy must have introduced them. That scoundrel. And to think I vouched for him with hostesses."

"Timothy introduced Sherman to Juliet?" Timothy, who had benefited greatly from her death and continued to try to leech money from Dorian like a parasite. Dorian rested his elbows on his knees as pieces of the story clicked together. "When do you think it started?"

His mother glanced pointedly between him and Caro. "Must we speak of this with an audience?"

"Caroline has been vital to this entire effort. Please continue."

The dowager sighed in capitulation. She might not agree, but she wasn't going to fight it.

"How long, Mother?"

"When Juliet's mother died, she grieved so very hard. I

worried for her, and I know you did too. I insisted she join me in Bath until she was ready to sail to you."

Dorian studied his mother as her pause grew into a lapse in conversation. She stared into the fireplace, and he could see she was shifting events in her mind to make sense of it, as he had.

"Letters began to arrive. So much correspondence. Weeks passed, and then months. Her mood was much improved, so I initially thought the letters were from friends. You wrote so faithfully, of course, but I knew they weren't all from you." It sounded like she was trying to relieve him of the worry that he should have done more.

"I remember she left for London to attend a masquerade, right as her mourning period ended. She was so excited to go; I tried to tell myself she was eager to rejoin society. After that, I received the occasional letter from her, usually full of plans for that school she was building. Never another word about joining you. By that point, I had my suspicions but hoped I was wrong. At least she was discreet."

Small consolation, that. "When did Timothy show up with Sherman?"

"I suppose about a week after I brought her to Bath."

That made sense. Timothy introduced them, and their game had begun.

"When you last saw Juliet, how was she?"

"She was out of her mind with the fever. Ranted about her cousin betraying her and being played false. I thought it was the illness speaking. I'd seen Timothy recently, and he hadn't mentioned a falling-out."

A timeline began to form.

Julie had been grieving her mother. Timothy introduced her to Sherman, who then took advantage of Dorian's absence and Juliet's grief. Along the way, they managed to steal thousands of pounds from her under the guise of a charitable school. Somehow Juliet discovered at least part of their deception and fell ill soon afterward. "The school she spoke of doesn't exist."

"You think Timothy helped Sherman swindle his own cousin?" Caro sounded appalled.

His mother didn't seem to know if she was going to rage or cry. Her expressions ran the gamut of emotions.

Dorian nodded as he pressed his palms against his eye sockets. God, he was tired. "I think they worked together for the money. I don't know if romancing her was part of the plan, but we know from Sherman's letters there was most definitely an affair."

"You found the letters?"

"The late duchess kept them hidden in books. As I'm processing the duke's donation, we are inspecting each volume to ensure there are no letters within that could fall into the wrong hands." It was just like Caro to pinpoint exactly what his mother's concern was and address it directly. Caro turned her attention to him. "So, knowing this, why not approach Timothy and find Sherman that way?" Caro asked.

"It's tempting. But I think, given that I already have your solicitor friend, Mr. Bellmore, looking into the legalities of Timothy's actions over the last few months, gathering information might be more important than confrontation right now. When I corner Timothy for a confession, I want to know all I can. If he's as deep into this as it sounds, I intend to bring legal consequences against him."

"Lord, the scandal, Holland. Think of the scandal!" Gloria said, throwing up her hands.

But Dorian was already shaking his head. "I don't care about the bloody scandal, Mother. These men are stealing from women and breaking their hearts. If we can stop them from doing it again, surely that's worth being in a few gossip columns."

The smile Caro gave him made him feel like not just a duke, but a king. "If Lord Bixby knew of the fraud, he's culpable. There might very well be more than one villain in this situation. The scandal could be larger than you think, Mother. Prepare yourself."

Chapter Twenty-Three

Any day that began with a letter from the palace was going to be complicated. Dorian read it through for a third time.

England, Austria, Prussia, and Russia had signed a treaty, documenting their unified position against Napoleon. They'd each pledged soldiers and promised peace among their countries for the next twenty years. No small feat in diplomacy.

The palace requested his return to service. In glowing terms, the letter cited work he'd done earlier in the war, while alluding to the tasks he'd undertaken in places he wasn't "officially" allowed to be. With so much happening on the Continent, he could be of use there. If the palace had their way, he would be on a boat within six weeks. Due to the burden of the title, they were being generous with the allotted time to get his affairs in order. Or so they said.

Hastings entered the morning room and cleared his throat softly. "Mr. Gerard Bellmore from Morris, Haredale, and Wilson is waiting in your study, Your Grace."

A welcome distraction. Dorian shoved the letter in his pocket, then set his cup in its saucer with a rattle. "Mother, I hope you have a pleasant day. I'll see you this evening for the Markhurst soiree."

Dorian would much rather send a carriage for Caro and

stay in, but he'd promised to attend Lady Markhurst's event, as she was a particular friend of Gloria's. Since he was not in his mother's good graces at the moment, he couldn't cry off.

The dowager had said exactly one thing to him since entering the room. "You'll be as old as he was in a month."

When he studied his mother in the morning light of the breakfast room, it was easier to remember the way she'd been when he was a boy. His parents might not have been wildly passionate about each other, but they'd been well matched. Where Gloria was strong-willed, his father had been easy to please. Content to let her have her way if it made her happy, but unmovable on things for which he cared deeply.

She'd mourned him far longer than expected. In some ways, she still did. As he rose, the set of her mouth struck him as familiar, and he paused. His mother was afraid.

This determined push for his marriage was motivated by fear. Fear that she'd lose him. Fear that the one thing that had kept her going for the last thirty years—being the Duchess of Holland—would be moot. Fear that she'd lose everything a second time. And that, he understood.

Before he left, he pressed a kiss to her powdered cheek. She closed her eyes as if to soak it in, and Dorian made a mental note to be more affectionate. "Enjoy your breakfast, Mother."

Weariness pulled at him. He hadn't slept well the night before. The letter from the king was a bomb waiting to blow up something in his life—he just wasn't entirely sure what that was yet. And the longer he sat with the idea of finding Sherman for answers, the more he wondered if those answers were worth finding.

In the brief time he'd had with Caro, he could spot differences between this affair and his marriage. It wasn't the passion, or the sighs and lazy exploration of skin. After all, their physical relationship was wrapped in the newness of them, and time would impact that.

No, the real difference was in him. Dorian made time to talk with her for hours about everything and nothing, because Caro was not only a lover but a friend. And he had to treat her as both.

A successful relationship just might come down to attention and intention. Not taking anything for granted.

When he'd married Juliet, they'd been young. His friends were still raising hell about Town or taking a grand tour. Dorian became a husband before he had the time to become a man. As he grew older, he proved how difficult it was for someone without enough maturity to be a good man, to be a good husband. Rather than being cruel, he'd been complacent.

Dorian knew—rather ashamed to admit it, really—that he was a better friend to Caro than he'd been to Juliet. Thankfully, Caro had several truly decent friends, and one of them was in his study right now. Mr. Gerard Bellmore greeted him with a smile. "Hello again, Your Grace."

They shook hands, then Dorian waved him to a chair and took his seat behind the desk. "Any progress?"

"Well, you were right. She gave her money to a charlatan, thinking she was funding a school in Kent that doesn't actually exist." Removing a stack of papers from his satchel, the solicitor placed them on the desk, then nudged the pile toward Dorian.

The papers appeared to be ledger pages and banking receipts. "This is the proof?"

"Short of a signed confession, yes."

"Excellent. The charlatan in question is connected to Juliet's cousin. Have you found recourse for my severing of ties? Assuming his larcenous arse isn't rotting in prison, of course."

Another stack of papers appeared from the satchel and were placed on the desk. "Yes, Your Grace. After looking over your marriage contracts, I've found several options. Your path depends on how far you wish to distance yourself from him."

The cover letter detailed the key clauses. Dorian barely spared the solicitor a glance as he read. "Which of these options is the legal equivalent of pushing him off an extremely tall building into the Thames?"

Mr. Bellmore chuckled. "It's my duty as your legal counsel to advise you that pushing someone off a building is illegal under any circumstance. That said, I believe this is the course of action you want if you can't get his friend to implicate him in the fraud and theft charges." He pointed toward a note at the bottom of the page. "Since you've more than fulfilled your promised support, in both real funds and emotional and societal transfers toward her family, and as there are no longer privately held ancestral funds to pass on to a next of kin, this states you're well within your rights to terminate support. I've drafted a letter stating this and, with your permission, will send notices to every institution you bank with notifying them that Timothy Parker's credit is hereby terminated. I'll send a copy to Mr. Parker and inform him that all future communication will be handled by our firm."

God, Timothy would hate that. "And if he doesn't simply go away?"

"Then the legal recourse falls on him to prove you're somehow in breach of contract."

"Were you able to ascertain anything regarding a plan or explanation for the recent debts in her name?"

"Those are a little trickier. He is definitely making promises in the late duchess's name, which is obviously illegal. However, when faced with the consequences dealt by the judicial system, or those from the underworld thugs he's dealing with...your best option might be to publicly denounce your financial support. There may be social consequences and a bit of a scandal. But if everyone knows he's not under the protection of the duchy any longer, the rubbish might see itself out."

One stack of ledgers detailed the financial downfall of Juliet, all in the name of what she believed to be love for another man. The other pile of papers was the marriage contract he'd signed so many years ago, when he would have believed it to be impossible for them to end how they did. Yet here they were. Not growing old together after all.

"Thank you, Mr. Bellmore. Notify the banks and creditors of Timothy's change in status and deliver the firm's notice to him. He and I have some unfinished business, then I never want to see him again."

Mr. Bellmore stood, gathering the satchel. "All I ask is that the unfinished business not be resolved atop any buildings."

Dorian laughed. "I will do my best."

"Much appreciated, Your Grace."

Constance Martin said this man was a close friend of Caro's. A solicitor would be a great match for a vicar's daughter turned shopkeeper. Dorian had to wonder if Mr. Bellmore had thought so too.

"It recently came to my attention that we share a mutual friend. Caroline Danvers."

Mr. Bellmore's smile was immediate and so genuine a flare of jealousy bit at him. Maybe one of her theater proposals had been from him. "She mentioned she was working in a private library in Bloomsbury. Was it yours? She hasn't shared details. Caro is very discreet."

"Funny, but she assured me of your discretion as well. You speak highly of each other." He had to ask. "I realize it's a personal question, but have you considered taking the friendship further? She's a beautiful woman, after all."

The solicitor studied him for a moment, and Dorian had the sense he was taking his measure. "May I ask if you've grown close during her time here?"

"We have."

"Your Grace, may I sit and speak on a private matter?"

Dorian motioned to the chair once more. If he and his solicitor wanted the same woman, it could make a working relationship awkward to say the least. But better to find out now.

Mr. Bellmore had seemed unflappable on the few occasions they'd met face-to-face. At the moment, his knuckles were white where he gripped the strap of his satchel.

"I proposed to her recently. She declined."

Ah, so his suspicion had been correct. "She mentioned she'd had a proposal—two in one night, actually—but she didn't say who."

The solicitor eyed him speculatively, and Dorian had the feeling they were both trying to determine the relationship the other had with Caro.

"I'm in love with her." There. The truth was out in the world, and there could be no misunderstanding between him and the solicitor. Fiddling with the lid on his inkwell, Dorian chuckled. "I haven't said it out loud until just now."

"Not even to her? Then why tell me, Your Grace?"

The light from the window behind him cast a prism from the silver inkwell cap to the polished surface of his desk. In the beginning, he'd begged Caro to speak the pause, as they called it. He was doing so now. "I need to know if you're a better man for her than me, Mr. Bellmore."

The solicitor chuckled. "Not to state the obvious, but you're a duke."

Circling the silver cap with the pad of his finger, Dorian spoke. "I have a dukedom she doesn't want. Asking for her hand would put her in the position of everyone watching and judging her, which she also doesn't want. I have plenty of money, which she refuses to let me spend on her. My position doesn't matter, Mr. Bellmore. Not to her."

"Caro is a friend, Your Grace." He cleared his throat and squeezed his eyes closed. When he opened them, there was fresh resolve in his expression. "What I am about to share might very well get me fired. If that is the case, then rest assured I will complete the tasks asked of me today before handing your file to another associate."

"That's rather dire, Mr. Bellmore. I won't fire you or your firm if you're in love with her too. Please believe that."

"I asked Caro to marry me because the partners in my firm will only promote married, stable men. Since my partner of seven years, Leo, and I are happy, promotion doesn't seem likely. He and I suggested an arrangement we thought would offer her stability, while making me look like the kind of family man the firm wants." The solicitor's gaze was direct, but a white line of tension around his mouth made it clear he was worried about how this information would be received.

That wasn't how Dorian had expected this conversation to go. But the details made sense now. Two proposals—Mr. Bellmore and his partner. "After seven years, I'd say it sounds like you're already a stable family man, Mr. Bellmore."

The solicitor visibly exhaled. "We're happy, Your Grace. But you can see where I am in a difficult position."

"Yes, I can. And I understand now why Caro didn't tell me you and Leo were the ones who proposed. As you said, she's discreet." Which made him respect her even more.

"She suggested we move with her to Kent and that I set up a private practice there. I'm not too keen on the idea. With you in her life, I wonder if she will be moving after all."

"The cottage. I watched her fall in love with the property. It's perfect for her. Another of Caro's dreams that is the opposite of what I offer. It might be worth visiting the village, Mr. Bellmore. You might be happy there. Although..." An idea grew and Dorian's smile grew with it. "What would it take for you to set out a shingle in London? Step away from the firm you're with currently and be your own man?"

Mr. Bellmore laughed, but there wasn't much humor in the sound. "So many things."

"Such as?"

"A client list capable of sustaining overhead expenses. Larger savings than I currently have, so I could hire a barrister willing to work with an unknown firm. Connections to build the firm into something that could sustain everyone involved for the future."

"Wouldn't those same things be needed in Kent?"

"In a smaller village, my expenses would likely be less overall. I could scale the needs to a manageable size."

Dorian leaned back in his chair and rested his chin on one fist. "It sounds like what you need is a wealthy benefactor. Perhaps a duke you've impressed with your abilities and discretion."

The solicitor blinked, then stared. "Your Grace, I don't know what to say."

"Say you'll consider it." Dorian thought through what he wanted to say. He was dealing with a solicitor, after all, and details mattered. "This offer isn't dependent upon my relationship with Caro. You've done excellent work for me, Mr. Bellmore. I hate to see anyone's life hindered because they love someone other people deem unacceptable for whatever asinine reason."

"With all due respect, Your Grace, anyone who deems Caroline Danvers unacceptable has either never met her or isn't worth knowing."

Although the idea was all of three minutes old, the rightness of it felt as solid as the wood desk in front of him. The men who'd sat here, held this title before him, had done things their way. This was the next step toward being a duke he could be proud of.

And the solicitor was right. Anyone who thought a woman like Caro wasn't worthy of a duke, just because her father hadn't sat at a desk like this or held a title like his, was not worth knowing.

"I suspect this whole situation with Timothy will cause a stir, because we know he won't slink off into the night quietly. And if I can convince Caro to take a chance on a life with me, there will surely be even more scandal. Despite those looming issues, the Holland name carries enough weight and funds to help you become established on your own, Mr. Bellmore." Dorian stood, and the solicitor followed. He offered his hand. "I hope you'll consider my offer. In the meantime, we deal with Timothy and see this thing through."

When the solicitor left, looking happy but a bit stunned— which made Dorian inordinately satisfied—he checked the time. Bixby had agreed to meet at three o'clock this afternoon. Which meant he'd have time to visit the library and see Caro once she arrived later this morning.

And after Bixby, he would visit the jewelers. Because every duchess deserved a ring.

* * *

"He's using the store to shuffle letters to his mistress, isn't he?" Hattie said when the customer left the shop. At Caro's nod, she wrinkled her nose. "I thought I recognized the shady air about him. I thought Mr. Sanders was better than that. Why is it they always think we don't know what they're up to? Do they believe we're not going to notice, just because we're women? I should warn her off when she comes in. She might not know he's married."

Caro shrugged and plucked Mr. Sanders's letter from Hattie's hand. "You could casually mistake her for his wife or ask after their children. I think they have three. But meddling beyond that would be entirely up to you. I'd say something..." In the office, she placed the letter in the appropriate box.

Mr. Sanders wasn't the first man to use the bookshop mail system to hide communication from his lovers, and he wouldn't be the last. *It would be an easy way for a man to run romantic schemes with multiple women. Especially when he's the kind of man who rents rooms by the week and slinks away in the dead of night.*

"Walter wouldn't be the type to do that. Right?" Constance's voice reached where she stood in the office. That she was even asking the question made Caro want to shake her and demand she rethink this whole marriage.

"I've met Walter once, darling." She joined her cousins on the sales floor. "Only you can know if he's the kind who would have an affair. Have you heard from him since your row?" In Caro's opinion, any man marrying a woman should make an effort to befriend her closest friends. Even more so if those friends doubled as family. Any man who didn't see the wisdom of that was a fool.

Constance still looked troubled, but she kept her hands busy by tidying a display of botany books, sketch pads, and water paints near the counter. "He sent one note. It was all very vague. If I'm interpreting the letter correctly, Walter arrived safely to...wherever. But excise men were in the town, so they're meeting at another location. I still don't know if he will be home in time for the wedding."

"I'm sorry, luv. I know this is weighing heavily on you, and I hate that. But Connie, I wouldn't be a good friend to you if I didn't say something. In my opinion, the question you should be asking is not if he is going to be home in time. It's if you *want* to marry him after the way he treated you. If his expectations of what your life together will look like don't match yours, you need to call it off." Of all people, Caro felt the burden of loving a man who lived a vastly different life from hers. If Dorian were a cloth merchant like Walter Hornsby, and loved her too, Caro would be throwing a lifetime of reservations to the wind and planning her own wedding.

Somewhere between him asking to know her and becoming her friend, she'd learned to trust him.

Which meant, she realized with a pang, she needed to tell him about her writing. Maybe he'd be flattered...Yes, she'd hope for that.

Even though their relationship wasn't bound for marriage, Dorian deserved her honesty. And thanks to their time together, there was enough Blanche in her to be that brave.

"Your future together should be one you both want; otherwise, what are you doing?" Hattie said. "And that applies to both of you." She waved a finger between Connie and Caro.

The sales floor of the bookshop wasn't the time or the place to ponder her doomed romantic relationship, so Caro changed the subject. "Connie, you know who might be the kind of man to use a mail account for nefarious purposes? Sherman."

While she couldn't in good conscience tell Dorian's private business without his permission, she could clarify for Hattie. "A friend discovered their spouse was having an affair and wants to find the lover. I wonder if perhaps the person they're looking for might use a mail account like Mr. Sanders."

"I'll check our records. If he doesn't have an account here, he might have one at another shop." Constance latched onto the distraction as Caro hoped and hurried to the office.

If she found a way to contact Sherman that didn't interfere with the possible legal case Gerard was building against him and Timothy, Dorian would have the chance to question the man outside a courtroom. Maybe then he could lay this whole business to rest.

"A chance to catch a dodgy one in the act—I like it." Hattie grinned.

A moment later, Constance returned with the file of mail account contracts and set it on the counter. "We are assuming he used his real name, of course, but let's see if we get lucky. Chatsworth, Foster, Kingston, Thompson—whoops, too far." Fingers flew as she flipped and shuffled paper. "If he's here, what will you do? Set up a meeting? Pose as his lover and tell him to go to the devil? What's the plan?"

"No plan yet. This is all speculation." Caro leaned over to look at the names scrawled at the top of each page, although they were upside down and at times the handwriting was abysmal.

Pouting out her lip, Constance set down the stack. "Snood, but no Snyder. Should we send queries to other stores?"

"I'll do it," Hattie said, pulling a stack of papers in front of her.

"Disappointing, but not surprising. Connie, if you'll cover the store, Hattie and I can deliver notes to the other shops. The walk will do me good."

"I'll begin by making a list of all the lending libraries and places offering mail service," Hattie said.

"At least we have a plan. It might not work out, but it's something I can do. Thank you for your help," Caro said. "I need to get to Bloomsbury and finish the library." The project that had brought her into the duke's home and changed her life forever was nearly done. She pasted on an unbothered expression and focused on what needed to happen next. "Connie, could you clear a place on the interior wall in the back for the crates? They'll be delivered later today. Avoid the area near the door. And maybe set down wood, so the men can stack the crates on top. We don't want the books ruined if that room floods again."

Constance's grin was sunny to the point of being nearly manic. "Anything to distract me from my problems."

Chapter Twenty-Four

❦

As the hack rattled through the streets in a now-familiar route toward the ducal townhome, Caro made lists in her head. They'd finish the library sorting today, and the packing wouldn't take long now that she knew what went where.

Several more of the valuable books needed to be mailed to their new homes. The letters she'd sent to the bookshop's collectors were bearing fruit. It looked like the long hours on this project were going to be the financial boost the store had hoped for. A small part of her was sad not to have a business reason to be in Dorian's home. Perhaps she'd been hiding somewhat behind the excuse of working in the library. After today, when she was there, it would be because she was there only for him. In his bed.

With every visit, she recognized a paradox. The more at home she felt in his rooms, the more she became aware that the luxurious space would never be her home. To be simultaneously relishing every moment while already grieving the inevitable end of their love affair was taking a toll.

And it had become a love affair. There were moments when she'd swear Dorian had fallen in love too.

The seconds when his eyes met hers and held such admiration, it was impossible to imagine not seeing that expression for the rest of her life. And during those hours spent in bed, with his body warming her back while the fireplace heated her front, as his hands drew lazy lines along her skin and they talked about whatever was on their minds.

She loved him, and even if he felt the same way, she didn't know if that would be enough to change their future. Or even if it should.

London passed in a blur as she worried at her bottom lip. She wouldn't tell Dorian about her mail-delivery idea to catch Sherman unless one of the shops found him in the records. It did no good to get Dorian's hopes up or argue about his concerns—at least not until it was too late for him to stop her.

The hack dropped her off in front of the white townhome. As she climbed the steps, Caro noted absently that despite the house's grand appearance, it no longer intimidated her. Hastings opened the door and greeted her warmly. Howard was prepared in the library with crates and men.

It was moving day.

Footmen hammered crates closed while she labeled each with a number to correspond with the inventory lists she'd built over weeks of work. While easily placed titles, like Mr. Lipscomb's mythology books, had already been delivered to the bookshop or directly to collectors, much of the library was bound for the hands of everyday people.

Dorian had been in meetings all morning, but she hoped he would have time to go over the final inventory sheet before she left.

All too soon, it was finished. Maids were cleaning the empty bookshelves with lemon oil. Men carried crates down the hall to load them into a waiting cart.

Anticipation made butterflies take flight in her belly when she knocked on his door. This phase of the project was complete, and that felt like an achievement. His voice saying,

"Enter," made those butterflies flutter for entirely nonprofessional reasons.

She stepped inside, then closed the door behind her. It had once been intimidating to be in Dorian's study, with all the polished wood and fine furniture. Now the room felt cozy and familiar.

"Sorting and processing are complete. I'll notify you of each sale when the valuable volumes go to collectors. The collectables are marked for Martin House. Everything else is being loaded into a cart as we speak. Those can go to the shop as well, or we can take them to charities or other stores."

Dorian stood and met her as she crossed the room. He dropped a kiss on her lips. "I thought the shop was going to take the noncollectible books for your lending library."

Something about him today seemed more relaxed and at peace than she'd seen outside of his bedroom, and it made her smile fondly. "We can certainly use many of the books, but I had an idea. If you wanted to spread your generosity and build goodwill within the community, there are several schools, women's homes, and orphanages in the city that could benefit from the collection. You've said the late duchess spent a great deal of time working with charities. She wanted to build a school." Caro stroked her hand over his jaw. "No matter how it ended, there were sweet years too, and those shouldn't be forgotten."

Dorian kissed her palm. "That's an excellent idea. You're a good woman to think of it, especially given all you know," he said. "Perhaps you can help me make a list of places, and Howard will schedule those deliveries."

"Already done." She handed him a paper, and he chuckled.

"Everything is organized and labeled, I take it?"

She shrugged. "Color coded, actually. If you opted to give everything to Martin House, the cart driver would receive this inventory." She showed him a paper with directions to deliver the lot to her shop. "But since you like my idea, he will get this one instead." She produced a different paper with a flourish. "This one assigns each delivery location a color that corresponds with a crate marked with the same color."

He studied her face, and she wished she could read his mind. "Let me into the pause," she said. As always, the reminder made them smile.

Dorian dropped a lingering kiss on her lips. "I was thinking how impressive you are and that I'm lucky to know you. Organizing the running of an entire estate, or even the British army would be well within your abilities."

He opened his arms, and she walked right into them. "It feels odd to not have a professional reason for being here anymore. Without the appeal of being covered in library dust, will you still want me?" she asked, only half in jest.

"God, yes. I will always want you here. Every day. Every night. I'm nowhere near done with you, Caroline Danvers. I don't think I ever will be."

From anyone else, that would have been a declaration. In a world where he wasn't a duke, she'd have taken it as one. However, this wasn't that world. As she'd told Hattie, this was a fantasy. And she desperately wished to cling to the fantasy for as long as she could.

Her mind spun the fairy tale to new heights. Of sitting in an ugly paisley chair by the fire, writing while he pored over ledgers and paperwork at his desk. Perhaps making space for a desk of her own across the room, so she could look up from her work whenever she liked, to let him catch her smiling at him. Rising onto her tiptoes, Caro pressed her mouth to his. "We will find our way through. I don't know exactly how that looks, but we will."

In answer, strong hands gripped her bottom, lifting her

against him as he stalked toward the desk before the giant window she'd observed him against so many times. The window she'd imagined in her mind when she wrote Phoebe on her knees before Lysander, licking and sucking tormented admissions of loss and vulnerability so the hero in her story could find healing and love.

He set her down on the polished surface, never breaking their kiss.

While her real-life duke wasn't nearly as damaged and haunted as Lysander, Caro related more deeply to this story than any others before. Perhaps because this book, *Phoebe Takes the Duke*, although not finished, was the one she'd written while falling in love with the man behind the title and perfectly polished facade.

He'd inspired *A Dalliance for Miss Lorraine*, but that had been the public version of him. The man on those pages bore little resemblance to the one in her arms now.

As always, desire flared hot and fast between them. For several long, glorious, gasping breaths, she allowed herself to be lost in him. She sucked his bottom lip between hers until the only thing she could taste was Dorian, and the liquid heat at her core ached from the hard length of his arousal pressing against her.

"I think you missed me last night." She smiled against his mouth, and his laughter tasted sweet.

"What gave me away? I was trying to be aloof and mysterious." He nipped and teased along her jaw.

"This house is crawling with servants, and in a few moments the driver will need his marching orders," she reminded him.

"Bloody people ruining my plans to finally fuck you on this desk," he grumbled against her throat.

She laughed quietly. "And to think I used to believe you

truly were aloof and mysterious." She slid off the desk to her knees and pressed a palm against the impressive tent in the placket of his breeches. "Allow me to show you how much I appreciate your plain speaking." The buttons of his breeches opened beneath her eager fingers.

"I thought you said we didn't have time to— Bloody fucking hell, your mouth is a miracle," he gasped.

Phoebe had seduced Lysander this way, and a thrill went through Caro that she could have the chance to play out the scene. She sank into the experience. The salty musk of him, amplified by his body heat, filled her nostrils and tickled her tongue. Such an amazing contrast of silky soft skin over hardened flesh. When she withdrew, the suction made a faint *pop*. "What did you think about while we were apart? Tell me."

Her fingers wrapped around the base of his cock and stroked, meeting her lips as she drew him deep once more.

Dorian's answer came between heavy breaths. "I couldn't sleep, because I missed you. The bed felt too empty, so I imagined you there. Thought about the way your pussy gets so wet—fuck, Caro, do that again. I yelled your name when I came."

Between his legs, his testicles were a firm weight in her hand as she rolled her palm and fingers along them. "Tell me more."

"More?"

She licked the bulge of a vein along the bottom side of him from root to top. "I'll suck for as long as you speak."

When her finger ventured behind his bollocks to smooth skin, his responding chuckle ended abruptly with a groan. He rested his hands on the edge of the desk for support as his knees shook.

"You speak. I suck," she repeated.

When he began to talk, she took him deep once more and made him gasp. "I didn't sleep that first night we were home from Kent. The bed was too empty, even though you'd never been in my room be-before." He stuttered when she pressed another finger behind his tight testicles, then scraped a nail over the puckered flesh just beyond. "I kept remembering how I panicked when I thought you'd left me at the inn. It unnerved me."

She drew back. Above her, his blue eyes were serious, swamped with desire. The memory of her not being there when he awoke had kept him awake all night? When he didn't elaborate, she raised her eyebrows in silent question and flicked her tongue over the wide head of his cock.

True to their agreement, he started to speak and she rewarded him with a firm pull into her mouth. "I want you so much it scares me. All day, every day." As her movements quickened, so did his words. "I want to help you make these dreams you have come true. Even though I'm scared that a life with me isn't one of them."

Hands and mouth working in tandem, she carried him along toward his own release. The thrusting of his hips grew frantic and his voice broke. Caro pressed her knees together, trying to ease the ache between her thighs.

"I'm close; if you don't want me to—"

She sucked deeper in answer, making her opinion on the matter quite clear. His hands threaded into her hair, guiding her head, and she moaned.

With a low curse, he came.

Dorian was still trying to catch his breath as she carefully refastened his breeches, then got to her feet. She perched on the desk between where his hands still clutched the edge.

"You're quite proud of yourself, aren't you?"

"I am." She grinned. "Do you think anyone heard us?"

"God, I hope not. The servants are discreet but the dowager is another matter. My mother and I are not seeing eye to eye on things at the moment." Dorian gently tucked her hair back into order, and her heart flipped at the sweetness of the gesture. "Do your best to avoid her if you can. It's in everyone's best interests. However, we have things to discuss, you and me. I've committed to an event this evening, but would you join me for dinner tomorrow night?"

"I'd like that. But now I should go direct the driver." They did have things to discuss, and she'd have to draw on Blanche's bravery. Just then, she didn't require Blanche's help to summon a saucy smile and leave Dorian with an image that would wreck his composure whenever he thought about it. "Before I go, I need you to know one thing."

"What's that?"

Caro rose on her toes and whispered in his ear. "Sucking your cock made me so wet it's dripping down my thighs right now."

Grinning, she ducked under his arm and darted to the door. His deep groan had her giggling as she fled the study and returned to work.

Chapter Twenty-Five

ight I ask what you intend to do with this information?" Lord Bixby's study was a tidy, sparse affair: all sleek, dark wood and minimal objects to accumulate dust. If Dorian didn't know for certain the townhome had been part of the man's family holdings for decades, he'd think Bixby had just moved in and hadn't unpacked beyond the most essential items.

Dorian took a seat on the opposite side of a massive desk that was empty except for an inkwell and a candlestick with a taper that had burnt down to the nub and not yet been replaced. "Are you asking if I intend to do Sherman bodily harm, or are you more concerned with the larger impact on your family?"

The other man offered a tight smile. "Sherman and I have never been close. His mother married poorly but is still dear to my mother. Thus the pressure to provide introductions in hopes that he could restore that branch of the family's standing. Everything I do is for my family, Your Grace. Specifically, my sisters. You may have noticed the bare spots on the walls as you entered and lack of valuables displayed about on tables."

He'd noted a lack of tables altogether, but Dorian wasn't going to say that.

"I see by your expression you understand what I'm saying." Bixby folded his hands on the desk, and Dorian wondered for the first time if he'd misjudged the man entirely. "To clarify, we are not in dire straits. However, economies are in place. Luxuries have been sold to fund their dowries. I've had to be creative at times. Thankfully, within our circle, favors and information often hold more sway than ready coin."

"You blackmail people."

Bixby's laugh was a sharp bark. "Blackmail implies I receive funds. I don't want people's money. In that way, my cousin and I differ. It might be a fine line but a distinct one in which I take solace. Sherman's actions are always self-serving. It's the one way in which he's reliable. I, on the other hand, seek to protect and move my family forward. I'm only a baron, Your Grace, and I have three younger sisters to see settled. I'll do what I must for their futures. If that means I barter information so they can have a place at the finest tables, then so be it."

"I will do what I can to protect your sisters, as long as I have your word you'll forget what you know after this meeting." Bixby he might need to prosecute. But Dorian would dower the sisters himself if it came to it.

Offering his hand to shake, Bixby said, "After this conversation, I will have no knowledge of any involvement between Sherman and your family."

"No involvement between Sherman and my family— dead or alive, extended or dear."

"Agreed. We provide mutual protection for those we love."

They shook on it, then got down to the heart of the matter.

Bixby asked, "From our conversation over whist, am I to gather you know of the connection between Timothy and Sherman?"

"Timothy introduced Sherman and Juliet." Oddly enough, his throat didn't clutch at their names. In fact, the pit of betrayal, anger, and that general sense of "how dare you" that had made him lose his breath upon sight of the first letter had disappeared beneath a layer of cool resolve. Answers were within reach. Equally within reach were doubts that Sherman would have the power to tell him a damn thing he hadn't already figured out or was willing to learn on his own with Caro. She didn't see a duke first, like Juliet had. Caro saw a man and would demand he be a better man if he needed to.

"If you're here, you haven't confronted Timothy. Why is that?"

"He and I have never been friends. However, since he was Juliet's last remaining relative after her mother passed, I didn't think it kind to cut him off. Now that Juliet is gone, I've hired legal counsel to assist in blocking Timothy from the dukedom's pockets. When I confront him, I want all of my paperwork and information in place. Ideally, I will only have to deal with him one more time, then I can pretend he doesn't exist. Even if he molders in debtors' prison."

"As you probably know, Sherman and Timothy met during their later school years. Father funded his education in hopes that Sherman would make something of himself. When I inherited the title, Sherman and his enthusiasm for underachieving came along with it." A quirk tilted his lips, and Dorian smiled back. Nearly every family he knew had at least one person determined to send everyone else to Bedlam or the poorhouse, depending on the day.

"So imagine my surprise when, once I introduced Sherman to friends in London, he stopped asking for money. At the time, I was dealing with another family matter and, frankly, didn't think anything of it beyond a sense of relief.

Had I considered the possibilities, charming and wooing the wives of my friends and then extorting money from them wouldn't have come to mind as a likely scenario."

He had to hand it to him—Bixby had a compelling way of telling a story. "Just when we think we've considered every way they can create problems, they find new kinds of trouble."

"Indeed. I was incensed. Demanded he give the money back, but he'd already spent it. Sherman promised he'd never do it again, but I don't think the man has ever met a lie he didn't want to get to know better. It's as if he's incapable of telling the truth. He breathes duplicity instead of air."

"I spoke to a man who wrote a series of love letters for him. He isn't even wooing honestly. He cobbles those letters together in a script of sorts."

"I don't doubt it. My cousin is not exceptionally intelligent, hardworking, or good-looking. What he is, is cunning and determined to *take* in any given situation. If he's offering you anything, there will be something in it for him. There's always an ulterior motive. At first, he chased the low-hanging fruit. The unhappy wives, the widows with heavy pockets. Then he grew either bored or cocky."

"You think Juliet was targeted rather than convenient?"

"Absolutely. You two were a well-known love match. Every lady in London wanted to be her, and all the men wished to be you, with a beautiful woman staring at us like we'd hung the stars. With you gone to the Continent, he saw a chance to test the waters. See if she was lonely or weak in any way."

"And she was. If I have the timeline correct, the relationship developed after her mother died."

"That coincides with what I know. Timothy provided the introductions while she was grieving and you were elsewhere." Bixby leaned back and folded his hands over his stomach. "Sherman has two tactics: the role of secret admirer, and the role of friend. No woman will ever look at him and upend her skirts or her purse because of his looks. So, he plays the part of the friend until an emotional bond has formed and he can twist their regard into something romantic or at least a sense of responsibility. The secret-admirer path works best during the Season, when he can woo via letter, then meet during a masquerade ball to hide his face. Depends on the woman and how susceptible he thinks she is to judging a book by the cover, as it were."

So, they'd likely been friends before he'd preyed on the relationship and turned it romantic with his letters. Gloria had mentioned a masquerade in London. "And the money?"

"Again, depends on the woman. But they've all had their own funds to some degree. Some like the idea of a kept man. Especially those who know their husbands have mistresses. Others, as I believe was the case with Juliet, prefer to believe their funds are helping a charitable cause."

"Like a school in Tippering."

Bixby nodded. "Like the nonexistent school in Tippering. Which, by the way, has been fully funded by three women that I know of. There's also a menagerie of rescued animals in the Lake District, a widows' shelter near Bath, and an orphanage in India. All imaginary but well supported by his various women."

One word made Dorian cock his head. "You refer to them all as women but not lovers. Is that a deliberate choice?"

For the first time since the conversation began in earnest, Bixby looked uncomfortable. "It's highly unlikely he ever bedded your wife or anyone else's in a way that would have resulted in pregnancy."

"And why is that?"

"The man has the clap. Picked it up over a decade ago. Mercury treatments haven't helped, and frankly, he couldn't call his soldier to attention if his life depended on it. Not that there aren't other ways to bed a woman, obviously. But at least we needn't worry over him leaving a fleet of bastards about."

Dorian blinked. "I see. Thus, the need for emotional and romantic approaches versus old-fashioned passionate bed sport."

"It's a cold comfort, I know. But for all their professions of affection, it's doubtful they ever made it to a bedroom."

A long sigh escaped, but he couldn't say it was one of relief. "Cold comfort, indeed. Thank you for your time. One last question—where can I find your cousin?"

"Last I heard, he has rooms on Rupert Street."

"I checked. He's not there anymore."

"Then I'm afraid Timothy is your best chance at tracking him down." Something in his demeanor shifted from relaxed to curious. "I have a question for you, though."

"Certainly. You've been more than forthcoming with me."

"Is what they are all saying true? Is the book about you?"

"What book?"

"Blanche Clementine's latest novel. Speculation is running rampant. I'm surprised you haven't heard. It's been all over the drawing rooms and gossip rags."

Dorian shook his head in confusion. "I've read Blanche Clementine's books but haven't had a chance to do more than begin her newest."

Lord Bixby's curiosity morphed into something almost predatory, and he leaned forward with a toothy smile. "Everyone is convinced the hero in the book is you. And if that's the case, then you have been a very naughty—but intriguing—boy in your private affairs."

* * *

Shakespeare was correct when he said "I am to wait, though waiting so be hell." Waiting was mind-numbingly boring, with an anxious undercurrent that prevented sleep. But then, Shakespeare had been waxing poetic about love—or at least, about people in the heady throes of lust. Not a spinster waiting to spring a trap on the former lover of her current lover's dead wife. Good old William would appreciate the convolutedness of the situation.

"What if he doesn't take the bait? How do we live with ourselves if we are *this* close to catching him, but he doesn't show up?" Constance asked from the pillow beside Caro.

"I appreciate your willingness to accept my crusade for justice as your own, but I don't want you to worry too much about this." They'd spoken of little else since finding Sherman Snyder's mail account at the Matthewses' place, a bookshop closer to Piccadilly and Mayfair.

Connie's blonde curls flopped onto Caro's face as her cousin rolled toward her.

"I'd much rather let my mind spin about this than my own problems. Thank you for finding someone with a situation dramatic enough to provide ample distraction."

"Anything for you, Connie," Caro said dryly.

"I still say we should put a bag over his head," Constance said.

"If he can identify us, it can only spell trouble. A sack over his head solves that problem," Hattie commented from the other side of the bed.

"What if he's exceptionally tall or brawny? We might not be able to reach him to toss a flour sack over his head with any kind of accuracy." Caro nibbled at her bottom lip. Kidnapping was complicated.

A moment passed, and she swore she could hear Constance's brain mulling it over. Finally, Connie said, "Best plan is to incapacitate him, then put the sack over his head."

Why do I feel like she's about to suggest bludgeoning him?

"If I bash him with a rock—"

"Mercy, Constance." Hattie jerked her head off the pillow. "No blood. Not if we can help it. Ideally, we leave no marks."

The mattress shook as Constance cackled evilly. "Except for the ones on his soul as we shed a light on his many misdeeds."

"You're enjoying this far too much," Caro commented.

"There is no such thing as enjoying the downfall of a villain too much, and as a reader of Blanche Clementine, I am appalled to hear her suggest such a load of rot."

"Well, speaking as someone who actually *is* Blanche Clementine, I can assure you there's a difference between fiction and reality."

Constance heaved a sigh. "Rubbish."

"Fictional villains can't retaliate with real consequences. This man could. What if he hurts us, or sees our faces, or gets away? Or all three?" Practical Hattie, always ready with a problem.

"Please don't bother me with facts when I'm being dramatic." Constance's hand covered Caro's in the dark, then fumbled to find Hattie's too. "However, you make excellent points. Hattie, you'll help us plan. Between the three of us, there's nothing we can't do."

True. They seemed to be a triad of strengths and weaknesses that complemented each other. Once the account was found, it was the matter of a moment to bring the young bookseller, Miss Eliza Matthews, in on their plan to catch "a bad, bad man," as Constance had put it.

Caro had written a vague note and left it for him to collect. They hoped the scrawled *Not much time. I must see you. Leave word when we can meet at this store. Urgent!* was sufficient incentive.

Unless the handwriting was too unfamiliar and he smelled a trap.

Or he didn't collect his mail for another month.

Eliza would know if letters were flowing through the store, but what if he'd just ended things with someone and therefore, again, smelled a trap?

This plan could go wrong in a million ways, and every possible scenario played out in Caro's mind. However, the mail-service payment was due on his account this week, which raised their chances of Sherman visiting Matthews Bookstore and finding their bait.

Then they'd get him to answer Dorian's questions. But how, exactly?

"Caro, I can hear your brain spinning. Stop. We will figure this out, and then Hattie will make contingency plans with extra contingency plans," Constance said. "Now go to sleep. We might have a busy day of villain kidnapping tomorrow. At the very least, you'll need all your energy to think of new ways to shag your duke, away from his silver dragon of a mother."

Caro kicked her beneath the covers, and Constance giggled. "I'm terribly proud of your current life choices, darling Blanche. Just in case that wasn't clear."

Chapter Twenty-Six

*T*he ring he'd selected the day before sat atop his bureau, its stone winking in the morning light with the fractal colors that had caught his eye in the jeweler's shop. If a gem could flirt, this one did.

Mounted in a halo of diamonds, the pinkish-orange sapphire reminded him of illustrations of flowers he's seen from India. It was a ring fit for a queen. Or a duchess. He slipped it into his pocket, where it would stay until he placed it on Caro's finger this evening.

Hopefully.

Once he knew her answer, he would respond to the letter from the palace. He wouldn't make the same mistake with her that he'd made with Juliet. If Caro married him, Dorian would say no to his king.

And that would not be well received. He swallowed around a lump of worry. The problem with King George and with Prinny was that one was mad and the other was petty. Petty and powerful. There would be repercussions for his refusal.

"Holland, I need to speak with you," Gloria called into his dressing room.

"I'll just be one more minute, Mother."

Except, she was there already, in the doorway, wearing an expression that said she'd seen the ring. "So that's the way it is, is it?" Gloria settled into the chair beside his dressing mirror and took a second to arrange her gown around her so the filmy material lay in perfect waves to the floor. "When were you going to tell me?"

"When there was something to tell. I don't know if she will say yes. Until she does, it isn't any of your business."

Lines around her mouth tightened. "Anything having to do with the duchy is my business."

"The duchy, yes. The current duke, no."

"They are one and the same, son."

He felt his jaw flex. "No, they're not. And it grieves me to hear you say otherwise."

Silence settled in the room, but not for long. "She's not beautiful like Juliet was."

Like hell she wasn't. Caro's face was a source of endless fascination, her body a landscape he wanted to lose himself in. Most beautiful of all was her mind, with its sharp intelligence and sly wit. The way her chin grew even more pointed when she was being stubborn, and the way her cheeks rounded when she teased him . . . Anyone who didn't see the absolute breathtaking essence of Caroline Danvers was missing one of the great wonders of the world.

However, his mother's tactic was obvious, so he kept these thoughts to himself.

"I suppose it has been five years. A man can't be expected to be without companionship. That doesn't mean you need to marry her."

Again, he let her statement go unanswered. Straightening cravat folds that didn't need straightening in the mirror, he smoothed all expression from his face and waited for her to say her piece. Depending on her final stance after his rebuttal, he might need to send his mother back to Bath for the foreseeable future. But he hoped it wouldn't come to that.

"You've the look of your father. Whenever I broached a topic he didn't want to discuss, he'd make the same face you are right now. It was usually only regarding matters he felt so deeply about that he couldn't be swayed. Is that the case here?"

Would he end things with Caro if his mother stomped her perfectly shod foot and demanded it? Absolutely not. "I won't be swayed, no."

Gloria squinted and pursed her mouth tighter. "I see. Is she blackmailing you, or holding something over your head?"

A laugh shocked him when it rose hard and fast. "Blackmail? That's your first assumption?"

She lifted one shoulder in a delicate shrug. "You're a man of considerable means. And she is…I'm assuming she isn't from a notable family or money, or you would have said so by now. And you claimed you didn't need another love match."

"I thought I could marry for duty. Marry to sire an heir and put the dukedom first." Truth slipped from his tongue. The words felt right and, now that they were flowing, refused to stop. "But if the reason for doing so is because I might die young, doesn't it make more sense to make the best of the life I have? Whether it's for another month, or another fifty years? If I only have months left before fate intervenes, then I want to spend those months with Caro. And if I don't get more than a short life with her, I need to know if you'll help her navigate society without me here."

She heaved a sigh, but a softening in her expression gave him hope that he might not have to pack her into a carriage and send her to Bath after all. "If you want a woman who will be accepted in our circles, you are choosing poorly."

"If you knew her, you would understand. There's a presence about Caro, especially when she's relaxed. A confidence that puts everyone else at ease as well. She's an extraordinary woman."

"So are any number of women who are far more accept-able companions." Her tone was gentle but still made his teeth lock together.

"None of them would ever forget I am a duke. Caro treats me the same as she would the butcher or the chimney sweep. Perhaps even harsher, to be honest. When I'm high-handed, she reminds me that my feet are made of clay."

"High-handed? You're Dorian Whitaker, fifth Duke of Holland. Of course you're high-handed. What utter rot."

He sat in the nearest chair and interlaced his fingers so he wouldn't fidget. Ink stained the inside of his right pointer finger, and he rubbed at it. After hours at his desk, there was always a blotch on that spot. Caro liked to trace the smudge when they were together. Smiling, he murmured, "I'm just a man. Blessed to be part of a wealthy, titled family. I could have easily been born to a blacksmith or a peddler. The title is a responsibility, Mother, one bestowed entirely by chance. England would be a better place if we remembered that more often, I think."

"She has you speaking nonsense if she's convinced you you're nobody special." She bristled.

Dorian shook his head. Gloria might never understand. After all, he was still learning this very thing. "On the contrary—I'm the most special man in her life. Besides per-haps her uncle."

"You're as stubborn as your father was." She sighed, and some of the steel disappeared from her spine. "He was also wise and kind and led with his heart. Please be careful, son. Your heart has already been through so much. It might not be the most reliable guide."

"True. But it's the only one I have. And I've worked very

hard to rebuild it over these last few years. I need to listen to it if I'm to continue to be a man I can face in the mirror."

"There will be a scandal."

"Probably." Let them be scandalized.

"I suppose this answers one aspect of the problem, then."

He cocked his head. "What problem?"

"The reason I wanted to speak with you. Everyone is going on about that Blanche Clementine book, but despite the chatter, no one would speak with me directly about it. They kept saying I needed to read it and see what I thought about the hero."

Dorian groaned up at the ceiling. "Lord, this again."

"You've read it?"

"No. I started it and then set it aside. But yesterday, Lord Bixby told me what everyone is saying. It's utter nonsense, Mother."

She was silent a moment. "I don't think it is. I've just finished it, and I think there is truth to what they're saying. Dorian, this is a problem, and we need to get to the bottom of it. While I see and appreciate the fiction in the story, the ton is reading it, and they believe what they're reading is true. The hero is utterly depraved. A slave to his basest desires. The things he does to that heroine…" Twin flags of pink stained her cheeks. "That book is the result of a creative obsessed mind."

Dorian laughed ruefully. "What am I supposed to do about that? If the ton is so set on seeing facts where there's only fiction, I can't dissuade them otherwise."

"We must get the author to print a statement in the paper decrying your involvement in the book. This has to be why Lady Humphry gave you your walking papers. How many others will turn their backs on us, believing you're some kind of sexual deviant?"

Dorian shook his head. God, what was this latest hero *doing*? Unbidden, the memory of the blonde woman at the Waterstone ball rose in his mind, when she'd pressed against his groin and propositioned him. Other things, moments he'd dismissed over the last month, began to make sense. Awkward pauses in conversations as he passed. The way the game room had fallen silent when he and Oliver entered, searching for Bixby. Hell, Bixby had practically foamed at the mouth when he'd asked about the book. Even Lady Agatha had made a sly reference to the talk, hadn't she? How had she phrased it? That they expected *interesting things* from him.

Well, shit.

"Unfortunately, the author is notoriously reserved. In fact, she's only signed one copy of her work, and I have it." She preened a bit at that, and he couldn't help but smile. "Your bookseller's shop was able to convince her publisher to have her sign a single copy. They are who can get us to the author. We need to go to Martin House and convince Blanche Clementine to clear your name."

"Eliza Matthews sent a message." Hattie waved a missive sealed with a blob of green wax.

Caro scrawled an address on the label of a signed copy of Ann Radcliffe's *A Sicilian Romance* and set it on top of the other books from the Holland library going out to collectors today. "Open it; see what it says."

No matter what it contained, it couldn't be better than the royalty check she'd received from her publisher that morning. It had been well above anything she'd made thus far with her writing. On top of the stack of outgoing mail, along with the books, was a letter to the Adamses informing them she didn't need to lease after all. She could pay the asking price for their cottage. Just in time too. The last letter she'd received said the couple wanted to move at the end of April, which left a little over a month to put everything in place.

She ran a finger over the delivery direction. Home. Hers.

Joy and satisfaction nearly brought tears to her eyes. She'd done it. Gerard would help guide the legalities of purchasing the cottage. But in this letter was her promise to buy her new home, and she was a woman who kept her promises.

Thank God for Gerard. He'd certainly been busy lately. Between dealing with Dorian's situation and negotiating the next contract with her publisher, it was a miracle he had time to sleep. Last night, he'd dropped by on his way home. Even tired after a long day, he'd been so excited to share Dorian's offer to sponsor his solicitor's office. When she saw Dorian tonight, he would be on the receiving end of her most effusive thanks. A ripple of anticipation coursed through her at the thought.

Nothing could ruin this day.

Hattie broke the seal on Eliza's note, then let out a soft whoop. "Sherman took the bait. He's meeting us in the back room of the Matthews Bookstore at six o'clock."

Just like that, Caro's palms started to sweat. She was supposed to have dinner with Dorian tonight, but not until seven. If their plan went the way she hoped, they could meet at the Matthews Bookstore, deal with Sherman, then retire to Bloomsbury in time to dine and celebrate.

"Our game of cat and mouse is officially in play, then."

"Meow, meow, darling pussycats," Hattie said, and Constance laughed somewhere outside the office.

A moment later, Connie appeared at the door. "Caro, the silver dragon and your duke are here." Though Connie whispered it, Caro desperately hoped the dowager hadn't overheard their nickname for her.

She capped her inkwell, then brushed her hands on her apron as she left her office. "Your Grace," she said, curtsying. *Should I have said, "Your Graces," because there are two of them?* "This is an unexpected but welcome surprise."

That little bubble of happiness she felt every time she saw Dorian popped when she noticed his expression. Dark eyebrows pinched into the V she hadn't seen in weeks, and his mouth was firmly set in the implacable line she used to associate with him. Before her eyes, the man she'd grown to love slid on the mask she used to believe was real. "What's wrong? What happened?"

Dreadful scenarios filled her head. Someone had died. Or maybe something less drastic, and he'd decided to take back the donation for some reason.

She glanced at her cousins to see twin looks of confusion.

"Have you been selling many copies of the new Blanche Clementine book?" he asked, not helping her confusion one bit. And yet, a tremor of unease sent a warning through her. Like the expectant silence before a boom of thunder, when you knew a storm was coming but you didn't yet know how bad it would be.

Caro stepped around the sales counter and looked between Dorian and his mother. Was this about how much they'd charged the dowager for the signed copy? She exchanged a look with her cousins and saw her worry reflected there. "Yes, we've sold out our stock several times over. Shops all over town are enjoying the interest readers have taken in the book."

"Everyone's talking about it. Patrons are clamoring for copies," Constance said.

"While I'm glad your shop is benefiting, I find myself in the middle of an embarrassing situation." Dorian's voice was as grim as she'd ever heard it. He removed his hat and spun it in his hands, running the rim through his fingers. It was what he used to do when he visited the store. He'd once confessed that Lord Southwyn teased him about his tendency to turn icy and ducal when nervous. Despite that composure, some part of him always fidgeted.

"I'm sorry... I don't understand." Sure, people were talking about her book, but that was outside her control and ultimately a good thing. The last few releases had met moderate success. Through random chance, this was the one that ended up circulating through drawing rooms and groups of friends who didn't usually read that kind of book. From there, they probably discussed the naughty bits behind their fans, until everyone was talking and no one wanted to be left out of the conversation. It was how publishing worked.

"Whoever read one of the first copies seemed to think the novel is about me, and the idea has caught fire. I'm sorry—"

The dowager interrupted. "The hero character is also a duke, looks like Holland, and is grieving the loss of his wife. Like my son, he served as a diplomat. Unfortunately, the methods he takes to move on from his loss are extremely graphic in nature and unflattering to a man of Holland's status."

Caro stifled a wince. The dowager wasn't going to be a Blanche Clementine reader, then. The events in the book could describe any number of people. Except the dukedom, of course.

Dorian's tone was more conciliatory, obviously trying to balance his mother's indignation. "The character bears an eerie resemblance, according to the chatter. However, the chatter is abundant and doesn't seem to be quieting."

"My friends and enemies delighted in laughing at us to my face. All the while refusing to tell me why. I had to purchase my own copy to understand that my son is the subject of an erotic novel detailing sexual escapades lurid enough to have everyone in society reaching for their smelling salts."

"But not before turning the next page," Constance quipped, then bit her lip when no one laughed. "Apologies. Misplaced humor."

Two of the customers milling about headed over to the display of Blanche Clementine books in the window, probably to see what everyone was going on about. Caro counted five others eavesdropping on the drama unfolding in the middle of the store, and only one of them was trying to be subtle about it.

"Dor— I mean, Your Grace. You're familiar with this author's work. We all are. Surely any number of us can and do imagine themselves or specific people in the roles of characters. It's a work of fiction. From an author you've appreciated in the past, I might add."

Her cousins watched silently, waiting to see how she would handle this. She'd planned to tell him about her writing that evening at dinner, where they'd be private and she could explain everything. How she'd needed to create a happy ending for someone, since she'd believed it impossible for herself. That she'd started with sweet romantic tales, until realizing erotic stories made more money. And by then, her dream of a cottage had taken root, so she'd written the fastest route to freedom. This wasn't how or where she'd imagined that conversation taking place.

"Blanche Clementine is clearly well educated, evidenced by the craftsmanship she displays in her writing. That means she's likely from my social set. If this book *is* about me, she's been nursing a fascination or even an obsession for God only knows how long." Dorian lowered his voice and she leaned in to hear. "I've already had one reader attempt to take liberties. How much worse would meeting the author herself be? People with obsessions can be dangerous."

A reader had done what? She bristled. Why hadn't he said something?

"It's pathetic, is what it is," his mother said. "She hides behind lurid penned fantasies about someone who is likely beyond her social sphere, rather than settle for a relationship in the real world."

A thread of truth made the words sting. That Dorian didn't know he and his mother were talking about her in such disgusted tones wasn't a consolation.

The bell over the front door tinkled, and a group of ladies walked in, then stopped. Judging by their fine gowns and beautiful hats, they were society women. Caro's pulse pounded in her ears. This was becoming more public by the minute, and knowing the silver dragon, there'd be no stopping the conversation until she was satisfied.

"Your Grace, it's fiction. People will eventually realize there are more differences than similarities, and all this will pass," Hattie tried.

"Everyone I know, as well as anyone who reads the papers, believes the Duke of Holland is having a licentious affair with some unknown woman who recorded their bedroom exploits for the world to read." The dowager would not be swayed.

With a shaky hand, Caro brushed a curl of hair off her face, and part of her was gratified to see Dorian track the movement with concern. "Would it be such a horrible thing to be someone's inspiration for a hero in a novel?"

"If it means the whole world reads a dirty book and believes I did everything detailed inside, then yes."

At the frost fair, he'd stood in their stall and corrected Oliver for describing her books as dirty. She might have fallen in love with him a little at that moment, hearing him champion her work. Now the closing of her heart was an unmistakable feeling. Like a door slamming and being locked from the inside. All the tenderness and devotion she'd fostered for him scurried behind that barrier and hid.

Later, she would cry and rage and probably curse the day she met him. But right now, Caro took a moment to look at Dorian—perhaps for the final time.

Because of their affair, the pieces of Blanche Clementine she'd needed most were woven tightly into the fibers of her being. Despite knowing Blanche would separate her and the duke, Caro couldn't reject those parts of herself again.

Perhaps this was what Gerard and Leo had praised that night in the theater—this feeling of unsentimental inevitability.

She was always going to choose the path that would be truest to herself. As painful as it was to hear the duke's response, this was where she'd have arrived anyway when the time came. No matter when that secret came out, Caro would remain Blanche Clementine, and she would still be proud of her work.

"Your Grace, while I understand the situation in which you find yourselves, I'm not sure what you expect Martin House to do about it." Practical Hattie to the rescue.

"I expect you to approach the publisher with a request as you did before. Blanche Clementine must publish a public statement in every paper in London denying she took any inspiration from the Duke of Holland. If she does not comply within the week, we shall sue for defamation."

The threat fell in the room, and everyone went silent.

If the Hollands sued, they only needed to claim the book

had damaged his reputation. Unfortunately, it would fall to Caro to prove she hadn't been writing about Dorian. And given their relationship, those would be murky waters to navigate.

Tremors rocked her hands, so she folded them at her waist. It felt as if her heart were going to beat from her chest. In some ways, this was like that day with her father all over again. At least she would not be homeless or alone when it was over.

But a suit could destroy her career and steal her livelihood, and it would probably impact her family's shop by extension.

Playing innocent was an option, of course. Agree to contact the publisher, then write a notice to the papers. Continue to hide, then leave this whole affair—and Dorian—in the past.

For two heartbeats, it was tempting. Safe.

Caroline glanced at her cousins. Hattie had moved to stand beside Connie with a composed expression that couldn't quite hide the sympathy. Regardless of what she chose, they were here, and God knew they'd seen each other through worse.

Despite the silver dragon's threats, Caro couldn't believe Dorian would bring a lawsuit against her if he knew she was Blanche. He might never speak to her again after making his feelings clear regarding her work, and God knew she wasn't inclined to trust him with her heart after this. But at his core, he was a good man. That's why she'd fallen in love with him.

Funny that in the end, it wouldn't be his title that stood in the way of their relationship but hers. Just as he couldn't give up his dukedom, she wouldn't give up being an author.

No matter how much someone loved a man, that emotion could not survive denying or losing parts of oneself along the way. Isn't that what she'd been hoping Constance would realize before her wedding day?

No more hiding. "Contacting the publisher won't be necessary."

"I insist—" the dowager began, but Caro continued, addressing Dorian as if his mother hadn't spoken.

"Your Grace, allow me to address your hypocrisy first. They're not dirty books. They're erotic novels. Novels you've enjoyed and encouraged your friends to read."

He had the decency to appear slightly abashed at that, but she could not soften now or she would cry in front of everyone. "I am truly sorry that my actions have placed you in this position. I never meant to cause harm. You didn't ask to be a muse, after all."

His beloved face wavered from confused to betrayed, then to lost within a blink. "Caro..."

"I am Blanche Clementine." Around the store, several gasps filled the silence. She allowed herself one last look at the planes of a face she'd kissed countless times. "I love you." Lifting her chin, she continued. "But I also love me. And I'm proud of my work and my success. When faced with the choice of losing you or loving myself, I will choose to remain my own woman."

"Caro, what are you—"

She cut him off with a hand in the air. "By speaking your mind without knowing whom you were discussing, you allowed me to hear the truth of the matter." She turned to the dowager. "If it will make you feel better, I will have a statement printed in the papers. I'm confident I can write something convincing. After all, that is what I do."

Dorian appeared frozen in place. She stepped closer to ensure her next words would be just between them—and unfortunately, his mother. "Thank you, you beautiful man, for letting me into your life for a short while. You have been my hero in so many ways. I put too much of my heart on the page without realizing it, and I'm sorry that has caused you grief. I hereby release you from hero duty." A trembling in her belly threatened to unravel all the parts she'd only recently knit together, but she forced her body into a curtsy. "Goodbye, Your Grace."

Chapter Twenty-Seven

◆

Six o'clock arrived far too fast, and Caro felt no more prepared to meet Sherman as she stood in the dark storeroom of their friend's bookshop than she had that morning when she read the note. Albeit for entirely different reasons.

After the duke and silver dragon left that morning, every other customer in the place bought her books, and she'd signed each one. Three of the women had even told her, "Well done, Blanche." The moment had been bittersweet.

And then Constance had placed her hands on her hips and asked, "What about Sherman?"

Hattie quickly surmised that the duke had been the "friend" they were helping. But given that Hattie was a vault with iron-tight lips that never spilled secrets, Caro wasn't concerned. Connie had once joked that Hattie spoke to no one except God—and she might even keep secrets from him.

In the end, they decided to see it through. Not because they had anything to gain from revenge against Sherman Snyder, but because countless women were not able to seek revenge against him and men like him. After all, if the cousins had the opportunity to remove one predator from London and didn't take it, then they weren't the kind of people they claimed to be.

So, for the sake of his victims and to spare future women

he would hurt, the cousins arrived at the Matthews Bookstore as planned and got into position.

A single lantern with its wick trimmed low burned on the far wall, casting barely enough light to see. As it was, Caro could just make out the vague shape of a body in the corner. By its location, she knew that dark shadow was Hattie, armed with rope and a cricket bat as an emergency weapon. *Please, God, don't make us have to bludgeon the man.*

Although Connie would be thrilled about that, and Caro knew her cousin could use another reason to smile.

Caro stood at the wall, where she'd be almost hidden by the door but not impeded by it. In the middle of the room, just beyond where the beam of light from the bookstore would land when the door opened, sat a simple wood chair.

Outside, Eliza Matthews's voice was a light lilt, playing her part to perfection. "You can't stay long. If my father finds out I let this meeting happen, I'll never hear the end of it."

As the latch in the door released, a triangle of light illuminated Constance. Wearing Hattie's black cloak with the hood up to shield her face and hair, she wore the dark-green gown they'd picked up from the secondhand seller a few blocks from the shop. While the cost had been dear, the effect was vital to creating the several seconds needed to make this whole mad caper a success.

Light shone on exactly what they needed it to—Constance's considerable bosom, on display and framed rather nicely by the extremely low-cut gown and cloak pulled back on her shoulders. Between lack of light and dark fabrics, the high, rounded globes of her pale breasts shone like twin half-moons in the night.

"What is this about?" A man of average height—thank you, Lord, as Caro was the one responsible for throwing the sack over his head—entered the room.

Eliza hissed, "Five minutes, and not a second more. I mean it," then pulled the door closed.

They pounced. Caro tugged the flour sack over his head, then moved aside as Hattie yanked the man's arms behind him and tied his wrists with a rope. They'd practiced the maneuver last night, but this might have been her fastest time yet.

Practice might make perfect after all.

Constance pushed him into the chair, then proceeded to wrap him in rope they'd left on the floor for exactly this purpose. Around his torso to the chair back, then around his lap and legs, until he and the wood were one and the same.

"What the fuck is this? Unhand me!" His struggles made the chair hop on the floor, but their knots held firm. Brash curses and crude oaths flowed in a vile river.

"He has quite a mouth on him, doesn't he?" Constance said.

"Who said that? The one with the tits? Who are you?" Sherman bellowed, but half-heartedly, as if he'd realized bluster would get him nowhere.

"Half the population has tits, odious man," Hattie said. She turned to Caro and gestured toward the rather non-threatening picture Sherman made as the fight disappeared from his posture. "*Your friend* is going to be here soon, right? Because if he keeps talking, I might let the violent one hit him to shut him up." Connie's teeth flashed white in the dim room.

It seemed like hours had passed since Sherman walked in the door, but Caro knew it had only been minutes. Subduing the man had taken less time than expected, if she was honest. This afternoon she'd written to Holland, telling him when and where to meet, but she hadn't told him why.

Given the events of this morning, she didn't know if he

would show up. Regardless, she and her cousins had decided on a course of action if the duke did not arrive as expected.

Stuck in a back room with her cousins and a man tied to a chair, Caro couldn't help but wonder how Dorian would react when he arrived. If he arrived.

"Is this it? You kidnap me, tie me up, then slowly kill me from boredom?"

"It's not kidnapping. We haven't taken you anywhere you didn't want to be," Constance said. "I could have stood here in this dress and you probably would have stayed put without the rope, and you know it."

"Ah, you're the one with the tits," he said.

Constance shook her head. "How you managed to woo anyone away from their spouse is beyond me. Once you open your mouth, it's obvious you're a pig."

"Is that what this is about? Is one of you a bloke? Fuck, if you're a husband or brother, I'm sorry. I'll leave her alone—I promise. Never speak to her again, no more letters. On my honor."

"An easy oath when you have no honor," Hattie growled, still clutching the cricket bat as she raised the wick on the lamp to chase away the shadows.

"Who exactly are you swearing to leave alone? Do you even know?" Hearing him speak made Caro's skin crawl.

"Uh...well. I can't help it if women think I'm irresistible. They line up, and who am I to deny them the comfort of a loving friend?"

"So you don't know who would hire us or who would want to dispose of you, because there are too many people on the list? You *are* a pig." Disgust dripped from Hattie's tone.

"Disposed of? Now, let's not get hasty, ladies—and gentleman, if there's one in the room keeping quiet."

Constance grinned at them. *This is fun*, she mouthed.

Hattie scrunched her face and mimed, *Are you mad?*

Constance shrugged.

The duke would be here any moment if he chose to come, and he would finally get the answers he sought.

Seeing him hurt had made the impact of a person like Sherman Snyder all too real. People like this man, who lived entirely selfish lives, uncaring of others except to use them for their own gain, made her sick. Literally sick to her stomach. That Dorian, or rather, the duke, might lump her into the category of people who'd hurt him might be a pain she carried forever. She needed to stop thinking of him as Dorian.

"Why do you do it, Sherman?" Caro asked.

"Because I can, you bitch. Why else?"

Acid churned with anger. Anger on behalf of the duke and every person Sherman had put through hell. Every broken heart that didn't have to happen. Every penny and pound stolen to support a villain. Sherman was a predator. But tied to a chair with a bag over his head, this predator was at his most vulnerable, and that gave her a vicious thrill she'd never experienced before.

"I'm glad you have the bat, Hattie. Caro would be using it right now, I think," Constance said.

Caro blinked and drew in a shuddering breath as if surfacing from underwater. At her sides, her fists ached from clenching. There were probably half-moons from her fingernails dug into her palms. "You're right. He deserves it, doesn't he?"

"And now he knows two names. Well done." Hattie threw up her hands, knocking the cricket bat on the ceiling. Their prisoner wasn't as relaxed as he'd like them to believe, because the thump of the bat made Sherman jump.

Light flooded the room when the door opened. Awareness shivered over Caro's skin an instant before a familiar

voice cut through the air with the force of a whip. "Do I want
to know what is going on?"

Dorian placed his hands on his hips and took in the scene
before him. Caro stood between him and a man with a sack
over his head, who'd been tied to a chair for some reason.
The dark-haired cousin that didn't like him held a cricket
bat, while Constance stood by wearing a gown cut in a way
rarely seen outside brothels or Continental ballrooms.

Dorian carefully closed the door behind him, then
approached Caro like he'd approach an easily spooked animal. God, it had only been hours, but it felt like years.

He'd hoped the note was an olive branch, a chance to discuss what had happened. While that clearly wasn't the case,
he couldn't for the life of him fathom what he'd just walked
into. "I haven't been bored even once since you walked into
my library. But I have to ask. Who's the man in the chair?"

"Sherman Snyder," she said simply.

He felt his eyes go wide. No matter what his thoughts
were about this woman right now—and God knew they
were a muddled mess—there was no denying she was
impressive. But then, he'd already known that. "How did
you manage this?"

"I didn't do it for you. I did it for all the women he's hurt."
She waved toward their captive. "You wanted answers. Ask
away. Our only request is that you ensure he doesn't hurt
anyone else."

The man in the chair's voice held a whiny, nasal tone the
flour sack couldn't muffle. "Who's here? There's a man, after
all. I knew a few women couldn't do something like this on
their own."

"Every time you open that mouth, I like you less. And I

thought you were an arse to begin with," Constance said. She glanced at Dorian as she spoke, and it occurred to him that if these three women could do this to a man who hadn't personally wronged them, then he might be in real trouble.

Yet Constance didn't move closer, and while Hattie glared menacingly, her cricket bat remained at her side.

"Since there's only one chair, and it's occupied, am I safe?" he asked.

Amusement lit Caro's eyes for a second, then disappeared. "Yes. But we can leave if it makes you more comfortable."

"How long has he been here?" Dorian circled Sherman, assessing his condition. Although they'd used enough rope to tie off a ship, they hadn't made the loops around his elbows and wrists too tight. Not tight enough to lose circulation, at any rate.

"I'm not sure how long it's been. I asked you to arrive fifteen minutes after we were due to meet him. Were you late?" Caro answered.

"No. I'm about five minutes early." He exhaled, trying to think clearly. "All right. Does he know who you are?"

"Two of our given names. No surnames," Hattie said, glaring at Constance. One cousin had slipped up, and he felt a stab of pity for the blonde. Hattie seemed the type to hold a grudge.

"Can Sherman identify anyone in this room?" he asked.

"One pair of spectacular tits!" the man in the sack said.

Dorian glanced around. Sherman referred to Constance's revealing gown, thank God, and not the only pair of breasts in the room that, in Dorian's opinion, were perfect in every way.

A few feet away, Sherman Snyder, the man who'd stolen, then broken Juliet's heart, shifted in the chair. Honestly, the whole thing was rather inconceivable. Judging by what he could see, Juliet's lover wasn't tall, or broad, or built like a man who spent time in a boxing ring or doing any kind of strenuous activity. Average in every way. How had the playwright described him? Human paste. Bland and dull to the point of making you want to drink to rid yourself of the memory of him.

"Can someone loosen the knots? My shoulders hurt."

Dorian curled his lip. Even the man's voice was annoying.

"Don't you want to question him? We've been trying to run him to ground for weeks. Thus far, he hasn't done much beyond obsessing over you-know-who's breasts, and admitting to a lengthy list of people who would wish him ill," Caro hissed.

She was right. Of course she was—it was Caro. The damned woman was frequently correct. An appealing trait in a woman who was willing to not only face his dragons but capture them and tie them to a chair so he could deal with them more efficiently. No wonder he'd been so convinced she was his future.

Dorian simultaneously wanted to tuck the loose section of hair behind her ear and demand an explanation as to why she'd ended things without giving him the opportunity to explain. Or think. Or come to grips with her secret identity.

A muddy mess of feelings might be filling him, but one thing was clear as crystal. "We need to get you and your co-conspirators safely away from here, so this worthless man can't retaliate for what you've done tonight."

"But...your answers. The letters. Don't you want to understand?"

To his surprise, being in the same room as Sherman only brought confirmation of what he'd begun to suspect. "What can he tell me? His twisted version of events? We knew different sides of the same woman. Neither of us was given the full truth—only what she let us see. I was and am far from perfect, as everyone in this room would agree." The cousins nodded a little too enthusiastically, but Caro watched him with a blank expression. "This pathetic man can't be trusted to pinpoint my failings with any kind of honesty. The mistakes I made in that relationship aren't ones I...I made with you. I don't need his opinion on a damned thing. All I need is your safety."

"Fine; then we move to plan B," Hattie said.

"What is plan B?"

"Where we don't ask for resolution of the past, but we ensure he won't ever hurt a woman again," Caro said.

That, he could fully support. "May I?" He pointed at their captive.

Considering his next move, Dorian stepped closer to the chair, then motioned for the women to stand behind their captive. He leaned in so he was mere inches from the man's ear. "Sherman Snyder, everyone in this room knows the kind of man you are. My legal team has documented thousands of pounds you've stolen from powerful people."

Savage satisfaction surged through him as the flour sack began to tremble. "Fraud and theft are hanging offenses, and there's a list of peers who would line up to watch you swing. You've swindled, threatened, manipulated, and hurt too many people to escape consequences."

Sherman's breathing heaved through the room, lacing the air with his rising panic.

"If I ever hear of you scheming to harm another soul, or if you try to find the people in this room, I will go to the newspapers with every scrap of evidence I've collected. After that, I'll take the lot of it to King George, Queen Charlotte, and Prinny himself. Natural consequences will follow, and there's not a soul alive that can shelter you from them. Do you understand me, Mr. Snyder?"

Under the rough fabric covering his face, the man gulped loudly. "I know who you are. This bag doesn't disguise your voice."

Dorian glanced up to confirm the women were out of sight, then lifted the front of the sack far enough to look Sherman in the eye. "Unlike you, I don't need to hide behind scripted letters or masquerade masks. You misrepresent yourself, but I do not. I am Dorian Whitaker, fifth Duke of Holland, and you are a worthless pile of shit who will never harm another woman."

Sherman's eyes were blue but, like the rest of his face, a nondescript shade. The playwright had been brutally accurate in his description, as unflattering as it had been. Sherman had a large nose on an oddly flat face, as if he'd been hit with a brick at some point. With no looks to speak of and an absence of a winning personality, it was no wonder he had to lie his way into people's good graces.

"If I do what you say, then what?"

"I'll keep what I know to myself. Think of this meeting as a warning. Now you know the evidence I have against you. And we both know I'll happily use it if you try to cross me or mine again. Are we clear?"

"Yes."

Dorian let the sack fall back over Sherman's face, then addressed the women. "What is your exit plan?"

Constance hurried to the door. After a pattern of taps and knocks, it opened, and the bookseller who'd let him into the bookshop stood waiting.

"Did you get what you needed?" The woman didn't spare a glance for the man tied to a chair.

Booksellers were dangerous creatures, Dorian thought.

Constance and Hattie slipped from the room. Caro gave her friend a hug, then kissed her dark-brown cheek. "Yes. Thank you, Eliza."

Dorian nodded to the shopgirl. "I won't leave you to deal with him."

She shrugged. "The door isn't far if you want to drag him outside."

"Excellent." He dug in his pocket for money, then handed it to her. "This should cover the chair if we cause damage. Thank you for your help this evening."

Dorian tipped the chair onto two legs and proceeded to drag it across the floor, as Sherman cursed loudly.

"Shut your mouth, man. They trussed you up like a hog; you won't fall off unless you flail about. In which case, I'll throw your sorry arse out with the rest of the rubbish."

Once Eliza waved good night and locked the door behind them, they paused. His coach waited, and at the end of the alley, traffic passed with plenty of hacks to hire. "May I offer you a ride home?" he asked the women.

"No, thank you, Your Grace." The honorific from Caro made him hiss in a breath.

"Then I'll wait here until you're safely in a hack."

The women didn't say goodbye. He watched until they'd hailed transportation at the end of the dark alley. What if this was the last time he saw her? But what was there to say?

Everything and nothing. The letter from the palace sat in his desk drawer in the study, waiting for a response. While he was inclined to accept the assignment and leave London, that felt a bit like slinking off to escape the gossip frenzy that would ensue once word spread about their public confrontation in Martin House. He couldn't leave Caro to weather that alone, even if she didn't need or want his support.

Besides, running off to war seemed too close to chasing a death wish. Not something to commit to on the day your future blew up in your face.

"Fuck," he said.

"Difficult night?" The dry comment came from the sulky man in the chair.

Silently, Dorian untied the knot securing Sherman's wrists. It would be several moments before the man could fully unravel the twists and layers of rope.

Leaving him mostly bound to the chair, Dorian climbed into his carriage and called to the coachman to drive.

If they were lucky, footpads might find Sherman before he wiggled free and see an easy target. Dorian just couldn't make himself care about the man anymore.

Chapter Twenty-Eight

❦

Constance's wedding day dawned as bright as the bride's
mood.

Overcast and without any sign of the sun.

Since Caro's mood was also suffering due to man problems, she couldn't blame her. That didn't mean she wasn't worried. Especially when Connie stared at nothing, silent and subdued as the family entered the church early that morning.

Walter's return from the coast two nights ago should have been met with celebration by everyone, but Caro and Hattie couldn't muster the enthusiasm. Hattie because she had too many opinions on the marriage, and Caro because she'd gone numb at some point since leaving Dorian in the alleyway behind the Matthewses' bookshop.

Hattie gave their normally cheerful cousin a concerned look, then caught Caro's eye and mouthed, *What do we do?* Right. They should do something.

"Connie, might we steal you away for a moment? We'd like one last chance to hug you before you're an old married woman." Caro forced cheer into her voice as she and Hattie tugged the tight-faced bride toward the back of the church.

"Talk to us," Hattie demanded in a low hiss.

Constance's cheeks were pale, and dark circles only enhanced the wild look in her eyes. "My heart has been beating too fast all morning. I feel like I'm going to be ill—or maybe faint, and I've never fainted in my life. Not for real, anyway." She pressed a hand to her belly. "Tell me I'm doing the right thing."

Caro wrapped her arms around her, then Hattie embraced them both. "If you have doubts, there's no one forcing you to go through with it today."

"Everyone knows we're supposed to get married." Constance's voice was barely audible.

"That is not reason enough to tie yourself to someone," Hattie said.

"Did something else happen with Walter, or is this just an overall sense of…" Caro began.

"Wanting to run away? Panic? Sweating through my wedding gown, even though it's dreary and cold today?"

"I, for one, am in full support of you leaving. Eventually you'll find someone who wants the same things you do," Hattie said.

"When we're apart, all I can think about is that fight when he yelled and said those things. But then I see him, and I feel happy again. Then I start questioning if what Walter wants is better. Betsy has that kind of marriage, and she seems happy. We're twins—why can't we be alike in this way? What can't I want that too and just be *happy*?"

Sobs shook Connie's shoulders, and Caro tightened her arms around her. "Darling, you're the most cheerful person I know. It's Walter that doesn't make you happy."

"He thinks I'll change and be more like Betsy. He said it like he was looking forward to it. But *I like me*."

Tears pricked at Caro's eyes. "Don't say that as if it's a bad thing. You have a true north within you, and that is worth protecting."

"You can't marry someone who thinks changing you is something to look forward to. There's not a bloody thing wrong with you," Hattie said.

Slowly, Constance straightened, forcing them to loosen their arms. They kept her in the circle of their embrace as she wiped her eyes and firmed her chin. "I want to go home."

Caro heaved a sigh. "Thank God. I was afraid we'd have to drag you from the altar by your hair, and it would be a shame to ruin that hat. Now, do you want to tell them, or would you like one of us to do it?"

But Connie was returning to her usual self now that she'd made up her mind. She raised her voice to be heard throughout the room. "Thank you all for coming, but I won't be getting married after all. Walter, I'm terribly sorry. I'll explain everything when I can. But for now, I am going to go."

With the early hour, the hack made short work of the ride to Martin House. Tears dripped silently from Constance's chin as they unlocked the new back door that had been installed two days before. Wood crates stood by the door like sentries, full of Juliet's books.

In the last week, Caro had found herself thinking of the late duchess more often by her first name. After seeing the books she'd collected and loving the man Juliet had once married, Caro couldn't help feeling she knew her. At least a little.

Upstairs, they helped Constance out of the gown they'd retrimmed for the wedding and set aside the bonnet she'd created for the special day. Scents of the wedding breakfast filled the house from the kitchen.

And silently, they all crawled into the bed they shared each night. Except, instead of taking the places they'd established almost two years ago, they tucked Constance in the middle. Hattie by the wall. Caro on the outside edge defending them from the world. They wrapped their arms around her and didn't press for conversation.

Rain fell against the windows as it often did during a late-March morning in London.

No one spoke. But then, no one had to.

Dearest Readers,

Firstly, thank you to those who have enjoyed my stories since the beginning. I'm grateful to each of you for being part of my journey. Secondly, I'd like to offer a warm welcome to my new readers.

Now, on to my purpose for writing to you all. It has come to my attention that certain readers believe A Dalliance for Miss Lorraine *was born from my relationship with a specific high-ranking member of society.*

I'd like to lay those rumors to rest.

During the writing of A Dalliance for Miss Lorraine, *this particular peer and I had never shared more than five minutes of conversation at one time. I hate to disappoint you, dear readers, but the duke who falls in love with Miss Lorraine is an amalgamation of my own concept at the time of my perfect man. Looking back, I realize I allowed my personal preferences to inhabit one character far more than I have in the past, which means this book is dear to my heart.*

In conclusion, I'd like to state unequivocally that A Dalliance for Miss Lorraine *is a work of fiction.*

Thank you for reading,
Blanche Clementine

The newsprint blurred on the page. Dorian rubbed his eyes and heaved a sigh.

Of course Caro had followed through, because in addition to being an excellent keeper of secrets—his and her own—she was a woman of her word. He hoped she realized Gloria's threat of a lawsuit was empty now that they knew Blanche Clementine's identity. Even so, she'd fulfilled her promise down to the literal letter.

Last night's abandoned brandy glass sat on the table beside the chair, next to this morning's cup of tea. The cut crystal of the glass played with the light from the fireplace, similar to the way it made Caro's ring sparkle from its spot on his pinky finger.

It seemed like forever ago when he'd sat in this chair and drunkenly hallucinated Juliet. Or perhaps it was a dream. Truthfully, he hoped it had been her ghost. The idea gave him comfort. There was a time when he'd have tried his damndest to duplicate that night for just a few more moments with her. So much had happened since then that if she were to appear, he wouldn't know where to begin.

No—that wasn't true. He knew exactly where he'd start. Caro. He'd talk about Caro. About how he'd not only fallen in love, but he'd done so with a woman society deemed unacceptable. He'd show Jules the ring and hope she would be happy for him despite the unavoidable scandal of the Duke of Holland marrying a bookseller.

He'd been prepared not to care, because it was actually Dorian Whitaker marrying Caroline Danvers.

Given the chance, he'd tell Juliet's ghost about the night he'd walked in on Sherman Snyder tied to a chair. Even a week later, the memory of Caro and her girls catching Sherman cheered him as he turned the ring this way and that to admire the play of color.

Despite a decade of marriage, he couldn't say what Jules would think about the kidnapping of her lover. Once upon a time, he thought he knew her inside and out, but he clearly hadn't. The fact there was a lover to kidnap was proof of that.

Even though he had only been with Caro a short time, he could imagine in his mind her and her cousins referring to the kidnapping by a suitable caper name like The Great Catch and Release. He hoped, when they discussed it, they were proud of themselves. They should be. He hoped they laughed. And he hoped Caro remembered that when it came down to it, despite how they'd ended things, Dorian cared more about protecting her than asking the questions that had once haunted him.

If Juliet were here, he would ask her opinion on the king's letter. It shamed him to remember how little discussion there'd been the first time he was summoned to war. At the time, he'd felt answering the call was a matter of duty and service to his country. Those things had felt more important than what he'd wanted, or what Juliet needed. He would welcome the chance to apologize for that.

Juliet's ghost would have to accept that he'd severed all ties with her loathsome cousin. Rather than waiting for the rest of the valuable books in the library to sell, Dorian would cut a cheque for an estimated value. Today, he would enclose it with Mr. Bellmore's legal notice.

Several merchants had sent panicked letters after learning that the dukedom no longer supported Timothy's line of credit. A year ago, Dorian might have disregarded the worried words of the business owners and let them handle their accounts as they saw fit.

This week, he'd replied to each of them and asked to be invoiced for anything purchased on credit before they'd received notice. Anything after that handshake would be

Timothy's responsibility. But he didn't want the merchants to suffer.

Dorian had finally taken a stand. Now he would like to hide from the world and nurse his broken heart. Sprawled as he was in one of the ugly wingback chairs, someone might mistake him for being jug-bit from the night before.

Alas, he wasn't drunk. Just sad. Drapes still covered the windows, blocking out the world, and he wanted them to stay that way for a while longer, so he raised the wick on an oil lamp and opened the book he'd already read twice this past week. Funny, he'd started to read it the night he met Juliet's ghost, then set it aside. Perhaps he wasn't supposed to have read it until he'd fallen in love with the author.

Blanche Clementine wrote one hell of a great story. He'd always thought so. Knowing what he knew now, the novel played out in his head as if read in her voice. It was the next-best thing to having her beside him.

As he sipped his cold tea distractedly, a passage leapt from the page with new significance.

There were numerous mentions of the hero's hands. This one made him look from the page to his fingers. Ink stained the hero's right pointer finger, so Lorraine knew he'd spent the day working and taking care of people.

A dark smudge marked the usual identical place on Dorian's finger. One could map his hands by the way she'd written them. Long fingers, dark-gold hair, the silvery scar on his palm under the thumb. The hero had earned that scar in a sword duel.

Dorian's was from a far less romantic slip of the blade while cutting an apple about a decade ago.

Maybe it was because he could hear Caro reading the words on the page to him, but this book felt different from her others. *A Dalliance for Miss Lorraine* wasn't only about the trials and triumphs of a pair of lovers—this was a love letter. It might have been a love letter to a stranger, but that stranger had been him. Or at least, the version of himself he'd shown the world.

When he'd been one hard emotional blow away from losing his ability to breathe, Caro had seen a hero.

Although broken and bitter, he'd still been enough to inspire her. It was humbling to realize how much grace she'd shown him when he was struggling.

If there was any version of him on the page in the next book, Dorian was curious to see how it would differ from this one. The relationship between them had changed so drastically. Of course, given how he acted in her shop, the next character she based on him would probably be a villain. Or a dead body floating in a canal.

A Dalliance for Miss Lorraine should have been a success without people connecting him to it. The things about the author that had won him over in real life were evident on the page. Not just to him, but to everyone who read it. That alone should have ensured readers flocked to her work.

She'd been right, as she often was, to walk away. If she'd bent and bargained or pleaded and cajoled for his forgiveness while he'd been angry . . . well, she wouldn't have been Caro.

Society would look down their noses at her, but the irony was that at every turn of their relationship, she'd required him to rise to meet her, not the other way around. To win her body, he'd had to stop hiding his desire. To win her affection, he'd had to let go of the icy reserve he'd used as a shield. To win her respect, he'd had to see the world through a more equal lens instead of the hierarchy of titles he'd been taught.

This was no different. Any woman who commanded attention without needing words would never be content with being partially adored. She knew her heart was more valuable than that and wouldn't hand it over easily.

If he wanted Caroline Danvers and all the ramifications that would bring with the ton, he would have to not just accept but celebrate Blanche Clementine as well. Convincing her he was willing to do that would be a challenge.

In Kent, she'd dreamed aloud for him as she shared her heart's desire. He'd watched her fall in love with the Adams cottage. At the time, that had inspired a selfish response. Instead of feeling gratitude for her willingness to be vulnerable, he'd feared her leaving.

Staring at the matching ugly chair across from him, Dorian smiled. He could live in Kent. People would think him mad if he ran away to live with an author in a cottage. But if their opinion didn't matter enough to stop him from wanting to marry a bookseller, or being openly proud of her identity as an author of erotic fiction, then why would their judgment be enough to sway him in this?

When the roses along the cottage fence began to bloom, he wanted to be there to share in Caro's wonder over the riot of color. And when night temperatures fell to freezing, he would keep her warm.

He'd offered to buy it for her, and Caro refused because it made her feel like a mistress. Now he needed to buy that property to help convince her that he wanted his wife to have everything her heart desired.

Dorian set his book on the table. He needed to talk to his solicitor.

"What do you mean the cottage isn't for sale? Are you sure?" Gerard Bellmore nodded, the picture of calm as always. Dorian was the opposite of calm. "Damn it."

It had been a good plan. He was going to buy Caro the cottage of her dreams and bring her the key, with the ring tied to it. Dorian was going to apologize for disparaging her work and tell her he'd do everything within his power to make her dreams come true.

A simple apology wouldn't be sufficient.

Dorian needed to show Caro he'd been paying attention. That he'd been listening. After all, wasn't that the lesson he'd learned from Juliet? Despite offering every creature comfort, he'd failed to fully offer himself. It wasn't an excuse for her choices. But he could learn from the mistakes he'd made before he made them again.

Oh... So why was his plan contingent on offering creature comforts?

He thumped back into the chair feeling as if he'd been slapped.

"Are you quite all right, Your Grace?"

"Yes. I'm having a bit of an epiphany. I assume Caro told you what an unmitigated arse I was? She ended things, and rightly so."

The solicitor nodded, but if he was agreeing with the summary of events or acknowledging he already knew of them, Dorian wasn't sure.

"Wait. Did the book sell enough that she bought the house?"

"Since she's already disclosed her nom de plume, I feel comfortable sharing that I am the legal representation for Blanche Clementine."

Dorian leaned forward. "Are you negotiating with the publisher for a more favorable contract? Because we both know that whatever she was being paid before is less than what she deserves."

Mr. Bellmore raised one eyebrow but kept silent.

"Damn it, you are annoyingly discreet."

That earned him a smile.

"I assume, then, if you are involved with her contracts, Caro would also ask for you to draw up paperwork for a significant transaction, such as purchasing property."

Mr. Bellmore neither confirmed nor denied.

Dorian chuckled ruefully. "Blink once if I'm correct."

A small smile, then the solicitor slowly blinked one time.

The humor was short-lived. Dorian rested his forehead in his palms. "I need to convince Caro that I only want what is best for her and that I am proud of her. Not just Caro, but Blanche. Hopefully, once the anger has abated somewhat, she will realize she wants me as much as I want her." His hands fell to the desk, and he stared at her friend. "How do I show a woman I've wronged that she can trust me? I don't want to live without her. But I'm not sure what else I can do to prove my sincerity. Her heroes would make a grand gesture. That was supposed to be the house. She fell in love with that cottage, and I wanted to give her something she loved."

Gerard cocked his head, still silent.

"You know more than you're letting on. But you won't say, because you're so bloody discreet, and her friend. Fuck, Bellmore. I can't see the forest for the trees. Please help." An idea occurred to him. "Cross-examine me."

"I don't understand, Your Grace."

"Cross-examine me, like I am a witness on the stand in court."

"I'm not a barrister. I'm a solicitor—"

Dorian waved away the protestations. "Using the information you have, ask me questions to help me find a new plan."

Finally, his legal counsel heaved a sigh and asked in a

voice that would not be out of place in the courtroom, "Very well, Your Grace. Are you in love with Caroline Danvers?"

That was easy. "Yes. Very much so."

"What is it you love about her?"

"Countless things. She's confident. Her sense of humor. God, her laugh. It lights up a room, doesn't it? Her mind— it's amazing what she's created in her novels." As he stared at the shining surface of his desk and his eyes lost focus, he turned his gaze inward. "The bravery she's shown in not only putting her work out into the world but claiming it like she did last week. I'm proud of her. I love the way that stubborn chin of hers gets really hard right before she tells me I'm being a prig." The solicitor's low laugh pulled him back to the moment.

"And if she returns your devotion, what do you think she loves about you?"

Dorian rubbed at the ink smudge on his hand as if it held the answer. "She doesn't care about a coronet. My money doesn't matter—it makes her uncomfortable, I think. Hell, it took her weeks to relax in this place." He waved a hand toward the study. "I can't imagine what she'd think of the Dorset estate. It's an honest-to-God castle." Dorian and Mr. Bellmore winced in unison.

When writing Lorraine's hero, she'd loved his hands. Not just the body parts themselves, but specifically the signs of work on his hands. There had been a few evenings when she'd read on the sofa while he finished the last of his work for the day or pored over books explaining modern water-filtration systems and the latest innovations in farming equipment. Those had been nights she asked about his projects—investments previous dukes had considered too costly when their benefits would be immediately felt by tenants and employees rather than the ducal coffers.

"Caro likes when I use my position to help people. She was so excited to donate my library to all those schools and orphanages." The memory of that day made his throat dry. God, he missed her. A glance at the solicitor showed him watching with a sympathetic smile.

"Anything else?"

"She loved it when I asked her to speak the pause." At Mr. Bellmore's obvious confusion, he explained. "Before she spoke, she would hesitate, then say something exceedingly professional and polite. The first time we kissed, I asked her to say whatever it was she thought during that pause, because that was where the real Caroline was. It became a sort of code for us. Speak the pause. Let me in. Say what's on your mind. I think if there's one thing Caro might love about me, it's that I have always wanted to know the real her."

"What else did she say she wanted besides the house? Think, Your Grace."

Dorian recalled the conversation in the coach. "Something that was just hers that couldn't be taken away. That's why I was going to put the cottage in her name and have it in a trust, separate from my estates. No matter what, it would be hers."

Mr. Bellmore nodded encouragingly. "Work from there. Ask yourself what you can give Caro that no one else can. And I'll give you a hint: it's not a house."

Chapter Twenty-Nine

To my dearest Blanche Clementine,

Thank you for your letter clarifying the gossip surrounding your latest release. As always, your words were effective and phrased with care. I've long been an admirer of your work and thought A Dalliance for Miss Lorraine *one of your finest novels yet. Entirely fictitious, yes, but an excellent piece of literature.*

While your letter was factual in every way, it lacked context to provide the full tale. If nothing else, your readers appreciate a repentant hero as well as a good story, so please indulge me for a moment as I tell mine.

I can't point to the exact second I fell in love with you. It was likely something as simple as seeing you smile over the pages of a book. This feeling came upon me by degrees until loving you was as permanently ingrained as that scar on my hand (which I did not receive in a duel).

When you told me who you were, I acted like an [redacted]. I didn't respond like anyone's hero, least of all yours. Although I instantly regretted it, we both appreciate the power of words. Especially when used to judge, demean, and hurt.

My love, I hurt you. For me to detail my remorse, it would take all the newsprint in London.

I beg you to allow me to apologize in person. If there is any room in your heart for a second chapter, for us, please consider allowing me to be your hero.

I will be waiting where we met at eight o'clock in the evening this Friday. Should you decide to leave me to wait, I will respect your choice.

Yours in the truest sense,
Dorian Whitaker, Fifth Duke of Holland
(and longtime Blanche Clementine reader)

"What are you going to do?" Constance asked.

Caro wiped away the tears that had begun as soon as she realized what she was reading. "Damn it, Dorian," she said, sniffling.

"He apologizes prettily, doesn't he?" Hattie put the kettle on and opened the cupboard where they kept the teacups. Hattie was right. This called for tea. When she opened the next cupboard and reached for the bottle of whisky, Caro wanted to laugh through her tears.

"He apologizes prettily and publicly," Constance said.

That wasn't by accident.

"It's a proposal is what it is." Hattie poured the whisky into the cups. "Tea is coming soon enough. This will hold us over till then." They sat at the small table in the kitchen with a fresh loaf of Aunt Mary's bread between them. It smelled like yeasty heaven. Caro sliced them each a piece and placed the butter crock where everyone could reach it.

"A duchess...mercy." Constance took a drink, then coughed. "There's a nice symmetry to it. Her letter countered by his letter. Think he put it in all the papers like you did?"

"Oh, I'm sure he did. The public nature is deliberate. Dorian knows I hated growing up feeling like everyone was watching me." She'd slathered her bread with butter, but now she just held it. Eating had been difficult this past week. Food sounded great until she took that first bite. Then her throat closed and her stomach churned. Caro handed the slice to Constance.

"Is he trying to be a prick, then?" Constance's posture shifted in a blink from relaxed to combative.

"He's giving me a taste of what it would be like to be his duchess. And he's doing it in a way that takes the pressure of judgment off me. If anyone is embarrassed by these public letters, it will be him. By telling everyone he loves me, he's protecting me *during* the speculation, not *from* the speculation."

"Not a prick, then. That's rather beautiful. No wonder you're a writer." Constance relaxed again before taking a bite of her bread.

"Holland is an intelligent man. He knows this will cause an uproar and is clearly prepared for it. Now that Caro's claimed her identity as Blanche Clementine, their relationship will inspire speculation beyond just the difference in their stations. Every time you publish a book, expect more attention. You've seen how many new customers we've had in the store since you told everyone who you are. That is a sampling of what is to come."

"Thank you for the increase in book sales, by the way," Constance said. "Father is positively giddy."

"Consider this carefully, Caro. That's what I am saying. If you don't want that life, no one will blame you. Even if you love him, it might not be worth it." Hattie fetched the kettle and went about the ritual of adding boiling water to tea leaves, then carried the pot to the table.

"I do love him."

"I thought love was worth anything," Constance said. "That's what I've always believed."

"It's not worth sacrificing a part of yourself," Hattie corrected gently, and Caro knew they were all recalling Connie's flight from the altar. "You have the cottage. Running away to live in obscurity in Kent while publishing delicious books is an option."

"True. Caro, you're awfully quiet." Constance nudged her hand.

"I'm thinking. You make excellent points. I'm not from his social sphere. I might never be accepted there. Claiming my pen name publicly means I've removed myself even further from the ton." Accepting Dorian's offer, although he hadn't stated a proposal in so many words, would make obscurity impossible.

Caro poured herself a cup, then sipped her whisky and tea. Mellow warmth seeped into her belly.

If she had Dorian by her side, would finding a way to live in his world be worth it? Maybe there was a compromise somewhere between the glittering ton and a tiny cottage.

"That man adores you and made sure everyone in London knows it." Constance topped off her whisky with a dollop of tea. "He is accepting the scandal and the speculation. Embracing it instead of running from it. The real question is, will you?"

Caro took a bracing sip. "I think the real question is if their opinions should matter more than my love for him."

"To love." Constance raised her teacup.

"To the duchess," Hattie said, raising hers.

They looked expectantly at Caro.

"To bedeviling the silver dragon for the remainder of her days."

* * *

Dorian clenched his fingers, then flexed them as he had been doing for the last thirty-five seconds.

He knew because he'd been counting.

Thirty-seven seconds now.

A deep breath in and out helped settle the pounding in his chest. Not entirely, but enough to keep the invisible iron bands around his ribs at bay. They'd been waiting to clench down and steal his air all day.

The gaslight cast a yellow hue on the wet cobblestones around him, barely cutting through the blanket of fog that crept and settled along the street. Another deep breath in, full of fresh rain and a trace of someone's meal from a home above one of the storefronts.

A bell tinkled, and relief swamped him. Caro stood in the doorway, wrapping her worn knit shawl around her shoulders.

Curls at her temples tightened into ringlets in the damp air.

"I had a speech prepared, and now I've forgotten it."

She cocked her head, offering a hesitant smile. "Then give me the pause instead. I don't need pretty, practiced words. Just honest ones."

More of the tension in his chest loosened. "I love you. I should have told you the instant I realized, but I was scared."

Her smile grew. "That's a good beginning."

"If you don't want to see me after tonight, I understand. And you won't have to see me, because the king wants me to go back to the Continent. I don't say that to make you feel like I'm going to run off to war if you tell me to go to hell. But you won't have to worry about me coming into the shop."

"Is that why you wanted to meet? To say goodbye?"

He removed his hat and ran a hand through his hair. "No. I don't want to go. I want to stay here with you. I want to make a life *with you*. However, declining the appointment risks repercussions. I'm trying to be forthcoming about everything we're up against right now." Heaving a sigh, he stared up at the sky. "I told you I had a speech prepared. It was a good speech." And it hadn't been a depressing list of the things keeping him up at night.

A small sound that might have been a laugh made him look back at her. "I don't know why I described your work that way. You were right to call me a hypocrite. Caro, you're incredibly talented." He reached out for her, then thought better of it and let his hand fall to his side. "I'm sorry for hurting you."

"Thank you." Her voice was rough and so sweet after thinking he may never hear it again. "I should have told you about the writing. I'd like to say the secret haunted me every day, but that wouldn't be true. I've hidden it for so long; talking about it feels strange. Not that it matters, but I had decided to tell you."

She was too far away to touch but close enough that when she licked her lips, the lamplight made them shine, and he ached for her. How tightly she clutched at the shawl told him she didn't want to be touched right now, so he kept his distance.

"My father found the tin where I kept the letters from my publisher and the royalties I'd saved. That's why he disowned me. Called me horrible names—some of which your mother echoed last time we saw each other."

Dorian winced. The finality of her reaction made even more sense now. In her shoes, he'd have done the same.

"I suppose what I'm saying is that I'm no stranger to

judgment, so I hid that part of me—Blanche—because it was safer." It took all of his self-control to stay where he was and not engulf her in a proper hug.

"I don't ever want you to hide who you are from me. Or what you're thinking, or anything else. I love all of you, including Blanche Clementine."

"I love you too, you know. For so many reasons, Dorian. But I'm scared of what it means to be with you like this, where everyone can see. Especially now that I'm claiming my work. That part of me always felt closer to the surface when I was with you, and it will likely only grow stronger. Soon enough, I may just wander around your rooms naked all the time. Who knows!" She threw up her hands, and it was fucking adorable.

"The idea of missing the chance to watch you walk around naked all the time makes me want to rage and wail." Hope pulsed through him, daring him to take a step toward her. "One more reason to tell the king I won't return to the Continent. I can't risk missing that, no matter how petty Prinny might act over me telling the palace no."

She matched his step with one of her own. "What if I wanted to travel the Continent with you? Have you considered that?"

"I want you with me every day, everywhere. I don't care if that's Kent or Greece or Prussia. I'll beg if that's what it takes."

The speech he'd prepared might have been more dignified, but this was honest. When he dug in his pocket and retrieved the ring, his hand didn't shake. "My plan was to buy your cottage and bring you the key with this on a ribbon." The ring caught the light, and her eyes went wide. "Except, you're both the impressively talented Caroline Danvers and the wildly successful Blanche Clementine, so you'd already purchased the home of your dreams."

When he took another step, she met him with one of her own again. A foot or two of wet pavement separated them now as he held out the ring. "If I'd known about your father stealing your savings, I probably would have tried to get it from him, along with anything else of yours. But knowing you and your cousins—"

"We already tried. He spent it almost right away."

He nodded. "Right. You'd said you wanted something that was just yours. Something no one could take away from you. But I can't buy your home, and you earned back the money your father took. All I can...Caro, all I can offer is me." His voice was rough with emotion. "I'm yours. No one can take me away from you."

When she reached out a hand and cradled his jaw, he inhaled at the contact. His nose filled with the orange-blossom scent she dabbed on her wrists, and the lingering threat of the iron bands disappeared from his chest. "I've missed you," he said.

"Are you sure, Dorian?" She removed her hand, and he wanted to snatch it back, but she was counting obstacles and listing them on her fingers. "Shake my family tree as hard as you like, but you won't find so much as a mad baron. I won't stop writing. I love what I do, and the happiness I put out into the world has value. Not only is my family in trade, but I am proud of this shop, and my aunt and uncle. Dorian, I'm a walking scandal. Also, your mother hates me." She added that last bit as if it were an afterthought.

Swallowing around the hope clogging his throat, he clasped the hand of reasons she'd raised between them. "Caro, please wear my ring. Be my wife. Tolerate being my duchess." He placed a kiss on each fingertip. "As to my mother, I can't make promises, but I hope she will come around. If she doesn't, we will live in the cottage while she's in London. The rest of the year, she's in Bath. Of course, if we have children, she might melt entirely and worship at your feet like I do."

Caro grimaced. "I don't want the silver dragon at my feet, thank you."

His laugh echoed off the storefronts around them. "God, I love you. I truly do."

But she didn't join him in laughing. "Dorian, my mother died in childbirth. I'm not opposed to having babies, but you need to understand that I will be terrified until they're safely delivered."

Finally, he wrapped his arms around her and rested his cheek atop her head. "We can't predict the future. Hell, I might die too soon, and then you'll have to wrangle my mother without me."

"If this is how you plead your case, you'd be a lousy barrister." Her jest was watery with tears, but he loved her all the more for the effort.

"We can wait to have children or hope for the best. I just want you. What else do you need in order to say yes?"

Caro pulled back just enough to meet his gaze. "Living in society with everyone watching will be taxing. I'll need my cottage as a retreat. And while I'm thrilled to support charities, I won't be the kind of duchess Juliet and your mother were."

"You'll be far too busy writing novels to scandalize the ton and set their bedsheets aflame." He grinned, hope nearly making him burst.

Her answering smile warmed him from the inside out. "You're really all right with Blanche?"

"I'll give copies away at our engagement ball."

She raised a brow. "Engagement ball?"

"Or we get married by special license. Or elope. I just want *you*, Caro. Although I do fancy the idea of introducing you to society as my bride and daring them to say an unkind word to our faces."

"No more hiding," she whispered.

"Because we have nothing to hide. Please, Caro. Marry me."

Slowly, she raised her hand, and he slipped the ring on her finger.

"And then the duke and duchess live happily ever after?" He placed a lingering kiss on her mouth.

"Of course." The smile she gave him transformed her face into a perfect heart shape. "I wouldn't write it any other way."

Epilogue

Two years later, in a colorful cottage in Kent

The fireplace in their cottage crackled, and all was right in the world. Dorian wrapped his arms around his wife and spread his fingers over the dome of her belly.

After a little over a year on the Continent, they'd realized they were expecting and returned home. Prinny had been happy to release Dorian from his assignment since the war was drawing to a close. Besides, no one wanted Caro anywhere near battlefields and soldiers' camps when she carried the child to a dukedom without an heir. And everyone knew Dorian would march through hell before he'd leave his wife.

Sweat cooled on their skin from their lovemaking. Caro tugged the quilt higher over their bodies just as he began to feel the chill. They'd barely made it to their bed before he was inside her, insatiable for each other as ever.

"Happy birthday, Dorian."

He smiled against her nape and laid a kiss on the soft skin. "Thank you."

"How do you feel being thirty-eight?"

"Even more grateful than when I was thirty-seven. This will be a wonderful year."

She covered his hands on her belly. "A lot of changes."

"Yes, but we are ready. If you can march with soldiers across Europe, charm diplomats, and win over my mother— all while writing novels—then you're ready for motherhood."

She laughed. "You said we were ready, but that list was all about me. What about you?"

"Yes, well. I marched with you, I didn't punch the diplomats when they were too thoroughly charmed, and I didn't say 'I told you so' too often when my mother finally thawed. I didn't write any novels, but I don't think that should disqualify me from our next chapter."

"You inspired novels, though. There's a part of you in every hero I write. Oh, don't let me forget to bring that copy of *A Soldier for Samantha* to your mother."

"She always gets the first signed copy. I remember."

He pushed onto his elbow, then dropped a kiss on her nose, her pointed chin, and finally her lips. When she pushed him onto his back, he rolled and brought her with him. She straddled him, gloriously round and full, with her tangle of dark curls draped over her shoulders.

"God, you're the most gorgeous sight I've ever seen."

Her smile was sweet, but he knew it could turn wicked in a blink. And he loved her for it.

The tips of her breasts brushed his chest when she kissed him. Alas, the possibility of deepening the kiss disappeared when she sighed, then shifted to roll off the bed.

"I'm hungry. If you want to make love again, we need to eat first." Caro walked, naked, out of the bedroom. A moment later, cupboards in the kitchen opened and closed, then something hit the floor and she cursed. It didn't sound like anything broke, but bending and getting up again was a bit of a process for her these days.

"Whatever it is, leave it. I'll be there in a minute," he called as he searched the floor for the breeches he'd abandoned earlier, then hastily pulled them on.

Tomorrow they'd return to London until the baby was born. Their search for a midwife Caro trusted had been a bit of an adventure, but they'd finally found one—a no-nonsense woman who didn't coddle his duchess but did have an excellent record of safe deliveries. They'd agreed on that midwife, because after meeting her, Caro had slept peacefully for the first time in weeks. That had been enough for Dorian to put the woman on retainer and set aside thoughts of hiring a doctor.

Besides, if they didn't go to London, their cottage would be bursting with friends and family within a week, and no one would leave until the child turned five. As it was, they'd often had visitors since their return from the Continent. And when they weren't visiting, her cousins sent letters and newspaper clippings with their commentary written in the margins. Caro had a collection of them she'd saved from the last two years.

One had been particularly memorable. In October 1814, the Horse Shoe Brewery near St. Giles flooded. The article explained that the brewery's wooden vats burst, sending hot beer pouring into the streets, drowning several people. Newspapers enjoyed their grisly details, and whoever wrote the article took particular glee in reporting the deaths of two of the victims. Sherman Snyder, who was found impaled with a piece of wood, then drowned in beer. His companion, also drowned, was identified as Timothy Parker. Above the article, Constance had written, *I didn't do it*. Hattie scrawled under that, *I didn't either. But he deserved worse.*

It had been a macabre sort of justice. Far better than what Dorian could have imagined. At the time, Caro had shaken her head and said she wished she could think of endings like that for her villains.

As much as she'd miss the cottage, Dorian knew Caro was excited to see her cousins again. Martin House was hosting an event next week to celebrate the release of her latest book. In a bid to avoid too much speculation, she'd made this hero blond, missing an eye, and she had him walk with a limp. A dashing and handsome war hero, obviously, but one bearing no physical resemblance to Dorian.

"Did we eat all of the cheese Jeffrey brought over last week? I could have sworn there was..." Caro's voice faded to mutters.

Jeffrey and Bryan were their neighbors—delightful gentlemen farmers with a talent for making goat cheese. Jeffrey often dropped by to share his latest flavor experiments with Caro. Bryan had taught Dorian to bake bread and how to chop wood without breaking his back or risking losing a toe to the axe.

"I used the rest of the rosemary-and-lemon-balm spread on my toast, but there was a little of the apricot honey you like in the larder. Look behind the pickled beets."

"You ate the rest of the rosemary? That's it. I'm killing you in the next book."

The toothless threat made him grin as he padded through the main room. Caro had insisted they leave Mrs. Adams's brightly painted wood trim as it was and decorated their home with colorful art and textiles from their travels.

There wasn't a bit of crystal or marble to be seen, except the crystal whisky glasses she'd bought for his thirty-sixth birthday. Because, she'd explained with the dark humor they'd adopted for the subject, if he died young, she'd need to get drunk while still looking like the lady she was now.

The love of his life was in the kitchen, humming under

her breath as she sliced fruit and cold chicken, then placed it on a plate with the rest of the cheese. All of that bare skin was a delightful temptation, but he restrained himself to a playful nip on her shoulder.

"I'll put the kettle on." He stoked the fire, then gathered a few more items from the pantry to round out their simple feast.

Naked afternoons were truly the highlight of his life thus far, and he refused to give them up. After all, their rooms in London had locks, and he intended to use them.

Soon enough, they'd be surrounded by servants who'd be shocked to see a duke and duchess making their own meal, much less their own bread.

Curious onlookers in the ton struggled to understand why his and Caro's world didn't revolve around the latest *on dit* circling the ballrowom, or who'd lost their vouchers to Almack's since the last Season.

But then, no one needed to understand. This was their haven. Where they weren't Blanche Clementine, or a former bookseller, or a duke and duchess.

Here, they were Dorian and Caro. And that was enough.

Author's Note

London's first recorded frost fair was held in AD 695. The last one took place in February 1814, when the Thames froze between London Bridge and Blackfriars Bridge. Yes, the ice really was so thick they partied on it for days and had bonfires large enough to roast whole oxen. And yes, they actually paraded an elephant on the river to convince people it was safe. It must have been quite a sight.

In October 1814, two of the twenty-two-foot-tall brewing vats at the Horse Shoe Brewery burst, causing a fifteen-foot-high beer tsunami. Tragically, the flood took eight lives, all of which were women and children. Since I've never met a beer I didn't think tasted like piss, the idea of drowning in hot porter is my idea of hell. So of course, I had to use it in this story.

An ancient Sumerian stone tablet is thought to be one of the earliest examples of erotic writing credited to a female author. Which just proves women have been romanticizing sex and writing about it for as long as men have been drawing penis doodles on walls and in book margins. In England, Aphra Behn (1640–1689) is credited as one of the first women to make a living as a writer. Erotic poetry is listed in her body of work. Thanks, Aphra.

DON'T MISS MORE SWEEPING HISTORICAL ROMANCE WITH THE MISFITS OF MAYFAIR!

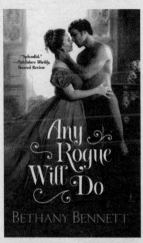

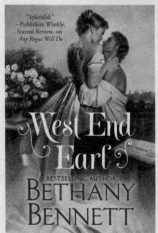

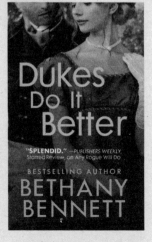

About the Author

Bethany Bennett grew up in a small fishing village in Alaska, where required life skills included cold-water survival, along with several other subjects that are utterly useless for a romance writer. Eventually settling in the Northwest with her real-life hero and two children, she enjoys mountain views from the comfort of her sofa, wearing a tremendous amount of flannel, and drinking more coffee than her doctor deems wise.

You can learn more at:
    Website: BethanyBennettAuthor.com
    X: @BethanyRomance
    Facebook.com/BethanyBennettHistoricalRomance
    Instagram: @BethanyWritesKissingBooks

Fall head over heels for charming dukes and sharp-witted ladies in these swoony historical romances from Forever!

BOOKSHOP CINDERELLA
by Laura Lee Guhrke

As an unmarried woman with no prospects, Evie Harlow is content with running her quaint bookshop. Until Maximillian Shaw, the devilishly attractive Duke of Westbourne, saunters in with a proposition: To win a bet, he'll turn her into the season's diamond. Slowly, Evie follows Max's lead and becomes the star of high society, even as their time together results in chemistry she's never felt before. But when Evie's reputation is threatened, will she trust that Max's feelings for her are more than just a bet?

MY ROGUE TO RUIN
by Erica Ridley

Lord Adrian Webb never meant to get caught up in a forgery scheme. But now a blackmailer is out to ruin him, and the most alluring woman he's ever met is trying to put him behind bars. Every time Marjorie Wynchester thinks she has Adrian figured out, her assumptions turn on their head. He's a heartless scoundrel. A loyal brother. A smooth liar. A good kisser. So is winning her affections just another attempt to avoid the law? Or maybe he's not such a rogue after all?

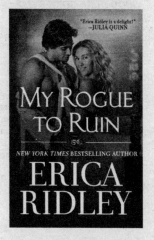

Connect with us at Facebook.com/ReadForeverPub

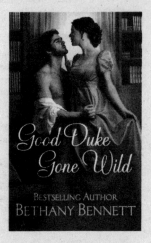

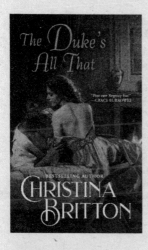

WAKE ME MOST WICKEDLY
by Felicia Grossman

To repay his half brother, Solomon
Weiss gladly pursues money and
influence—until outcast Hannah
Moses saves his life. He's irresistibly
drawn to her beauty and wit, but
Hannah tells him she's no savior. To
care for her sister, she heartlessly
hunts criminals for London's underbelly. So Sol is far too respectable
for her. Only neither can resist their
desires—until Hannah discovers a
betrayal that will break Sol's heart.
Can she convince Sol to trust her? Or
will fear and doubt poison their love?

THE PARIS APARTMENT
by Kelly Bowen

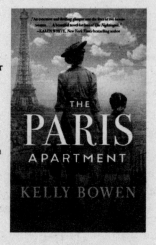

LONDON, 2017: When Aurelia
Leclaire inherits an opulent Paris
apartment, she is shocked to discover
her grandmother's secrets—including a treasure trove of famous art
and couture gowns.

PARIS, 1942: Glamorous Estelle
Allard flourishes in a world separate
from the hardships of war. But when
the Nazis come for her friends,
Estelle doesn't hesitate to help those
she holds dear, no matter the cost.
Both Estelle and Lia must summon
hidden courage as they alter
history—and the future of their
families—forever.